PS
525
.I8
M3

OCT '75   APR 1992

APR '95

KALAMAZOO VALLEY COMMUNITY COLLEGE
LEARNING RESOURCES CENTER
KALAMAZOO, MICHIGAN 49009

29097

The Masquerade

AMS PRESS
NEW YORK

THE MASQUERADE

An Historical Novel

By

OSCAR MICHEAUX

Author of

The CASE OF MRS. WINGATE

BOOK SUPPLY COMPANY

Publishers

40 MORNINGSIDE AVENUE

NEW YORK

1947

29097

Library of Congress Cataloging in Publication Data

Micheaux, Oscar, 1884-
　　The masquerade : an historical novel.

　　Reprint of the 1947 ed. published by Book Supply Co., New York.
　　I. Title.
PZ3.M5809Mas8　　[PS3525.I1875]　　813'.5'2　　73-18595
ISBN 0-404-11406-7

Reprinted from the edition of 1947, New York
First AMS edition published in 1975
Manufactured in the United States of America

AMS PRESS INC.
NEW YORK, N. Y. 10003

ACKNOWLEDGMENT

For a long time I have been desirous of bringing forth a novel dealing with the conditions our country faced from about 1855 to 1870. Since retiring from the production of Motion Pictures in 1940, and returning to writing, I have written and caused to be published, three novels, which plots I was able to select very successfully from among the stories I filmed while making pictures some years ago. I had merely to select and rewrite whatever one of the old stories I liked best, which in fact, was not nearly so arduous as creating a new theme entirely, and, due to the fact that the story had been worked out very carefully when it was filmed, I found that it made a better and more convincing novel after I had worked it back to story form.

Accordingly, after deciding to do an historical novel as my next publication, I went back to my old file of motion picture scenarios and found one that just fitted my purpose: a scenario from a novel by Chas. W. Chesnutt, published almost fifty years ago. I had filmed the novel twice. First, as a silent picture in the early twenties, and as a talking picture early in the thirties. It dealt with a "free" Negro family in North Carolina. It began shortly before the outbreak of the Civil War, and ended shortly after the close of the conflict. The story made no mention, however, of Abraham Lincoln, the Dred Scott Decision, John Brown, or the Civil War, all among the most turbulent, grave and exciting events in our history, and which events were taking place during the period of this story. But the story provided a splendid background to work in these characters and events as I saw fit, and which I desired to do, and I feel that the reader will be pleased with the way it has been handled.

I am very happy, in the meantime, for the privilege of having known Mr. Chas. W. Chesnutt, who died in 1932, and acknowledge with gratitude, the assistance provided by his book of that period which I have drawn upon in the rounding out and completion of this novel.

Respectfully,

Oscar Micheaux
New York City, New York
January 15, 1947

*Dedicated to
those who believe in liberty
and freedom for all.*

Chapter One

IT IS THE YEAR 1857. Ever since *"Uncle Tom's Cabin,"* a novel by Harriet Beecher Stowe, exposing the horror and cruelty of slavery began publication in 1851 as a serial story in the *National Era*, America had begun to grow more restless than before regarding the institution of slavery.

Then, on March 6th, 1857, exactly two days after the inauguration of James Buchanan, a Southerner, and the choice of the South as President of the United States, there was handed down by the Supreme Court of the United States a document called the DRED SCOTT DECISION, of which Roger Brooke Taney of Maryland, Chief Justice of the Supreme Court, at the time, was the author.

This decision shook America from stem to stern—as the country, especially the North, never had been shaken before. Since few people know and ever have read the facts in this case, let us reach back into history—more than a hundred years—to 1834, in fact, and detail briefly the facts in the case.

In 1834, Dr. John Emerson, a surgeon in the United States Army, went from Missouri, a Slave State, to Illinois and later to Fort Snelling, an outpost in the Territory of Wisconsin. He took with him a Negro slave named Dred Scott.

Ordered back to St. Louis, Dr. Emerson left Fort

Snelling in 1837. With him went Dred Scott and a Negro woman by the name of Harriet, whom Dred Scott married while on the steamboat on the Mississippi River before it reached the boundary of the State of Missouri. In due time Harriet gave birth to a daughter, and, later, to another daughter in St. Louis.

Dr. Emerson died in 1844. The Negroes then became the property of his widow, but Mrs. Emerson moved to Mass., leaving the Negroes in St. Louis under the care of Taylor Blow, son of Peter Blow who had been Dred Scott's master in Virginia.

Taylor Blow was at a loss as to know what to do with Dred Scott and his family. He finally took Scott to the law firm of Fields and Hall in St. Louis in the hope of finding some solution to the problem. After listening to a recital of the events from the time Scott was taken into Illinois and Wisconsin, the lawyers being of the Abolition minded sort advised Scott to sue for his freedom. This, Scott proceeded to do, setting forth the contention that under the Missouri Compromise Act (which prohibited slavery in the domain north of the Compromise line, except in the state of Missouri) he had been emancipated by reason of his residence in Illinois and Wisconsin.

After years of litigation, the case of Dred Scott came before the Supreme Court of the United States at the December term of 1856, on a writ of error.

The paragraph in the decision which brought forth all of the criticism—the storm of criticism that was to come, (the italics are the author's) follows:

"*They have, for more than a century, been regarded as beings of an inferior order, and are alto-*

gether unfit to associate with the white race, either in social or political relations; and so far inferior in fact, that they have no rights which the white man is bound to respect; and he might justly and lawfully be reduced to slavery for his own benefit. He may be bought and sold and treated as an ordinary article of merchandise and traffic wherever a profit might be made of it."

Among the countless number of criticisms, by almost every leading and outstanding man of that day, Abraham Lincoln said: "It is not only erroneous, but vile and monstrous." As stated above, while the decision was ready and could have been released in December, 1856, it was not published until March 6, 1857—two days after the inauguration of James Buchanan.

Regarding this, Abraham Lincoln, in a public speech shortly after, asked: "Why was the decision held up? ... Why the delay for reargument? Why the incoming President's advance exhortation in favor of the decision? And why the hasty after-endorsement of the decision by the President and others?"

In March, 1858, Senator Seward, of Ohio, accused Taney and Buchanan of conspiracy. He charged that Dred Scott had been used as a mere "dummy" in a political game.

Roger Brooke Taney in his prediction that the decision would stand the "test of time and the sober judgment of the Country, and would endure for a hundred years, perhaps longer," was decidedly in error and he lived to see that it added only fuel to the bitter controversy going on between the North and the South which was not decided until Lee surrendered to General Grant at Appomatox

Court House a few years later, after the most viciously fought war of all time.

We now go back to the year of 1855, to the career of Abraham Lincoln, and that of an adversary of great ability; a man whose brilliant intellect not only made him well known to the people of his time but also intrigues the reader of today; and because of the events that followed, his name will be discussed for generations to come.

That man was Stephen A. Douglas. He was born in Vermont but migrated to Illinois where he engaged in politics. At this time, 1855, he had just arrived in Springfield, Illinois, from Washington.

Called the "Little Giant" (he was only five feet two inches tall), he was powerfully built for a man of his height, with an unusually large head upon which he wore a buff of long, carelessly kept hair. One was aware of his striking personality at a glance—seeing him left no doubt as to his remarkable genius and influence.

He arrived in the capital of Illinois early one night and was met at the railroad station by a brass band and torchlight procession which escorted him to the hotel, where he was requested to deliver a short address.

"I have come home," he said, "as I have done so many times before, to give an account of my stewardship. I know the democrats of Illinois. I know they always do their duty. I know, democrats, that you will stand by me as you have always done. I am not afraid that you will be led off by those renegades from the Party (he was referring to several men who had been prominent in the Democratic Party but who had recently deserted the ship) "who have formed an unholy alliance to turn the glorious Democratic Party

over to the Black Abolitionists." He was striking especially at Abraham Lincoln. "Democrats of Illinois," he yelled loudly. "Will you permit it?" The street shook with voices en masse: "No! No! Never! Never."
Douglas' blue eyes flashed; his lips trembled. "I tell you," he went on firmly and passionately, "the time has not yet come when a hand full of traitors in our camp can turn the great State of Illinois, with all her glorious history and tradition, into a Negro worshipping, Negro-Equality Community! Illinois has always been, and always will be, true to the constitution and the Union!"

And he gracefully wished them goodnight. The torches, the brass band, and the crowd vanished; the street was empty!

On the afternoon of the next day, Douglas spoke; he talked for almost three hours. Had not the Missouri Compromise been practically wiped out by the Omnibus Bill of 1850? Was not the real question whether the people should rule, whether the voters in a territory should control their own affairs?

If the people of Kansas and Nebraska were able to govern themselves, were they not able to govern a few miserable Negroes? The crowd went along with him. They seemed to enjoy it, and cries came: "That's so! Hit 'em again, Stephen, etc., etc., etc." The speech over, three ringing cheers were given for the "Little Giant," and he left the auditorium a very happy and proud man.

Abraham Lincoln, who occupied one of the front seats, had listened to him carefully and had whispered occasionally in the ears of friends who, judging from their chuckles, had found his remarks quite amusing. When it was over, Lincoln walked down the main aisle at Douglas' side, joking with the Senator.

Only a few years before, Douglas had made Lincoln a loan of $100.00, Lincoln having signed a note and later repaid it. They had argued together on the streets, in courtrooms, churches, schools and grocery stores.

To a pretty young woman Abolitionist who told Douglas after his speech, that she didn't like his address, Lincoln interposed, "Don't bother young lady. We'll hang the judge's hide on the fence tomorrow." And he did.

When the young woman insisted later to Lincoln that he had no business laughing and joking during such a brutal speech, Lincoln answered that maybe he ought to feel a little guilty. As to Slave-holders' way of looking at slavery, it didn't hurt him so very much. "I have heard it all my life," he said, "And as the boy said about skinning eels, 'it don't hurt 'em so very much; it has always been done. They're used to it.'"

There had been a saying around the Court-Houses, "With a good case, Lincoln is the best lawyer; but in a bad case, Douglas is the best lawyer a State ever produced."

Chapter Two

THE NEXT AFTERNOON Lincoln stood before the same crowd Douglas had spoken to. As stated, Lincoln had listened to Douglas' speech from a front seat in the State House Auditorium, but Senator Douglas sat on the platform from where Lincoln delivered his address, and interrupted him at intervals to the dissatisfaction of the many persons present to hear Lincoln.

Before it started, Lincoln came in, pushing and squirming his way to the platform where he was to reply to Douglas' speech of the day before. After being introduced, he questioned if he was just the man who should be selected to reply to the Senator, mentioning the world-wide fame of Senator Douglas, his high position in the United States Senate and the power he held there as a debator. He was going to discuss the Missouri Compromise, presenting his own view of it, and in that sense his remarks would not be specifically an answer to Senator Douglas, though the main point of Douglas' address would receive respectable attention. "I do not propose to question the patriotism or to assail the motives of any man or class of men, but rather to confine myself to the noble merits of the question." With these apologies and explanations out of the way, he was set for his main speech.

He began with a short history of the United States and Slavery. He dug back into beginnings and traced out the growth of Slavery. "Wherever slavery is, it has first been introduced without law. The oldest laws we find concerning it, are not laws introducing it, but merely regulating it as an already existing thing."

He gave five sound reasons for hating it as a monstrous injustice. And he added, "Let me say that I think I have no prejudice against the Southern people. They are just what we would be in their situation. If Slavery did not now exist among us, we should not instantly give it up. This I believe of the masses North and South. Doubtless there are individuals on both sides who would not hold slaves under any circumstances, and others who would gladly introduce it anew if it were out of existence.

"We know that some Southern men do free their slaves, go North and become tiptop Abolitionists, while some Northern ones go South and become most cruel Slavemasters. When Southern people tell us that they are no more responsible for the origin of Slavery than we are, I acknowledge the fact. When it is said the institution exists, and that it is very difficult to get rid of in any satisfactory way, I can understand and appreciate the saying. I surely will not blame them for not doing what I should not know how to do myself."

Was this oratory? Debating? The man, Abraham Lincoln, was speaking to thousands of people as if he and another man were driving in a buggy across the prairie, exchanging their thoughts and views. He was saying that, if all earthly power were given him, he wouldn't know what to do as to Slavery.

There were not ships and money to send the slaves anywhere else; and when and if shipped anywhere else outside America they might all perish; might all die. "What then? Free them all and keep them among us as underlings? Is it quite certain that this would better their condition? I think I would not hold one in slavery at any rate, yet the point is not clear enough for me to denounce people upon.

"What next? Free them and make them politically and socially our equals? My own feelings will not admit of this, and if mine would, we well know that the thought of the great mass of the white people will not. Whether this feeling accords with justice and sound judgment is not the sole question, if indeed any point of it. A universal feeling whether well or ill founded, cannot safely be disregarded. We cannot, then, under the circumstances, make them equals. It does seem to me that some system of gradual emancipation might be adopted, but for the tardiness in this, I will not undertake to judge our brethren of the South."

And yet while he could not say what should be done about slavery, where it was already established and operating, he was sure it would be wrong to let it spread North. "Inasmuch as you do not object to my taking my hog to Nebraska, therefore I must not object to you taking your slave. Now I admit that this is perfectly logical, if there is no difference between hogs and Negroes."

The South had joined the North in making the law that classified African Slave Traders as pirates and provided hangings as the punishment. "If you did not feel that it was wrong, why did you join in providing that men should be hung for it? The practice was no more than bringing Negroes from Africa to such as would buy them. But you never thought of hanging men for catching and selling wild horses, wild cattle or wild buffaloes or wild bears."

The speaker at times was, in a way, lost from his audience, as though language had not been invented for what he was trying to say. He referred to the man whose business it was to operate a sort of "Negro Livery Stable," buying and selling slaves. "He watches your necessities and crawls up to buy your slave, at a speculating price. If you cannot help it, you sell to him; but if you can help it, you drive him from your door. You despise him utterly. You do not recognize him as a friend, or even as an honest man. Your children must not play with his children, but they may rollick freely with the little Negroes, but not with slave dealers' children.

"If you are obliged to deal with him, you try to get through the job without so much as touching him; you hope that he will not offer to shake hands, for if he did, you would have to refuse to. You instinctively shrink from the snaky contact. If he grows rich and retires from business, you still remember him, and still keep up the ban of non-intercourse upon him and his family. Now why is this? You do not so treat the man who deals in corn, cotton, tobacco or potatoes.

"Over the country are 433,643 free black men. At $500 a head, worth $200,000,000. How comes this vast amount of property to be running about without owners? We do not see free horses or free cattle running at large. How is this? All these free blacks are the descendants of slaves, or have been slaves themselves; and they would be slaves now, but for something which has operated on their white owners. What is that *something*? Is there any mistaking it? In all these cases it is your sense of justice and human sympathy continually telling you that the poor Negro has some material right to himself—and those who deny it and make mere merchandise of him, deserve kickings, contempt—and death! And now why will you ask us to deny the humanity of the slave, and estimate him as only the equal of a hog? Why ask us to do what you will not do yourselves? Why ask us to do for nothing what two hundred millions of dollars could not induce you to do?"

He drew a line between his position and that of the Abolitionists. "Let it not be said that I am contending for the establishment of political and social equality between the white and the blacks. I have already said the contrary."

He reasoned that the application of what Douglas called the "sacred right of self-government" depended on whether the Negro was a man. "If he is not a man, in that case he who is a man, may as a matter of self-government, do just what he pleases with him. But if the Negro is a man, is it not to that extent a total destruction of self-government to say that he, too, shall not govern himself? When the white man governs, that is self-government; but when he governs himself and also governs another man, that is more than self-government—that is despotism. If the Negro is a man, why, then, my ancient faith teaches me 'that all men are created equal!' And that there can be no moral right in connection with one man making a slave of another. What I do say is that no man is good enough to govern another man without the other's consent. I say this is the leading principle, the sheer anchor of American Republicanism."

The speech was three hours long. Through most of it,

Lincoln spoke as though he were not debating or trying to beat or crush an opponent, but rather as though he was examining his own mind, his own facts and views, his own propositions and the demonstrations of them.

And again he was no philosopher at all; he was a sad, lost man chanting a rhythm of the sad and lost. "Little by little but steadily as man's march to the grave, we have been giving up the old for the new faith. Nearly eighty years ago we began by declaring that all men are created equal; but now from that beginning we have run down to another declaration that for some men to enslave others is a 'sacred right of self-government.' " (He was hitting what Douglas had said and declared loudly, full on the chin.) "These principles cannot stand together. They are as opposite as God and the devil. Whoever holds to the one, must despise the other."

He painted the "Liberal party throughout the world," watching slavery, fatally violating the noblest political system the world ever saw." And he intimated his knowledge of the movement on foot to extend slavery from the black race to certain lower grades of white labor in saying: "Is there no danger to liberty itself in discarding the earliest practice and first precept of our ancient faith? In our greedy chase to make profit of the Negro, let us beware lest we 'cancel and tear to pieces' even the white man's charter of freedom."

The speech came to an end. The crowd that heard it scattered out of the State House to their homes. Douglas felt the sting. He frequently interrupted Lincoln, but to no avail. The cold logic of the tall man held every man's and woman's attention who heard it, all of whom went away thinking and talking about what he said. The papers, North and South, commented on it and the slavery question anew, and became more interested in what it would all come to in time as a result. It was for years the bone of contention between the North and South, and was by now obvious to every American that somewhere, sometime and somehow, it would reach a showdown with such results as only time could tell, which brings us up to the real beginning of our story.

Chapter Three

IN THE LITTLE TOWN of Fayetteville, North Carolina, perched on the banks of the Cape Fear River which flowed to the sea, there lived, among approximately 5,000 other people, two professional men, who visited the offices of each other, and who had much interest in common.

One, Archibald Straight, was a lawyer, and had served at one time as Judge of his county. The other, younger than the Judge by a few years, was a physician, known as Doctor Green.

They were, at this hour, as was almost everybody all over America, especially those who took life seriously, debating the *Dred Scott Decision* and its effect on the nation as a whole.

"I tell you, Judge Straight," Dr. Green was saying, "the decision was fine and a perfect clarification of the circumstances, regardless of what the North insists on calling it. It put the Negro race, if you can call them a race, in their place and right where they belong, and I think the country will quit arguing so much about the Slavery question from now on and let us Southerners alone; leave us to attend to it as we best know how, and them to attend to their own affairs and quit meddling so much in ours."

"All very well, Dr. Green. That is how *you* see it, view it."

"Naturally. A man has a right to his opinion, hasn't he?"

"Oh, of course, Dr. Green, of course."
"Well?"
"But it is not going to turn out as you say."
"Then how is it going to turn out?"
"To be frank and honest with you, doctor, I really don't know."
"But you have an opinion, don't you?"
"Of course. By all means, of course."
"Then what is your opinion?"
"That we are about to face the most serious crisis in the history of the country."
"How do you arrive at such an opinion?"
"By several ways—almost every way."
"You are not clear, Judge Straight. All you imply seems vague and indefinite. Please try to make it plainer."
"I will if you'll agree to face facts and conditions, views and convictions as they are, and not as you would like to have them."
"I agree to that—now shoot."

As they talked, Judge Straight did not see the door to his office, or at least he was not looking in that direction, but Dr. Green was, and as he looked out of the door which was open, a curly haired mulatto boy of about fifteen years of age walked up and was about to mount the steps that led to the entrance when he happened to raise his eyes which met those of Dr. Green's who looked at him curiously. The boy bowed lightly and pausing, backed up, hesitated, then turning, walked away.

Dr. Green watched him, still curiously. Judge Straight, who was talking, looked at Dr. Green and upon seeing his eyes elsewhere, turned to follow the direction until it rested upon the object. When they did, the boy walked past his window, turned to look through same, and, upon finding both men looking at him curiously, quickened his step and went on his way.

Out of the sight of both men, they turned to look at each other, a question in the eyes of both. Dr. Green was the first to speak.

"Who is that boy?"

"That boy?" Judge Straight repeated, then turned to look in the direction the lad had taken, then turned back to Dr. Green.

"That was Johnny Northcross, Molly Northcross' son. You know her, don't you? They live out of town aways, on the old Wilmington Road in a nice little cottage setting back quite aways from the road. They call it The House Behind the Cedars."

"Yes, I remember now. I've seen the lad before, of course, many times, but just now . . ."

"What?" The Judge was curious.

"He was coming here. Your face was turned the other way and I knew you didn't see him, but I did. He started to enter the office. I think he was coming here to see you, but noting that I was here, it seemed to—sort of change his mind."

"Yes?" The Judge now turned and looked wonderingly out of the door that opened on the street.

"Yes, I am sure he was on his way to see you—in fact, I know he was for he seemed to have dressed up for the occasion."

"That is rather strange," the Judge said, musingly, then turned back to Green.

"I wonder what he wanted to see me about?"

"Couldn't say," said the Dr., shaking his head, "But he was coming in the office for that purpose, I am sure."

"Well," the Judge went on as if to dismiss any serious thought about the boy, "If he was, he'll be back. He'll perhaps knock around for awhile and come back, so forget about it and let's get back to what we were talking about."

"Of course, yet—"

"—Yet, Dr. Green. What now?"

"I'm still thinking about that boy."

"Johnny Northcross?"

"And that's his name?"

"Of course. Just a nice little colored boy, very mannerly and, for a Negro, intelligent too."

"Who does he belong to?"

"To his mother. He's a free Negro, you know."

"A free Negro? Yes, come to think of it, I remember. Now let's see, who's his father, since you say he belongs to his mother, and is a free issue?" Judge Straight smiled. Dr. Green was looking at him a bit oddly.

"I thought you knew that, too . . ."

"Well, if you want the truth, he looks a great deal like Richard Northcross, one of our wealthier planters, but of course—"

"He couldn't be related to Richard. I regret to advise you, but he is."

"Now what're you talking about?"

"About that boy's father. He's Richard Northcross, our wealthy planter." Dr. Green turned to look at Judge Straight quickly, then relaxed into a half smile of understanding.

"Another one of those cases, eh? Well, it's little wonder that the North is so critical about slavery. What happened and how? You seem to know. Tell me the story, the old, old story."

"This boy's mother belonged to Jefferson Wainright, you remember him?"

"The plunger who went broke many years ago and moved away?"

"Exactly. Well, this boy's mother, Molly, belonged to Wainright's wife, but Wainright knew that she was his blood daughter by one of his slave women, and he presented her to his second wife, who was years his junior before he went broke. When he was sold out at auction to satisfy his debtors, he had Richard Northcross to bid Molly in. She was then very young, but old enough to satisfy men when and if it came to that—and it soon did, shortly after Northcross bought her. He made his wife a present of her, and Mrs. Northcross assigned her to the duties of personal maid.

"When Molly was eighteen, she turned up pregnant. Northcross married her off to one of his slave men, whom she had been sort of going with, so I am told, which is mostly grapevine gossip and I shouldn't be telling you about it."

"I've asked you to, so, go ahead. I'm finding it interesting."

"When the baby came, it was as white as snow, and, the man Northcross had married her off to—a coal black darkey—knew it wasn't his, the Negro knew it too, so he ran away. Northcross never made any effort to track him down and find him. Sort of guilty around the conscience,

I guess. Well, Northcross' wife knew whose child it was and as soon as Molly was strong enough, she hustled her right off that job. She made Northcross provide for Molly and her child, so he purchased the cottage where she has lived since, that house behind the Cedars. He has kept her there since and has continued to be intimate with her, for she has had two children since, one of whom is still living. A little girl, I imagine, two or perhaps three or four years of age, and that's another one of those stories, so common all over the South."

Dr. Green suddenly started and consulted his watch.

"Dang it," he cried, jumping to his feet. "I just remembered that I have an appointment at my office—and I'm overdue now." He crossed quickly to the door, where he turned only long enough to wave at Judge Straight, then he was gone.

As he left the office, he turned to look up the street in the direction in which Johnny Northcross had gone, and saw him, standing on a corner one block away, with his eyes in his direction. He thought again about the clean, curly headed lad and since he saw him leaving the Judge's office, wondered what it was he wanted to see the Judge about.

Chapter Four

ALTHOUGH NO PROVISIONS had been made anywhere in North Carolina to educate Negroes—not even free ones, Johnny Northcross possessed a very complete literary training and was in his second year high school in 1857.

This had been made possible by the wife of Fritz Obermark, who operated a tavern in Fayetteville, and who had come to America from Germany a few years before, bringing his wife and children with him.

The Obermarks objected to slavery; objected to it so much until they refused to send their children to the public school, due to the school's refusal to accept even free Negroes as students. Mrs. Obermark, before her marriage to Fritz, had been a high school teacher in Germany and was thorough in her work down to the last detail—in short, Mrs. Obermark was a good teacher.

So shortly after settling in Fayetteville and opening his tavern for business, Fritz built a small school on his farm on the outskirts of Fayetteville and installed his wife as teacher. She proceeded to teach her own children and offered to teach Negroes for a small fee; all who wished to attend. Many free Negroes, therefore, were given an opportunity to educate their children, among whom was a Negro family living near, by the name of Fowler, of whom we will say more about later in this story. Among the others, was Johnny Northcross.

The Obermarks, as quickly as they were able to, installed a library in their little private school and sought all the books that were available. Since they opposed slavery, they were soon regarded as Abolitionists, and soon got in touch with Abolition Societies all over the North. When Mrs. Obermark wrote of what she was doing, or at least trying to do, and that she needed funds to develop a library, she soon got the funds—and no end of books, among which was more than one copy of "Uncle Tom's Cabin." Naturally all her pupils, old enough to understand what it was about, read quickly, and re-read, Mrs. Stowe's immortal book.

By the time he was fifteen years old, Johnny Northcross had read it three times, and was terribly moved by it. But it was not until he read the *Dred Scott Decision*, which put him to thinking all out of proportion to what he had before, and, in the end, made him determined to do something for himself about it. He decided to talk with Mrs. Obermark concerning it, since he had heard her express much indignation regarding the subject. He sought a time when they were alone, to broach the subject, and he did one afternoon after school had been dismissed.

"According to the Dred Scott Decision, Mrs. Obermark, no colored person can ever hope to be anything, regardless of how hard he may try,"

"Oh, Johnny, that is not true, it is not true at all and you must not feel that way," Mrs. Obermark cried, very much surprised and taken aback. "You are intelligent and ambitious, and you will be a successful man some day. Just be patient and after you've finished school, go forth into the world and prove yourself. That is the way to look at life, Johnny."

"But, according to this decision, that is impossible. It says in plain words, and seeks to show and prove, that Negroes are beings of an inferior order and that we are unfit to associate in any way with white people; that we may be bought, like they buy cotton and tobacco in town; and that we may also be sold to the highest bidder. My mother was sold at auction."

"But you are free, Johnny. Nobody owns you."

"That is true, but I am not a citizen; I have no rights that anybody is bound to respect. Then how can I, under such circumstances and conditions, ever hope to be anything; ever hope to be anybody—and I do want to be something. I had hoped to be somebody."

"You *are something now*, Johnny. A very intelligent and ambitious boy. In less than two years you will have learned all that I can teach you. Then—"

"—What?"

"You will go forth into the world and make a name for yourself; soon become somebody." Johnny Northcross shrugged his shoulders.

"You're very kind, Mrs. Obermark. But according to Mr. Justice Taney, it just can't be done. He used up—oh, so many words to convince everybody who reads that very long decision, that Negroes can never hope for anything, free or otherwise."

"Old Judge Taney is a Southerner, and filled with race prejudice. Don't take his vile decision of the Dred Scott Case seriously. Think more about what brave men—like Abraham Lincoln say."

"President Buchanan says the decision is right and proper. How is a Negro to think, and what is he *to* think, when the President of the United States himself commends the decision?"

"I hate to ask you, or tell you to disagree with the President of the United States. It does not seem right and proper, but President Buchanan is a Southerner, too, and being from the South, it is not surprising to hear him express agreement with the Dred Scott Decision. Just refuse to think about anything except that when you finish school and go forth into the world, you'll make your way and in the end, be a successful man. That's the way you must feel and think, Johnny, the way you must feel and keep on thinking."

"I thank you for so much encouragement, Mrs. Obermark, but they say that Abraham Lincoln is an Abolitionist; that he is radical and vain. They say—"

"—Regardless of what they say, Johnny. The thing for you to do is to keep up with Abraham Lincoln. Some day he may be President of the United States, and—"

"—If that happens, they say, the South will secede from the Union, and there will no longer be a United States."

"The South may secede from the Union, that is possible; but if Lincoln becomes President, he will not accept their secession; he will compel them to stay in and be a part of the Union. He is a fine, brave and intelligent man, Johnny and I want you to follow him, what he says, and what he proposes to do."

"Meantime, I'm thinking about myself now. You say that I can be something. Well, I'd like to be—a lawyer."

"A—what, Johnny?"

"A lawyer, Mrs. Obermark."

"A lawyer, Johnny?"

"Yes, Mrs. Obermark. Do you think I can?"

"Well, if that is what you've made up your mind to become, I—suppose so; but you could succeed in something else much quicker, I think, and also much easier than to become a lawyer."

"Nevertheless, that's what I want to become, a lawyer, a great lawyer."

Mrs. Obermark was taken aback. When she insisted that Johnny would succeed, she hadn't thought about his becoming a lawyer. It did not take her long to understand how far fetched was such an ambition; how difficult, how very difficult this would be for him. She had hoped he would take up some sort of trade. Negro men—even though slaves, were often fine carpenters, blacksmiths, mechanics. There were some free Negro contractors and builders. All these lines were open to them, which was why she had insisted that Johnny could be somebody; could succeed—but now to want to be a lawyer, well, that was so different, and so difficult for even a free Negro in the South, that she hardly knew how to encourage him, or to even try to encourage him.

"You should, I feel, if you want to be a lawyer, wait until you have finished your education—that is, the kind that I can give you, Johnny, before you decide fully about becoming a lawyer."

"I'm sorry, Mrs. Obermark, but I've been thinking about it for a long time."

"About what for a long time, Johnny?"

"Of becoming a lawyer."

"Oh, you have, have you, Johnny?"

"For a long time, Mrs. Obermark."

"And that is why—you've been reading into those law books in the library?"

"That is why, Mrs. Obermark. I could read a whole library of law books. I feel like I could read all the law books that I see in Judge Straight's library."

"Judge Straight's library?"

"Yes, Mrs. Obermark."

"Do you know Judge Straight."

"Yes, Ma'am; but I doubt if he knows me. I've run errands for him and he should know me; but he may not. He is a very great man, Mrs. Obermark, and I am sure he must be very wise in the ways of men."

"He is, Johnny. Judge Straight is a very learned man, and a very good man."

"That is what I've thought, and why I've decided to go to him and talk to him about my plans."

"Your plans, Johnny?"

"Yes, Mrs. Obermark. My plans to become a lawyer."

"Oh."

"I feel that he will tell me the best way to become one."

"You think so?"

"That's how I feel. I think he can best tell me how to go about it; the best way and all that, you know."

"You think so?"

"I am sure he will. Don't you think he will?"

"I—I rather feel that he will. At least Judge Straight will be honest with you, and, since you seem to have made up your mind about it, I think Judge Straight is just the man you should see and talk to about it."

"That's what I had decided, and I'm going to see him tomorrow morning."

Johnny took his books and went home then, leaving Mrs. Obermark to close the school and go home, thinking; thinking about Johnny Northcross and his strange ambition.

Chapter Five

AFTER JOHNNY NORTHCROSS reached home, he did the chores, for his mother had several cows that had to be milked, hogs that had to be fed and a team that had to be bedded down each night. He ate his dinner, talked with his mother and played with his young sister, Rowena; then did some reading and checking of his studies for the next day, then it was bed time.

He retired earlier than usual, not to sleep, for he was not sleepy at all. He wanted to think, and to plan some more about how to become a lawyer. "Lawyers have first to be educated," he surmised. If he studied hard, he would learn in another year just about all Mrs. Obermark had said that she could teach him. He had, as has been shown, decided to call on old Judge Straight the next day and have the talk, but after further consideration, it would be best to call and talk with Judge Straight after he had completed his education; at least all that Mrs. Obermark could teach him and all that he could secure in Fayetteville.

He lay awake for two hours before he could decide fully to wait another year before calling on the old Judge and lay his cards on the table.

During that period, the controversy in the North and especially in Illinois over the Slavery question, developed greater intensity, and every week the papers which the wealthy white ladies of Fayetteville took and would give to him when he went to take butter and eggs and vegetables which they produced, grew more interesting, and he would read what they said about it with keen interest.

Especially interesting to him, was the series of proposed political debates between Abraham Lincoln, regarded now as one of the leading Abolitionists of the country, and Senator Stephen A. Douglas, of Illinois, whose State Sovereignty favored the South and the perpetuation of Slavery. The first debate was to take place at Ottawa, Illinois, August 21, 1858.

Johnny Northcross knew that the major part of the debate at least, would appear in the following week's papers, so he made himself patient and waited for the days to go by. In due time he was given the papers that carried the debate, and chose a time when he would not be interrupted, and have nothing to do so that he could read at least one side, perhaps the other later.

He unfolded the paper, and there before him, covering one entire page, was Senator Douglas' argument. He read it with eager anxiety.

"Ladies and gentlemen. I appear before you today for the purpose of discussing the leading political topics which now agitate the public mind. By an arrangement between Mr. Lincoln and myself, we are present here today for the purpose of having a joint discussion, as the two great political parties of the state and union, upon the principles in issue, between these parties; and this vast concourse of people gathered here from all over, shows the deep feeling which pervades the public mind in regards to the questions dividing us.

"Prior to 1854 this country was divided into two great

political parties, known as the Whig and Democratic parties. Both were National and patriotic, advancing principles that were universal in their application. An old line Whig could proclaim his principles in Louisiana and Mass. alike. Whig principles disregarded boundary or sectional lines. They were not limited by the Ohio river, nor by the Potomac, nor by the lines of the Free and Slave states, but applied and were proclaimed wherever the Constitution ruled; or the American flag waved over American soil. So it was and so it is with the great Democratic Party, which, from the days of Jefferson until this period, has proven itself to be the historic party of this nation. While the Whig and Democratic parties differed in regards to a bank, the tariff, distribution, the specie circular, and the sub-treasury, they agreed on the great Slavery question, which now agitates the Union. I say that the Whig party and the Democratic party agreed on this Slavery Question, while they differed on those matters of expediency to which I have referred. The Whig party and the Democratic party jointly adopted the compromise measures of 1850 as the basis of a proper and just solution of this Slavery question in all its forms. Henry Clay was the great leader, with Webster on his right and Cass on his left, and sustained by the patriots in the Whig and Democratic ranks who had devised and enacted the compromise measures of 1850.

"In 1851, the Whig party and the Democratic party united in Illinois in adopting resolutions endorsing and approving the principles of the compromise measures of 1850 as the proper adjustment of the question. In 1852, when the Whig party assembled in convention at Baltimore for the purpose of nominating a candidate for the Presidency, the first thing it did was to declare the compromise measures of 1850 in substance and in principle, a suitable adjustment of the Slavery question. (applause) My friends, silence will be more acceptable to me in the discussion of these questions than applause. I desire to adjust myself to your judgment, your understanding and your consciences, and not to your passions or your enthusiasm. When the Democratic convention assembled in Baltimore in the same year, for the purpose of nominating a Democratic candidate for the Presidency, it also adopted the compromise measures of 1850 as the basis of Democratic action. Thus you see that up to 1853-4, the Whig party and the Democratic party both stood on the same platform with regards to the Slavery question. That platform was the right of the people of each State and Territory to decide their local and domestic institutions for themselves, subject only to the Federal Constitution.

"During the sessions of Congress of 1853-54, I introduced into the Senate of the United States a bill to organize the Territories of Kansas and Nebraska on that principle which had been adopted in the compromise measures of 1850, approved by the Whig party and the Democratic party in Illinois in 1851, and endorsed by the Whig party and the Democratic party in National conventions in 1852. In order that there might be no misunderstanding in relation to the principle involved in the Kansas and Nebraska bill, I put forth the true intent and meaning of the act in these words: 'It is the true intent and meaning of this act not to legislate Slavery into any State or Territory, or to regulate their domestic institutions in their own way, subject only to the Federal Constitution.' Thus you see, my friends, that up to 1854, when the Kansas and Nebraska bill was brought into Congress for the purpose of carrying out the principles which both parties had up to that time endorsed and approved, there had been no division in this country in regard to that principle except the opposition of the Abolitionists. In the house of representatives of the Illinois legislature, upon a resolution asserting that principle, every Whig and every Democrat in the house voted in the affirmative, and only four men voted against it, and those four were old line Abolitionists.

"In 1854, Mr. Abraham Lincoln and Mr. Trumbull entered into an arrangement, one with the other, and each with his respective friends, to dissolve the old Whig party on the one hand, and to dissolve the old Democratic party on the other, and to connect members of both into an Abolition party, under the name and disguise of a Republican party. The terms of that arrangement between Mr. Lincoln and Mr. Trumbull, have been published to the world by Mr. Lincoln's special friend, Mr. James H. Matheny, Esq., and they were, that Lincoln should have Shield's place in the Senate, which was then about to become vacant, and that Trumbull should have my seat when my term expired. Lincoln went to work to Abolitionize the old Whig party all over the State, pretending that he was then as good a Whig as ever; and Trumbull went to work in his part of the State preaching Abolitionism in its milder and lighter form and trying to Abolitionize the Democratic party and camp. In pursuance of the arrangement the parties met in Springfield in Oct. 1854, and proclaimed their new platform. Lincoln was to bring into the Abolition camp the old line Whigs, and transfer them over to Giddings, Chase, Fred Douglas and Parson Lovejoy, who were ready to receive them and christen them in their new faith. They laid down on that occasion, a platform for their new Republican party, which was to be thus constructed. I have the resolutions of their State convention then held, which was the first mass State convention ever held in Illinois by the Black Republican party, and I now hold them in my hands, and will read a part of them and cause the others to be printed. Here are the most important and material resolutions of this Abolition platform:—

" '1. *Resolved,* That we believe this trust to be self-evident, that when parties become subversive of the ends for which they are established or incapable of retaining the true principles of the Constitution, it is the right and duty of the people to dissolve the political bands by which they may have been connected therewith, and to organize new parties upon which principles and with such views as the circumstances, and the exigencies of the nation may demand.

" '2. *Resolved,* That the times imperatively demand the reorganization of parties, and repudiating all previous party attachments, names and predestinations, we unite ourselves together in defense of the liberty and constitutions of the country, and will hereafter co-operate as the Republican party, pledged to the accomplishments of the following purposes: To bring the administration of the government back to the control of its first principles; to restore Kansas and Nebraska to the position of Free Territories, that as the Constitution of the United States vests in the States, and not Congress, the power to legislate for the extradition of fugitives from labor, to repeal and entirely abrogate the Fugitive Slave Law; to restrict Slavery to those States in which it exists; to prohibit the admission of any more Slave States into the Union; to abolish Slavery in the District of Columbia; to exclude Slavery from all the Territories over which the General government has exclusive jurisdiction; and to resist the acquirement of any more Territories, unless the prospect of Slavery therein forever shall have been prohibited.

" '3. *Resolved,* That in furtherance of these principles we will use such Constitutional and lawful means as shall seem best adapted to the accomplishment and that we will support no man for office under the General State government who is not positively and fully committed to the support of these principles, and when personal character and conduct a guarantee that he is reliable, and who shall not abjure old party allegiance and ties.'

"Now, gentlemen, your Black Republicans have cheered one of those propositions, and yet I venture to say that you cannot get Mr. Lincoln to come out now and say that he is in favor of each one of them. That these propositions, one and all, constitute the platform of the Black Republican party of this day, I have no doubt; and when you were not aware for what purpose I was reading them, your Black Republicans cheered them as good Black Republican doctrines. My object in reading these resolutions was to put the question to Abraham Lincoln this day, whether he now stands, and whether Mr. Lincoln today stands, as he did in 1854, in favor of the unconditional repeal of the

Fugitive Slave law. I desire him to answer whether he stands pledged today, as he did in 1854, against the admission of any more Slave States into the Union, even if the people want them. I want to know whether he stands pledged against the admission of a new State into the Union, with such a Constitution as the people of that State may see fit to make. I want to know whether he today stands pledged to the abolition of Slavery in the District of Columbia. I desire him to answer whether he stands pledged to the prohibition of the slave trade between the different States; I desire to know whether he stands pledged to prohibit Slavery in all the Territories of the United States, north as well as south of the Missouri Compromise Line. I desire him to answer whether he is opposed to the acquisition of any more Territory, unless slavery is prohibited therein. I want his answer to these questions. Your affirmative cheers in favor of this Abolition platform is not satisfactory. I ask Abraham Lincoln to answer these questions in order that when I trot him down to lower Egypt (he meant Cairo and extreme Southern Illinois) I may put the same questions to him. My principles are the same everywhere. I can proclaim them alike in the North, the South, the East and the West. My principles will apply wherever the Constitution prevails, and the American flag waves. I desire to know whether Mr. Lincoln's will bear transplanting from Ottawa to Jonesboro, Arkansas. I put these questions to him today distinctly, and ask an answer. I have a right to an answer for I quote from the platform of the Republican party, made by himself and others at the time that party was formed, and the bargain made by Lincoln to dissolve and kill the old Whig party, and transfer its members, bound hand and foot, to the Abolition party, under the direction of Giddings and Frederick Douglas.

"In the remarks I have made on the platform, and the position of Mr. Lincoln upon it, I mean nothing personally disrespectful or unkind to that gentleman. I have known him for nearly twenty-five years. There were many points of sympathy between us when we got acquainted. We were both comparatively boys, and both struggling with poverty in a strange land. He was more successful in his occupation than I was and hence more fortunate in this world's goods. Lincoln is one of those peculiar men who perform with admirable skill everything which they undertake. He was then just as good at telling an anecdote as now. He could beat any of the boys wrestling, or running a footrace in tossing a copper; could ruin more liquor than all of the boys of the town together (somebody called loudly "Liar") and the dignity and impartiality with which he presided at a horse race or a fist-fight excited the admiration and won the praise of everybody that was present and participated. I sympathized with him because he was struggling with difficulties and so was I. Mr. Lincoln served with me in the legislature in 1836 and we both retired and he subsided, or became submerged, and he was lost sight of as a public man for some years. In 1846 when Wilmot introduced his celebrated proviso, and the Abolition tornado swept over the country, Lincoln again turned up as a member of Congress from the Sangoman district. I was then in the Senate of the United States and was glad to welcome my old friend and companion. Whilst in Congress he distinguished himself by his opposition to the Mexican war, taking the side of the common enemy against his own country; and when he returned home he found that the indignation of the people followed him everywhere, and he was again submerged, or obliged to retire into private life, forgotten by his former friends. He came up again in 1854, just in time to make the Abolition, or Black Republican platform, in company with Giddings, Lovejoy, Chase and Frederick Douglas, for the Republican party to stand upon. Trumbull, too, was one of our contemporaries. He was born and raised in old Connecticut, was bred a Federalist, but removing to Georgia, turned nullifier when nullification was popular, and as soon as he disposed of his clocks and wound up his business in Georgia, migrated to Illinois, turned politician and lawyer here and made his appearance in 1841 as a member of the legislature.

"These two men, having formed this combination to Abolitionize the old Whig party and the old Democratic party, and put themselves into the Senate of the United States, in pursuance of their bargain, are now carrying out that arrangement. Matheny states that Trumbull broke faith; that the bargain was that Lincoln should be the Senator in Shields' place, and Trumbull to wait for mine; and the story goes that Trumbull cheated Lincoln, having control of four or five Abolitionized Democrats who were holding over in the Senate, he would not let them vote for Lincoln, and which obliged the rest of the Abolitionists to support him in order to secure an Abolition Senator. There are a number of authorities for the truth of this besides Matheny, and I suppose Mr. Lincoln will not deny it. Having formed the new party for the benefit of deserters from Whiggery, and deserters from Democracy, and having laid down the Abolition platform, which I have read, Lincoln now takes his stand and proclaims his Abolition doctrines, and expressed his opinion anew regarding slavery. Let me read a part of them. In his speech at Springfield to the convention which nominated him for the Senate, he said:

" 'In my opinion it will not cease until a crisis will have been reached and passed. *A house divided against itself cannot stand.* I believe this government *cannot endure half slave and half free.* I do not expect the Union to be dissolved; I do not expect the house to fall; *but I do expect that it will cease to be divided!* It will all become one thing, or all the other. Either the opponents of Slavery *will arrest the further spread of it,* and place it where the public mind shall rest in the belief *that it is in the process of ultimate extinction, or its advocates will push it forward until it shall* become alike lawful in all the states—old as well as new, North as well as South.'

("Good, good!" and cheers)

"I am delighted to hear you black Republicans say 'good!' I have no doubt that doctrine expresses your sentiments, and I will prove to you now, if you will listen to me, that it is revolutionary and destructive of the existence of this government. Mr. Lincoln, in the extract from which I have just read, says that this government cannot endure permanently in the same condition in which it was made by its framers—divided into Free and Slave States. He says that it has existed for about seventy years thus divided and yet he tells you that it cannot endure permanently in the same principles and exist, divided into **Free and Slave States.** Hamilton, Jay and the great men of that day, made this government free to do as it pleased on the subject of Slavery. Why cannot it exist on the same principles on which our fathers made it? They knew when they framed the Constitution that in a country as wide and broad as this; with such a variety of climate, production and interest, the people necessarily required different laws and institutions in different localities. They knew that the laws and regulations that would suit the granite hills of New Hampshire and Vermont, would be unsuited to the rice plantations of South Carolina, and they therefore provided that each State should retain its own legislation and its own sovereignty, with the full and complete power to do as it pleased within its own limits, in all that was local and not national. One of the reserved rights of the states was the right to regulate the relation between master and servant, on the Slavery question. At the time the Constitution was framed, there were thirteen states in the Union, twelve of which were slave-holding States, and one a Free State. Suppose this doctrine of uniformity, preached by Mr. Lincoln that the states should all be Free or all be Slave had prevailed, and what would have been the results? Of course the twelve Slave-holding states would have overruled the one Free state, and Slavery would have been fastened by a constitutional provision on every inch of the American Republic, instead of being left, as our fathers wisely left it, to each state to decide for itself. Here I assert that uniformity in the local laws and institutions of the different states is neither possible or desirable. If uniformity had been adopted when the government was established, it must have eventually been the uniformity of Slavery everywhere, or else this uniformity of Negro citizenship and Negro equality everywhere.

"We are told by Lincoln that he is utterly opposed to the Dred Scott Decision and will not submit to it, for the reason that he says it deprives the Negro of the rights and privileges of citizenship. Do you desire to strike out of our State Constitution that clause that keeps slaves and Free Negroes out of the state, and allow the Free Negroes to flow in, and cover your prairies with Black settlements? Do you desire to turn this beautiful state into a free Negro colony, in order that when Missouri abolishes Slavery, she can send one hundred thousand emancipated Slaves into Illinois, to become citizens and voters on an equality with yourselves? If you desire Negro citizenship; if you desire them to come into this state and settle with the white man, if you desire them to vote on an equality with yourselves, and to make them eligible to office, to serve on juries, and to adjudge your rights, then support Mr. Lincoln's and the Black Republican party, who are in favor of the citizenship of the Negro. For one, I am opposed to Negro citizenship in any and every form. I believe this government was made on the white basis. I believe it was made for white men, for the benefit of white men and their posterity forever, and I am in favor of confining citizenship to white men, men of European birth and descent, instead of conferring it on Negroes, Indians and other inferior races.

"Mr. Lincoln follows the lead and example of all the little Abolition orators, who go around and lecture in the basement of schools and churches, reads from the Declaration of Independence that all men were created equal, and then asks: How can you deprive a Negro of that equality which God and the Declaration of Independence awards to him? He and they maintain that Negro equality is guaranteed by the laws of God, and that it is asserted in the Declaration of Independence. If they think so, of course they have a right to say so, and so vote. I do not question Mr. Lincoln's conscientious belief that the Negro was made equal, and hence is his brother; but for my own part, I do not regard the Negro as my equal, and positively deny that he is my brother or any kin to me whatever. Lincoln has evidently learned by heart Parson Lovejoy's catechism. He can repeat it as well as Farnsworth, and he is worthy of a medal from Father Giddings and Frederick Douglas for his Abolitionism. He holds that the Negro was born his equal and yours, and that he was endowed with equality by the Almighty, and that no human can deprive him of these rights, which were guaranteed to him by the Supreme Ruler of the universe. Now I don't believe that the Almighty ever intended the Negro to be the equal of the white man. If He did, he has been a long time demonstrating the fact. For thousands of years the Negro has been a race upon the earth, and during all that time in all latitudes and climates wherever he has wandered, or has been taken, he has been inferior to the race he there met. He belongs to an inferior race and must always occupy an inferior position. I do not hold because the Negro is our inferior that therefore he ought to be a slave. By no means can such conclusion be drawn from what I have said. On the contrary, I hold that every right, every privilege, and immunity consistent with the safety of society in which he lives. On that point I presume there can be no diversity of opinion. You and I are bound to extend to our inferior and dependent beings every right, every privilege, every facility and immunity consistent with the public good.

"The question then arises what rights and privileges are consistent with the public good? This is a question which each State and each Territory must decide for itself. Illinois has decided it for herself. We have provided that the Negro shall not be a Slave, and we have also provided that he shall not be a citizen, but protect him in his civil rights, his life, his person and his property, only depriving him of any political rights whatsoever and refusing to put him on any equality with the white man. That policy of Illinois is satisfactory to the Democratic party and to me, and if it was to the Republicans, there would be no question upon the subject. But the Republicans say that he ought to be made a citizen, and when he becomes a citizen, he becomes your equal, with all your rights and privileges. They assert the Dred Scott Decision to be monstrous because it denies that the Negro is or can be a citizen under the Constitution. Now, I hold that Illinois had a right to abolish and prohibit Slavery as she did, and I hold that Kentucky has the same right to continue and protect Slavery that Illinois had to abolish it. I hold that New York had as much right to abolish Slavery that Virginia has to continue it, and that each and every State of this Union is a sovereign power, with the right to do as it pleases upon this question of Slavery and all of its domestic institutions. Slavery is not the only question which comes up in the controversy. There is a far more important one to you, and that is, what shall be done with the Free Negro? We have settled the Slavery question as far as we are concerned; we have prohibited it in Illinois forever; and in doing so I think we have acted wisely, and there is no man in the state who would be more strenuous in his opposition to the introduction of Slavery than I would. But when we settled it for ourselves, we exhausted all our power over that subject. We have done our whole duty and can do no more. We must leave each and every other State to decide for itself the same question. In relation to the policy to be pursued toward the Free Negroes, we have said that they shall not vote whilst Maine, on the other hand, has said that they shall vote. Maine is a Sovereign State, and has the right to regulate the qualification of votes within her limits. I would never consent to confer the right of voting and of citizenship upon a Negro; but still I am not going to quarrel with Maine or New York for differing from me in opinion. Let Maine take care of her own Negroes, and fix the qualifications of her own voters to suit herself, without interfering with Illinois, and Illinois will not interfere with Maine. So with the State of New York. She allows the Negro to vote, providing he owns two hundred and fifty dollars worth of property, but not otherwise. I would not make any distinction whatever between a Negro who held property and one who did not.

"Now my friends if we will only act conscientiously and rigidly on this great principle of popular sovereignty, which guarantees to each State and Territory the right to do as it pleases on all things local and domestic, instead of Congress interfering, we will continue at peace with one another. This doctrine of Mr. Lincoln's among the institutions of the different States, is a new doctrine, never dreamed of by Madison, or the framers of this government.

Mr. Lincoln and the Republican party set themselves up as wiser than these men who made this government, which has flourished for seventy years, under the principle of popular sovereignty, recognizing the right of each State to do as it pleased. I believe that this new doctrine as preached by Mr. Lincoln will dissolve the union if it succeeds. They are trying to array all the Northern States in one body, against the South to excite a sectional war between the Free states and Slave states, in order that the one or the other may be driven to the wall.

"I am told that my time is up. Mr. Lincoln will now address you for an hour and a half, and I will then occupy a half hour in replying to him."

Chapter Six

JUDGE STRAIGHT, WHO HAD BEEN reading Douglas' speech aloud to himself and to Doctor Green, paused now, removed his glasses which he proceeded to wipe with his handkerchief, put them back on and glanced at Dr. Green, a question in his eyes.

"Well," Dr. Green began, thoughtfully, "that's Douglas' side of the argument. What do you think of it?"

"I'd rather hear what you think of it before expressing myself, if you don't mind, Doctor."

"Sounded sincere, but rather unusual, coming from a Yankee."

"I agree with you. Born in Vermont, Douglas is more of a Yankee than Lincoln, who was born in Kentucky," smiled Judge Straight. "I wonder if Douglas isn't straddling; playing both ends against the middle, understand what I mean?" Judge Straight said.

"Oh, he's a politician, all right—but so is Lincoln."

"Just different kinds of politicians," Judge Straight said, his eyes cast down in thought. Then, raising them: "One point Douglas made, and that *is* a point."

"Yes?"

"That if Lincoln's doctrines succeed, it will dissolve the Union."

"That is a most serious point, yet it is possible." Dr. Green said and paused. His face was most thoughtful and serious. He turned to Judge Straight.

"Just how could this be done. I mean, what procedure would have to be employed?"

"That's simple enough. Secession."

"Secession? You mean that the Southern States might—secede from the Union? That would be dissolution all right."

"Exactly."

"But can they do that?"

"I see nothing to keep them from seceding but a strong President."

"What about Buchanan?"

"Weak as water."

"Yeah?"

"Couldn't be weaker."

"He was the choice of the South. In fact, they seemed to have forced his election on the country."

"Because he assured them, and they believed him, that he wouldn't interfere with the slavery question. Don't you recall that the Dred Scott Decision was held up until after he was inaugurated; and that he commended the decision highly?"

"Of course, but I didn't know that was the reason it was held up," Dr. Green said with a frown.

"That was why—and you see what the public at large is saying about it."

"And they don't ever seem to get through talking about it, criticising it and tearing it to pieces."

"And they won't quit talking about it and tearing it to pieces, either. They'll be doing so long after both you and I are dead."

"Just what is this country coming to, anyhow—and it is all about slavery? Will the North ever let us alone and leave us to handle the Negro in our own way?"

"Never as long as the South insists on holding him in slavery."

"Wasn't the Dred Scott Decision supposed to have settled that; the position of the Negro both North and South, so Chief Justice Taney said?"

"But Abraham Lincoln has just said, 'A house divided against itself cannot stand.' "

"Yet Douglas made a very intelligent reply to that, in his speech which you've just read."

"But his argument in favor of the most," he said, "lacked conviction. The thing failed to get over. After reading it, what are you thinking, about what Douglas said or what he quoted Lincoln as saying? In addition to his 'House Divided' argument, his 'This country cannot endure permanently half slave and half free.' That argument goes home; it puts you to thinking," Judge Straight insisted. "It keeps you thinking, and all Americans who have heard it and will hear it—and there is everything to prove it."

"What, for instance?"

"All this slavery agitation. Lincoln says that it will all in the end be one way, or the other, meaning it will be 'all slave' or 'all free.' Well, since the North has freed the slave of her own volition, and declares over and over again that slavery is a crime against civilization, and that all men are created equal, do you believe that any of them are going to back water and repermit slavery back in their domain?"

"No," Dr. Green replied, shaking his head.

"Then there is but one thing left, if the country is to endure permanently."

"Slavery will have to go," Dr. Green ventured.

"And there is where the trouble lay. The South will never consent to that without a fight, they will secede from the Union, one by one or in a body.

"There is the greatest problem of it all. President Buchanan will do nothing to prevent it. As stated, he's a weak man and should never have been made President of these United States, but the South put him in. That is why Lincoln dissolved the old Whig party. It had outlived its usefulness. It accepted slavery as an institution, against the wishes of the tide of Abolitionism, sweeping the North. In fact, there was little or no difference between Whiggery as it stood and Democracy, except the South preferred the Democratic party. So it was easy to put over Buchanan as they did in 1856, with the result that we now have the Republican party, a new institution, that opposes slavery as its main issue, and, take it from me, they are determined to abolish slavery, one way or the other in due time—and they have the man at the head of it, with the will to carry out and put into effect their platform."

"You mean Abraham Lincoln, of course," said Dr. Green nodding his head up and down.

"Well, Judge, let us look forward two years. Both parties will be out in the open to elect a candidate for President. Who will it be? Name the man that will be put forward by the Democrats first."

"Stephen A. Douglas."

"Stephen Douglas! But he's a Northerner."

"Straddling on the slavery issue, designed to hold the

South and hoping to carry some of the Northern states. After Buchanan, a Southerner is out. The South cannot elect a president alone. Some Northern states have got to vote along with her."

"I can understand that. Then you feel at this time that it will be Douglas? Versus who?"

"Abraham Lincoln."

"Good Heavens, no!"

Archibald Straight shook his head sadly, but firmly. "He's just as sure to be nominated by the Republican party as if he were already nominated."

"And if he is—"

"He is pretty sure to become the next President of these United States."

"And in the event that he is elected?"

"The South is liable to secede."

"And that will be the end of this country under its present name, the United States of America?"

"It could be, if Abraham Lincoln was another James Buchanan."

"Now what do you mean?"

"Just what I say, Dr. Green. If Abraham Lincoln was no stronger willed than our present Chief Executive, James Buchanan."

"Then you think that as president, Lincoln might object?"

"I mean more than that."

"More?"

"That Lincoln will not accept secession."

"But if they secede, how can he prevent it?"

Straight looked at Green and smiled. Then raising a

finger, went on. "Lincoln will declare that they are a part of the Union and will refuse to recognize secession."

"Then that means war?"

Straight nodded his head up and down.

"Then, while we are at war, Lincoln may—"

"—Declare the slaves free."

"But in such an event, it will be a long war, a long and bitter war, but the South should win."

"If war comes, that will be how they feel about it, but in the history of most wars, perhaps all that stretch over years, it is always the side with the greatest resources, with the most money, who win—in the end."

"But it will be different if the North and South ultimately find themselves at war."

"Perhaps."

"Well," Dr. Green said, rising to his feet with a deep sigh. "I hope none of this will happen. Nothing but the election of Abraham Lincoln and his ideas about the Negro could cause the South to want to break up the Union." Both men were standing now, and Dr. Green turned toward the door. Straight followed him. At the door both paused and looked out into the street. It was a beautiful North Carolina day, as clear as crystal and was pleasant outside. Turning back to Judge Straight, Dr. Green, his face very serious, said,

"I certainly hope it won't happen, Judge. I hate to picture our great Union being broken up, torn asunder. Knowing what we do and seeing things as far in advance as we can, they surely ought to be able to work out some sort of compromise."

"If we had a strong willed President we might be able

to. While I don't want to hear this repeated," and Straight paused to glance around, "I think the best way to avoid what is bound to be the greatest catastrophe of all times, would be to put through a constitutional amendment to purchase the slaves from their owners outright and set them free."

"That would be the cheapest way in the long run," Dr. Green said nodding his head.

"But it would take a strong man in the White House to work that out. The country needs a President who is a leader—and Buchanan is only a figurehead—and a mighty poor one at that." Both men, as Judge Straight concluded, shook their heads sadly, and Dr. Green turned to leave the office. As he stepped forward, both happened to look up the street and their eyes fell upon Johnny Northcross, coming in that direction.

"Are you looking at what I see, Judge?"

"I can't help seeing what you are looking at."

"Do you recall that about a year ago he came to call on you?"

"I do, but he never came back."

"He's on the way back now," and with a smile and a slap on the back, Green left the office and Judge Straight went back to his desk.

Chapter Seven

JUDGE STRAIGHT had no more than got seated and opened a newspaper when he heard footsteps coming up to his office, enter, and pause briefly when inside, whereupon he raised his eyes and met those of Johnny Northcross, looking straight at him with a sort of bold, defiant expression.

"Well," he began, "Young man, what can I do for you?"

John Northcross crossed the room then and paused across the table, at which the Judge sat, looking up at him.

"Sir," Johnny Northcross began, "I want to be a lawyer."

"God bless my soul," the Judge exclaimed, in shocked surprise, but somewhat amused, due to the suggestion seeming so far-fetched, coming from a Negro boy.

"It is a singular desire from a singular source and expressed in a singular way. Who the devil are you that wishes so strange a thing as to becoming a lawyer—everybody's servant. Have a seat," and he pointed to the chair which Dr. Green had just vacated.

"And everybody's master," Johnny replied calmly. "I refer to becoming a lawyer." He pulled the chair back then and sat down, turning as he did so to face the old Judge.

"That is a matter of opinion and open to argument, young man," the Judge now went on. "There may be, I admit, a small grain of truth in what you say." As previously shown, Judge Straight knew Johnny—just knew him. He had never as far as he could recall, exchanged words with him. So being, he preferred to reply in words of apparent ignorance.

"Who are you, anyhow, Mr. would-be-lawyer?"

"John Northcross, sir."

"John Northcross, eh?" the Judge repeated thoughtfully, thinking the while of Richard Northcross, the boy's father. He looked at the boy closely now, to compare him with his father. Then he relaxed and smiled just a little. The boy was the image of his father. Judge Straight smiled to himself as he considered the irony of it.

"And, where do you live, Johnny?" He decided not to let the boy think or feel that he knew who his father was, nor anything that went with it.

"A short distance out of town. On the old Wilmington Road in a place they call The House Behind The Cedars."

"That is near the Obermarks, isn't it? On the right side of the road as you go out of town?"

"Yes, sir."

"I've noticed it. Whom do you live with?"

"My mother, Mis' Molly Northcross."

"I see," the Judge mused. "She's a widow, isn't she?"

"Yes, sir."

"And you want to be a lawyer?"

"Yes, sir."

"How'd you let such a—desire, pop into your head?"

"I like the idea. I've read some law books. I like it."

"You want to be a lawyer. You are aware, of course, that you are a Negro."

"I am white and I am free, as all of my people have

been before me," Johnny replied, boldly, defiantly. This is what he had decided to do—be bold and defiant and claim to be white. He knew Richard Northcross was his father, that he was illegitimate; born out of wedlock; but he had thought about all that; had thought it all out months before. He was looking straight at Judge Straight now. Long ago he had decided that this was what he should do. Maybe the bluff would work. In the next moment, however, he became aware that it wasn't working, still he decided to continue his defiance.

"You are black, and you *are not* free," Judge Straight exclaimed, and met his effort at defiance and challenged it.

"I say that I am white, and I am free. All my people are free."

"Some of them," the Judge replied calmly. He didn't intend to tell the boy which ones were free.

"You are black my lad, and you are not free, and it is just about impossible for you, under those circumstances, to become a lawyer. No person of African extraction has ever become a lawyer in Fayetteville, so I'm surprised at you coming forward with such a suggestion. It is vain."

"I still want to become a lawyer."

"But consider the difficulty of realizing such an ambition in the South. You may be, perhaps, a 'Free' Negro; but at that you are not a citizen. You cannot travel without your papers; you cannot vote. You could not secure accommodations at an Inn; you cannot be out after nine o'clock at night without your permit. If a white man struck you, you dare not return the blow, and you could not testify against him in a court of justice."

"If he struck me and I could not return the blow, according to what you say, and I could not testify against him in a court of justice, then it would not be a court of justice. It would be a court of injustice."

"Perhaps you're right, but they still call it a court of justice, and, regardless of what you say about being white, I repeat, you are black and you *are* not free."

"It all sounds so strange; so unlike all that you white people say, that you write about, what you preach—but don't practice."

"Did you ever hear of the Dred Scott Decision?"

"I read it," the boy replied calmly. Judge Straight started, and looked at Johnny with a new expression in his eyes.

"You read it? Then—"

"It may all be true, what that decision said; but the Declaration of Independence says that 'all men are created equal.' What about that?"

"I'm afraid they were not thinking about—colored men when the framers conceived that, Johnny."

"Abraham Lincoln says that it meant all men, regardless of their color, creed or previous condition of servitude. What about that?"

"That's what Abraham Lincoln said; but Abraham Lincoln is only a politician. Judge Taney, the author of the Dred Scott Decision, said otherwise. Judge Taney is Chief Justice of the United States Supreme Court—and his word, and what he said about Dred Scott is law, the law of the land."

"Regardless of all that, Judge Taney meant 'Negroes.' I still insist that I am white and I am free, and I want to become a lawyer."

"Somewhere, sometime you had a black ancestor. One touch of Negro blood makes the whole person black and you won't be able to get away with claiming to be white."

"Why shouldn't it be the other way, if the white blood is so much superior?"

"Because it is more convenient as it is—and more profitable."

"It is not right."

"I agree with you, but that is the way it is, and, I'm afraid, the way it's got to stay."

"I had thought that I might *pass* for white. There are lots of white people darker than I am."

"Humph. Everybody around here knows you; and know you to be a Negro. Where did you get the becoming a lawyer idea, anyhow?"

"It is not an idea. It is an ambition."

"Have you talked to anybody else about—this ambition of yours?"

"I have," the boy replied.

"Your mother, perhaps?"

"No," Johnny replied, shaking his head. Judge Straight looked very much surprised. "Then pray who?"

"To Mrs. Fritz Obermark."

"You mean, Fritz Obermark, the tavern keeper's wife?"

"I went to school to her. She taught me all I know."

"Did she teach you to want to become a lawyer?"

"No sir."

"If you spoke to her about it, what was her reaction? What did she say?"

"She didn't say."

"What do you mean. You say that you talked to her

about it, now you advise that 'she didn't say.' "

"Mrs. Obermark is a very kind woman."

"I agree with you. A fine woman, a Christian woman." Nodding his head in agreement, Johnny went on to explain:

"After I read the Dred Scott Decision, and that a Negro has no right which a white man is due to respect; that we are no more than a bag of potatoes, a bale of cotton or a sack of corn, and that we may be bought and sold by anybody who desired to make a profit, I was very discouraged."

The Judge nodded his head up and down understandingly, and listened to the boy's story with keen interest.

"But I've been reading what Abraham Lincoln has been saying up there in the North, and I have lived on in the hope that what Judge Taney decreed in the Dred Scott Decision, might somewhere, somehow, be wrong, so I decided to talk about it with my teacher."

"That was the proper thing to do."

"She said that what Judge Taney said was not true; that his decision was cruel and inhuman; and that I should not think about it; that I should, in fact, try to forget it as much as I could. She said, and has always said, that I could succeed—that I *would* succeed and be a very successful man some day if I tried hard enough."

"Are you willing to try hard? Very hard?"

"Very hard, Judge. I am willing to do anything to be somebody."

"But just why a lawyer? It would be far easier for you to succeed doing something else. What did Mrs. Obermark suggest?"

"She implied that I could in some other way, though she didn't say that I couldn't become what I want to be, a lawyer."

"And that was how it started; you talked with Mrs. Obermark; you told her that you wanted to be a lawyer. Well, she must have said something, one way or another."

"I told her that I was going to talk to you about it."

"Oh, you did? What did she say to that?"

"She said that was the proper thing to do; that you were a fine gentleman and a wise man; that you would best tell me, and to come and talk to you." The Judge felt flattered, in spite of himself. He had been inclined from the outset to regard the boy lightly. Now he looked hard at him, a slight frown on his face.

"And you are—really serious about what you say, of becoming a lawyer?"

"I couldn't be more serious about anything."

"This is all so strange and unusual, also—impossible. I hate to tell you to give up such an ambition."

"Please don't tell me to give it up." Thereupon the Judge looked hard at him again, and rising to his feet, strolled across by the window and looked out at a huge magnolia tree that stood in the back yard. Johnny sat where he left him, staring up at the Judge hopefully.

Judge Straight was in a quandary. Off hand he was ready to dismiss the whole thing as the insane dream of a foolish boy. He turned to look at the boy, and their eyes met. Judge Straight was annoyed. He couldn't ignore the anxiety and expression in the eyes of this boy who wanted to be a lawyer. He presently returned to his chair and called the boy by name.

"Yes, sir, Judge Straight?" anxiously, hopefully.

"I am going to drive out of town tonight to see a man. What you've talked about is right now—well, we won't talk about it any more, but if it is convenient, come back to my office tomorrow and see me—anytime will do." The Judge rose to his feet then and waved the boy, who was trying to shower him with thanks and gratitude, toward the door and following him to it, closed and locked it behind Johnny.

Chapter Eight

NOT FAR FROM where Molly Northcross lived, out on the Wilmington Road in The House Behind the Cedars, lived a family, a Negro family by the name of Fowler, Henry Fowler and his large family, a wife and twelve children.

Henry Fowler was a tall, black and powerfully built man and one of the best carpenters and brick and stone masons in the state. He was so good, in fact, that over twenty-five years before, when slaves were not priced as high as at this period of our story, Henry Fowler purchased and paid for himself. One thousand dollars was the price he paid, $500 cash and the balance in notes, which he paid off in less than one year—and then he bought his wife a beautiful, healthy, brown-skinned Slave woman, for whom he paid (part cash and notes) $600.

So at the time of our story, Henry Fowler had been free most of twenty-five years and had, during that period, bred and raised his twelve healthy and strong children, seven boys and five girls, all of whom were born free, and so Henry Fowler and family were the most prosperous and highly respected of the Free Negroes who lived in and around Fayetteville.

The family and Molly Northcross called themselves neighbors, although the Fowler's two hundred acre farm was three miles away from The House Behind the Cedars. All the Fowler children had attended Mrs. Fritz Obermark's private school and the older ones had learned all that she knew how to teach them, and were intelligent, well raised children.

Fowler was a building contractor, and had been for many years. They complained that his prices were rather high; but most preferred to pay them on the grounds that when Henry Fowler built your house, your barn or anything else you wanted erected, frame, brick or concrete, it *was built*—and would stand the test of storms, wind, rain —and years!

Henry Fowler and his family were reading people, and kept themselves well informed on topics of the day, including the furious controversy going on all over the North regarding the slavery question.

"They say," he said one night at the dinner table, after they had finished their meal, but had not gotten up from the table. "They say," he repeated, "that if Abraham Lincoln gets the nomination for President on the Republican ticket, the South will promptly, if he's elected, secede from the Union and set up their own government, under the name of the Confederate States of America."

"God help us," echoed Matilda Fowler, his wife.

"Why do you say that, mama," said Selena, their oldest daughter, who had just been graduated from Oberlin College, Oberlin, Ohio. The family was very proud of her.

"Why, my dear," her mother replied. "Can't you see what will happen to our people; I mean our people still in slavery? The entire controversy is about the slavery question. The North wants slavery abolished; the South wishes to retain it. If they secede from the Union, the Negro down here may never be free."

Selena was thoughtful. In all they had talked about at Oberlin, so very much of which was about slavery, no one had ever put it that way. Yet—turning to her father.

"What do you think about it, papa?" Fowler lowered his paper thoughtfully.

"I agree with your mother. Our people's only hope for an early freedom, if this happens, is for Abraham Lincoln, if he be elected, and the South secedes, to prevent it—and he can only do so by force of arms."

"But if the South should win?" Selena suggested.

"Then it might be a long, long time before the race is freed, if ever. But that won't happen."

"The South says it will," Selena went on, her face serious. "All the Southern papers declare that if the states go to war, the South will win and win quickly."

"If she wins," observed her father, judiciously, "it will have to be quickly, but from what I have learned about Abraham Lincoln, he is not the kind of man that gives up quickly. If the South forces a war by attempting to secede, we are going to learn a great deal more about Abraham Lincoln than we now know."

"You think so?"

"All you've got to do is follow his speeches. I've read all that Douglas has said, and all that Lincoln says in reply to him."

"What do you think of Douglas?"

"A politician, pure and simple, playing both ends against the middle."

"What do you mean by 'playing both ends against the middle'?"

"Trying to satisfy both sides, the North and the South,

in the hope of getting enough votes to be elected President."

"They tear everything he says to pieces at Oberlin."

"Oberlin is a hot bed of Abolitionism," her father said calmly. "We expect that from there."

"Frederick Douglas spoke there a month ago. I wrote you about it."

"Yes, we know. How was he received?"

"They raved about him. People came to hear him from all over Northern Ohio. He was magnificent. I was proud of him. Oh, father. He just makes you feel things. He says that within ten years there will be no slavery anywhere in the United States. He said that it will have to go. He also said a great deal about a man he called John Brown."

"A conscientious Abolitionist. He has been turning Kansas upside down. They say that he is crazy."

"I don't believe it," Selena said, insistently. "The South wants us to feel that all Abolitionists are crazy. They say that Harriet Beecher Stowe is crazy—or at least was when she wrote Uncle Tom's Cabin; they call it a pack of lies. They say there never was a man as mean as Simon Legree; that a man just couldn't be that mean."

"They also say," interposed Mrs. Fowler, "that the Dred Scott Decision was all right."

"They *would* liken us to a sack of wheat and a bale of cotton," cried Selena indignantly. "Oh, you ought to hear how they deride it at Oberlin! They say that Roger Brooke Taney should be impeached for writing it. They call it the most infamous document ever conceived by the mind of man."

"All of this agitation about slavery can't go on indefinitely," Fowler said. "It's got to break up somewhere, somehow."

" 'A house divided against itself cannot stand,' " Selena quoted. "Ah, those are words by Abraham Lincoln that will never be forgotten as long as America lives. Also, 'this country cannot endure permanently, half slave and half free.' "

"Immortal words, Selena," Mrs. Fowler cried, and made a supplication. "Immortal words. The Lord will not let this crime against himself and man endure. Someday we will all be free, now let us pray." Whereupon she bowed her head in prayer and Henry Fowler offered the prayer.

When it was over, they rose from the table, just as Leonard, one of the younger boys of the family, burst into the room, crying:

"Johnny Northcross has disappeared! Johnny Northcross has disappeared! Nobody has seen him for three days! He's disappeared!"

"What do you mean, boy, disappeared?" his father cried, grabbing him and forcing him to face him.

"That's what happened. I was by his house. His mother says he has." All the family had gathered now around Leonard and his father. All were excited.

"All his mother will say is that 'He's gone. My Johnny's gone!' and falls to crying."

Henry Fowler paused and turned to look in the faces of his family.

"Well, Henry," Mrs. Fowler cried. "What are you going to do, just stand there speechless? Have the boys hitch horses to the buggy and let's get up to Molly's and see what this is all about. It must be a mistake."

A half hour later the Fowler family joined others in the yard of the house behind the Cedars and went into the house where they found Molly crying. Neighbors who had arrived sooner were comforting her as she sat crying. Her small daughter, Rowena, clung to her skirts and she was crying, too, although she was too young to know what it was all about. But she understood by the seriousness on everybody's face that something had happened.

Henry Fowler, who was looked up to by the Negroes as a sort of leader, came forward and stood over Molly. The others moved back respectfully to permit him to question her.

"Is what we hear true, Molly? It must be a mistake."

"It ain't a mistake, Mr. Fowler. Johnny's gone, gone, jes' gone." And again she lowered her eyes and gave up to tears, using her apron to dry them.

"But—what do you mean, 'just gone,' Molly? How could a big boy like Johnny just—disappear?"

"That's how it happened, Mr. Fowler. Johnny just disappeared. Disappeared three days ago."

"But maybe he—got lost in the woods. If that's so, we'll find him. Perhaps he may have gone to visit—old Mose Allen, the hermit, who lives deep in the woods. Johnny is sort of—venturesome, you know. If so, we'll go look for him. We'll—"

"Tain't no use, Mr. Fowler. You won't fin' him."

"Maybe he—might have gone to see Della, the Conjure Woman?"

"He didn't believe in Conjurism. He was afraid of old Della. He didn't go there. I don't know where Johnny went, 'cept that he's gone. He told me he was going away, and that he'd never come back; that nobody that's living around here would ever see him again."

"But why?" Henry Fowler insisted, in amazement.

"Please don't ask me. All he said when he came home the last time was that because of that old Dred Scott Decision, a niggah couldn't be anything and never would be, and that he couldn't stand it and was going away for good. He said goodbye to me and little sister, and said that he'd never come back. And then—he just walked out the door and I ain't seen him since."

Henry Fowler had listened to her carefully, and saw that he could learn no more about Johnny from her at the present time, so motioning to the others, he went outside and they followed him. Outside he turned to them and said:

"Johnny was always inclined to dream somewhat, now that I come to think of it. He has evidently gone away, but I'm sure that he'll come back soon. It does all seem strange and peculiar, but I advise you all just to be patient, and wait and not bother his mother any more for awhile. She's all upset now, so it'll only make her suffer more if we continue to hang around and bother her, so go back to your homes and wait, just be patient. I'm sure Johnny'll return soon."

He left Selena there to help comfort the distracted Molly, and loading the rest of the family he had brought with him into the buggy, they returned to their home, where when alone again with Matilda, he resumed his query regarding Johnny.

"Why did he go away like that, Henry," Mrs. Fowler asked, and looked at him curiously. "He must have had a reason. What reason?"

"I didn't say what I thought up there where all could hear it, Matilda. But Johnny always possessed peculiarities. He is one of these many Negroes that would like to be white, perhaps he planned to go North somewhere and pass for white, who knows? I wouldn't put it past him."

"He could do that, of course, but why would he leave like that, his mother to be so unhappy and all that?"

"Negroes like that develop strange ambitions, nobody knows what kind of an idea they may get."

"Do you think he'll ever come back?"

"Some day, maybe, but not soon. I'm sure of that, not soon," and Henry Fowler shook his head, rose to his feet and went outside.

And so it was. Johnny Northcross *had* disappeared. As far as those who knew him all his life were concerned, the earth could have just opened and swallowed him. That was how completely he disappeared—and was never seen by those who knew him, except one, in Fayetteville again.

Chapter Nine

WE LEAVE NORTH CAROLINA, Molly Northcross and the Fowler family, and move Northward, to a small town at the junction of the Potomac and Shenandoah Rivers, near where the states of Maryland, Virginia and West Virginia intersect. It is late in the year of 1859, and a strange event is taking place.

Abolitionists had been writing, singing and praying for Negro freedom for thirty years. The sweet tempered Reverend Samuel J. May had long ago tried to slow down his fellow Abolitionist, William Lloyd Garrison, with saying at one of their meetings, "Mr. Garrison, you are too excited—you are on fire." The reply of the veteran agitator, was, "I have need to be on fire, for I have icebergs all around me to melt."

At the yearly meeting of the Anti-Slave Society in Framingham Grove, near Boston, on a fourth of July, Garrison had read the Fugitive Slave Act, had then read the court order of a Federal Judge, handing a Fugitive Slave back to its owner, and had then lighted matches to both documents, crying as they burned, "And let all the people say Amen!"

The "Amens" were shouted and then Garrison raised high above his head a copy of the Constitution of the United States, read its clauses that sanctioned slave property, declared it the source of all other atrocities, termed it the original "Covenant of death and agreement with hell," set a lighted match to it and held it up burning as he cried, "So perish all compromises with tyranny, and let all the people say 'Amen'."

Henry Ward Beecher had held mock auctions of slave women in his Brooklyn church; "Uncle Tom's Cabin" was selling in editions of hundreds of thousands of copies; of writing, talking and singing there had been much. In hundreds of runaway slave cases in the North, there had been little and big riots and clashes; in Kansas, had been civil war and terrorism.

Now out of Kansas came a man who stole horses, ran slaves to freedom and for the sake of retaliation and terror, burned barns, and killed men who dared block his way, without trial or hearing. Asked why he had killed young people, he had answered "nits grow to be lice." He had come to Kansas from Ohio and New York, a child of Mayflower Pilgrim fathers. Both his grandfathers had fought in the Revolutionary war; at his house his 19 children had partaken of prayers and scripture readings morning and night as they were reared in his solemn household. As he mixed with the Abolitionists of the Eastern States, he told them action was wanted, bold deeds! Not a Moses giving laws, nor a Jeremiah with lamentations, but a Samson not afraid to pull down a temple if it brought his own death. A lesson could be taken from Joshua whose Ram's Horn brought down the walls of Jericho. "One God and man can overturn the Universe," he said often.

He was through with talk. Some agreed with him. The thousands of dollars he wanted for rifles, pikes, wagons and stores were given to him by wealthy and respectable citizens who secretly agreed to call the affair a "speculation in wool." They spoke and wrote to each other, asking "How is our speculation in wool getting along?"

On Monday, Oct. 15th, 1859, telegraph dispatches to all parts of the United States carried terror and strange news. At the junction of the Shenandoah and Potomac Rivers, where the states of Maryland and Virginia touch borders in a rocky little town called "Harper's Ferry," the telegraph wires had been cut, a United States government arsenal and rifle factory captured, the gates broken and the watchman made prisoner, and Virginia Slaveholders taken prisoners and locked up, and their slaves told they were free and should spread the word of freedom to all slaves everywhere.

All this happened between Sunday night and Monday daybreak. It was a Monday mystery. What was happening? Was a slave revolt starting? Would the next news tell of rebellion? Slaves repeating the Nat Turner insurrection? Only on a wider scale, with a list of men, women and children butchered in their looted or burned homes? The country breathed easier on Tuesday, when Captain Robert E. Lee, commanding 80 Marines, rushed a little Engine house, where eighteen little men inside had fought till all were dead or wounded except two.

In a corner of the engine house they found an old man with a long, flowing beard, who said that his name was John Brown.

"Who sent you here?" they asked.

"No man sent me here," he replied, calmly. "It was my own prompting and that of my maker, or that of the devil, which ever you please. I acknowledge no man in human form."

"What was your object in coming?"

"I came to free the slaves," he said. His gaze into space made him seem saintly; like a messenger from above.

"And you think you were acting righteously?"

"Yes, my friends, righteously. I think you folks are guilty of a great wrong against God and humanity. I feel it right to interfere with you to free those you hold in bondage. I hold that the Golden Rule applies to the slaves, too."

"And do you mean to say that you believe in the Bible?"

"Certainly I do."

"Don't you realize that you are a seditionist, a traitor, and that you have taken up arms against the government of the United States?"

"I was trying to free the slaves. I have tried moral persuasion for the purpose, but I don't think the people in the Slave states will ever be convinced that they are wrong."

"You are mad and fanatical."

"And I think you people of the South are mad and even more fanatical. Is it sane to keep millions of men and women in Slavery? Is it sane to think that such a system can last? Is it sane to suppress all who would cry out against this system? And to execute all who would interfere with it? Is it sane to talk of war rather than give it up?"

The state of Virginia gave him a fair trial on charges of murder, treason and inciting slaves to rebellion. Northern friends gave him able lawyers; he was found guilty; a judge pronounced the sentence—he must hang by the neck until he was dead, dead, dead!

He looked the judge in the eyes and spoke calmly, as though he had thought it all out long ago, and as though he might be speaking to all Americans and the world and to future generations.

"Had I taken up arms against the rich, the powerful the intelligent, the so-called great, or in behalf of any of them or their friends, or any of their class, every man in this court room would have deemed it an act worthy of reward, rather than of punishment. Yet the court acknowledges the validity of God. I see a book kissed here which is called the Bible, and which teaches me that all things I would have men do unto me, so must I do unto them. I endeavored to act up to those instructions. I fought for the poor, and say it was right, for they are as good as any of you. God is no respector of persons. I believe to have interfered in behalf of this despised poor, I did no wrong, but right. Now if it be deemed necessary that I should forfeit my life for the furtherance of the end of Justice, and mingle my blood further with the blood of my children, and the blood of millions in this Slave country whose rights are disregarded by cruel and unjust enactments, I say, let it be done!"

Word came from friends who planned to steal him away from the death watch. He sent back word that he would be more useful to freedom when dead. He knew he could show men how to die for freedom, without a quaver or a flicker of fear. Afterward his ghost would come back and walk over the earth and tear at men's hearts with questions about freedom and justice and God. He would be a memory among young men. It is the young who count. For himself, he was fifty-nine years old, but the average age of those who had captured Harper's Ferry with him, and flamed in a scarlet deed before the world, was twenty years and five months.

Yes, he would go to his hanging. He would write a last message; before going to the noose he would hand another prisoner a scrap of paper with the writing: "I, John Brown am now quite certain that the crimes of this guilty land will never be purged away but with blood. I had, as I now think, vainly flattered myself that without much bloodshed it might be done."

On the day of his doom, the Shenandoah Valley was swept and garnished by sky and weather beyond the 3,000 guardsmen with rifles and bayonets. He could see blue haze and a shiny sun over the Blue Ridge mountains.

"This is a beautiful country," he said, smiling as he gazed out over the timbered mountains. "I never had the pleasure of really seeing it before."

And he may have thought that he missed many Shenandoahs of life, shining valleys that would have lighted him into pronouncing the word beautiful, wistfully, yet he was not a wistful man. He was a man of doom; believing in his right to doom others and the power of God to doom wrongdoers everlastingly.

Speaking through his bars, he had told one, "All our actions, even all the follies that led to the disaster, were decreed to happen ages before the world was made." It was all settled for him, so long before and he was only walking as God had ages ago preordained that he should walk. The

Sheriff asked, "Shall I give you the signal when the trap is to be sprung?"

"No, no," came the even word from the white beard. "Just get it over with quickly."

What John Brown believed came true; his ghost did walk. The Governor of Virginia, the jailer who had kept him in the lock-up, talked about the way he died, without a quaver or a flicker, cool, serene; he died as great Virginians had died; he was an artist at dying.

Emerson, Thoreau, Victor Hugo, compared him to Christ, to Socrates, the great martyrs who had met death bravely, firmly. Wendell Phillips said, "The lesson of the hour is insurrection." The Abolitionists chanted hallelujahs. The Anti-Slavery men had regrets. Stephen A. Douglas called for a law to punish conspirators, quoting Lincoln's House Divided speech and Seward's Irrepressible conflict speech to which that Republican politicians and their "revolutionary doctrines" had incited John Brown.

Lincoln spoke at Troy, Kansas, on December 2, the day John Brown was hanged, and made an appeal to Southern sympathizers. "Old John Brown thought slavery was wrong, as we do. He attacked slavery contrary to law and it availed him nothing before the law that he thought himself right. He has just been hanged for treason against the state of Virginia; and we cannot object, though he agreed with us in calling slavery wrong. Now if you undertake to destroy the Union contrary to law, if you commit treason against the United States, our duty will be to deal with you as John Brown has been dealt with. We shall try to do our duty."

The plunge of John Brown into the darker valley beyond the Shenandoah kept echoing. Sweet Louise Alcott referred to him as "Saint John the Just," and Longfellow whispered to his diary that the hanging of Brown marked the "Day of a new revolution, quite as much needed as the old one."

Brown had been so calmly and so religiously glad to be hanged publicly before all men and nations, that he could not be dismissed lightly from the thoughts of men. Even those who agreed with Stephen A. Douglas, speaking in the Senate, that Brown was a horse-thief and murderer, were puzzled at the old man writing to his family: "A calm peace too, fills my mind by day and by night," and to a Clergyman, "Let them have me; I forgive them, and may God forgive them, for they know not what they do."

The hanging of John Brown renewed the nationwide agitation against slavery. The number of Anti-Slave Societies increased in numbers, then somebody conceived the idea to draw huge paintings, to be displayed along the highways, all over the North. These paintings showed John Brown on the gallows, the rope around his neck, his long gray beard flowing all over his breast. His eyes were large and raised to heaven, his hands outstretched, reminding one of some strange and saintly patriarch, making appeal to God. On the same long billboard, was the scene of a beautiful octoroon slave girl, on her knees, hair down over her shoulders, eyes down, bent and crying while a brutal auctioneer stood over her, his mouth wide with the words, "How much am I bid?" Below, hands up, pointing at the girl, were a group of slave-traders, some with a string of blood hounds, held in the other hand, all seeming to bid for the helpless girl. Beneath these huge paintings that could be seen from a quarter mile away, were these captions: *"This is Slavery."* And under Brown's picture, *"He gave his life to end this sin against God and man. Will you join with us to drive it from the face of the earth?"*

The response was terrific. John Brown became a martyr, and lives as one to this day. Perhaps he will continue as a martyr until the end of time. Although slavery got started almost with the first settlement of the country, and had grown and flourished for a hundred years or more without many people paying to it so much attention, it now possessed seemingly, the minds of all the people in the North. "Down with it, down with it and — long live John Brown!" rang and echoed louder and louder the country over.

The more conservative people shuddered with fear as to what it would come to. Lincoln's "House divided against itself, cannot stand," speech became a byword. Everybody seemed to have learned it by heart and seemed never to get tired of saying it, repeating it over and over. Also, "The country cannot endure permanently half slave and half free." And the people believed it, they said it, sang it, preached it, and in this state of excitement, 1859 rolled out and 1860, the fatal year in the history of America, came in.

Chapter Ten

IT IS NOW THE YEAR 1860. We pass over the early months of that year with regrets as the nomination of Abraham Lincoln for President on the young and new Republican ticket, was most interesting; but if all the interesting events in Abraham Lincoln's life were chronicled, it would take a whole shelf of volumes, so we pass over the nomination and come directly to the election campaign in the fall of that year.

The campaign between Lincoln and Stephen A. Douglas, nominee for President on the Democratic ticket, was more interesting, controversial and exciting than their series of debates in Illinois in 1858.

Douglas was stumping the country; it seemed a losing fight; he went on, tireless; his friends were amazed at the way he wore out, went to bed, rested, got up and came back to the fight again.

He told a Boston crowd: "When you asked your representatives why the Pacific Railroad had not been made, why the mail systems had not been reformed and carried on with vigor, why you have no overland mail route to the Pacific and no steam lines, you are told that the slavery question occupied the whole session. All great measures that affect the commercial interests, the shipping interests, the manufacturing interests, the industrial interests of the country, have been lost for want of time. There never will be time unless you banish forever the slavery question from the halls of Congress and remand it to the people of each State and Territory."

And he told a New York crowd: "If Lincoln should be elected, which God in his mercy forbid (a voice 'Amen' and laughter) he must be inaugurated according to the Constitution and laws of the country. . . . Yet if the withdrawal of my name would tend to defeat Mr. Lincoln, I would this moment withdraw it."

Democrats of the Southern wing of the party sent Jefferson Davis to dicker with Douglas; if all contenders would shake hands and join on one candidate they would sweep the election; Douglas said it couldn't be done; too many of his friends would go for Lincoln.

Among business interests in the East, Douglas was able to stir a fear of what would happen if Lincoln were elected and the country was split with civil war; trade would go to pieces.

"I think there will be the most extraordinary efforts ever made to carry New York for Douglas," Lincoln wrote to Thurlow Weed, the New York Republican political boss. "You and all others who write me from your state think the effort cannot succeed and I hope you are right. Still, it will require close watching." Replying to a Southerner, he wrote of receiving many assurances from the South, "that in no probable event will there be any formidable effort to break up the Union." He hoped and believed "The people of the South had too much good sense and good temper to attempt the ruin of their government rather than see it administered as it was administered by the men who made it."

Again and again came letters—just precisely what would he do with slavery if elected? Would it not be wise to say plainly that he wouldn't interfere? One he answered, "Those who will not heed or read what I have already publicly said would not read or heed a repetition of it." He quoted: "If they hear not Moses and the prophets, neither will they be persuaded though one rose from the dead."

Replying to a pro-Douglas Louisville editor, he wrote, "For the good men of the South—and I regard the majority of them as such—I have no objection to repeat seventy and seven times. But I have bad men to deal with, both North and South; men who are eager for something new upon which to base new misrepresentations; men who would like to frighten me; or at least fix upon me the character of timidity and cowardice" (he was hinting at James Buchanan). What he would write would be seized upon as an "awful coming down." The letter closed, "I intend keeping my eye on these gentlemen and not to unnecessarily put any weapon in their hands."

Dick Yates, who was soon to become Governor of Illinois, and whose son was elected and served a term or two as such, more than forty years later, was telling of a pretty young bride who handed a bridegroom a thousand dollars after their wedding night. And the bridegroom told her, "Lizzie I like you very much, but this thousand dollars doesn't set you back any." From this Yates went on, "If Lincoln has all the other qualifications of a statesman, it doesn't set him back any with us who know and love him, to know that he was once a poor hard working boy.

"We know old Abe doesn't look very handsome, and

some of the papers say he is positively ugly." Yates was also saying on the stump, "Well, if all the ugly men in the United States vote for him, he will surely be elected."

Enemy newspapers rolled up his past, claiming that he had said that Thomas Jefferson was a slave-holder who "brought his own children under the hammer, and made money out of his debaucheries," particularizing that "A daughter of this vaunted champion of Democracy was sold years ago at public auction in Louisiana, and purchased by a society of gentlemen who wished to testify by her liberation their admiration of the Statesman who "dreamt of freedom in a slave-embrace."

This Lincoln designated as a base forgery, "which my friends will be entirely safe in denouncing."

The campaign was in its last week. Millions of people had by this time read his words of two years ago in The House Divided speech. They struck the soft, weird keynote of the hour. "If we could first know where we were, and whither we are drifting, we could better judge what to do and how to do it."

Twice, since he had first spoken, the corn had grown from seed to the full stalk and had been harvested.

In a book he had carried, it was said, "All rising to power is by a winding stair." As he went higher it grew colder and lonelier.

The last leaves were blowing off the trees, and the final geese honking South. Winter would come and go before seed corn went into the ground again.

At last came the day of election, Nov. 6, 1860. From nine o'clock on, Lincoln sat in the Springfield telegraph office. Lyman Trumbull arrived from Alton and summarized reports. "We've got 'em, we've got em!" Then came a telegram. "Hon. A. Lincoln: Pennsylvania 70,000 majority for you. New York safe. Glory enough. S. Cameron."

Out in the streets, and up around the State House, crowds surged, shouting: "New York, 50,000 majority for Abe Lincoln." Lines of men locked arms and sang "Ain't I glad I joined the Republicans." They sang and cried until they were hoarse.

The count showed Lincoln winning by 1,856,452 votes, a majority of nearly a half million over Douglas. But fifteen states gave Lincoln no electoral votes—and in ten Southern states he didn't get a count of one popular vote!

Chapter Eleven

EVENTS THEN CAME as by clock at a signal—and Lincoln's election was the signal!

South Carolina legislators voted to raise and equip 10,000 volunteer soldiers; Georgia and Louisiana legislators voted $1,000,000 and $500,000 for arms and troops.

South Carolina through its legislature declared itself a sovereign and independent state and seceded from the Union of states on December 20, 1860. With a flag of its own, with oaths of allegiance, forts, post offices, custom houses of the Federal government were taken. Before New Years' Day it was known that the whole row of cotton states would follow South Carolina, with a view to forming a Southern Confederacy. And in the same weeks, for whatever it portended there was also the accomplished fact that a great chain of railroads, making a complete rail transportation line from Bangor, Maine to New Orleans, had been completed.

A crisscross of facts was operating. Robert Toombs was saying: "It is admitted that you seek to outlaw $4,000,000,000 of property of our people in the Territories. Is not that a cause for war?" But was secession the softest way of managing this property? Jefferson Davis had his doubts. And Alexander Stephens had written five months before, shortly after Lincoln's nomination on the Republican ticket, "I consider slavery much more secure in the

Union than out of it if our people are but wise. Property suffers in revolutions," he pointed out. "The institution is based on conservatism." Stephens had noted the diminishing supply of slave labor and wrote his belief that without fresh supplies from Africa, slavery would be replaced by free competitive wage labor.

Among the fire-eaters clamoring for secession were those who made a business of buying, breeding and selling slaves. A planter from Georgia had told the National Democratic Convention, "I have had to pay from $1,000 to $2,000 a head for good niggers, when I could go to Africa and buy better darkies—all I can bring back for $50 a head. I tell you and plead with you, gentlemen of the Democratic party, of which I am a life long member, to put in your platform at this convention, a promise to restore the slave trade—and I will subscribe $100,000 to your campaign fund!" This was too much for Democrats, who upheld slavery even, and he was hooted down.

A reporter on the New York Tribune dug up a strange fact in South Carolina. On the tax lists in Charleston, for the year 1861, he found the names of 132 "colored people" who paid taxes on 390 slaves which they owned; the class included eleven Indian families who had consorted with Negroes.

Secession was the creed of state sovereignty, which Douglas had said so much about in the years before. It was now kicking back and proving a boomerang for not even the learned Douglas had thought or foreseen that it would give the State the right also to secede from the Union as they were now doing, and stand by themselves in a separate existence when it chose to do so.

John C. Calhoun and other figures of austere life and heroic proportions had taught this with a logic that to Southerners seemed inexorable and unconquerable. Yet the fact must be recorded with this, that Davis, Stephens and other high counselors of the South, in their letters and speeches at this time, did not advise secession. The leaders were Yancey, Rhett and others. They cried, "The irrepressible conflict is about to be visited upon us by the Black Republican Lincoln and his fanatical, diabolical Republican party."

Once secession was accomplished by its radical manipulators, Southerners, till then conservative and advising against disunion, fell in line as patriots whose first oath of allegiance was to their sovereign State, their country. They quoted Decatur:

"Our country! In her intercourse with foreign nations, may she always be in the right, but our country right or wrong." And the *Charleston Mercury* published dispatches from Northern cities under the heading "FOREIGN NEWS."

Those who demurred, reasoned and lifted warnings against disunion and secession were many, but their efforts were useless against the onrush of those who took Lincoln's election as a signal for a time of change. There were those who looked on Lincoln as Alexander Stephens did in a letter to J. Henley Smith, a fellow Georgian, five months before the election, saying:

"What is to become of the country in case of Lincoln's election, I do not know. As at present advised, I shall not be for disunion on the grounds of his election. It may be that his election will be attended with events that will change my present opinion, but his bou-election would not be sufficient in my judgment to warrant a disruption —particularly as his election will be the result, if it occurs at all, of the folly and madness of our own people. If they do these things in the "green tree," what will they not do in the dry? If, without cause, they destroy the present government, the best in the world, what hopes have I that they would not bring untold hardships upon the people in their efforts to give us one of their own modeling? Let events shape their own course. In point of merit as a man, I have no doubt Lincoln is just as good, as safe and sound, as far as the South is concerned, as Buchanan, in spite of all the criticism heaped on Buchanan by the North, and would administer the government so far as he is individually concerned as safely and as honestly and faithfully in every particular. I know the man well. He is not a bad man. He will make as good a President as Fillmore did, and perhaps better, in my opinion. He has a great deal of practical common sense. Still, of course, his party might do mischief. If so, it will be a great misfortune, that our people brought upon us . . . We have nothing to fear from anything so much as unnecessary changes and revolution in government . . . I shall, of course, vote for Douglas."

The "Green Tree" grew. One by one the six cotton states of the lower South joined South Carolina in leaving the Union and declaring their right to self-government and self-determination, under the "state-sovereignty idea." A strange silence met all this. Nothing was heard from Stephen A. Douglas for or against it, at this time. He seemed to be standing quietly on the sidelines, looking on, wondering perhaps, why he hadn't thought that perhaps his preachment hadn't encouraged the secession idea, now that it was here.

The Southern delegates met at Montgomery, Alabama on Feb. 4th, 1861, 30 days before Abraham Lincoln was to be inaugurated. They organized a provisional government, called The Confederate States of America, electing Jefferson Davis, of Mississippi, President and Alexander Stephens, of Georgia, as Vice-President. Conventions in North Carolina and Arkansas, deliberated, and joined the Confederacy. In Tennessee, the voters balloted 105,000 to 47,000 in favor of secession, the Union strength coming from the Mountainous sections, where there were few and hardly any slaves, showing that the whole idea of seceding and breaking up the Union was due to disagreement between the North and the South with regard to Negro slavery.

In Virginia, three to one of 130,000 votes, were in favor of "The Mother Of Presidents" going into the Confederacy. The one third against it were from the western part of the State, which disagreed so completely that it "seceded" from Virginia, stayed in the Union, and became West Virginia.

In Texas, Governor Sam Houston refused to call the legislature and tried to stop secession—but was bowled over.

Arsenals, supplies, post offices and ships were taken over by the new government. No one was arrested—as John Brown had been two years before, tried for treason and hanged, for capturing one single arsenal. Fort guns fired on a ship at sea. President Buchanan, the vaciliator, nervous, distracted and intoxicated most of the time, proclaimed Fast Day publicly, and moaned privately that he was the "last President of the United States."

"The Union is falling to pieces all around me and I don't know what to do about it" he was quoted as saying.

Well meaning men of splendid intentions and generous hearts sprang forward with compromises, arrangements, and suggestions; special committees and conferences of duly appointed delegates met, spoke, protested, argued and adjourned. Southern congressmen resigned and left Washington; there were enough votes one January day to admit "Bleeding Kansas as a State in the Union." The *Charleston Mercury*, in an editorial, derided, *"What a Union!"*

While Southern radicals were calling Lincoln a fanatical, diabolical Abolitionist, Wendell Phillips sneered at him and called him the "Slave hound" of Illinois. Robert Toombs read to the new Georgia legislature a defense of Secession written and published by Horace Greeley. The advice of Greeley was: "Let the crying sisters depart in peace."

Boston heard Phillips declare: "Let the South march off, with flags and trumpets, and we will speed the parting guests. Let us not stand upon the order of her going, but go at once. Give her forts, arsenals and sub-treasuries. Give her jewels of silver and gold, and rejoice that she has departed. All hail disunion!"

Frederick Douglas, the great Negro Abolitionist, after a visit to see Lincoln, in Springfield, was asked what he thought of secession. He replied quietly: "It is not what *I* think about it," and turned his eyes in the direction of

Lincoln's home which he had just left. "Wait until that man back there speaks. It is what *he* thinks of and about it, that counts." Smiling, a smile the reporters did not understand until Lincoln read his inaugural address on the facade of the Capitol, one month later, he went on his way.

Chapter Twelve

WHILE ALL THIS was going on, secession and disunion, let us turn back for a moment, to little Fayetteville, resting quietly on the banks of the Cape Fear River and see how our old friends Judge Straight, Dr. Green, and, in the country, the Fowlers were taking it.

"Well," sighed Dr. Green, "secession seems about complete now with Texas overriding its Governor and coming in. I think that just about completes the Confederacy, and we are no longer a part and parcel of the United States of America." Judge Straight smiled, and grunted.

"Says who?" he said, looking hard at Green, who turned to him in some surprise.

"Says who? What do you mean?"

"Says I, and I mean that all this seceding, grabbing post offices, arsenals, custom houses and etc., is all very premature."

"It has already been done. The Confederate States of America is now a fact, a Republic within itself. What do you mean by calling it premature?"

"Just what I said, and which is just what it is, no more."

"You talk in riddles or parables or—will you explain *why* it is not now a government in itself?"

"Wait until Abraham Lincoln speaks."

"Abraham Lincoln! He's the cause of the whole thing. If

he hadn't thrust himself into the situation, this—none of this, would have happened."

"Listen to me, Dr. Green. Haven't you studied and weighed this whole thing, thought it out clearly and without bias?"

"I've certainly given it a lot of thought."

"It's too bad the whole South didn't do so, before it went to such an extreme, by which I mean, seceding from the Union and setting up this so-called 'Confederacy,' without even waiting to see what Lincoln was going to do."

"But every effort was put forth to ascertain his views—what he planned to do and all that, but up to now even, there has been no answer."

"There was none due."

"None due!" Dr. Green exclaimed in shocked surprise. "Now what do you mean?"

"That Abraham Lincoln was duly elected as fifteen other presidents have been before him. He said a lot of things before and during his campaign for the Presidency. His speeches, the platform and all that had been published widely, and everybody knew just where he stood, and what he stood for before they voted for and elected him."

"He was known as the greatest Abolitionist in the country."

"Very true, but he said time and again, that he would, if elected, uphold the Constitution. He couldn't himself change that, so why all this breaking up and seceding before the man is even inaugurated?"

"It's because they expect him to do something radical about slavery."

"The whole country has been against the spreading of

it. They haven't permitted a slave State to be admitted in years. Slavery has long since been confined to where it is."

"But the South felt sure that if he were elected, he planned to interfere with it. They have seceded in order to beat him to the punch."

"Like a group of children, small children. Why couldn't they wait until he was inaugurated; wait until they heard and read his inaugural address; it is most certain that he will set forth such plans, if any, with regards to the institution at that time. At least, in all courts it is the rule to hear a least one side of the case, and both sides most times before rendering a decision. If the South *had* to secede, they could have at least waited until Lincoln was inaugurated, heard and read his address to the Nation, after which they could have seceded and broke up the Union just as well afterwards as before."

"Well," Dr. Green sighed, "there is plenty of logic in what you say, but they have seceded and set up their own government where the North can no longer bother them about keeping Negroes in Slavery, so that is that."

"I have the feeling that the trouble hasn't really started yet." Dr. Green looked quickly and intently at him.

"If Lincoln in his inaugural address, does not recognize the Confederacy, and these States right to secede, and says they are still a part and parcel of the Union, the same as all the States that haven't seceded, then what?"

"Then it is war."

"War sure enough, and a real war."

"The North will then have to conquer the South, and restore the status quo."

"Which is exactly what I expect them to do."

"You don't seem to take our Confederacy very seriously."

"I have no right to, for it has been conceived and set up on a foundation of sand, and sand gives way; it may let you down. It is sand, loose sand, you know."

Selena Fowler found herself back in Fayetteville, after a vis't to Charleston, South Carolina, the glamour city of the central South of that day; a city full of tradition—dating back to the earliest settlement in America. It was proud of this tradition, and liked to boast about it.

As has been shown, South Carolina was the first state to secede, laying down a pattern by doing so, for all the other cotton states which followed.

Miss Fowler went to Charleston just before Thanksgiving, 1860 and did not return to Fayetteville until well into February, 1861—and she returned to her parent's home with plenty to talk about for weeks afterward.

"My, what a place, what a place!" she exclaimed, when the family walked into the large sitting room with its huge fire-place, the light from which illuminated the room so completely that lights were hardly necessary.

Important conversations in the Fowler home customarily took place after dinner, and, usually, if some member of the family had something very important to report or talk about, they waited until all the family were gathered in the large sitting room where it was very comfortable.

Selena took the seat proffered her, which was arranged so that she could tell about her trip facing most of the family.

"You mean," her father said, "about the war and—all that?"

"I mean about, just about everything," Selena replied, hardly knowing just where to start.

"Well, I read that there is great activity down there, preparing for the—expected war."

"And how!" Selena exclaimed, and shook her head as if to emphasize how active it was.

"All you see and hear are recruits, drilling, drilling and drilling everywhere, morning, noon and night."

"You don't mean to say so," her mother exclaimed, seeming amazed. "Who are they preparing to fight?"

"The North, mother, the North and the Yankees—and how they seem to want to fight."

"Well, I declare. Getting all ready to fight with the War not started?"

"It is in full blast in Charleston—and how badly they want to fight. Why, they're just War crazy."

"It's an outrage," her father commented, his face serious. "The people of the whole State should be ashamed of themselves. Talking about Lincoln starting the war, when the man has done nothing but get elected to the Presidency —and he didn't do that, even. The people did it."

"Not the Southern people, and especially not Charlestonians. I doubt if he got a hundred votes in that town."

"How did they manage to reach such a—radical conclusion, anyhow, dear?" her father queried curiously. All eyes now went to Selena, who, taking her time, started to tell them how.

"In the first place, Charleston, seemingly, more than anywhere else in the South, resents, more than any other

Southern spot, the North's continued interference with their slavery question. They argue that the Negroes who are being held as slaves are not kicking and seem satisfied, so why has the North got to shed so many tears about the situation?

"They honestly feel this way about it. Why, would you believe that there are more than 100 Negro families down there, free Negroes, who own slaves, Negro slaves?"

"Oh, no!" her mother exclaimed.

"The records show that they paid taxes on almost 400 Negro slaves—owned I tell you, by Negroes themselves."

"And what kind of people are these Negroes?" from her father.

"Good looking ones, mostly, almost white with a few mixed with Indians. They live mostly, these slave owners, in a very fine section of town and to themselves, and are as proud as rich Southerners themselves."

"God help us," Mrs. Fowler cried, throwing up her hands.

"Why, they went so far as to try to organize a Negro Unit to get ready to help the whites there, lick the North."

"Hush your mouth!"

"They certainly did. The only thing that seemed to challenge it was that, they all wanted to be officers."

"What do you mean?"

"When they reported, it was found that nobody had enlisted to fight exactly. The set up was: forty-three officers and one private." The whole family laughed uproariously.

"What are they saying about Lincoln down there?"

"Just about everything. They say he'll never be inaugurated; that there are at least a half dozen spots where he is to be assassinated on the way to Washington, so he will never get to be president at all.

"There are other rumors which say he will; and that he will be inaugurated in Chicago, under the watchful eye of the Army, and will go to Washington afterwards, but that he will be killed before he gets to sign a single bill."

"What do they have to say about his silence; just why he hasn't said what he plans to do, if and when he ever becomes President?"

"They have an answer for that, too—in fact, they seem to have an answer for everything in Charleston. One of the big boasts is, that if they try to force Lincoln on the country—disregarding the fact that he has been duly elected, and is due to take his seat, that a Confederate Army will be waiting just outside Alexandria, Virginia, and will promptly cross the Potomac, march into Washington and take over the Capitol and everything else and install Jeff Davis as President and Alexander Stephens as Vice-President instead of Lincoln and Hamlin.

"Another thing they are whispering is that Hamlin has some Negro blood and that he will have to be killed at the same time with Lincoln, as having a Vice-President with Negro blood would be a greater disgrace than letting Lincoln take his seat." All of which brought more laughter from the family, it was so obviously untrue and absurd.

"Charleston is filled with Slave-Traders, and it is talked around there that after the South has licked the North and taken the whole country over, the first thing Congress will do is to repeal the law that prohibits importing any more Negroes as slaves. They say they will repeal all laws that confine slavery to slave States, and pass a new one that permits owners to have slaves anywhere and everywhere in the United States; and that slave-traders will be allowed to import all the Negroes from Africa for new slaves that they can bring. They declare that a movement is on foot to import 50,000 from West Africa to be shipped to Texas, mostly, and, that after the War is over and the South has licked and killed off most of the Yankees, the brave young Confederates who have been responsible for winning the war, will be given free land in Texas and be permitted to purchase up to five or six slaves at a top cost of $500 each as a reward for winning the war."

Chapter Thirteen

IN JUSTIFICATION OF SECESSION, the South Carolina convention issued two papers. One, An Address to the People of the Slave-holding States, reported by R. B. Rhett; the other, a Declaration of the Causes of Secession, reported by C. B. Memminger. Respecting the members or the delegates to the convention's point of view, this declaration to us, seems so interesting that we have decided to reproduce in full same herewith, with the exception of two long and early paragraphs, going back to 1787.

"The people of the State of South Carolina in convention, assembled, on the 2nd day of April, A.D. 1852, declared that the frequent violations of the Constitution of the United States by the Federal government, and its encroachments on the reserved rights of the States, fully justifies this State in its withdrawal from the Federal Union; but in deference to the opinions and wishes of the other slave-holding states, she forbore at that time to exercise this right. Since that time, however, these encroachments have continued to increase, and further forbearance ceases to be a virtue.

"And now the State of South Carolina, having resumed her separate and equal place among nations, deems it due to herself, to the remaining United States of America and the nations of the world that she should declare the immediate causes which have led to this act.

"The Constitution of the United States in its fourth Article, provides as follows:

"No person held to labor or service in one state under the laws thereof, escaping into another, shall, in consequence of any law or regulation therein, be discharged from such service or labor, but shall be delivered up, on claim of party to whom such service or labor may be due."

AUTHOR'S NOTE: *One of the most unpleasant sights of that period to Northern people, opposed by sentiment and human sympathy to slavery, was the spectacle of seeing a helpless Negro, who had run away from bondage, being turned over by the local sheriff to slave-hunters from the South, who were invariably wicked and vile of character and speech. The more such recoveries, the greater the objection grew toward it, hence the local state laws nullified the Federal Fugitive Slave Act which was passed against the will of most Northern legislators, but who acquiesced to keep "peace in the family of States."*

We return now to South Carolina's Cause for Secession.

"This stipulation was so material to the compact, that without it that compact would not have been made. The greater number of the contracting parties held slaves and they had primarily evinced their estimate of the value of such a stipulation by making it a condition in the Ordinance for the government of the territory ceded by Virginia, which obligations and the laws of the General government, have ceased to effect the objects of the Constitution.

"The States of Maine, New Hampshire, Vermont, Massachusetts, Connecticut, Pennsylvania, Illinois, Indiana, Michigan, Wisconsin and Iowa, have enacted laws which either nullify the acts of Congress, or render useless any attempt to execute them. In many of these States the fugitives are discharged from the service of labor claimed, and in none of them has the State government complied with the stipulation made in the Constitution. The State of New Jersey, at an early day, passed a law in conformity with her Constitutional obligation; but the current of Anti-Slavery feeling, running so high, has led her more recently to enact laws which render inoperative the remedies provided by her own laws and by the laws of Congress.

In the State of New York, even the right of transit for a slave has been denied by her tribunals; and the States of Ohio and Iowa have refused to surrender to justice fugitives charged with murder, and with inciting servile insurrection in the State of Virginia. Thus the constitutional compact has been deliberately broken and disregarded by the non-slave-holding States; and the consequence follows that South Carolina is released from her obligation. . . .

We affirm that these ends for which this government was instituted have been defeated and the government itself has been destructive of them by the action of the non-slaveholding States. Those States have assumed the rights of deciding upon the propriety of our domestic institutions; and have denied the right of property (property referred to in all cases was that of human slaves) established in fifteen of the States and recognized by the Constitution.

They have denounced as sinful the institution of slavery; and have permitted the open establishment among them of societies, whose avowed object is to disturb the peace of, and *eloin* the property of the citizens of other States. They have encouraged and assisted thousands of our slaves to leave their homes; and those who remain, have been incited by emissaries, books and pictures, to servile insurrection.

For twenty-five years this agitation has been steadily increasing until now it has secured to its aid the power of the common government. Observing the forms of the Constitution, a sectional party has found within that article establishing the executive department, the means of subverting the Constitution itself.

A geographical line has been drawn across the Union (they were referring to the Mason Dixon line) and all of the states North of that line have united in the election of a man to the high office of President of the United States whose opinions and purposes are hostile to slavery. He is to be entrusted with the administration of the common government because he has declared that *"This government cannot endure permanently half slave and half free,"* and that the public mind must rest in the belief that slavery is in the course of ultimate extinction.

This sectional combination for the subversion of the Constitution has been aided in some of the States, by elevating to citizenship, Negroes, persons who, by the supreme law of the land, are incapable of becoming citizens. (Please recall the Dred Scott Decision). And their votes have been used to inaugurate a new policy, hostile to the South and destructive of its peace and safety.

On the fourth day of March, next, this party will take possession of the Government. It has announced that the South shall be excluded from the common territory; that the Judicial Tribunal shall be made sectional, and that a war must be waged against slavery until it shall cease throughout the United States.

The guarantees of the Constitution will then no longer exist; the equal rights of the States will be lost. The slaveholding States will no longer have the power of self-government, or self-protection and the Federal government will have become their enemy.

Sectional interest and animosity will deepen the irritation; and all hope of remedy is rendered vain, by the fact that the public opinion at the North has invested a great political error with the sanctions of a more religious belief.

We, therefore, the people of South Carolina, by our delegates in convention assembled, appealing to the supreme Judge of the world for the rectitude of our intentions, has solemnly declared that the Union heretofore existing between this State and the other States of North America is dissolved, and that the State of South Carolina has resumed her position among the nations of the world, as a separate and independent State, with full powers to levy war, conclude peace, contract alliances, establish commerce, and to do all other acts and things which independent States may of right to do.

Chapter Fourteen

IN THE MANY stories on the life of Abraham Lincoln, the story of a plot in Baltimore to assassinate Lincoln as he passed through that city on his way to Washington, became so persistent that Alan Pinkerton, the great detective of that period and many decades after, was sent with a large staff to investigate. He succeeded in arresting a large number of men, but broke up such a danger if there ever were any real danger, and accordingly, Lincoln reached Washington safely and on the 4th day of March 1861, in the early afternoon, gave the world the finished address which follows below. His speech went to a wide realm of readers, who searched and dug into every line and phase of it. Reason and emotion wove through it —and hopes, fears, resolves. It was momentous to Lincoln and the Country because it told why he would make a war if he saw a war as justified and inevitable. He read the address.

"Fellow citizens of the United States. In compliance with a custom as old as the government itself, I appear before you to address you briefly, and to take, in your presence, the oath prescribed by the Constitution of the United States, to be taken by the President, before he enters on the execution of his office. I do not consider it necessary at present to discuss those matters of administration about which there is no special anxiety or excitement.

"Apprehension seems to exist among the people of the South that by the accession of a Republican administration, their property and their peace and personal security are to be endangered. There has never been any reasonable cause for such apprehension. Indeed, the most ample evidence to the contrary has all the while existed and been open to their inspection. It is found in nearly all the published speeches of him who now addresses you. I do but quote from one of these speeches when I declared that 'I have no purpose directly or indirectly to interfere with the institution of slavery in the states where it exists. I believe I have no lawful right to do so, and I have no inclination to do so.' Those who nominated and elected me, did so with full knowledge that I had made this and many similar declarations, and had never recanted them. And more than this, they placed in the platform for my acceptance, and as a law to themselves, and to me, the clear and emphatic resolution, which I now read:

"*Resolved,* That the maintenance inviolate of the rights of the States and especially the right of each State, to order and control its own domestic institutions according to its own judgment exclusively, is essential to that balance of power of which the perfection and endurance of our political fabric depend, and we denounce the lawless invasion by assumed forces of the soil of any State or Territory, no matter under what pretext, as among the gravest of crimes.'

"I now reiterate those sentiments; and in doing so, I only press upon the public attention the most conclusive evidence of which this case is susceptible; that the property, peace and security of no section are to be in any wise endangered by the now incoming administration. I add, too, that all the protection, consistent with the Constitution, and the laws that can be given, will be cheerfully given to all the states, when lawfully demanded, for whatever cause—as to one section as to another.

"There is much controversy about delivery up of fugitives from service or labor. The clause I now read is as plainly written in the Constitution as any other of its provisions:

"No person held to service or labor in one State, under the laws thereof, escaping into another, shall in consequence of any law or regulation therein, be discharged from such or labor, but shall be delivered up on claim of the party to whom such service or labor may be done.'

"I take the official oath today, with no mental reservations, and with no purpose to construe the Constitution of laws by any hypocritical rules. And while I do not now choose to specify particular acts of Congress as proper to be enforced, do suggest that it will be much safer for all, both in official and private stations, to conform to and abide by all those acts which stand unrepealed, than to violate any of them, trusting to find impunity in having them held to be unconstitutional.

"It is seventy-two years since the first inauguration of a President under our National Constitution. During that period, fifteen different and greatly distinguished citizens have in succession administered the executive branch of the government. They have conducted it through many perils, and generally with great success. Yet, with all this scope of precedent, I now enter upon the same task for the brief constitutional term of four years, under great and peculiar difficulty. A disruption of the Federal Union, heretofore only menaced, is now formidably attempted.

"I hold that, in contemplation of Universal law and of the Constitution, the Union of these States is perpetual. Perpetuity is implied, if not expressed, in the fundamental laws of all governments. It is safe to assert that no government proper ever had a provision in its organic law for its own termination. Continue to execute all the express provisions of our National Constitution, and the Union will endure forever—it being impossible to destroy it, except by some action not provided for in the instrument itself.

"Again, if the United States be not a government proper but an association of States in the nature of contract, can it be peacefully unmade by less than all the parties who made it? One party to a contract may violate it—break it, so to speak, but does it not require a vote of all to lawfully rescind it?

"Descending from the principles, we find the proposition that, in legal contemplation, the Union is perpetual, confirmed by the history of the Union itself. The Union is much older than the Constitution. It was formed, in fact, by the Articles of Association, in 1774. It was matured and continued by the Declaration of Independence in 1776. It was further matured, and the faith of all the then thirteen States expressly plighted and engaged, that it should be perpetual, by the Articles of Confederation in 1778. And, finally, in 1787 one of the declared objects for ordaining and establishing the Constitution was to 'form a more perfect union.'

"But if the destruction of the Union by one or by a part only of the States be lawfully possible, the Union is less perfect than before the Constitution, having lost the vital element of perpetuity.

"It follows from these views that no State upon its own mere motion can lawfully get out of the Union; that resolves and ordinances to that effect are legally void; and that acts of violence, within State or States, against the authority of the United States, are insurrectionary or revolutionary, according to Constitution.

"I therefore consider that, in view of the Constitution and the laws, the Union is unbroken and to the extent of my authority I shall take care, as the Constitution expressly enjoins upon me, that the laws of the Union be faithfully executed in all the States. Doing this I deem only to be a simple duty on my part; and I shall perform it, so far as practicable, unless my respectful masters, the American people, shall withhold the requisite means, or, in some authoritative manner direct the contrary. I trust this shall not be regarded as a menace, but only as the declared purpose of the Union that it will Constitutionally defend and maintain itself.

"In doing this there need be no bloodshed or violence; and there shall be none, unless it be forced upon the National authority. The power confided to me shall be used to hold, occupy and possess the property and places belonging to the government, and to collect the duties and imposts; but beyond what may be necessary for these objects, there will be no invasion—no using of force against or among the people anywhere. Where hostility to the United States, in any interim locality, shall be so great and universal, as to prevent competent resident citizens from holding the Federal Offices, there will be no attempt to force obnoxious strangers among the people for that object. While the strict legal right may exist in the government to enforce the exercise of these offices, the attempt to do so would be so irritating, and so nearly impracticable withal, that I deem it better to forego, for the time, the uses of such offices.

"The mails, unless repelled, will continue to be furnished in all parts of the Union. So far as possible, the people everywhere shall have the sense of perfect security, which is most favorable to calm thought and reflection. The course here indicated will be followed unless current events and experience shall show a modification or change according to circumstances actually existing, and with a view and a hope of a peaceful solution of the National troubles and the restoration of fraternal sympathies and affection.

"That there are persons in one section or another who seek to destroy the Union at all events and are glad of any pretext to do it, I will neither affirm nor deny; but if there be such, I need address no word to them. To these, however, who really love the Union, may I speak?

"Before entering upon so grave a matter, as the destruction of our National fabric, with all its achievements, its memories, and its hopes, would it not be wise to ascertain precisely why we do it? Will you hazard so desperate a step while there is any possibility that any portion of the ills you fly from have no real existence? Will you, while the certain ills you fly to are greater than all the real ones you fly from—will you risk the commission of so fearful a mistake?

"All profess to be content in the Union if the Constitutional rights can be maintained. Is it true then, that any right, plainly written in the Constitution has been denied? I think not. Happily the human mind is so constituted that no party can reach to the audacity of doing this. Think, if you can, of a single instance in a plainly written provision of the Constitution that has ever been denied. If by the mere force of numbers, a majority should deprive a minority of any clearly written Constitutional right, it might, from a moral point of view, justify revolution—certainly would, if such right were a vital one. But such is not our case. All the vital rights of minorities and of individuals are so plainly assumed to them by affirmations and negations, guarantees and prohibitions, in the Constitution, that controversies never rise concerning them. But no organic law can ever be framed with a provision especial to every question which may arise or occur in its practical administration. No foresight can anticipate nor any document of reasonable length contain, express provisions for all possible questions. Shall fugitives from labor be surrendered by National or State authority? The Constitution does not expressly say. May Congress prohibit slavery in the Territories? The Constitution does not expressly say.

"From questions of this class spring all our Constitutional controversies, and we divide upon them into majorities and minorities. If the minority will not acquiesce, the majority must, or the government must cease. There is no other alternative, (The South in seceding, was guilty of this and they knew it as well as did Lincoln) for continuing the government is acquiescence on one side or the other.

"If a minority in such case will secede rather than acquiesce, they make a precedent which will in turn divide and ruin them; for a minority of their own will secede from them whenever a majority refuses to be controlled by such minority. For instance, why may not any portion of a new Confederacy, a year or two hence, arbitrarily secede again, precisely as portions of the present Union now claim to secede from it? All who cherish disunion sentiments are now being educated to the exact temper of doing this.

"Is there such perfect identity of interests among the States to compose a new Union, as to produce harmony only, and prevent renewed secession? Supposing that, in a State, one county or two or three, decide to secede from the rest of the counties in that State, where would the State soon be—any State; every State?

"Plainly the central idea of secession is the essence of anarchy. A majority held in restraint by Constitutional checks and limitations, and always changing locality with deliberate charges of popular opposition and sentiments, is the only true sovereignty of a free people. Whoever rejects it does of necessity fly to anarchy or to despotism. Unanimity is impossible; the rule of a minority, as a permanent arrangement is wholly inadmissible; so that rejecting the majority principle, anarchy or despotism in some form is all that is left.

"I do not forget the position assumed by some, that Constitutional questions are to be decided by the Supreme Court; nor do I deny that such decisions must be binding, in any case, upon the parties to a suit, as to the object of that suit, while they are also entitled to very high respect and consideration in all parallel cases by all other departments of the government. And while it is obviously possible that such decisions may be erroneous in any given case, still the evil effect following it, being limited to that particular case, with the chance that it may be over-ruled and never become a precedent for other cases, can better be borne than could the evils of a different practice. At the same time the candid citizen must confess that if the policy of the government upon vital questions affecting the whole people, is to be irrevocably fixed by the Supreme Court the instant that they are made, in ordinary litigation between parties in personal actions, the people will have ceased to be their own rulers, having to that extent practically resigned their government into the hands of that eminent tribunal. Nor is there in this view any assault on the court or the Judges. It is a duty from which they may not shrink to decide cases properly brought before them, and it is no fault of theirs, if others seek to turn their decisions to political purposes.

"One section of our country believes slavery is right, and ought to be extended, while the other believes it is wrong and ought not to be extended. This is the only substantial dispute. The fugitive slave clause of the Constitution and the law for the suppression of foreign slave-trade, are each as well enforced perhaps as any law can ever be in a community where the moral sense of the people imperfectly supports the law itself. The great body of the people abide by the dry legal obligation in both cases and a few break over in each. This, I think cannot be perfectly cured, and it would be worse in both cases after the separation of the sections than before. The foreign slave-trade now imperfectly suppressed, would be ultimately revived, without restriction in one section, while fugitive slaves, now only partially surrendered, would not be surrendered by the other.

"Physically speaking, we cannot separate. We cannot remove our respective sections from each other, nor build an impassable wall between them. A husband and wife may be divorced, and go out of the presence and beyond the reach of each other; but the different parts of our Country cannot do this. They cannot but remain face to face and intercourse, either amicable or hostile, must continue between them. Is it possible then, to make that intercourse more advantageous or more satisfactory after separation than before? Can aliens make treaties easier than friends can make laws? Can treaties be more faithfully enforced between aliens than laws can among friends? Suppose you go to war, you cannot fight always; and when, after much loss on both sides, and no gain on either you cease fighting, the identical questions as to terms of intercourse are again upon you.

"This country with its institutions, belongs to the people who inhabit it. Whenever they shall grow weary of the existing government, they can exercise their constitutional right of amending it, or their revolutionary right of dismembering it or overthrow it. I cannot be ignorant of the fact that many worthy and patriotic citizens are desirous of having the National Constitution amended. While I make no recommendations of amendments, I fully recognize the rightful authority of the people over the whole subject, to be exercised in either of the modes prescribed in the instrument itself; and I should, under existing circumstances, favor rather than oppose a fair opportunity being afforded the people to act upon it. I will venture to add that to me, the convention mode seems preferable in that it allows amendments to originate with the people themselves instead of only permitting them to take or reject propositions originated by others which might not be precisely what they would wish to either accept or refuse. I understand that a proposed amendment to the Constitution—which amendment, however, I have not seen, has passed Congress to the effect that the Federal government shall never interfere with the domestic institution of the States, including that of persons held to service. To avoid misconstruction of that what I have said, I depart from my purpose not to speak of particular amendments as far as to say, that holding such a provision to now be implied as constitutional law, I have no objection to it being made express and irrevocable.

"The chief magistrate derives all his authority from the people, and they have conferred none upon him to fix terms for the separation of the States. The people themselves can do this also if they chose; but the executive as such has nothing to do with it. His duty is to administer the present government, as it comes to his hands, and to transmit it, unimpaired by him, to his successor.

"Why should there not be a patient confidence in the ultimate justice of the people? Is there any better or equal hope in the world? In our present difference is either party without faith of being in the right? If the Almighty ruler of nations, with this eternal truth and justice, be on your side of the North, or on yours of the South, that truth and that justice will surely prevail by the judgment of this great tribunal of the American people.

"By the frame of the government under which we live, this same people have wisely given their public servant but little power for mischief. And have, with equal wisdom, provided for the return of that little to their own hands at very short intervals. While the people retain their virtue and vigilance, no administration by any extreme of wickedness, or folly, can very seriously injure the government in the short space of four years.

"My countrymen, one and all, think calmly and well upon this whole subject. Nothing valuable can be lost by taking time. If there be an object to hurry any of you in hot haste to a step which you would never take deliberately, that object will be frustrated by taking time; but no good object can be frustrated by it. Such of you as are now dissatisfied, and, on the sensitive point, the laws of your own framing it; while the new administration will have no immediate power, if it would, to change either. If it were admitted that you who are dissatisfied, hold the right side in the dispute, there still is no single good reason for precipitate action. Intelligence, patriotism, Christianity and a firm reliance on Him who has never yet forsaken this favored land, are still competent to adjust in the best way, all our present difficulties.

"In your hands, my dissatisfied countrymen, and not in mine, is the momentous issue of Civil War. The government will not assail you. You can have no conflict without being yourselves the aggressor. You have no oath registered in heaven to destroy the government, while I shall have the most solemn one to 'preserve, protect and defend it.' "

Thus flowed the reasonings, explanations, watchwords, that ended his long silence.

"I am loath to close. We are not enemies, but friends. We must not be enemies. Though passion may have strained, it must not break our bonds of affections. The mystic chords of memory, stretching from every battle field, and patriot grave, to every burning heart and hearthstone, all over this broad land, will yet swell the chorus of the Union, when again touched, as surely they will be, by the better angels of our nature."

Chapter Fifteen

ABRAHAM LINCOLN FELT strangely relieved when he completed his address. It had been on his mind for weeks. He had suspected, before he was elected, that there would be trouble activity from the South in the event that he was elected. But he hardly expected it to go as far as it had. As he watched the States, from his home in Illinois, after he was elected, proceed to withdraw from the Union steadily, he became fully aware of his position long before the time came for him to go to Washington.

He all but knew, and hadn't expected Buchanan to do anything to discourage it, although as the Southerner's choice, four years before, he felt that Buchanan might have held up secession until after he was inaugurated. However, he realized when he failed to, just how weak and cowardly Buchanan was; and that if the Union was to be reconstituted, as it were, it would be up to him, after becoming President to restore the status quo.

He was compelled to stand where he was for two and one half gruelling hours to shake hands with thousands, most of whom, if not all, wished him well. They studied him, observed his grave face and were grateful as they walked away, that they had shaken hands with a man who would either fail or succeed in the greatest task ever imposed on a President.

They loved and admired his speech and told him so,

over and over again as they passed by and clasped his hand. They admired the logic, the sound reasoning and the timeliness of all he said; but many realized as well as Lincoln did, that it would fall on deaf ears in the South, that was bristling and anxious to be at war. The Mexican War had been only a skirmish and over with very quickly without much bloodshed or loss of life. Lincoln was able to foresee that peculiar and unfortunate mania which make people crave to fight—especially as the South was viewing it, when they thought their rights were being interfered with —the right to maintain and extend slavery as they wished. While the whole South clamored and succeeded in bringing secession, charged Lincoln and his Abolitionists' ideas as the cause of bringing it about, at heart it knew that it was not Lincoln singly at all. They knew that a wave of Abolition had been sweeping over the North for years; that Uncle Tom's Cabin had been the first incident to inspire it more rapidly than before; and that The Dred Scott Decision-had added fuel to the flames, also that the hanging of John Brown, a year before election, added the straw which finally broke the camel's back.

The South knew that it was a house divided against itself, and that somewhere, somehow and sometime, the house would fall. So it chose Lincoln's election as the psychological moment to tear it down.

The South possessed a group who wielded great and almost undue influence in rushing her into secession prematurely. This was the same group which had been shaping the policy and destiny of the South, politically, for years untold. These were the slave-traders and large slave-owners.

In all that has been said or shown with regards to the relation between the North and the South, there was not shown any serious difference of opinion on important issues. The dissension was confined exclusively and positively to the Slave-question and it was the slave-issue that had now torn the two sections asunder.

Not all the people of the South favored slavery. It was a problem which they found themselves born into. They consoled themselves with the feeling, when it annoyed their consciences too much, to say to themselves that they never created it, they found it. It was an institution that the present generation had inherited, and no leader seemed to come forward with a program or a pattern bold enough and brave enough to change it.

Meanwhile the slave-traders, breeders and exploiters of slave-labor, found it profitable, seared their consciences, if many ever had any, and planned how to make it more profitable. Naturally it was they who found Northern sentiment so confounding to their trade. From Southern Tenn. north, there was growing a larger number of runaway slaves. They talked, the whole North, of an "Underground Railroad," stretching all the way from Cairo almost to Pittsburgh, where slaves found their way—and then were helped across the Ohio River by Abolitionists.

In the limited number of cases when they were able to trace and locate the fugitives, somewhere North of the Ohio, they were compelled to go to a Federal Judge and get a court order to carry the slave back. Unless they could succeed in doing this secretly, and if by any chance those who were succoring or concealing the runaway, discovered it, the officer or officers were threatened, and often attacked and forced to run away themselves to avoid being beaten, not to count being ostracized. Often if those hiding the runaway had the chance and the time, they frequently took the runaway to another section—even into Canada which granted no extradition. On the whole, the North gave the South no co-operation whatever, in helping to return runaway slaves.

Behind secession, Lincoln knew, there was much of this, and, with secession being urged and clamored for by the slave-traders and heavy slave-owners, was all that, that has been detailed above. Once free of Northern interference, the slave-trader and slave-breeder felt that he could operate without molestation or interference. These men had planned in the meanwhile, that if and when this finally happened, they would get a bill through in the Confederate Congress to restore the slave-trade, after which they could put headhunters in Africa to work, rounding up thousands of native Africans to be brought across the seas and placed in service.

After Lincoln finally completed the two and a half hours of hand-shaking, he was driven to the White House, seated beside Buchanan. He sat there quiet and solemn, his mind occupied with the problems soon to be, and they exchanged few, if any, words. Buchanan knew that Lincoln neither liked nor admired him, and had criticized him often and roundly because of what Lincoln knew to be true, that Buchanan was a political pawn and a coward. So seated side by side as they rode from the Capital to the White House, the incoming and the retiring President had little if any interests in common.

Arriving at their destination, Buchanan admitted Mr.

Lincoln to the White House and said, with a grin, "I hope you will be as happy here, Mr. Lincoln, as I am to leave it," and grinned again.

There were, of course, parties, people to meet, and the inaugural ball to have to attend, all of which Lincoln went through as cheerfully as he could, all the while, conscious and semi-conscious of the events soon to come. He knew that war would start; that the South, sooner or later would commit an overt act—and war then would break loose in all its fury—and that is what he dreaded.

As all the world soon knew, it burst out a little over thirty days later when South Carolina's Rebel Army hurled 3000 shells into Fort Sumter, forced its surrender, brought down the Stars and Stripes and raised the Confederate flag high where it furled in the air and seemed to throw defiance at the Union and all that went with it—the war was on!

"If the South wins, Father," Selena Fowler said, "Negro freedom will be as indefinite as Judgment Day, won't it?"

"Yes, dear," her father replied, soberly—"if the South wins." Selena looked at him quickly.

"You don't think the South will win, Father? They're saying it will all be over in six months; that the South will clean the North up in less time than that, but they give the North six months before surrendering." Henry Fowler smiled wanly.

"If it's over in six months, the South will win, I admit; but it will take twice that long at least for the North to get organized. The North is a large place; more than twice as many people up there, and as many States, with many more times the greater wealth."

"But they argue—"

"Yes, Daughter, I know all about what they argue. That is the way they feel—now. It will be two years before they begin to be convinced that they will not win; that they cannot win."

"Well, Father. In the event the North does win—what do you think they will do with the Negro—then?"

"All I say, dear," he sort of sighed, "is only a hazard. But I have the feeling that since they have forced the war on Lincoln, certainly against his will; and that he is an Abolitionist by practice and preachment and won't owe the South any appeasement, now, that somehow, sometime and somewhere before it is all over, there will come about someway and somehow, the complete freedom of the Negro."

"God be praised!" Selena exclaimed, her eyes up to heaven.

"It is obvious," her father went on, "that since slavery is the entire cause of the war, and that if the Negro is not in some way emancipated, we would be right back, when the war was over, where we started. Peace, then, would be only a breathing spell, and then another war all over again."

"That sounds logical."

"It is logical. The fact is, the South wouldn't be able to fight another one. They are so enraged, and angry, and so violent now because they've got to fight the war they've started, that they will be so exhausted when it is over they will be prostrate, completely prostrate."

"That means broken with no slaves to work for them to make back some of what they are losing, and will continue to lose."

"That's it. They are so proud, and so boastful, that it will be a hard pill to swallow, but swallow it they must. They asked for it."

"Do you think, before it is over, that they may call on us colored people, to help out? That will mean colored soldiers."

"I am sure they will have to. It's my belief that it's going to be a long war, and when wars run into years, they call on just about every able bodied man available."

"If that happens, what about—your sons, my brothers?"

"They will have to do their duty. I shall wait and while waiting, will prepare."

Chapter Sixteen

As PREDICTED AND expected, the South got way out in front during the early months of the war, reporting no end of victories before the North could even seem to get organized for war. This made the people back home in the South very cheerful, buoying their hopes and giving them reasons to believe that the war would be over very soon and that the South would come out victorious, in the end, as was being reported from the front, at the beginning.

And, as was also to be expected, many people of the North and quite a few from the South whose sympathies were still with the Union regardless of the fact that the States in which they lived had seceded from the Union, began to become very much discouraged and there was no end to complaint and criticism, much of which was directed at Lincoln himself. Some of the criticism and complaint amounted to downright and unfair abuse.

As early as July, 1862, Lincoln had already prepared and read an early draft of a proclamation which he had almost decided to issue. He read it to his Cabinet on July 22, 1862, and it agreed to the document, but a few thought it would be taken more seriously—in fact, would have greater effect if it were proclaimed after the Union armies, growing stronger and more effective daily, yet who had failed to win a major battle thus far, had won a major battle. Lincoln acquiesced to this suggestion, and turned his eyes back to the battle-fields and shortly after there was fought the great battle of Anteitam Creek, with all its slaughter of men and horses. This was the major battle the Union had been hoping to win, and all the North and their sympathizers in the South, became imbued with a great and new hope.

Meanwhile, one of the most influential men of that day was Horace Greeley, editor and publisher of the *New York Tribune*. Greeley had been growing restless by the weeks. The fact that he had committed himself unfavorably when secession started, by his words: "Let the erring sisters go in peace," kept him earlier from expressing himself, as he now did, on the progress of the war.

Though not formally allied with the Garrison Abolitionists, he had, through the columns of the *New York Tribune*, persistently denounced slavery. His criticism was framed in an open letter to Lincoln, headed by the caption:

THE PRAYER OF TWENTY MILLIONS

In it, he demanded that Lincoln definitely commit himself to emancipating the slaves, as the hardest single blow he could shoot, or that could be shot at Southern Rebellion. In this attitude, Greeley spoke for a large and powerful anti-slavery element in the North. Lincoln's reply, justifying the war as one for the preservation of the Union, is one of the most notable of his pronouncements. Greeley's Prayer of Twenty Millions follows:

"To Abraham Lincoln
President of the United States
Dear Sir:

I do not intrude to tell you—for you must know already—that a great portion of those who triumphed in your election, and of all who desire the unqualified suppression of the Rebellion now desolating our country, are sorely disappointed and deeply pained by the policy you seem to be pursuing with regards to the slaves of rebels. I write only to set succinctly and unmistakably before you what we require, what we think we have a right to expect, and of what we complain.

I. We require of you, as the First Servant of the Republic, charged especially and pre-eminently with this duty, that you *execute the laws* . . .

II. We think you are strangely, and disastrously remiss in the discharge of your official and imperative duty with regards to the emancipating provisions of the new Confiscation Act. Those provisions were designed to fight slavery with liberty. They prescribe that men loyal to the Union, and willing to shed their blood in her behalf, shall no longer be held, with the nation's consent, in bondage (he meant the Negro slave) to persistent, malignant traitors, who for twenty years have been plotting and for sixteen months have been fighting to divide and destroy our country. Why these traitors should be treated with tenderness by you, to the prejudice of the dearest rights of loyal men, we cannot conceive.

III. We think you are unduly influenced by the councils, the representations and menaces of certain politicians hailing from the border slave States. Knowing full well that the heartily, the unconditionally loyal portion of the white citizens of those States do not expect nor desire that slavery shall be upheld to the prejudice of the Union—for the truth of which we appeal, not only to every Republican residing in those States, but to such eminent loyalists as H. Winter Davis, Parson Brownlow, the Union Central Committee, of Baltimore—and to the *Nashville Union*—we ask you to consider that slavery, the inciting cause and sustaining base of treason. The most slave-holding sections of Maryland and Delaware being this day, though under the Union flag, in full sympathy with the rebellion, while the free labor portions of Tennessee and Texas, though writhing under the bloody heel of treason, are unconquerably loyal to the Union ... It seems to us the most obvious truth, that whatever strengthens or fortifies slavery in the border States, strengthens also treason, and drives home the wedge intended to divide the Union. Had you from the beginning, refused to recognize in those States, as here, any other than unconditional loyalty—that which stands for the Union—whatever may become of slavery—those States would have been, and would be far more helpful and less troublesome to the defenders of the Union, than they have been, or now are.

IV. We think that timid counsels in such a crisis calculated to prove perilous, and probably disastrous. It is the duty of a government so wantonly, wickedly assailed by rebellion, as ours has been to oppose with force, in a defiant, dauntless spirit. It cannot afford to temporize with traitors. It must not bribe them to behave themselves, nor make them fair promises in the hope of disarming their causeless hostility. Representing a brave and high spirited people, it can't afford to forfeit anything better than its own self-respect, or their admiring confidence, for any government, even to dispel the affected apprehensious armed traitors that their cherished privileges, may be assailed by it, is to invite, insult and encourage hopes of its own downfall. This rush to arms of Ohio, Indiana, Illinois, is the true answer at once to the rebel raids of John Morgan and the traitorous sophystries of Beriah MacGoffin.

V. We complain that the Union cause has suffered, and is now suffering immensely from mistaken deference to rebel slavery. Had you, sir, in your inaugural address, unmistakenly given notice that, in case the rebellion, already commenced, were persisted in, and your efforts to preserve the Union, and enforce laws, should be resisted by armed force, *you would recognize no lawful person as rightfully held in slavery, by a traitor*. We believe the rebellion would therein have received a staggering, if not fatal blow! At the moment, according to the returns of the most recent elections, the Unionists were a large majority of the voters of the slave States. But they were composed in good part, of the able, the feeble, the wealthy, the timid—the young, the reckless, the aspiring and the adventurous, had already been largely lured by the gamblers and Negro-traders, the politicians by trade and the conspirators, by the unjust, into the toils of treason. Had you by then proclaimed that rebellion would strike the shackles from the slaves of every traitor, the wealthy and the cautious would have been supplied with a powerful inducement to remain loyal.

VI. We complain that the Confiscation Act which you approved is habitually disregarded by your generals and that no word of rebuke for them from you has yet reached the public's ear. Freemont's proclamation and Hunters Order, favoring emancipation were promptly annulled by you; while Halleck's number three, forbidding fugitives from slavery to rebels to come within his lines—an order as unmilitary, as inhuman, and which received the hearty approbation of every traitor in America—with scores of like tendency—have never provoked even your remonstrance . . . And finally we complain that you, Mr. President, elected as a Republican, knowing well what an abomination slavery is, and how emphatically it is the cause and essence of this atrocious rebellion, seem never to interfere with these atrocities, and never a direction to your military subordinates which does not seem to have conceived the interests of slavery rather as against that of Freedom.

VII. On the face of this wide earth, Mr. President, there is not one disinterested, determined, intelligent champion of the Union cause who does not feel that all the attempts to put down the rebellion, and at the same time hold up its exciting cause are preposterous and futile—that the—rebellion if crushed out tomorrow, would be renewed within a year if slavery was left in full vigor—that army officers who remain to this day devoted to slavery can at best be but half-way loyal to the Union—and that every hour of deference to slavery is an hour of added and deepened peril to the Union. I appeal to the testimony of your ambassadors in Europe. It is freely at your service, not at mine. Ask them to tell you candidly whether the seeming subserviency of your policy to slave-holding, and slave upholding is not the perplexity, the despair of statesmen of all parties, and be admonished by the general answer.

VIII. I close as I began with the statement that what an immense majority of the loyal millions of your countrymen require is a frank, declared, unqualified, ungrudging execution of the laws of the land, more especially, of the Confiscation Act. That act gives Freedom to the slaves, coming within our lines, or those who may live at anytime near—We ask you to render it due obedience by publicly requiring all your subordinates to recognize and obey it. The rebels are everywhere using the late Anti-Negro riots in the North, as they have long used your officers treatment of Negroes in the South, to convince the slaves that they have nothing to hope for from a Union success—that we mean in that case to sell them into a bitter bondage to defray the costs of the war. Let them impress this as a truth on the great mass of their ignorant and credulous bondmen —and the Union' will never be restored—never! We cannot conquer ten millions of people united in solid phalanx against us, powerfully aided by Northern sympathizers and European allies. We must have scouts, guides, spies, cooks, teamsters, diggers and choppers from the blacks of the South, whether we allow them to fight for us or not, or we shall be baffled and repelled. As one of the millions who would gladly have avoided this struggle at any sacrifice but that of principle and honor, but who feels now that the triumph of the Union is indispensable, not only to the existence of our country, but to the well-being of mankind, I entreat you to render a hearty and unequivocal obedience to the law of the land.

      Yours,
      HORACE GREELEY"

 President Lincoln saw fit to make reply to the letter from an old friend, and so, in a few days, Mr. Greeley found the following on his desk at the office of the *New York Tribune* in New York:

> EXECUTIVE MANSION
> WASHINGTON, D. C.
> AUGUST 22, 1862

Dear Sir:

I have just read yours of the nineteenth, addressed to myself through the *New York Tribune*. If there be in it any statements or assumptions which I may know to be erroneous, I do not here and now controvert them. If there be in it any inferences which I may believe to be falsely drawn, I do not here and now argue against them. If there be perceptible in it an impatient and dictatorial tone, I waive it in deference to an old friend, whose heart I have always supposed to be right.

As to the policy I 'seem to be pursuing,' as you say, I have not meant to leave anyone in doubt.

I would save the Union. I would save it the shortest way under the Constitution. The sooner the National authority can be restored, the nearer the Union will be 'the Union as it was.' If there be those who would not save the Union unless they could at the same time *save* slavery, I do not agree with them. If there be those who would not save the Union unless they could at the same time *destroy* slavery, I do not agree with them. My paramount object in this struggle is to save the Union, and is *not* either to save or destroy slavery. If I could save the Union without freeing *any* slave, I would do it. And if I could do it by freeing all the slaves, I would do it; and if I could do it by freeing some and leaving others alone, I would also do that. What

I do about slavery and the colored race, I do because I believe it will help to save this Union; and what I forbear, I forbear because I do not believe it would help to save the Union.

I shall do *less* whenever I shall believe what I am doing hurts the cause, and I shall do *more* whenever I shall believe doing more will help the cause. I shall try to correct errors when shown to be errors; and I shall adopt new views so fast as they shall appear to be true views. I have here stated my purpose, according to my views of *official* duty, and I intend no modification of my oft-expressed *personal* wish that all men, everywhere could be free.

Yours,
A. LINCOLN

Since Abraham Lincoln and his cabinet had been thinking and planning some radical and drastic move to shake the South from end to end, and, in that way seek to bring her back to her senses, which she seemed to have lost altogether, as they saw it, or weaken her in every possible way they could, and in that way make ultimate defeat so obvious that they would give up sooner than might otherwise be the case, Horace Greeley's carefully and thoughtfully as well as thoroughly conceived letter, urging emancipation, had much to do with what very shortly transpired.

Lincoln had long since come to realize that freeing the slaves was an inevitable step in ending a quarrel that had been going on for thirty years. North and South had quarreled and fought in Congress over the slavery issue until there was little more to fight about. He knew that if the South was willing to look at it fairly and squarely, there was but one thing left to do—end slavery in one way or by another.

But because the South claimed such a heavy investment in human flesh, and since the institution had grown into a giant before many of the present generation had been born; endless men, almost, calling themselves ministers of the gospel, had spent years explaining that God Almighty intended the Negro to be a hewer of wood and a drawer of water; the white man's slave, and while few actually made themselves believe it, they acted and pretended so so completely until many had succeeded in fooling themselves.

Most of all, they resented the North interfering in what they felt was their Constitutional right, and the Fugitive Slave Act upheld this assumption, and the North, to get along with Southern legislators perhaps more than for any other reason, had acquiesced, and was a party to that law and other compromises which continued slavery. Dislike to it in the North had long since become an obsession, so it was fight, fight, quarrel, quarrel—and fight eternally, over Negro slavery.

Chapter Seventeen

SLAVERY IN AMERICA, Lincoln knew, and every other sober minded American knew, was older than the Union itself —much older; almost as old, in fact, as white settlement itself. To attempt to change it by the mere stroke of a pen, in spite of what all the North was clamoring for, took courage, thinking, planning, consideration. Yet, admittedly, something serious had to be done. By now, considered a disease—the very worst a free country could have saddled into its Constitution, Lincoln finally concluded to take the move that made history, and is perhaps known to more people up to this day than any other document ever conceived.

Accordingly, therefore, on the 22nd day of September, 1862, he issued, effective January 1, 1863, the:

EMANCIPATION PROCLAMATION

By THE PRESIDENT OF THE UNITED STATES OF AMERICA

A Proclamation

Whereas, on the 22nd day of September, A.D. 1862, a proclamation was issued by the President of the United States, containing among other things, the following to wit:

"That on the 1st day of January, A.D. 1863, all persons held as slaves, within any State or designated part of a State the people whereof shall be in rebellion against the United States, shall be then, thenceforward and forever free; and the executive government of the United States, including the military and naval authority thereof, will recognize and maintain the freedom of such persons and will do no act or acts to repress such persons, or any of them, in any efforts they may make for their actual freedom.

"That the executive will on the first day of January aforesaid, by proclamation designate the States, if any in which the people thereof, respectively shall then be in rebellion against the United States; and the fact that any State or the people thereof, shall be in good faith, represented in the Congress of the United States by members chosen thereto at elections wherein a majority of the qualified voters of such States shall have participated, shall, in the absence of strong countervailing testimony, be deemed conclusive evidence that such State and the people thereof are not then in rebellion against the United States.

"Now, therefore, I, Abraham Lincoln, President of the United States, by virtue of the power in me vested as Commander-in-Chief of the Army and Navy of the United States in time of actual armed rebellion against the authority and government of the United States, and as fit and necessary war measures for suppressing said rebellion, do, on the first day of January, A. D. 1863, and in accordance with my purpose so to do, publicly proclaim for the full period of one hundred days from the first day of above mentioned, order and designate as the States and parts of States wherein the people thereof, respectively are this day in rebellion against the United States the following, to wit:

"Arkansas, Texas, Louisiana (except—he named 13 parishes, one of which included New Orleans) Mississippi, Alabama, Florida, Georgia, South Carolina, North Carolina and Virginia (except the forty-eight counties designated as W. Virginia), and also as Berkeley, Accomac, Northampton, Elizabeth City, York, Princes Anne, and Norfolk, including the Cities of Norfolk and Portsmouth and which excepted parts are for the present left precisely as if this proclamation were not issued.

"And by virtue of the power and for the purpose aforesaid, I do order and declare that all persons held as slaves within said designated States and parts of States are, and henceforward shall be, free; and that the executive government of the United States, including the Military and the Naval authority thereof will recognize and maintain freedom of said persons.

"And I hereby enjoin upon the people so declared to be free to abstain from all violence, unless in necessary self-defense; and I recommend to them that in all cases when allowed, they labor faithfully for reasonable wages.

"And I further declare and make known that such persons of suitable condition will be received into the armed services of the United States to garrison forts, positions, stations, and other places, and to man vessels of all sorts in said service.

"And upon this act, sincerely believed to be an act of justice, warranted by the Constitution upon Military necessity, I invoke the conservative judgment of mankind and the gracious favor of Almighty God."

Opposition to the Emancipation Proclamation

Naturally the document met with a storm of criticism,

derision, defiance and all the angry words the South could think and hurl at it, but what was most surprising however, was the opposition it aroused in the North. The criticism, of course, was mainly from the Democrats, Northern Democrats. It was left to the legislature of Illinois, Lincoln's own home State, which had gone Democratic, and was known to be the stronghold of Copperheadism and a bigoted organization known as the Knights of the Golden Circle, to advance the most capricious criticism. They even met and passed the following resolution:

"Resolved: That the Emancipation Proclamation of the President of the United States is as unwarrantable in military as in civil law; a gigantic usurpation at once converting the war, professedly commenced by the administration for the vindication of the authority of the Constitution into the crusade for the sudden, unconditional and violent liberation of millions of Negro slaves; a result which would not only be a total subversion of the Federal Union, but a revolution in the social organization of the Southern states, the immediate and remote, the present and far-reaching, consequences of which to both races cannot be contemplated without the most dismal foreboding of horror and dismay. The proclamation invites servile insurrection—a means of warfare, the inhumanity of diabolism of which are without example in civilized warfare, and which we denounce, and which the civilized world, will denounce as an uneffaceable disgrace to the American people."

Chapter Eighteen

The Strange Case of Johnny Northcross is not exactly a story of the Civil War; the early events, however, running concurrently with important events that led up to the war, and its outbreak, must have brought the reader to feel that it is in most part, a war story.

It was the author's intention at the outset, however, to make the war, leading to the issuance of the Emancipation Proclamation, a part of the story. That having passed, we now return to the case of Johnny Northcross, the happenings at Fayetteville, the setting of our story, and to the people and circumstances surrounding it. Before doing so, however, let us pass briefly over the events which followed the Emancipation Proclamation, such as the greatest battle of the war, and Sherman's March to the sea, during which was fought the battle of Atlanta and the burning of that city, all for the purpose of splitting the South wide open.

The Northern armies were now converging in Northern Virginia, planning the ultimate invasion of and capture of Richmond, the Southern Capital, which had been moved from Montgomery, Alabama. Lee's army, we find now in the Valley of Virginia, heading Northward mysteriously, forcing Hooker's army to hold where they were to block whatever was Lee's purpose. That purpose was to keep Hooker's large army from concentrating toward Richmond, and with Lee heading Northward through the Valley of Virginia, presumably for Harrisburg, the Capital of Pennsylvania, caused Lincoln to retire Hooker, placing General George E. Meade in charge, who swung the armies about forthwith to block and intercept Lee's bold attempt to spread the war by driving on Harrisburg.

Accordingly, the two great armies made contact and came together at a little town southeast of Harrisburg, called Gettysburg, where on the morning of July 1st, 1863, began and was fought, the greatest battle of all times, *the Battle of Gettysburg*. All day and late into the night of July 1st; with reinforcements arriving to assist each army hourly, the mighty battle raged on. All through July 2nd, it raged, into the night of the second, into the third day of July, during which Longstreet's great assault was launched and finally repulsed.

It was Lee's hope to have caught Meade short of men and cavalry; and to have crushed his armies before they could reach full strength. This done, Lee planned to sweep for the Atlantic Coast, reaching there somewhere between Wilmington, Delaware and Baltimore, swing South, capture Baltimore—and then the most important prize of all, the City of Washington itself.

It was a daring and bold vision which depended on crushing Meade's army, thereby clearing the way. Robert E. Lee was too smart a general to leave a Union army behind to catch him in the middle, between Harrisburg and the East Coast. By nightfall of the third day of July, with the battlefield by this time an inferno of flying shells, the dead and the dying, Lee saw that Meade's army had reached full strength and would be able to hold out—yes, more; that it would ultimately crush his own armies. When the

sun rose, therefore, over the hills of the bloody battlefield the morning of July 4th, the Union scouts brought back the cheering news.
Lee was retreating!
And this retreat continued, into the Battle of the Wilderness, where he faced the great General Grant for months; through the remainder of 1863, into 1864 back, back, Lee continued and was forced to fall until in April of that year; the two generals met at Appomatox Courthouse and Lee surrendered to Grant, and the war was soon over; the South had been subdued; the slaves freed, and the country faced a new problem—to make the Negro a citizen all over the United States, and reconstruction with which we will not attempt to deal, but pass over everything and return to Fayetteville—and The House Behind The Cedars.

It is now the year of 1869, just twelve years since Johnny Northcross disappeared so mysteriously and had never been seen or heard of in Fayetteville since. Where did he go? Was he still living or had he died?

This brings back into our story the Fowler family, via a younger son whose name was Frank, a playmate and school mate of Rowena Northcross, who was only a child when her brother disappeared so mysteriously.

Rowena by now, had grown to young and beautiful womanhood, and was the belle of Negro Fayetteville—and Frank Fowler's suitor, although not declared, everybody seemed to understand that Frank liked Rena and Rena liked Frank and that some day this fine young couple would be wed. Everybody but Mis' Molly, Rena's mother, who had other plans, which we will explain more fully when we get to them.

Frank was too young to follow his brothers, five of whom had been sent by their father North to join the Union army and had fought there. When the war was over all the boys returned home but one, the middle one, whose name was Lawrence, and who had fallen at the Fort Pillow massacre. Henry Fowler brought the news, a telegram from the President himself, and Frank, who was then only old enough to understand a great sorrow, never forgot it.

They were dining. His father and two or three of the children had gone to Fayetteville and returned while the balance of the family were dining. He looked up as his father entered the room and knew there was something wrong. He stopped eating and waited, which wasn't long, for as his father reached his mother's side at the foot of the table, he burst into tears, the first time Frank had ever seen his father cry, as he laid the telegram by his mother's plate and sobbed:

"Lawrence is dead."

His mother, who had been expecting something to happen, threw up her arms and burst into tears. Selena and the other girls gathered around her, crying too, but sought to calm and pacify their mother. It was the first death in the family of fourteen and all took it grievously. All were sad for weeks and months; but that was in 1864.

Now we are relating events of 1869. Most of the older children had married and moved away to their own homes where many had children, but Frank near the last of the twelve children, lived at home with his parents. His father had taught all his boys industry. He had bought more land

and given several of the boys acres of their own. Of Frank, he had followed in his father's trade, a carpenter and mason.

For more than a year now, Frank had been contracting and building, and, since there had been little or no construction during the war, now that it was over and the country had become more settled, it seemed that just about everybody who owned land wanted buildings erected, and Frank had more than he could do.

From the beginning, Rena Northcross had assisted him, by helping him to draw estimates and keep his books. She had found it delightful work and Frank found her most efficient and helpful. Both were glad to be thrown together, and enjoyed each other's company.

Frank was now 22, Rena 18. He was tall, dark, with a flush of coarse brindle-like hair, a powerfully built and athletic type, over six feet tall. Rena was a cross between her father, Richard Northcross, and her mother, Molly, had fine silken, dark chestnut hair, could easily pass for white, which, however, as far as expression went, she seemed totally unconscious of.

She was rather tall for a girl, slender, shapely, but what Frank liked about her best of all was that she was so keen, so considerate of everybody's feelings, so thoughtful and intelligent.

Such was the state of affairs in Fayetteville and The House Behind The Cedars as we return to our real story, where we will continue until the end of this book.

It is night, or should we call it early evening? Anyway, it was growing dark in the Northcross household; Rena and her mother had dined, cleared the table, washed and dried the dishes and put them away. Molly was seated in her rocking chair, sewing at something and Rena sat at the dining room table, figuring out an estimate that Frank had left with her for a set of buildings which he wanted back the next day. They heard dogs in the neighborhood barking, which meant that somebody was near or approaching, and looked up, askance. Then they heard footsteps on their front porch. There was a pause while Molly and Rena looked at each other, then turned their eyes toward the front door, where, by this time the footsteps were directed and a moment later, there was a knock at the door. Again Molly exchanged glances with Rena, then nodding, said:

"I'll answer." Rising to her feet she crossed into the hall where she was out of the sight of Rena, who waited and listened.

Without opening the front door, but looking out as if through it, Mis' Molly called and Rena, hearing her, listened intently.

"Who's there?"

"A gentleman," came back the answer, then a pause. "Does Mis' Molly Northcross live here?"

"Yes," was the guarded answer. "I'm Mis' Molly Northcross. What do you want?"

"I have a message to you from your son, Johnny."

"Oh!" Molly exclaimed, in shocked tones. Rena, in the dining room, heard her and rose quickly and excitedly to her feet. A key turned, the door was opened, and, swinging it wide, Molly looked up and into the face of a smiling stranger.

"You've got a message from my son, you say?" she asked

with great anticipation. "Is he sick—or in—trouble?" She was so excited that she forgot to invite the smiling and pleasant stranger inside for the moment.

"No. He's well and doing well, and sends his love to you, and hopes you've not forgotten him."

"Forgot him? No, God knows I ain't forgot him! But come in, Sir, come in and tell me more about my son."

The stranger entered and Molly closed the door behind him and after she had closed the door, she chanced to turn and face the man, who at the same time was in the act of turning in the lighted hall to face her.

"When did you last see my son?" she inquired of him now, nervously anxious.

"I have never met your son," he replied, with a peculiar twinkle of the eyes which she did not understand. Her face fell.

"Then the message comes through you from somebody else?"

"No," he replied, calmly. "Directly from your son."

She scanned his face with a puzzled look. This bearded young gentleman who spoke so politely and was dressed so well, surely—no, it could not be! and yet—

He was smiling at her now through a mist of tears. An electric spark of sympathy flashed between them.

"John!" she suddenly cried, raising her arms. "John, my John! It *is* Johnny, my son!"

"Mother—my dear old mother!" he cried. The next moment his arms went out, and into his embrace went Molly Northcross, his old and happy mother.

Chapter Nineteen

WE NOW RETURN TO 1857—the day Johnny Northcross visited and had the prolonged conversation with Judge Straight at the latter's office in Fayetteville just twelve years before.

It will be recalled that Judge Straight rented a horse and buggy at the livery stable that night and drove into the country, presumably to see some one. Whom did Judge Straight drive into the country to see? He drove out to the Northcross plantation to see Richard Northcross; and concerning Northcross' illegitimate son, Johnny.

He found Northcross idle, lounging in the library, reading his papers.

"Well, Judge Straight," he cried, as the Judge was ushered into his presence. "I'm glad to see you; a sort of glad surprise for I was not expecting my old friend."

After being offered a seat, the Judge requested him to close the library door as his visit was of confidential nature, and he wished to be alone with Northcross.

By the serious frown upon the Judge's face, Northcross had construed that the visit concerned something serious, so seated to face the Judge, Northcross went directly to the point.

"What's up, Judge? By the serious frown you are wearing, and the fact that you've driven this far into the country to see me, I am sure it must be something rather serious, so let's come directly to it."

As Northcross talked, the Judge's eyes stared into space before him, thoughtfully. He now turned to Northcross.

"Are we—quite alone?"

"Quite alone, Judge, so you may proceed."

"I wouldn't wish Mrs. Northcross to overhear what I am here to talk about. It would not be best, in fact, if that be possible, for Mrs. Northcross to know anything about why I am here to see you."

"I can relieve your mind on that point, Judge. Mrs. Northcross is in Raleigh for a short visit." Relief was evident promptly on the Judge's face, and, relaxing, he turned to Northcross, got to his feet and stood over him, and went on:

"It might prove somewhat embarrassing to you at the outset, Northcross, but however you accept it, I feel it my duty to appraise you of a serious fact."

"All right, Judge, all right," Northcross exclaimed, rising now to face the Judge. "Go ahead with whatever it is. By now I have grown about used to anything that might pop up in my life. About the only thing I haven't experienced thus far is death. I haven't died yet, so go ahead with what you came to see me about, and have no anxiety about how I will accept it."

"Thank you, Richard," the Judge now said, "for taking it so philosophically." He looked back at the chair he had just risen from. "Well, let's be seated and I will begin."

Both took seats again, and, with Northcross' eyes on him, Judge Straight began.

"I'm here to see you about your son, Richard. Molly's boy."

Northcross started, almost violently, his jaw dropped, his eyes opened wide and he glared at Judge Straight cautiously and sharply.

"My—what?"

Judge Straight shook his head, patiently. "I was afraid I would surprise you, Northcross, perhaps shock you."

Northcross arose, trod the floor back, forth, then sat down again, his eyes for the moment, on the floor.

Judge Straight, who had remained seated, just waited, patiently. Finally Richard Northcross raised his eyes to the Judge, and the Judge went on:

"Shall I explain—how it happened?"

Nodding his head up and down, Northcross said:

"Yes, do Judge Straight. Please do." He swallowed then, deeply and Judge Straight went on.

"He came to the office today. I have seen and know him, as most people have and do in Fayetteville; but I don't recall ever having exchanged any words with him. But from his strange visit, and all he said, it was evident that he had planned to call on me for a long time. Well, today he called."

"Yes?" from Northcross, a bit anxiously.

"Yes. Today he came to see me, and spoke these words forthwith: 'Sir, I want to be a lawyer.'"

"A lawyer?" Northcross exclaimed, surprised.

"You're surprised—almost shocked. Well," the Judge went on amiably, "so was I. I was inclined to dismiss it as of no consequence, but he wouldn't let me."

"Wouldn't let you?"

"No," the Judge replied, shaking his head negatively.
"But—"
"You'd better hear me through first, Richard. I think you'll understand better."

The Judge paused and adjusted his position, then went on:

"As I was saying, I was inclined to dismiss the query, but not him. He apparently had been thinking it out for a long time, and was determined, now that he was before me, to see through what was on his mind."

"Strange—but interesting. Please go on, Judge Straight."

"I reminded him that he was a Negro, of course, and that he was aware of the fact. 'I am white,' he replied, stoutly. 'I am white and I am free,' he took care to remind me. Still not inclined yet to take him seriously, I sought nevertheless to discourage him so I replied, as convincingly as I knew how: 'You are black and you are not free.' He stuck out his arm, rolled up his sleeve and said: 'There are plenty of white people darker than I am. I want to be a lawyer!' I reminded him of the Dred Scott Decision, which he had read and he tore it all to pieces, quoted from Abraham Lincoln, and kept on insisting that he wanted to be a lawyer.

"Frankly, Northcross, the boy's persistence annoyed me at first, but as we talked on and I became convinced more and more that he was sincere, had thought out all he was there to see me about, carefully, I tried to show that if he really was as anxious as he insisted to be somebody, some trade or industrial pursuit would be far easier to acquire. He was interested in nothing else but of becoming a lawyer and stuck to it. I got up, walked over by the window and tried to think of some way to get rid of him. As I stood there, I turned once to look at him and our eyes met. And there was where he got me. There was an expression in that boy's eyes as he looked straight at me that I shall never forget until the longest day I live.

"I asked him if he had considered how difficult it would be for him to become a lawyer. His answer was a suggestion which I could see he had thought out carefully. He said, 'I have considered that I might pass for white.'" Judge Straight was silent for a moment as if to let Richard Northcross think, too. Northcross *was* thinking, too; he had been thinking all the while Judge Straight talked.

"Well, there it was," Judge Straight said and shrugged his shoulders. "What he suggested was so full of logic that I was taken aback. He *could* easily pass for a white boy anywhere he isn't known, which put me to thinking. As you know, Northcross, there is no chance for him to become much of anything as a Negro—even a Free Negro; but as a white man the boy might manage to become something, especially when he seems possessed with so much natural intelligence—so much resolute determination.

"Well, I was cornered; he had touched my human sympathies. All his life is before him. As stated, as a Negro, he could never become much of anything; but as a white man —well, who knows what heights he might reach in fifteen or twenty years?

"I didn't want to argue any more but I had to tell him something. So I told him to come back tomorrow. Meanwhile, I had decided when I told him to come back to come out here and see you and talk it over with you tonight."

"What am I to do about it?" Northcross wanted to know, speaking for the first time. His question seemed to Judge Straight rather blunt, and angered him slightly. He replied, and his reply was as blunt as Northcross' suggestion.

"What are you to *do* about it, Northcross? The boy *is* your son, isn't he, though born out of wedlock. You won't deny that—to me?"

"No, Archibald," Richard Northcross replied rising to his feet. "But you know as well as I do that—matters of that kind, we try to—"

"—Keep hushed as much as possible. It is not exactly any concern of mine and I have never said anything to you about your—past depredations, nor do I come here now as a condemner."

"I know, Judge, I know you have not. The whole thing is embarrassing when you come to think of it, to consider it, and it is unfortunate that so many of we—slaveholders allowed ourselves to be so—careless. It is true, my relations with the boy's mother is as old almost as slavery itself. Our fathers before us did it—the beautiful and passionate slave-girls were so tempting; we found having intercourse with them so easy, so convenient. Young, passionate, many of us found them far more satisfying to the loins than intercourse with our own wives. I found Molly so. Even to this day I would rather go see her than offer my wife sexuality. But all of this is beside the point. The mistake is history, Johnny Northcross is my son, the same as those by the woman I married. It's all because of this confounded thing called slavery." He seemed to think of something and while he had been striding back and forth, he suddenly sat down, leaned toward the Judge and stared hard at him.

"What do you think about all this agitation going the rounds about the institution, Judge?" Before the Judge had time, however, to frame an opinion, Northcross went on:

"What do you think of Abraham Lincoln and his Abolition preachments? I think he's going to bring about a big confusion in regard to it before it's all over. Well, Archibald, I hope he will, or something else will happen to bring the confounded practice to an end. It is the only way it will ever end—via some crisis, a war maybe; a war between the North that is against it, and the South that wishes it upheld.

"Do you know, Straight," he went on rising quickly to his feet, "that I am against slavery—and always have been?"

Judge Straight looked up at him, and Richard Northcross met his stare squarely, without a flinch.

"Yes, Archibald, I, a slave-owner and holder, with my father before me one, and his father before him a slaveholder—yet I am, and always have been unalterably opposed to the institution and between you and me, I have long prepared for the day when mine would be freed by me, or by a war that will end the dirty practice all over these United States—end it for good!"

"Are you sure you know what you are talking about, Richard?"

"Just as sure as your visit to me tonight. I am sure that within four years I shall no longer be a slave-holder; so sure that I will not, that for the last ten years I have sent thousands of dollars North to New York and Boston, so that if I am ostracised for taking action according to my conviction, I won't have to live as a poor man."

"This is a revelation!"

"Among the many things I have for years disliked about it, is these indigent, lying and hypocritical preachers who are subsidized by slave-breeders and traders, and stand in our pulpits and spend hours pretending to convince us or trying to, that it was ordained by the Almighty that the black man should be a slave—and point to ancient facts, twisted to fit their lies, to prove it. It is all so terribly wrong and mistaken. The truth is that the South has been rocked into a slumber, superinduced by downright laziness into believing these lies. The fact is, they're too Goddamned lazy to do anything about it.

"I've been following this man Lincoln—and the plan he has suggested to end it, since a majority of the American people are so set against it. That plan is a compensated emancipation by which he would have the Federal Government float a huge bond issue and purchase all the slaves and set them free."

"I've read his offer, which he repeats as often as prudent," observed Judge Straight; "but the public doesn't seem in the mood to consider it seriously."

"The South is too lazy to think about it on one hand, and then, the confounded slave-traders and breeders are the ones who are most cold to any plan to end slavery, because it is their way of making money. They know no other way, and they control the South politically so the rest of us are just helpless in their hands."

"That may be true, Northcross," Judge Straight observed judiciously, "but how can you account for the North's lack of enthusiasm? With a tide of Abolitionism sweeping the whole country up there, it would seem that they should show more interest in the plan. How do you account for this lack?"

"I've studied that, too, and here is why they are cold to it. They don't like the idea of paying for human beings. In fact, from what I've been able to find out, the idea of paying for a human being, even though the purpose is to set that person free is revolting to most. They insist on freedom without compensation—and, as you know, there is where they disagree. The South has had slavery so long and there is so much propaganda going on among us that it is right and just, and that the North leave us alone to handle the slavery question as we feel best, that there seems little possibility of emancipation on any kind of terms short of war—and war is destructive and expensive, but through a civil war with the North subduing the South is the only way I can see it ending."

"I'm afraid you're right, Northcross, afraid you are right and war is such an unhappy and terrible thing to anticipate."

"Especially when you feel convinced as I do, that it could be compromised and avoided—but I've talked clear away from the subject." They were both standing and had been unconsciously walking the floor.

"Well, let's get back to Molly and the boy, my boy, yes, my son, and as strange as it may seem, I love the lad just as much as I do my legitimate children." This caused the Judge to perk, and he replied.

"I'm indeed glad to hear you say that, and I hope you understand my position in the matter."

"I understand it fully, Judge Straight, purely an act of sympathy and a high regard for humanity. Just what more of we men who have begat children by our slave women need to possess. Well, I could have done worse. I freed Molly before the boy was born. At least the boy has never been a slave, so getting back to what you have called to see me about—but sit down, Judge Straight," he broke off abruptly to say, pointing to a chair. "Sit down."

Judge Straight obeyed, and Northcross then took a chair, made himself comfortable and turned to the Judge, his face serious.

"So the boy wants to be a lawyer, eh? I'm glad to hear that he desires to. High ambition. I like that."

"I'm glad to hear you say that, too, Richard. He not wants merely to become a lawyer. He's determined to become one."

"Good," Northcross exclaimed, and seemed highly pleased. "How do you feel about it, Archibald?"

"Well, I think he should have assistance in his ambition. That is why I took it upon myself to call out here and talk with you about it."

"I'm agreeable, but how can we go about accomplishing such an end?"

"By sending him away—far enough away to leave no connection with his past, his mother, his sister; away somewhere to study law, passing for white as he does so."

"I see. Our white people won't like such an idea, you know, if they found out about it. They are dead set against bright Negroes passing for whites."

"I understand fully, Northcross; understand so fully that I wouldn't be a party to it except under these circumstances—all because the boy is so determined to be a lawyer, and you know that would be impossible, almost, if he continued as a Negro."

"Of course. Well, we're in a crack, you because of my sins of iniquity," and Northcross smiled wryly. Judge Straight smiled the same way. "Well, Judge, had you formulated any plans?"

"I have, which follow. I know a law firm in Charleston, well enough to send the boy to with a letter, and not well enough for them to inquire too deeply, I hope, about the boy's parentage. I plan to write them that he is an orphan but sprang from good stock." Judge Straight looked at Northcross, and Northcross found himself raising eyes that met those of Judge Straight. Both lowered their eyes but both understood in that exchange of expression just what each had thought; and what Judge Straight had implied.

"The boy will have to change his name, and I have decided to suggest Walden, Johnny Walden." Northcross looked up, nodded agreeably. Judge Straight went on.

"I now suggest that the boy's father advance a limited sum of money for the education of the boy."

"A practical idea, Straight. Very practical. I, of course, am to provide these funds?"

"You, of course, Richard."

"Agreeable, Archibald, go ahead."

"All this is contingent on the boy being willing to forego his past completely. As I mentioned, he must forego his mother, his sister—he must forget Fayetteville and all the life and people around here whom he has known. When we send him away to Charleston to become this lawyer he seems so determined to be, he is to go as John Walden whom nobody here has ever known. Get the idea, Richard?"

"Fully, though that will be hard on Molly. She loves the kid so."

"I'm aware of it, but in taking this step to help the boy, we are diverting from our whole course of life and that of our friends. He must be willing to make a sacrifice for so great an opportunity."

"I fancy that he will be."

"That is what I think."

During the next few minutes they agreed on the sum to be turned over to Judge Straight to be sent to his friends in Charleston to defray all the boy's expenses. Judge Straight agreed to call on Molly and get her consent after he had laid the plans down to the boy, who needless to say was agreeable to every term and condition.

So, as we see, it was arranged thusly and Johnny Northcross quietly disappeared. His mother was not told whence he was going; just advised by Judge Straight to say that Johnny had gone—just gone. As we already know, Molly obeyed.

And now, as we also know, twelve years later Johnny came back.

Chapter Twenty

"I DIDN'T THINK," Molly sobbed, "That I'd ever see you again."

He smoothed her hair and kissed her. "And are you glad to see me, Mother?"

"Am I glad to see you? It's like the dead comin' to life. I thought I'd lost you forever. Johnny, my son, my darling boy!" she answered, hugging him tightly.

"It seems," he said, his voice coming as if from far away, "that I couldn't continue to live without seeing you, so all of a sudden, dear Mother, I decided to come back—and here I am," and he drew her close again, and again he kissed her.

"You've grown so tall," she said now holding him at arm's length and looking him up and down. "A fine gentleman! And you *are a* gentleman now, Johnny, ain't you? Sure enough? Nobody knows the old story. I stuck to what I promised; I just said 'you wuz gone', but how it hurt me, son. I cried for years, son, cried for years about you, I missed you so."

"I understand, mother, I understand, and how I hated to hurt you. But it seemed at the time that it just had to be. Slavery was everywhere; the Dred Scott Decision tried to convince the world that a Negro was nothing, could never be anything—and I wanted so to be somebody, mother. I always wanted to be somebody."

"And now, praise be to the Lord, you *are* somebody, ain't you Johnny? I'm sure you are, for you look like somebody, maybe a fine and outstanding gentleman?"

"Well, mother," he said, thoughtfully, as if weighing his words. "I've taken a man's chance; and have tried to make the most of it; and I haven't felt under any obligation to spoil it by raking up old stories that are best forgotten." He paused now to sweep his eyes around the hall and, in doing so, they fell and then rested on the old books which were there when he left. He pointed to them.

"There are the dear old books. Have they been read since I went away?"

"No, honey," she replied, shaking her head, "there has been nobody to read them 'cep'n Rena, and she doesn't take to those kind of books as you did. But I've kep' 'em dusted clean, and kep' the moths and the bugs out of 'em, for I hoped you'd come back someday, and knowed you'd lak to fin' 'em all in their places lak you lef' 'em."

"That's mighty nice of you, mother. You could have done no more if you had loved them for themselves. But where is Rena,"—he paused now to look around. "She must be grown up by now, a fine and beautiful child, I'll bet."

"I've been so glad to see you that I'd forgot about her," his mother replied a bit embarrassingly. Turning toward the dining room now, she called: "Rena, oh, Rena!"

The girl was not far away. She had been standing where her mother left her listening intently to every word of the conversation, and kept from coming in by a certain constraint that made a brother whom she had not met for so many years seem almost as much a stranger as if he had not been connected to her by any tie.

"Yes, Mama," she answered, coming forward.

"Rena, child," Molly began. "Here's your brother, Johnny, who's been away for so long. But he's come back to us at last, so tell him howdy."

As she came forward Johnny turned to meet her, and opening his arms, drew her to him, looked into her eyes fondly while she blushed furiously and kissed her affectionately. As had been stated she was a tall girl, but he towered above her in quite a protecting fashion; and she thought with a thrill how fine it would be if she could walk up the street with such a brother by her side! She could hold up her head before all the world, oblivious to any glance of pity or contempt. She felt a very pronounced respect for this tall gentleman who held her blushing face between his hands and looked steadily into her eyes as if with a well defined purpose.

"You're the little sister I used to read stories to and whom I promised to come and see some day. Do you remember how you cried when I went away?"

"It seems but yesterday," she murmured. "I've still got the dime you gave me."

He kissed her again, then turning they walked into the dining room and took a seat together on the old couch which was there when he left. He reached up, took his mother's hand and drew her down on the other side of him, then placed an arm around the waist of each. After kissing each again on the cheek with a loud smack he turned and looked into Rena's eyes fondly and said:

"You're a very pretty girl, Rena," and smiled, a smile in keeping with his feelings at the moment.

"Now, Johnny," Molly interposed at this point, with a

tender frown. "You'll spile her if you ain't keerful."

"No, he won't, Mama," Rena asserted, stoutly, "He's flattering me, I know. He talks as if I was some rich lady who lives on the Hill,"—(The Hill was the aristocratic portion of Fayetteville)—"instead of a poor—"

"—Young girl who has 'The Hill' to climb," Johnny replied smoothing her hair with his hand. Her hair was long, silken, glossy and smooth, with a wave like the ripple of a summer breeze upon the surface of still water. It was the girl's great pride, and had been sedulously cared for.

"What lovely hair. It has the proper wave to add to your beauty, Sister."

"Oh, Brother, you must not flatter me so," she protested, half seriously. "If you keep on, I can't promise that I won't get spoiled—and I'm sure you don't like spoiled people."

"No, I don't like spoiled people, darling; but I'm not afraid of spoiling you. Our mother, I can see, has reared you well." He smiled at Molly who was made very happy by him doing so. Then turning his eyes back to Rena, he went on a bit reminiscently:

"I think my little Albert favors his Aunt Rena somewhat."

"*Your little Albert,*" both women cried simultaneously, turning suddenly to him and in anxious surprise. "Then—you have—a—child?"

"Oh, yes," he replied calmly, "A very fine baby boy."

They began then to purr in proud contentment at this information and made minute inquiries about the boy and its mother. They inquired more coldly about the child's mother of whom they spoke with greater warmth when they learned that she was dead. They hung breathlessly on his words as he related briefly the story of his life since he left years ago the house behind the Cedars—how with a stout heart and an abounding hope and self-confidence he had gone out into a seemingly hostile world and made fortune stand and deliver. His story had for the women the charm of an escape from captivity, with all the thrill of a pirate's tale. With the whole world before him he had remained in the South, the land of his fathers, where, he conceived, he had an inalienable birthright.

By some good chance he had escaped military service in the Confederate Army, and, in default of older and more experienced men, had undertaken during the rebellion the management of a large estate which had been left in the hands of women and slaves. He had filled the place so acceptably, and employed his leisure to such advantage, that at the close of the war he found himself—he was modest enough to think, too, in default of a better man—the husband of the orphan daughter of the man who had owned the plantation, and who had lost his life upon the battlefield.

Johnny's wife was of good family, and in a more settled condition of society, it would not have been easy for a young man of no visible antecedents to win her hand.

In due time, after he had been graduated from the law school in Charleston, he had taken the oath of allegiance and had been admitted to the South Carolina bar. Rich in his wife's right, he had been able to practice his profession upon a high plane without the worry of sordid cares, and with marked success for one of his age.

"I suppose," he concluded, "That I have gotten along at the bar for lack of better men. Many of the good lawyers were killed in the war which almost ruined South Carolina, because I suppose, they seemed to have taken it more seriously than the rest of the South. Many of those who were not killed in battle, were disqualified; while I had the advantage of being alive and of never having been in arms against the government. People had to have lawyers and they gave me their business in preference to the carpet-baggers. Fortune, you know, favors the available man."

His mother drank in with parted lips and glistening eyes the story of his adventures and the record of his successes. As Rena listened, the narrow walls that hemmed her in seemed to draw closer and closer, as though they must crush her. Her brother watched her keenly. He had been talking not only to inform the women, but with a deeper purpose, conceived since entering the house and deepened as he had followed during his narrative the changing expression of Rena's face and noted her intense interest in his story, her pride in his success, and the occasional wistful look that indexed her self-pity so completely.

"And I 'spose you're happy, Johnny?" his mother advanced when he stopped talking.

"Well, Mother, happiness is a relative term and depends, I imagine, upon how nearly we think we get what we think we want. I have had my chance and haven't thrown it away, and I suppose that I ought to be happy. But then, I have lost my wife whom I loved very dearly and who loved me just as much, and I'm troubled about my child."

"Why?" they demanded. "Is there anything the matter with him?"

"No, not exactly. He's well enough, as babies go, and has a fairly good nurse. But the nurse is ignorant, and is not always careful. A child needs some woman of its own blood to love it and look after it intelligently."

Mis' Molly's eyes were filled with tearful yearning. She would have given all the world to have warmed her son's child upon her bosom; but she knew this could not be.

Up to this time Mis' Molly had not thought of the chasm between her son and her. Now it came back with such a shock that she found herself actually trembling at the thought of it. Johnny Walden had not been talking about the success of the boy who had gone away just twelve years ago. He had been relating the success of another lad—a *white* boy. The son who sat between her and his sister was not a *colored* boy. He was fully and unattainably white. All he had talked about was the success of a *white boy*.

And there lay the chasm; the deep river that could never be bridged. Johnny Walden had risen and was succeeding in South Carolina as a white boy, and it was there that the uncrossable line began. There was no reason under ordinary circumstances why she could not go to Charleston and take care of Johnny's little boy. Rena was old enough and responsible enough to look after their home. Then the boy could have what he needed, a flesh and blood care. But since her son was living as a *white man* in Charleston, was presumed to be a white man by all his friends and clients, taking her back with him would never do. Oh, of course it would be understood that she was just a good old mammy looking after the child. But she knew and she understood that he would know, that sooner or later, somewhere and sometime, somebody would begin to suspect the truth. In due time the truth *would* become a reality—and soon John's castle would fall!

No, John could never take her back with him to South Carolina—but he *could* take Rena. Yes, because people had been saying ever since she was born, and were still saying it. "Oh, Rena, you look just like a white girl."

"Did your wife leave any kin?" she asked Johnny, cautiously, carefully, but with some effort.

"No near kin, Mother. She was an only child."

"You'll be gettin' married again, maybe?"

"No," he replied. "I think not."

He was still looking at Rena, his purpose becoming more obvious, the longer he looked.

"If I had some relation of my own that I could take into the house with me," he said reflectively, "the child might be healthier and happier, and I should be much more at ease about him."

The mother looked from son to daughter with a dawning apprehension and a sudden pallor. When she saw the yearning in her son's eyes, she threw herself at his feet and cried out loudly:

"Oh, John! Don't take her away from me! Johnny, darlin' don't take her away from me for it will surely break my heart to lose her."

Rena dropped to her knees and placed arms about her mother's neck and cried words into Molly's ears:

"There, there, Mother. Never mind. I won't leave you, dear, Mama dear. Your Rena'll stay with you always and never leave you."

Johnny smoothed his mother's hair with a comforting touch, patted her cheeks, soothingly, lifted her tenderly to her place by his side, and put his arm about her.

"You love your children, Mother?"

"They're all I've got," she sobbed, "and they cos' me all I had. When Rena's gone, I'll want to go too, for I'll never see her again, and I can't bear to think of it. How would you like to lose your one child?"

"Well, well, Mother. We'll say no more about it. So let's change the subject and you tell me about yourself, and about the neighbors, and how you got through the war, and whose dead and whose married—and everything!"

The change of subject restored in some degree his mother's equanimity, and with returning calmness caused a sense of other responsibilities.

"Good gracious, Rena!" Mis' Molly cried, all of a sudden, just recalling. "Johnny's been in the house an hour, an' ain't had nothin' tu eat yet! Hurry to the kitchen and fix him a good dinner." No sooner spoken than Rena was up and gone. Turning to her son, "would you like—a piece of rabbit, John? Frank Fowler brought us two fresh-killed ones this morning when he left the work on his way by to have Rena figure out."

"Rabbit! Why, mother, by all means! I was reared on rabbit and have never lost my fondness for it. By all means fix some for me."

"Rena, oh, Rena?"

From the kitchen, "Yes, Mother?"

"Fix your brother some of the rabbit Frank brought us this morning; also some of that sweet potato pie we had for supper."

When Johnny heard the name of Fowler called, his mind, of course, went back to the large family who lived three miles away down the road when he went away. He remembered Frank as being about nine years old when he left. Now his mother was speaking of Frank, and the work he left for Rena to figure out when he was by that morning. What kind of work? From the way she spoke, Frank, whom he realized must have grown up and was now a man, must have some interest in common with the family. Perhaps with Rena. He would say nothing about it right now, but he would soon; very soon.

Now that he and his mother were alone for a few moments while Rena was preparing the meal, he decided to return to the subject that was uppermost in his mind.

"Of course, Mother," he said, calmly. "I wouldn't think of taking Rena away against her or your wishes. A mother's claim upon her child is a high and holy one. Of course she will have no chance here, where our story is known. The war has wrought great changes, has put the bottom rail on top, so to speak, for awhile at least; but it hasn't wiped *that* out. Nothing but death can remove that stain, if it doesn't follow us even beyond the grave. Here she must forever be a *Negro*—a nobody! Think of a pretty girl like her, living until death the life of a *nobody*.

"With me, she might have a chance to get on in the world; be a somebody. With her beauty and intelligence, she *might* make a good marriage. I did well, with nobody to push me forward so that I could meet, as I later in some way managed to do, the best people. Think of the advantage that she would have right off from scratch. If I mistake not, she has intelligence as well as beauty?"

"Yes," Molly sighed, sadly. "She's got good sense, plenty of good sense. She has been thinking of taking up school teaching. The Yankees have been starting them everywhere, fo' po' white people and niggers, too, so she was sayin' 'tuther day, that she could teach and take care of Frank's work, too."

"Now this Frank, you keep talking about, and his work. Is that the little Frank Fowler who used to play with her, and, they seemed rather—at so early an age, fond of each other?"

"Yes, Johnny, that's Frank."

"M-m. I see," Johnny said, a bit musingly. "Frank Fowler, eh?"

"Yes. He's a fine big man now and *so* industrious."

"Industrious? How?"

"He's a carpenter and builder."

"In the footsteps of his father. I hope he is as industrious. His father is a fine man—even if he is a Negro."

Mis' Molly looked at him quickly. Johnny did not meet her gaze.

"You spoke about Rena doing some work for him. What kind of work?"

"She keeps his books, works out his estimates for new construction. Oh, they are very fond of each other—get along fine together."

"What do you mean, get along fine together, Mother?"

"Well, just that, I guess. They seem to agree on and about everything."

"You wouldn't infer, that they are possibly—liking each other?"

"They might be. That's what everybody is saying."

"Please come to the point, Mother. The people are saying—what?"

"That they guess they'll be marrying each other by and by."

"Mother!" he exclaimed, and when Mis' Molly looked up, she found his eyes flashing fire.

"Why, Johnny! What's the matter?"

"The matter, Mother! What do you suppose I think is the matter? My sister, perhaps to marry a—*black man!*"

"Oh, Johnny, of course I understand you now. I'm sorry."

"Sorry? Why have you let it develop? I was just saying how, if you let her go back with me, she might meet and marry a gentleman, by that, I meant, of course, a white man."

"Yes, Johnny, I know what you mean and I said I was sorry. But Rena and Frank have been friends since they were babies; just seemed to take to each other from the start and they just grew up that way. I didn't want to see her get to like a dark man, but what could I do? Frank, even if he is dark, is such a manly fellow—just about everything a young man should be or could be. So what could I do? I've said nothing for it or against it. It just grew up and there it is."

"Well, that decides everything."

"Decides everything?"

"Rena must go back with me to Charleston when I return, regardless."

"Oh, Johnny, my son, please don't say that."

"It is said, Mother. But we must say no more now. We will undertake to get Rena off to bed as early as possible tonight, then you and I must have a talk, a long and serious talk—about Rena. That is all—now."

By the clink of dishes, both knew that the meal Rena was preparing was about ready, and no sooner had they thought about it than her cheerful voice called them. They turned and arm in arm marched into the dining room.

Chapter Twenty One

"Now, MOTHER, LISTEN to me closely and very carefully. I will be patient with you, for I know and understand that what I am going to talk about seems so far-fetched, strange and unusual in procedure that I hesitate to start talking."

"You are my son, Johnny. You have succeeded beyond my fondest dreams. I admire and appreciate whatever you plan to say, and I will try to understand you, son."

"Very well, mother. It is about Rena, my sister, your daughter. Beautiful, intelligent, sweet and her whole grown-up life before her."

Mis' Molly nodded her head understandingly.

"As it stands at this moment, there are two courses that she might follow, two lanes, as it is, leading into long years to come. Which shall she choose, that is for you and I to decide, I hope, tonight, dear.

"You tell me that she is very fond of Frank Fowler, her colored play and school mate. If she stays in Fayetteville, in all probability, she will marry him, and, since both are apparently healthy and normal, their marriage would bring about a new generation in a few years; a generation of *Negroes*.

"If she should return with me to Charleston, with her beauty, her intelligence and charm, she will meet a new set of people, a superior group of people, God's chosen people, white people. She could soon make a place for herself, an enduring place. The fact is, the place has already been made, just waiting for her to come forward and step into it."

"If she followed you over there, Johnny, she could never come back to me. I know what that means and you know what it means. If Rena steps over there, crosses that line, there is no returning. She will be gone from me forever—and I love her so, my las' one!"

"Yes, that is an unhappy—even a selfish outlook; but consider it the other way. She can stay near you and marry Frank Fowler, a *black* man, have a house full of brown children to join that long and hopeless brown procession with their heads bowed, marching away, away and away under that dark shroud, unknown and unknowing, but marching onward and away to—God knows where! Nobody can save them, for they have long since been condemned to remain hewers of wood and drawers of water. Nobody can change this outlook for Negroes—God *Himself* cannot change it!" He paused and drew closer:

"You see, mother. I am on the *inside*. As a white man I talk to them, and, thinking I am like themselves, white, they talk to me. We talk long and often among ourselves—about Negroes. It is always about Negroes. They talked about them before the war for years and years and years. Then when there was nothing left for them to talk any longer about, they went to war—with each other. The world knows the result! The North triumphed—for a while—and now they are trying to make of the Negro what it took hundreds of years for the white man to become. They think it will work—but the South knows otherwise. It will *not* work and it is *not* going to work for they *are not going to let it work!*

"This is what they talk about between themselves all the time. How and what to do about the Negro to topple him from that weak little pinnacle he seems to have attained with the help of carpet-baggers and scalawags. He talks about it and soon he will have plans ready to shove the Negro back, they say, where he belongs. I've lived as a white man long enough to learn much about them; Southern white people. They nurse their prejudice and hatred—especially toward the Negro. They're setting traps for them, and, sooner or later, watch what happens. He'll be forced out of politics as quickly as he has been put into it. He has just been put there. He doesn't know what it is all about, so, not knowing, he does not know how to defend himself. They will trick him. In time to come, I won't predict how long that will be coming, but he won't be able to vote at all. The North is not going to keep soldiers down here with loaded guns and drawn bayonets to protect his so-called rights forever. As soon as they get a sympathetic President, they'll get close to him; they know how to get what they want, and they'll show him that keeping these white men down South, away from their homes and their families is a mistake, and then gradually the troops of occupation will be withdrawn. As quickly as this has been accomplished, *watch these white people get busy!*

"They'll drive the Negro out of politics and the high places so fast and so completely until he won't be able to understand how it was done. I mean it, Mother,—even if they have to start a long period of lynching. They are already talking about an order whose members will dress all in white and carry fiery torches, who will ride through the night to frighten and drive Negroes out of these places of power that they have been lifted into.

"Now, beautiful Rena, is that what you want to happen to her? When she can just as easily return with me to Charleston, and with a little training etc, she can step out as a fine lady, marry a rich and fine gentleman in due time —and be free all her life. Not only her, but her children, her children's children, into the future, a hundred years hence, to be remembered and talked about.

"I know it will seem hard at the outset; but in ten, fifteen or twenty years at the most, Mother, you will die and then our last tie with the Negro race will be severed, soon thereafter, forgotten."

The tortured mother could endure no more. The one thing she desired above all others was her daughter's happiness. Her own life had not been governed by the highest standards, but about her love for her beautiful daughter there was no taint of selfishness. The life her son had described had been to her always the ideal but unattainable life. Circumstances, many beyond her control, and others for which she was in a measure responsible, had put it forever and inconceivably beyond her reach. It had been conquered by her son. It now beckoned to her daughter. The comparison of this free and noble life with the sordid existence of those around her broke down the last barrier of opposition.

"O Lord," she moaned. "What shall I do without her? It'll be lonely without her, Johnny, *so* lonely."

"You'll have your home, Mother—the house behind the

Cedars," Walden said, tenderly, accepting the implied surrender. "You'll have your friends and relatives, and the knowledge that your children are happy. I'll let you hear from us often, and will try to let you see Rena now and then. But you must let her go, Mother. It would be a sin against her to refuse."

"She may go," the mother replied brokenly. "I'll not stand in her way. I've got sins enough to answer for already."

Walden watched her pityingly. He had stirred her feelings to unwonted depths, and his sympathy went out to her. If she had sinned, she had been more sinned against, than sinning, and it was not his part to judge her.

He had yielded to a sentimental weakness in deciding upon this trip to Fayetteville. A matter of business had brought him within a day's journey of the town, and an overmastering impulse had impelled him to seek the mother who had given him birth and the old town where he had spent the earlier years of his life, although he had declared on leaving it so mysteriously, that he would never return—and meant it.

They talked and made plans until late into the night, then both retired. John was happy when he sank into the deep feather bed that he had slept on before he left home, and it was late the following morning when he awakened.

His mother and sister had risen at their usual time, and Rena was just finishing the estimate Frank had left with her when her mother came to the table and sat down to face her. Rena folded the estimate and put same into a catalogue envelope she kept at the house for the purpose, then turned to face her mother, a question in her eyes.

"Rena, how'd you lak to go and pay your brother, Johnny, a visit? I guess I might spare you for a little while."

The girl's eyes lighted up. She would not have gone if her mother had wished her to stay, but she had always regarded this as the lost opportunity of her life.

"Are you sure you don't care, Mama?" she asked, hoping and yet doubting.

"Oh, I'll manage to get along somehow or other. You can go and stay until you git homesick, and then Johnny'll let you come back home."

Mis' Molly said this with her eyes downcast, for she had a feeling that if Rena went, she would be like Johnny, never come back, except under cover of night. She must lose her daughter as well as her son, and this should be the penance for her sin. That her children must expiate as well the sins of their fathers, who had sinned so lightly, after the manner of men, neither she nor they could foresee, since they could not read the future.

The next boat by which Walden could take his sister away left early in the evening of the next day. He left them and went to a hotel, with the understanding that the next day would be devoted to getting Rena ready to return with him to Charleston.

Chapter Twenty Two

JOHNNY WALDEN, RECALLING that it was Judge Straight who had really given him his big chance in life, felt that it would show the proper gratitude if he called on the old Judge while in Fayetteville and expressed his thanks in person.

So, after standing at the front window inside of his mother's home and watching the road carefully to see that no one would see him, when he left, he ventured out and a half hour later called at Judge Straight's office. The Judge was not in but the door stood open and Walden entered to await his return. There had been few changes in the office. The dust was a little thicker, the papers in the pigeon hole of the walnut desk were a little yellower, the cobwebs in the corner a little more aggressive. The flies droned as drowsily and the murmur of the brook below was just as audible. Walden stood at the rear window and looked out over a familiar view. Directly across the creek on the low ground beyond, might be seen the dilapidated stone foundation of the house where once had lived Flora MacDonald, the Jacobite Refugee, the most romantic character of North Carolina history. Old Judge Straight had had a tree cut away from the creek side opposite his window, so that this historic ruin might be visible from his office; for the Judge could trace the ties of blood that connected him collaterally with this famous personage. His pamphlet on Flora MacDonald, printed for private circulation, was highly prized by those of his friends who were fortunate enough to obtain a copy. To the left of the window a placid mill-pond spread its wide expanse, and to the right of the creek, disappeared under a canopy of overhanging trees.

A footstep sounded in the doorway, and Walden turning, faced the old judge. Time had left greater marks upon the lawyer than upon his office. His hair was whiter; his stoop more pronounced; when he spoke to Walden, his voice had some of the thrillness of old age; and in his hand, upon which the veins stood out prominently, a decided tremor was perceptible.

"Good morning, Judge Straight," the young man said, removing his hat with the grateful Southern deference of the young for the old.

"Good morning, sir," the Judge replied with equal courtesy.

"You don't remember me, I imagine," Walden suggested, with a little smile upon his face.

"Your face seems familiar," the Judge returned cautiously, looking at him closely, "but I cannot for the moment recall your name. I shall be glad to have you refresh my memory."

"I *was* Johnny Northcross, sir, when you knew me."

The Judge's face still gave no immediate light of recognition.

"You sent me away to school...."

"Ah, now I remember you full well!" the Judge exclaimed of a sudden, extending his hand with great cordiality, and inspecting Walden more closely through his spectacles. "You went away a few years before the war."

"Yes, sir, to South Carolina."

"So you did, so you did. Well, I'm glad to see you again after so many, many years. I would have never known you, and I doubt if anybody else in this town will remember you. Meanwhile," and the Judge paused to point to a chair. "Sit down and tell me something about what has happened while you've been away."

Walden told him his story in outline, much as he had given it to his mother and sister, and the Judge seemed very much interested.

"And you married into a good family?"

"And have a child."

"A—boy?"

Walden nodded affirmatively, and smiled with pride.

"And you are visiting your mother?"

"Not exactly. I have seen her, but I am stopping at a hotel."

"H-m! Are you staying long?"

"I leave tomorrow."

"It's well enough. I wouldn't stay too long. The people of a small town are inquisitive about strangers and some of them have long memories. I remember your case well, which was strange and unusual and I was rather apprehensive regarding it. That you have been able to surmount the obstacles, became a lawyer as you so much desired to be, and have succeeded, is much for you to be thankful for and I am very much relieved. But custom is stronger than law, and in your case, custom *is* law. It will be worth your while here to be careful. Don't meet and talk with people you know—at least long enough for them to remember you."

After a few minutes longer with the Judge, Walden left him and made his way back to his hotel to await the cover of night when he planned to return to see his mother and sister out on the old Wilmington Road in the House Behind The Cedars.

Shortly after Walden left that morning to go into Fayetteville and call on old Judge Straight, Frank Fowler came by for the estimate that he had left with Rena to work out during the night; and he brought with him some partridges, which he had shot the day before.

"Oh, thank you, Frank, dear!" Mis' Molly exclaimed as she took them. Then, after a few words, turned and went into the kitchen, leaving Frank and Rena together. After Johnny left and before Frank came, she had warned Rena not to tell Frank or anybody else that they had had a visitor.

"It will take too many words to explain to our friends about Johnny; and the more we'd say in the effort, the more they would misunderstand, but would start talking and before long everybody would know as much as us, so just say nothing to Frank about it when he calls, dear."

"Just as you say, Mama," Rena replied; "but I'll have to tell him that I am going away."

"Of course, and I have thought all about that. Just say that you are going away to visit some friends of ours who are ill; and that you might be gone for two or three weeks. Tell him as little as you can, and get it over with quickly."

"Supposing that I let him drive me down to where this house is to be built, and I can tell him on the way there?"

Her mother frowned. She'd rather not see her go away that way; but soon she would be gone and never come back. That is what kept popping into her mind regarding her going back with Johnny. She'd never come back; he'd never come back; she might not ever see either again, and to hold back tears and not just break down completely, taxed all her strength. She had thought about it all the night through. Passing for white, she knew, was dangerous; it was risky and uncertain. The more she stayed away from their past; away from people she had been reared with and knew, the better the chance. Anyway it went, it was risky and dangerous, and she would be thinking about this for months to come, maybe years.

"Well, you may go with Frank; but don't stay long and don't talk much. Get back as quickly as you can and we'll put in the time getting you ready to leave on the next boat which leaves tomorrow night."

"If you'll drive me down to where you're going to erect these buildings, Frank, I'll like that."

"Of course, Rena. I'll be glad to," Frank replied, and was thrilled to have her ask him.

"But I can't stay long, Frank. We'll have to get back very shortly." She said these words for her mother's benefit; loud enough for Molly to hear her from the kitchen. and then she was relieved.

She was anxious to get away with Frank. Her brother's return had been such a surprise, and a thrill, that it had swept her off her feet—and made her at the time, forget Frank and their plans for the future. But after they pushed her off to bed, she lay there for hours, thinking about it and by the time morning arrived, she was in a deep quandary, profoundly disturbed over the outlook.

She realized after her brother had won her mother over to his plans for her, she would have to go back to South Carolina with him. He was now a rich man with a wide range, back there, of influence and friends. And while she was quite content with her life in Fayetteville, looking forward a year or two ahead as she was, to the time she would marry Frank and go live with him, all of which in one single night had been changed.

It left her upset and greatly excited. It meant her whole future life would be changed. She was happy and proud over the thought of her brother's success; of his ability to pass for white and get away with it; but she had never anticipated or craved such a thing. She was a colored girl, and had never considered that she might go away and pass for something that she was not. She could appreciate what a thrill this might be to some vain creature; to swell them up and set them to hating Negroes, for that was the way it always turned out. If they passed for white, they always hated and shunned Negroes thereafter—and she had never craved any such thing.

She had therefore been waiting anxiously for Frank to come by, and had planned to have him take her for a drive —not a drive for pleasure exactly, but a visit to their little glade in the forest, where they often went to talk and pass a happy hour with each other.

As they drove away, she looked back over her shoulder as if to see if they were being followed, which she knew, of course, was not true. But she was on the anxious seat and Frank noticed it. She wanted to talk to Frank, the one person she trusted implicitly. Convinced that no one could possibly hear them, she turned to the other, who seemed to be expecting some sort of outburst.

"Frank!" she all but exclaimed, and as he turned to her, her beautiful face was pathetic.

"Yes, Rena. There's something on your mind. I noticed it when I entered the house."

"There is, Frank. Oh, *so* much!"

"Do you—wish to—tell me about it, Rena?"

"If I don't, I'll go crazy—*crazy!*"

"Oh, Rena, what has happened—*so quick?* You were happy and composed yesterday morning. What has happened since to make you like you are?"

"Everything, Frank—*Everything!*"

"Great goodness!"

"I promised Mama I wouldn't talk, which means I'm not supposed to tell you what I am going to."

"Don't tell me if you don't want to, Rena."

"Oh, Frank, that is so—sweet of you! You understand me like no other person. I want to tell you what happened, dear—I want to tell you *everything.*"

Frank was by now disturbed, but there was nothing he could do but shrug his shoulders—and Rena went on.

"Do you remember Johnny, Frank?"

"Who disappeared so strangely long years ago?"

"Yes!"

"How could I forget it, Rena? I don't think anybody around here at the time has forgotten it."

"Well, Frank. Johnny came back last night."

"*What!*"

"He came back last night, stayed all night, and went

into town to see old Judge Straight today. He's stopping at the Fountain Hotel and will return to our house tonight again."

"*What mystery here?* Johnny Northcross, back."

"His name is no longer Johnny Northcross, Frank. He is now *John Walden,* and has been ever since he left."

Frank gazed hard at her and in amazement.

"He is also no longer a Negro. Ever since he left here, he has been *passing* for white. In Charleston where he lives, he married a wealthy white man's daughter. The girl's father was killed in battle, the girl, who married him, is dead. But he has a little boy. He lives in a mansion in Charleston, and—oh, Frank, he wants me to go back to South Carolina with him."

Rena broke into tears now and did not see Frank's eyes and mouth open wide. She covered her eyes with her kerchief and wept woe-begone for fully a minute before she could calm herself.

"So he wants to take you back with him, Rena?"

"Yes, Frank, to look after his little boy and meet his friends."

"Which means that you will have to *pass* for white also . . ."

"That is what I hate about it; I hate everything about it."

"But you will have to do as your brother and mother wish, Rena. Has your mother consented?"

"She had to. She didn't want to, but my brother is a great lawyer, convincing and persuasive. He practically forced mother to consent."

"Well," said Frank with a deep sigh. "That is that, Rena."

"But I don't want to go, Frank. Don't you understand? I don't want to go. I don't want to pass for white. I don't exactly like white people and never did. I don't want to go stealing over there like a thief in the night; frightened and scared. I don't want to be white, even if I can pass without any trouble."

"But if your mother has consented, and your brother is expecting you to return with him, it really doesn't matter just what you think or how you feel about it."

"But what about you, Frank? You haven't consented. Do you want me to go?"

"Of course not, dear; but what I want or think can't matter. You will have to go, Rena."

"But if I go I'd have to leave you, Frank. I don't want to leave you. I don't want to go. I want to stay right here."

"I'm sorry, dear. I know how you feel, but look at it their way."

"You mean my brother's way."

Frank shrugged his shoulders resignedly. "You say that Johnny is a rich and influential man now, has wealthy friends, all white people. Don't be silly, my dear. This is a rare and unusual opportunity. You must do as they ask you to."

"But what about you, Frank? I am thinking about you. If you say you don't want me to, I'll refuse and stay right here. After all, that is what I want to do."

"If you did, they would charge it to me—and hate me. I don't want your mother and your brother to hate me, Rena. You must go with him. I'll manage somehow."

Frank was not an outwardly emotional boy; but his heart at the moment was paining so; just seemed like it would break. He was dazed, bewildered. The world, which had seemed so bright and hopeful an hour ago, was whirling around him, and he could do nothing but try to be brave. Rena had hidden her eyes with her kerchief and was crying again. As he turned to try to comfort her, a large tear dropped from his eyes and ran down upon his work jacket. It was the end of everything for him. His castles had fallen, Rena was going away and he had to sanction it.

"You see, Rena, over there, with your brother rich and powerful, life can mean so much to you. Besides, you've said that he has a little boy that has no mother. The child needs a mother. You can be that mother. As for me, I'm a man. Father always told me that I must expect some kind of trouble in life. And he taught me to prepare for it, so please don't cry any more, but just prepare to go to Charleston with your brother, and don't worry about me. I'll manage to get along somehow. I will be here where I can comfort your mother. Think of what taking you out of her life is going to mean. You're all she has."

Rena was weeping now without restraint. Frank turned his mule about and drove her back toward the house behind the cedars. By the time they reached it, she had become resigned to her task, and was stronger. He helped her into the house and as they entered, her mother asked from upstairs if it were she, calling that she would be down in a few minutes. Frank turned to go and Rena grabbed him.

Although they had been schoolmates, playmates, and everybody was now expecting them to marry, they had never, in some peculiar way, exchanged a kiss. It was Rena who now broke that virtue, for, with a suppressed little cry, she threw her arms about him and kissed him, full on the lips, repeating it one, two and three times, then, as if she could stand it no longer, after squeezing him to her, broke and ran away and upstairs. Frank stood where she had left him a moment, tears welling up in his large, dark eyes, then as if to let nobody see him cry, turned abruptly and let the house.

Chapter Twenty Three

RENA AND HER BROTHER took the night boat to Wilmington, which left Fayetteville at eight p. m. Johnny ordered her to "meet him on the boat," by which Rena knew that he was taking no chance of them being recognized. Frank took her to the boat, and helped her aboard, all the way to her state-room. Inside, and alone, she again fell into his arms, she wanted to weep all over again but he would not let her, and took his leave almost immediately after the embrace.

"If anything goes wrong, dear. Remember. You can always come back to me. I'll be waiting." The next moment he was gone. Still weeping, but drying her tears, she dared open a window. She saw him as he crossed the deck below, walked across the gang plank hurriedly, climbed into his buggy, in which she had enjoyed the happiest moments of her life, when he drove her about the countryside—and he was gone. She waved at him hopelessly, knowing that he couldn't see her, drew the shade down and turned—to look into the eyes of her brother who had opened the state-room door unheard and was standing looking at her.

"Why, Johnny," she cried, frightened, "I—didn't hear you open the door. You frightened me."

He closed the door, after stepping into the room and crossed to her. "My state-room is next to this. I heard you when you—entered, and—"

"You—heard, *after* I entered?"

He nodded his head affirmatively, looking straight at her all the while.

"I'm sorry," she said, simply, and turned away. He came closer, up behind her and put his arms about her waist and leaning over, kissed her on her cheek.

"I'm not going to scold you for what you did, dear. I understand. It is hard to change to a new life overnight; hard to get away from those you've known—and liked, for such a long time." He paused then while she said nothing. Finally, he squeezed her upper arms which he held.

"I'll go out on the deck now, if you don't mind, and you can draw the curtain and look out if you like. After the boat leaves, I'll be back, and then we'll have a long talk, sister, a serious talk."

She turned as he was leaving and their eyes met as he was going out the door. He smiled at her oddly and closed the door. She heard his footsteps go down the narrow hallway to the deck, and then she sank upon a chair, strangely, or was it emotionally, exhausted.

A few minutes later the boat pulled out, backing up a bit, then the engineer reversed the motors, and the large flat boat swung out into the channel of Cape Fear River and headed Southeast for Wilmington, where it was due early the following morning—and Rena had left Fayetteville for the first time in her life for a long trip. Would she ever return? She closed her eyes in a fit of bewilderment and doubts. Sighing deeply, she rose to her feet and removing her hat and coat, decided to try and be brave.

Shortly afterward, her brother returned to her cabin, knocking on the door first. This, of course, was after their tickets had been taken up and they were not likely to be bothered again.

"I've ordered a light meal brought to your room, dear. We will eat it here, then—the talk."

The meal served and the dishes taken away, Walden turned to her, his face serious for that "talk."

"Now, dear sister. I didn't attempt to go into this back there," jerking his thumb over his shoulder in the direction of Fayetteville. "I felt it would be better to wait for this moment when I knew we would be all alone and sufficiently relaxed to digest everything properly."

"I agree with you, Johnny. I am sure that was the best."

"I suppose you understand what is before you, dear?"

"I—hope I do, Johnny, but I am anxious to hear what you have to say."

"A very important thing to explain, Rena, is, that your past life is behind you and that includes—Frank. It even includes our mother."

Rena sighed, audibly, and he moved closer, knowing that it hurt to the quick and she needed consolation.

"I know what I just said hurts, Rena—it even hurt me, more than twelve years ago, and I *wanted* to go away. I was so anxious to become a lawyer that when Judge Straight informed me that he had made arrangements for my education; that I must leave my past—even my name back there in Fayetteville, I was the happiest boy in all the world. Yet, as I stole away like a thief in the night, I was sad and unhappy. I kept thinking about mama and you, kept on and on and it seemed for a long time my heart would simply break and I would die.

"Yet, as you know, I did not die, but lived on, surmounted mighty obstacles and rose in due time to success. In time I forgot the grief, overcame my sorrow and the great loneliness that beset me, as it must now beset you, and—well, you know the rest of the story."

"It was all so wonderful, so brave on your part," she said quietly, "Mama and I are both proud of you. I'm sure that you know best, even if it does all but break my heart to leave Fayetteville and go away. I want you to know that in doing so, however, brother, that I've decided to be brave—and try to see it through as you did."

"I am happy to hear you say that, Rena; happy and encouraged. At least it won't be as hard for you on the one hand, as it was for me, for I was alone, on my own, whereas, everything is prepared for you. Just about all you have to do is to be brave and strong; resolute and determined—and forget the past. The future, that is up to me in a great measure—and I am prepared to see it through."

"Thank you, brother," she said, meekly. "I will do my best."

"Fine! Now where will we start?"

"Just a word before you do, Johnny," she said, laying a hand on his wrist. "I's saying this because, in anticipation of what is coming, this is so often on my mind."

"Go ahead, dear, and by all means tell me what this is that is so much on your mind."

"Well," she began, hesitatingly. "I've been told that meeting and mixing with white people is not as hard as when you encounter one of *us* in doing so."

"Us? What do you mean?"

"That meeting them when one is *passing* inclines to—make one self-conscious; un-nerves you. In short, frightens you when you meet their gaze. That is what I mean, and what is worrying me."

"Is that all that is worrying you, Rena? Go ahead, unburden yourself, dear."

"That's the worst of it."

"I'm so glad you brought that up—and now, dear. I was trying to find a way to come to it so that you would know. Now that I see it is on your mind, it relieves me."

"Thank you, Johnny. I am glad."

"If you were alone as I was, this could possibly upset you in the life you are about to step into. But there is where I can help so much. You see, to begin with, it is more our self-consciousness that makes us that way than anything else. We think that what we think they think, and give ourselves away when if we could just forget all about it, it wouldn't matter at all. What you must learn to do, Rena, is to *just think you are a white girl,* and it becomes much easier, so much easier. Now, you must in this case, not do much thinking at all. Just remember that you are my sister; and that all Negroes *think* I *am* a white man. So thinking, they don't turn to look at me the second time, and, the second time harder. As my sister, you understand, they will not doubt what you are and will not, therefore, look again at you with that penetrating expression, see?"

"Yes, I see, brother, and I also understand."

"Good, Rena, you are catching on readily. Now, I have not decided all this without doing a lot of thinking also. I've decided to place you in a private boarding school until next summer, the end of the term to be exact. In that school, you will meet a lot of white girls, the best white girls. You will learn through them and with them how white people think, act and do. This should get you accustomed to their ways of doing and to a degree, of thinking. Then, next June, when you leave the school and come to live with me, you are my sister, just out of boarding school. This will do away with much explaining about your past. When a girl is just out of boarding school, people rarely dig further into her past. They just take it for granted that you've been in school and before you went there, you were too young to know and understand much about anything that would interest them—and usually that is the end of it.

"Meanwhile, before you enter school, I will lay out what you are to do and say to the nice girls that you will meet there at the school. Leave that to me for the present. One of the many things I like about you, Rena, is your fine modesty and silence. If you were inclined to talk a lot, this move I am making would endanger us both, for, sooner or later your inclination to talk would crab the whole works for you would most surely say too much. I don't mind telling you at the outset that you and I both will for a long time—in fact, almost forever, be trodding on thin ice and just a slight mistake can and will ruin us. I have never forgotten that, but thus far nobody has decided to dig into my past and demand an accounting. They will be less inclined to about my sister, but all the while we must simply be careful."

"I agree with you fully, my brother, and I shall be careful at all times. I would be very unhappy if I felt a careless word or move on my part would upset all that you have struggled these long years to achieve."

"Well said, Rena. I will be patient with you at all

times and help you as much as it is possible for me to, to forget the past. Time only can heal that, and I have allowed for that." He rose to his feet now, and she followed suit. He crossed to the door and she came up beside him. He kissed her goodnight and went to his state-room.

Inside his stateroom and alone, John Walden relaxed completely—the first time he had permitted himself to do so since reaching Fayetteville, three days before. Relaxed, he began to plan his sister's future.

When he went to bed two hours later, he had concluded just how he would go about and engineer this great masquerade.

Chapter Twenty Four

IF WE WERE using captions at the beginning of each chapter, we would begin this chapter with the caption *"The other side—a Negro no longer!"*

Meanwhile, Rena, under the sponsorship of her brother, begins here and now, her great masquerade as somebody else, which inspired the title of this story. We will now proceed with the strange, and often sensational, events that follow, as the result of this masquerade.

Shortly after Rena finished her preliminary training at the girl's school, and returned to her brother's old colonial mansion on the outskirts of Charleston to make her home, the wealthy and aristocrats of the town staged a tournament, or a sort of pageant which was well attended by the better class, to some degree by the poor whites, and even a few Negroes bought seats and watched the activities from the bleachers.

Rena and her brother attended. At this tournament Rena was introduced to one of South Carolina's most attractive widows, a young woman by the name of Mrs. Janie Newberry. Since Mrs. Newberry was attracted to Rena's brother, she found the sister the exact vehicle to use for seeing more of Johnny. By showing kindness to Rena, she saw a means of making John more grateful to her.

At the tournament Rena also met a wealthy young aristocrat from North Carolina, who happened to be a client of her brother, by the name of George Wendell Tryon, scion of an old and wealthy North Carolina family. George was only 23, tall, athletic and handsome.

Back where Tryon lived, his mother had been planning his future, which included designs for his ultimate marriage to a beautiful blonde called Blanche—the rest of her name was Leary. Tryon had found her amusing and tolerable, but after meeting his lawyer's sister at the Tournament, he lost all interest in the girl his mother had selected for his wife, and had eyes for no other but Rena Walden; Rena had taken her brother's name when she returned with him to pass her future life, and to experience new associations as a white girl.

By this time Rena had begun to come to herself, although the past—her secret she preferred to think of it as —was almost constantly in her thoughts; and all this meeting white people, dining with them, dancing with them and listening to their talk, was still bewildering and confusing to her. As yet, however, she had not blundered, neither talked too much nor embarrassed her brother.

George W. Tryon was a fine fellow, and while Rena never let herself become infatuated with him, she found it possible to be nice and agreeable, and thought that if she were a white girl, and not merely masquerading as one, it would be quite easy to fall in love with him as he seemed, from their first meeting, to be falling in love with her.

She let him do the talking, as she allowed just about everyone she'd become acquainted with do, since "crossing over," but she had developed the tact of a good listener, and her silence and good listening, seemed to have won her friends. They called her "shy" and this accentuated her modesty, all of which added to her popularity—especially with George Tryon, who was soon a regular caller at her home, and took her out frequently.

By and by George Wendell Tryon told her that he loved her and asked her to be his wife. She delayed her reply, but promised to give him her answer in a week.

After George left her that night, she went to her brother, and said:

"George told me that he loved me tonight, and asked me to marry him."

"Oh, how wonderful, dear!" her brother exclaimed with great enthusiasm. "And did you—consent, dear?"

Rena shook her head negatively, whereupon the happy approval on her brother's face became clouded with a frown of anxiety.

"But Rena, dear, half the girls in Charleston would give their lives, if George Tryon asked them to marry him. He's the smartest catch of the season, wealthy, dignified, aristocratic—and a swell fellow. Why did you refuse him?"

"I did not refuse him, Johnny. I merely said that I would give him my answer in a week."

"Oh, that is better, much better, and takes a load off my mind. Why did you wish to wait a week, however?"

"I felt that I should talk to you about it first. The next reason was, Johnny, I'll try to be frank—I was afraid."

"Afraid? Afraid of what?"

"Oh, Johnny," she cried, bursting into tears. "You *know* what I am afraid of."

"There, there, dear. Of course I know; but you must not let that stand in your way. I've said, repeatedly, 'let the dead past bury its dead.' I've told you that you must *think* you are white—and defy all sentiments to the contrary."

"I've tried to, Johnny, and I'm still trying. But it's hard to forget that I—I am *not* a white girl. And if George knew the truth, would he want me then; would he love me just as much as he says he does?"

Her brother sprang to his feet. She could see that she had disturbed him; had upset his equilibrium. After a few strides he paused and stood over her.

"Unless we can forget and live down our 'skeleton in the closet,' there is neither future nor happiness for either of us, Rena, or for my little son, Albert. All our futures depend upon our being strong and resolute and—"

"—Being successful deceivers, John. I'm sorry, I know you are right, and I hate to upset you."

"Then why do you?"

"I don't know, I don't know. All I can think of is what George would say or do if he ever learns the truth."

"Let's look at it another way. In whatever move we take, you've got to take a chance. Let's consider if you married George and 'took the chance,' and that if you got through the first years and had children as a healthy and normal girl like you must expect."

"I follow you."

"After three, four or five years, he in some manner might find out, then what?"

"Yes, then what?"

"He would be confronted with the future of his own flesh and blood; his children, his children's children, then what *could* he do?"

"I—think he would have to—see it through, yes."

"That is the way to look at it. Oh, I know how much you dislike the idea of deceiving a man from the outset, but George Tryon is a sensible man. He would be shocked and angry. He would perhaps even hate you for awhile. But under such circumstances, however, he would have to cool off—in fact, he *would* cool off and consider the circumstances. He would in due time come to realize that while you may have deceived him, under the circumstances, he'd realize that there was no other alternative. He'd understand that you had done nothing wrong; that you were the nice, modest girl he fell in love with after all, only—"

"—That I was not what *he* thought I was all the while; that I was *not* a white girl and never had been; that I was a—*Negress*, the most despicable creature that God in all his power and glory could create; and that I had deceived him brazenly and willfully, for all the while I was letting him make love to me, I knew that I was a Negress, the daughter of a slave woman, an illegitimate—and a *bastard!*"

"Oh, my God, Rena, my God—and please hush! Hush this moment and say not another word."

"I'm so sorry, John. I hated to hurt you, but what I said was on my mind. I had to get it off, one time or another; one way or another. And now that I have, I feel better, stronger. Go ahead, Johnny, and say what you will."

"What is there left for me to say, after all you just said? I'm so shocked and mortified until I am—oh, just beaten."

He sat down then, weak and limp, and gazed for a time straight before him at nothing.

"Don't be discouraged, brother. I tell you, it was on my mind and until I could get it off—confess my feelings to somebody, I couldn't seem to go on. Now, let us look at it in its real light, after which we can go about making adjustments as I feel we should.

"First, I had thought of confessing the truth to George," she began, whereupon her brother became taut, sprang quickly to his feet, his mouth flew open. She raised a hand and stayed it.

"Please let me finish, dear. Before I had rehearsed the idea in my own mind, even, I dismissed it, for it would not have mattered so much to me. It would ruin you however, so the idea was out. What I am trying to explain, Johnny, is, that if I go through as you have planned, with this masquerade, I must prepare myself. I must, in short, admit to myself that I am masquerading; keep on thinking of it to myself in that way until I can feel justified in my act. In other words, to act, one can't go on feeling innocent and modest. They must 'play at it' all the while, be at least partially conscious of what you are doing. That is the way I see it. I've got to become an actress. Once I am complete in that role and have crucified my conscience, I might be able to tell George that I love him, too, and be his wife, bear his children, and then, if he ever learns the truth, stage a great scene: tell him cold and hard to his face that I fooled him; and that it is too late, if we have the children as we would have every reason to expect, to be mortified at his discovery and to brand me. I must be able to stand before him, cold and hard and say: 'Had I told you the truth before you married me, do you suppose that you ever would have? You know you wouldn't! I knew it and now you know it. But, in justice to myself, I was a nice girl, virtuous, pure and simple. I have made you a good wife, bore you lovely children, in spite of the fact that I was born out of wedlock, the daughter of an aristocrat slave-master, the offspring of a helpless mulatto slave woman. Knowing all this, and what you would have done had you known it before making love to, and marrying me, what do *you* think that I should have done?

" 'What is done, is done. Around us are your children, my children. If you must hate me, hate them, too; but I have them to love and caress until I die. There is no law against what I have done, and if you now wish to leave me, you must leave your children, too. Now my master, what?' "

"Oh, Rena, my sister, my child. I never knew all this was in you," he moaned, his face dejected, upset, bewildered, downcast.

She crossed to him and tried to comfort him.

"I am the same little sister that I have always been, Johnny. I love you and I love your little boy. I want to rear him to be—like his father. I can wish no more; but deceiving a man has been preached against in every novel of the kind that I ever read. All have pointed that a woman should 'confess' her sins, her past, to the man she would marry. You know, and I know, and George Wendell Tryon knows that I cannot confess *our* secret to him, so what? If we go on, I will have to at least harden myself and marry the man with no thought or intention of ever telling him the truth. Once that hard, I might be able to go through with it, otherwise, I have so many doubts and fears."

"Since it was in you, Rena, there was nothing left but for you to have your way. I am wondering, however, if—Frank Fowler hasn't some indirect influence over what you've just said? I don't mean that he has told you anything or communicated with you in any way. But if you are actually in love with that black boy, love him so much that all I said to our mother about the future of the Negro, doesn't matter."

"I'm sorry again, my brother. But Frank Fowler is the only man I ever loved; the only man I feel that I will ever actually love. But in coming here with you, becoming a part of your plan for my betterment, I forewent all which has been my past, including Frank Fowler."

"Then you don't love George Tryon?"

"No, Johnny, I do not; but I will marry him if you let me handle it my way."

"*Your* way, Rena?"

"As I explained. That is the only way I feel that I could go through with it. Otherwise, as I see it, to tell him that I love him would be a terrible lie. He is everything a *white* girl could love. In order to feel that I am a white girl, however, I've got to act it. To fall in love truly with a white man would be a lie; an encroachment. Somehow, I fear, I will always hate a deceiver. It is a common saying among our folks, I mean, Negroes, that we have no objection to our folks passing for white if they can better themselves by doing so, secure a better job in doing it, etc. On the other hand, we hate them when they try to do so out of **pure vanity**, for when they do, they in turn, hate us and seem to want to blame us if they fail. According to you, and logic, I had a chance to better myself by coming here with you. Surely from the standpoint of logic, any Negro who could walk into the best white society as you have installed me in Charleston, is far better off than continuing through life as a Negro—the best of Negroes.

"Strange, and I didn't want to; but you sold Mama on the idea, Mama told me to go. I am ready to go through with it as has been bargained, clear up until I die, now that I have started. All I wanted was for *you* to understand how I felt, brother. Once you know just how I feel, and realize that I will be playing a role when I do, then I am sure I can do it better. I wanted you to know just how I would do it. That is all, Johnny. Now get up and think it over for a week, until the time is due for me to give George my answer. Before I do, we will talk again, see?"

She got him to his feet then, sad and dejected. Yet, for Johnny Walden, there was no alternative but to do as she had asked him to.

Chapter Twenty Five

MRS. JANIE NEWBERRY, associated with several women's clubs in Charleston, gave a card party a few days after Rena's talk with her brother. It was in honor of Miss Walden. Only the wealthy, fashionable and elite of Charleston were invited, and some thirty or more attended.

Rena was duly presented to all those who had not met her. They met at two P. M. and the party lasted until 5:30 P. M. The afternoon was spent playing cards mostly, but along toward the end, it turned into gossiping. It seemed to have gotten started on the subject of Negro servants—in fact, "servants" seemed to have been the only topic discussed.

A Mrs. Caroline Milbank arrived somewhat late, and in explaining why, she started to explain or relate an experience. It seemed that she had visited New Orleans recently, and, while there, encountered the incident which she recited to those present with much story-telling effect.

"It was the talk of St. Charles Street when I arrived, or I should say that this person was the talk of social New Orleans when I arrived. She had become engaged to one of New Orleans' most promising young society men, and to say that he was madly in love with her, was putting it mildly. This debutante came from up on the Red River, commonly called 'The Cane River Country!' She was of a wealthy family who had owned quite a large number of slaves before the war, and still possessed all the land which had been in the family for more than a hundred years.

"This girl, whose name was Gertrude Poray, was sort of a creole type and as beautiful as any woman you ever saw. But to make a long story short, somebody had business up in the Cane River Country, and while there, learned the truth about Miss Poray."

"And what was that?" Mrs. Newberry wanted to know. The others held their breaths in anxiety.

"Miss Poray—was a Negress!"

"Go away from here!" Mrs. Newberry exclaimed, her mouth and eyes wide. Rena opened her eyes, too; but only swallowed.

"A nigger, so help me God!" Mrs. Milbank reiterated.

Exclamations of surprise were heard throughout the group, all alike—full of amazement!

"But—what," Mrs. Newberry said, "Ever possessed her to think she could get away with—such a fraud?"

"Well, they were rich, they had owned slaves; the family did not, and never had, associated with Negroes. Additionally, they *were* light enough to pass for white, so it didn't seem to upset her in the least."

"You—you mean she stayed on in New Orleans after they learned the truth about her; that she had nigger-blood in her veins?"

"Nothing different. She declared that she was just as white as any white person in New Orleans; that she was rich; that her parents had sense enough to avoid service in the civil war, that is, Confederate service, and that all New Orleans could go to Hades. That she was white, even if she did have Negro blood in her veins, and she'd like to see what they could do about it. Incidentally, the family owned the St. Louis-Royal Hotel where she was staying. So she stayed on in New Orleans until she was ready to leave and when she did, it happened to be on the same train I left on, passing for white, of course, and is in New York now, waiting to sail for Europe, where, I was told, she plans to make her future home; and where, no doubt, she can marry a white man without so many people objecting."

"The nerve of her! What did the man she was engaged to do about it?"

"Oh, he quit her the moment he heard that she had Negro blood; quit her cold—and ran away."

Laughter.

"Well, the effects of her masquerade was on when I left New Orleans. The best white people of New Orleans have decided to issue a questionnaire. I mean the social and elite. They are setting up a sort of 'Social Registry,' whereby every desirable person applying for membership, is to fill out this questionnaire, which will trace their ancestry back, preferably, to the family's arrival in America. If this cannot be done so handily, back at least to their great-grand parents. They are determined hereafter, before they admit people into their circle, to find out who they are and what they are, thereby avoiding any possibility of letting any more mongrels into it. I stopped over in Atlanta on the way home, and they were talking about doing the same thing there. They said that since the carpet-baggers had come down from the North and put the darkies into politics, there were attempts to do the same thing in Atlanta;

bright Negroes with money, intruding themselves into white society—the nerve of them!"

"I think we should set up something like that right here in Charleston," Mrs. Newberry declared, looking around, to be met by nods of approval from nearly everybody present, except Rena, who merely opened her eyes in feigned surprise whenever any of them happened to look at her.

"The ambition of every nigger who happens to be the off-spring of some rich white man by a mulatto slave woman—and all of you present know that Charleston is over-run with these kind of darkies, is to up and *pass for white*' and as I see it, unless we band together here, as you say they are doing in New Orleans and Atlanta, who knows how soon we'll wake up to find a lot of light-skinned Negroes in our midst, passing themselves off as one of us."

"The most disgraceful thing that could possibly happen to the proud people of our fair city," Mrs. Milbank said.

"Not all of you know it, but we have quite a number of Negroes right here in Charleston who owned slaves, and, as far as I have been able to ascertain, they have a little circle of their own and do not associate with the other Negroes. I think most of them will bear watching, however."

All present agreed with her, and as the meeting broke up, it was tentatively agreed that at an early date another meeting would be called with a view to setting up a local 'Social Registry' in Charleston, to find out who was who before accepting unknowns as members.

Mrs. Newberry drove Rena home after the party, talking all the while about her plans regarding the Social Registry.

"Don't you think it's a good idea, dear Rena?"

"I'm sure it is," Rena managed to say, and was relieved that Mrs. Newberry didn't look in her direction and had not looked at her directly during the discussion.

Dazed, after Mrs. Newberry drove away, she went to her room and went to bed; she was so spent and upset, that she sent word she had a headache and didn't care for any dinner.

Alone in her room, she permitted herself to relax and to think over what had been discussed at the party. She saw only one solution, if it could be called that; she could wait and watch to see if the Social Registry plans became a reality—and if they started to set such a thing up, there was but one alternative left to her—to disappear quietly or announce, for the protection of her brother, that she was leaving to make her home in New York. This, of course, would be a lie, for she knew nobody in New York and had never been there. It meant that she would return to Fayetteville, marry Frank Fowler, and forget as quickly as possible, with great relief, that she had ever tried to pass for white. Until then, however, she decided not to say anything about what had occurred to her brother, for the ordeal they had gone through a few days before was quite as much as she wished to see him burdened with for the present.

The next great problem on her mind, was her reply to George Tryon's proposal, which would be due in a few days.

For days following Mrs. Newberry's party in her honor,

Rena was beseiged by doubts and fears; misgivings dominated her every thought. Meanwhile, having been placed on the footing of an accepted lover, Tryon's visits to the house became more frequent. He wished to fix a time for the marriage, but at this point Rena developed a strange reluctance.

"Can we not know each other for a little while?" she asked. "To be engaged is a pleasure that comes but once; it would be a pity to cut it too short."

"It is a pleasure that I would cheerfully dispense with," he replied, "for the certainty of possession. I want you all to myself, and all the time. Things might happen. If I should die, for instance, before I married you—"

"Oh, don't imagine such awful things," she said, bravely, thinking of Mrs. Newberry and the prospect of the Social Registry.

"I should consider," he resumed, completing the sentence, "that my life had been a failure."

"If I should die," she went on, boldly, becoming conscious that she was beginning to develop her acting ability, and being able by now to realize that she was acting, "I should die happy in the knowledge that you had loved me."

"In three weeks," he went on, "I shall have finished my business in Charleston, and then there will be but one thing to keep me here. When shall it be, dear? I want to take you home with me."

Rena did some fast thinking. If she *had* to continue this masquerade; had to, for the sake of her brother, marry George Wendell Tryon and Mrs. Newberry did not start her Social Registry action before three weeks, she could marry George and go back to North Carolina to live with him as his wife. In that way she could avoid being checked as regards her antecedents. Well, she thought to herself, it is all an act, an act that might have to last a life-time, so why not play her part as she had planned and make herself, for the present at least, agreeable.

"I will let you know," she replied, with a troubled sigh, "in a week from today." It occurred to her only then that she had promised to give him his answer in a week, four days before. To her surprise—and relief, he did not complain. Instead, he said very patiently:

"I'll call your attention to the subject every day. In the meantime," he asserted, "I shouldn't like you to forget it."

Rena's shrinking from the irrevocable step of marriage was due to a simple yet complex cause. Stated boldy, it was the consciousness of her secret; the complexity arose out of the various ways in which it seemed to bear upon her future. Our lives are bound in such strange ways, with the lives of our fellow men. It had not been difficult for Rena to conform her speech, her manners, and, in a measure, her mode of thoughts, to those of the people around her; but when this readjustment went beyond mere externals and concerned the vital issues of life, the secret that oppressed her took on a more serious aspect, with tragic possibilities.

A discursive imagination was not one of her characteristics, or the danger of a marriage of which perfect frankness was not a condition, might well have presented itself before her heart had become involved. Under the influence of doubt, and fear acting upon love, the invisible bar to happiness glowed with a lambent flame that threatened dire disaster.

"Would he have loved me at all," she asked herself, over and over again, "if he knew the story of my past? Or, having loved me, could he blame me now for what I cannot help?"

There were two shoals in the channel of her life, upon either of which her happiness might go to shipwreck. Since leaving the house behind the cedars where she had been brought into the world without her own knowledge or consent, and had drawn the first breath of life by the involuntary contraction of certain muscles, Rena had learned in a short time, many things; but she was yet to learn, that the innocent suffer with the guilty, and feel the punishment the more keenly because unmerited. She had yet to learn that the old Mosiac formula, "the sins of the fathers shall be visited upon the children," was graven more indelibly upon the heart of the race than upon the tables of Sinai.

Then again came to her that question, would George Tryon still love her if he knew all? The man who loved the Negress in New Orleans, had thought he loved her until he learned the truth—then he was positive that it was all one great mistake and ran quickly away. Would George Tryon do the same things in regards her?

She had read some of the novels in the book-case in her mother's hall, and others at boarding-school. She had read that love was a conqueror, that neither life nor death, nor creed nor caste, could stay its triumphant course. Her secret was no legal bar to their union. If Rena could forget the secret, and Tryon should never know it, it would be no obstacle to their happiness. But Rena felt, with a sinking of the heart, that happiness was not a matter of law or of fact, but lay entirely within the domain of sentiment. We are happy when we think ourselves happy, and with a strange perversity, we often differ from others with regards to what should constitute our happiness. Rena's secret was the worm in the bud, the skeleton in the closet.

"He says that he loves me. He *does* love me. But would he love me if he *knew?*" She stood before an oval mirror brought from France by one of her brother's wife's ancestors, and regarded her image with a coldly critical eye. She was as little vain as any of her sex who are endowed with beauty. She tried to place herself, in thus passing upon her own claims to consideration, in the hostile attitude of society towards her hidden disability. There was no mark upon her brow to brand her as less pure, less innocent, less desirable, less worthy to be loved, than these proud women of the past who had admired themselves in this old mirror.

"I think a man might love me for myself," she murmured pathetically, "and if he loved me truly, that he would marry me. If he would not marry me, then it would be because he didn't love me."

She had the sudden impulse again to tell George everything and throw herself upon his mercy. Other than simply masquerading, she was everything he had built her up in his mind as being. Then, as quickly as the impulse had advanced itself, it died. The secret was not hers alone; it involved her brother's position, to whom she owed everything, and in less degree, the future of her little nephew, whom she had already learned to love so well. There was left to her but two courses of action: to marry Tryon or to dismiss him.

She let escape a deep and sickly sigh and taking off her clothes, went to bed, in the hope that sleep would make her forget, for that night, at least.

Hours passed before she went off to sleep, however. She kept thinking about George Tryon, trying to draw a picture of how he would look and how he would feel if he, in some way, should learn her secret. She also visioned how Mrs. Janie Newberry and Mrs. Milbank, and the others she had met at the card party, would look and feel if they, too, found out.

She was surprised when she awakened the following morning, feeling rested, that she had been able to fall asleep at all.

Chapter Twenty Six

Rena's heart was too heavy with these misgivings for her to keep them to herself indefinitely. She had decided to keep the matter of the proposed Social Registry to herself a while longer, but the rest she would take up with Johnny.

Accordingly, on the morning after the second conversation with Tryon in which he insisted that she give him her answer and set a date for the wedding, she went into John's study where he usually spent an hour after breakfast before going to his office. He looked up amiably enough, but beneath this attempt at amiability, she was sure she detected a slight frown. He read trouble in her face and conjectured, she felt sure, that he was in for another ordeal as of a few days before.

"Well, Rena, dear," he began, forcing a smile through his fear. "What is the matter this time? Is there anything you want—money or what? Understand me when I say that it is my desire to satisfy your every wish."

He had found her very backward in asking for things she needed. Generous with his means, he thought nothing too good for her. Her success thus far, had gratified his pride, and justified his course in taking her under his protection.

"Thank you, Johnny. You've given me already more than I need. It is something else." His frown deepened, he steeled himself for another trying ordeal. He hated ordeals. They upset and annoyed him, left him unfit for work ahead.

"I am not going to upset you as I did the other day, dear brother," she said and forced a smile. "I am sure that I will have no occasion to upset you that way again."

"Thank you, Rena," he said, and she was happy to see that he breathed a sigh of relief.

"George has been after me again regarding his proposal; and wants me to set a date for my marriage to him. It worries me. I'm afraid to marry him without telling him, and, as we debated the other day, I cannot tell him; I can never tell him. I suppose that if he found out afterward he would cast me off. But, as we also agreed, that is the chance I'll have to take. At the best, if he did, he would cease to love me, even if he didn't cast me off."

She would have liked so much at this point, to have told him what the man engaged to the creole Gertrude Poray had done when he found out in New Orleans, that she had Negro blood, but that would have added to the unpleasantness of the situation, which under the best circumstances was unpleasant enough.

"If he does not know it, I know I shall be forever thinking of what he would do if he *should* find it out; or, if I should die without his having learned it, I should not rest easy in my grave for thinking of what he would have done if he *had* found out."

Walden had listened with grave and serious face at her comprehensive statement. He rose and closed the door carefully, less some one of the servants might overhear the conversation. In such cases, he was more liberally endowed with imagination than Rena, perhaps, and not without a vein of sentiment, he had nevertheless a practical side that outweighed them both. With him, the problem that oppressed his sister had been in the main a matter of argument and self-conviction. Once persuaded that he had certain rights or ought to have them, by virtue of the laws of nature, in defiance of the customs of mankind, he had promptly sought to enjoy them. This he had been able to do by concealing his antecedents and making the most of his opportunities, with no troublesome qualms of conscience whatever.

But he had already perceived, in their brief intercourse, that Rena's emotions, while less easily stirred, touched a deeper note than his, and dwelt upon it with greater intensity than if they had been spread over the larger field to which a more ready sympathy would have supplied so many points of access;—hers was a deep and silent current flowing between the narrow walls of a self-contained life, like the spreading river running through a pleasant landscape.

Walden's imagination, however, enabled him to put himself in touch with her mood and recognize its bearings upon her conduct. He would have preferred her taking the practical point of view, to bring her round to which he perceived would be a matter of diplomacy.

"When did he last talk with you about it, dear?"

"Last night, Johnny."

"My poor, dear child," he began, with deep sympathy. "I'm afraid you're taking too tragic a view of this thing all around. Marriage is a reciprocal arrangement, by which the contracting parties give love for love, care for keeping, faith for faith. It is a matter of the future, not of the past. What a poor soul it is that has not some secret chamber, sacred to itself; where one can file away the things others have no right to know, as well as things that one himself, or herself, would fain forget! We are under no moral obligation to inflict upon others, the history of our past mistakes, our wayward thoughts, our secret sins, our desperate hopes, or our heartbreaking disappointments. Still less are we bound to bring out from the secret chamber the dusty record of our ancestry, whereupon I repeat:

Let the dead past bury its dead.
George Tryon loves you for yourself alone; it is *not* your ancestors that he seeks to marry."

Having listened to him carefully, she could appreciate now why they called him a good lawyer; a great lawyer. He had summed up her case, their case, and he had done so eloquently, logically. Unfortunately, she realized that she was not a lawyer, to be able to answer him in rebuttal, at which times, the logicalness and the eloquence is often shot full of holes. She only had one answer, which was a question: the same question she was repeating, over and over again, the question she was sure must have become monotonous to him, but in spite of its many repetitions, it was still new to her.

"But would he marry me if he knew the truth," she again persisted.

Walden paused for reflection. He would have preferred to argue the question, as he had been, in a general way, but felt the necessity, and the responsibility of satisfying her scruples, as far as might be. He had liked Tryon from the very beginning of their acquaintance. In all their intercourse, which had been very close for several months, he had been impressed by the young man's sunny temper, his straight-forwardness, his intellectual honesty. Tryon's deference to Walden as the elder man had very naturally proved an attraction. Whether the friendship would have stood the test of utter frankness about his own past was a merely academic speculation with which Walden did not trouble himself. With his sister the question had evidently become a matter of conscience,—a difficult subject with which to deal in a person of Rena's temperament.

"My dear sister," he replied. "Why should he know? We haven't asked him for his pedigree; we don't care to know it."

Especially when we have a live skeleton, resting in the closet so close by, she thought and would have liked to have said, but decided not to interrupt him. Meanwhile, he went on:

"If he cares for ours, he should ask for it, and it would then be time enough to raise the question. You will, in time, learn to love him, I hope, and will in due time, wish to make him happy if you marry him."

"Yes, oh, yes," Rena exclaimed with fervor.

"Well, then," Walden went on to say, "suppose we should tell him our secret and put ourselves in his power, and that he should then conclude that he couldn't marry you? Do you imagine that he would be any happier than he is now, or than if he should never know?"

Ah, no! She could not think so. One could not tear love out of one's heart without pain and suffering.

There was a knock at the door. Walden opened it to the nurse, who stood with little Albert in her arms.

"Please, suh," the girl said, with a curtsey, "The baby's been cryin' fo' Mis' Rena, and ah 'lowed she mought want me tu fetch'm, ef it wouldn't 'sturb heh."

"Give me the darling," Rena exclaimed, coming forward and taking the child from the nurse. "It wants its auntie. Come to its auntie, bless its little heart."

Little Albert crowed with pleasure and lifted its small lips for a kiss. Walden found the sight a pleasant one. If he could but quiet his sister's troublesome scruples, he might ere long see her fondling beautiful children of her own. Even if Rena were willing to risk her happiness, and he to endanger his position, by a quixotic frankness, the future of his child must not be compromised.

"You shouldn't want to make George unhappy," he resumed when the nurse retired. "Very well, would you not be willing, for his sake—to keep a secret—your secret and mine and that of the innocent child in your arms? What ever we do, or are doing what is unethical, it cannot be blamed on the child. Surely he has had no part in this—masquerade as you choose to call it. Would you involve all of us in difficulties merely to secure your own peace of mind? Doesn't such a course seem just a wee bit selfish? Think the matter over from that point of view, and we'll speak of it later in the week. I shall be with George all the morning, and I may be able, by a little management, to find out his views on the subject of birth and family, and all that. Some men are very liberal, and love is a great leveler. I'll sound him at any rate."

He rose to his feet then, and kissing the baby, left the

room to go to his office in downtown Charleston, leaving Rena to her own reflections, to which his presentation of the case had given the subject a new turn. It had never before occurred to her to regard silence in the light of self-sacrifice. It had seemed a sort of sin; her brother's argument had made of it a virtue. It was not the first time, nor the last, that right and wrong had been a matter of viewpoint.

Tryon himself furnished the opening for Walden's proposed examination. The younger man could not long remain silent upon the subject uppermost in his mind. "I am anxious, John," he said, "to have Rowena name the happiest day of my life—our wedding day. When the trial in Edgecombe County is finished, I shall have no further business here, and shall be ready to leave for home. I should like to take my bride with me, and surprise my mother."

Mothers, Walden thought promptly and decided to execute an understanding forthwith, are likely to prove inquisitive about their son's wives, especially when taken unawares in matters of such importance. This seemed a good time to test the liberality of his client's views, and to put forward a shield for his sister's protection.

"Are you sure, George, that your mother will find the surprise agreeable when you bring home a bride of whom you know so little and your mother nothing at all?" In addition to planning a shield for himself and sister, John happened to know that Mrs. Tryon had built up Blanche Leary to be her son's bride.

Tryon had felt that it would be best to surprise his mother. As he viewed it, she would need only to see Rena to approve of her, but she was so far prejudiced in favor of Blanche Leary that it would be wisest to present the argument after having announced the irrevocable conclusion. Rena herself would be a complete justification for the accomplished deed.

"I think you ought to know, George," Walden went on, without waiting for a reply to his question, "that my sister and I are not of an old family, or a rich family, or a distinguished family; that she can bring you nothing but herself; that we have no connection of which you could boast, and no relatives to whom we would be glad to introduce you. You must take us for ourselves alone. We are —new people."

"My dear John," the younger man replied warmly, "there is a great deal of nonsense about families. If a man is noble and brave and strong, if a woman is beautiful and good and true, what matters it about his or her ancestry? If an old family can give them these things, then it is valuable, indeed. If they possess them without it, then of what use is it, except as a source of empty pride, which they would be better without. If all new families were like yours, there would be no advantage in belonging to an old one. All I care to know of Rowena's family is that she is your sister; and you'll pardon me old fellow, if I add that she hardly needs even you. She carries the stamp of her descent upon her face and in her heart."

"It makes me glad to hear you speak in that way," Walden returned, delighted by the young man's breadth and earnestness.

"Oh, I mean every word of it," Tryon replied. "Ancestors, indeed, for Rowena! I will tell you a family secret, John, to prove how little I care for ancestors. My maternal great-great-grandfather, a hundred and fifty years ago, was hanged, drawn and quartered for stealing cattle across the Scottish border. How is that for a pedigree? Behold in me the lineal descendant of a felon!"

Walden felt much relieved at this avowal. His own statement had not touched the vital point involved; it had been at the best but a half truth. But Tryon's magnanimity would doubtless protect Rena from any close inquiry concerning her past. It even occurred to Walden for a moment that he might safely disclose the secret to Tryon; but an appreciation of certain facts of history and certain traits of human nature constrained him to put the momentary thought aside. It was a great relief, however, to imagine that Tryon might think lightly of this thing that he need never know.

"Well, Rena," he said to his sister when he went home at noon: "I've sounded George."

"What did he say?" she asked, eagerly.

"I told him we were people of no family, and that we had no relatives that we were proud of. He said he loved you for yourself, and would never ask you about your ancestry."

"Oh, I'm *so* glad," she exclaimed joyfully. This report left her very happy for about three hours, or until she began to analyze carefully her brother's account of what had been said. Walden's statement had not been specific,—he had not told Tryon *the* thing. George's reply, in turn, had been a mere generality. The concrete fact that oppressed her remained unrevealed, and her doubt was still unsatisfied.

She compared his case of one hundred fifty years ago

with hers as of the date. If an ancestor of hers had stolen over on the white side of society four generations ago, but had developed through the long years that followed with credit, she would perhaps be proud to boast of it at this time, the same as George had boasted of his that morning.

Rena was occupied with this thought when her lover next came to see her. Tryon came up the sanded walk from the gate and spoke pleasantly to the nurse, a nice looking mulatto girl who was seated on the front porch, playing with little Albert. He took the boy from her arms and she went to call Miss Walden.

Rena came out, followed by the nurse, who offered to take the child.

"Never mind, Mimy. Leave him with me," Tryon said.

The nurse walked discreetly over into the garden, remaining within call, but beyond the hearing of conversation in an ordinary tone.

"Rena, darling," her lover said, "when shall it be? Surely you won't ask me to wait a whole week. Why, that's like a lifetime."

Rena was struck by a brilliant idea. She would test him herself, then and now. Love was a very powerful force; she had found it the greatest, grandest, and sweetest thing in the world. Tryon had said that he loved her; he had said scarcely anything else for weeks, surely nothing else worth remembering. She would test his love by a hypothetical question.

"You say you love me," she said, glancing at him with a sad thoughtfulness in her large dark eyes. "How much do you love me?"

"I love you all one can love. True love has no degrees: it is all—or nothing."

"Would you love me," she asked, with an air of coquetry that masked her concern, pointing toward the girl in the shrubbery, "if I were Albert's nurse yonder?"

After a quick glance at the nurse, and relaxing into a new smile, he turned back to her:

"If you were Albert's nurse," he replied, with a joyous laugh, "he would have to find another quickly, for within a week we should be married."

The answer seemed to fit the question, but in fact, Tryon's mind and hers had not met. That two intelligent persons should each attach a different meaning to a simple form of words as Rena's question was the best ground for her misgiving with regard to the marriage. But his love for the moment, blinded her. She was anxious to be convinced. She interpreted the meaning of his speech by her own thought and by the ardor of his glance, and was satisfied with the answer.

"And now, darling," Tryon pleaded, "Will you not fix the day that shall make me happy? I shall be ready to go away in three weeks. Will you go with me?"

"Yes," she answered, knowing that she was lying, but she was by now resigned to whatever was going to happen. She was at last willing to gamble her future and forget the past, if she could get away with it. She was also at last on the great stage of life, and she had started acting. Would it last until she died?

Chapter Twenty Seven

THE MARRIAGE WAS arranged for the thirtieth of the month, immediately after which Tryon and his bride were to set out for North Carolina. Walden would have liked it much better if Tryon had lived in South Carolina; but the location of his North Carolina home was at some distance from Fayetteville, with which it had no connection by steam or rail, and indeed lay out of line altogether of travel to Fayetteville. Rena had no acquaintance with people of social standing in North Carolina; and with the added maturity and charm due to her improved opportunities, it was unlikely that any former resident of Fayetteville who might casually meet her would see in the elegant young woman from South Carolina, more than a passing resemblance to a poor girl who had once lived in an obscure part of the old town. It would of course be necessary for Rena to keep away from Fayetteville; except for her mother's sake, however, she would hardly be tempted to go back.

On the twentieth of the month, Walden set out with Tryon for the county seat of the adjoining county, to try one of the lawsuits which had required Tryon's presence in South Carolina for so long a time. This destination was a day's drive from Charleston, behind a good horse and the tria' was expected to last a week.

"This week will seem like a year," Tryon said ruefully, the evening before their departure, "but I'll write every day and shall expect a letter as often."

"The mail goes only twice a week, George," Rena replied.

"Then I shall have three letters in each mail."

Walden and Tryon were to set out in the cool of the morning, after an early breakfast. Rena was up at daybreak that she might preside at the breakfast-table and bid the travelers good-by.

"Johnny," Rena said to her brother that morning. "I dreamed last night that mother was ill."

"Dreams, you know, Rena," her brother answered with a smile lightly, "go by contraries. Yours undoubtedly signifies that our mother, God bless her simple soul, is at the present moment enjoying her usual perfect health. She was never sick in her life."

For a few months after leaving Fayetteville with her brother, Rena had suffered tortures of home-sickness; those who have felt it know the pang. The severance of old ties had been abrupt, but complete. At the school where her brother had taken her, there had been nothing to relieve the strangeness of her surroundings—no schoolmate from her own town, no relative or friend of the family nearby. Even the compensation of human sympathy was in a measure denied her, for Rena was too fresh from her prison-house to doubt that sympathy would fail before the revelation of the secret, the consciousness of which oppressed her at that time like a nightmare.

It was not strange that Rena, thus isolated, should have been prostrated by homesickness for several weeks after leaving Fayetteville. When the paroxysm had passed, there followed a dull pain, which gradually subsided into a resignation as profound in its way, as had been her longing for home. She loved and she suffered with a quiet intensity which her outward demeanor gave no adequate expression. From some ancestral source she had derived a strain of the passive fatalism by which alone one can submit uncomplainingly to the inevitable. By the same token, when once a thing had been decided, it became with her a finality, which only some extraordinary stress of emotion could disturb. She had acquiesced to her brother's plan; for her there was no withdrawing; her home-sickness was an incidental thing which must be endured as patiently as might be, until time should have brought a measure of relief.

Walden had made provision for an occasional letter from Fayetteville, by leaving with his mother a number of envelopes directed to his address. She could have her letters written, enclose them in these envelopes, and deposit them in the post-office with her own hand. Thus the place of Walden's residence would remain within her own knowledge, and his secret would not be placed at the mercy of any wandering Fayettevillian who might perchance go to that part of South Carolina. By this simple means Rena had kept as closely in touch with her mother as Walden had considered prudent; any closer intercourse was not consistent with their present station in life.

The night after Walden and Tryon had ridden away, Rena dreamed again that her mother was ill. Better taught people than she, in regions than the South Carolina of that epoch, are disturbed at times by dreams. Mis' Molly had a profound faith in them. If God, in ancient times, had spoken to men in visions of the night, what easier way could there be for Him to convey His meaning to people of all ages? Science, which has shattered many an idol and destroyed many a delusion, has made but slight inroads upon the shadowy realm of dreams. To Mis' Molly to whom science would have meant nothing and psychology would have been a meaningless term, the land of dreams was carefully mapped and bounded. Each dream had some special significance, or was at least susceptible to classification under some significant head. Dreams, as a general rule, went by contraries; but a dream three times repeated was a certain portent of the thing defined. Rena's few years of schooling at Fayetteville and her months at Charleston had scarcely disturbed these hoary superstitions which lurk in the dim corners of the brain. No lady in Charleston, perhaps would have remained undisturbed by a vivid dream, three times repeated, of some event bearing materially upon her own life.

The first repetition of a dream was decisive of nothing, for two dreams meant no more than one. The power of the second lay in the suspense, the uncertainty, to which it gave rise. Two doubled the chance of a third. The day following this second dream was an anxious one for Rena. She could not for an instant dismiss her mother from her thoughts, which were filled, too, with a certain self-reproach. She had left her mother alone; if her mother were really ill, there was no one at home to tend her with loving care. This feeling grew in force, until by nightfall Rena had become very unhappy, and went to bed with dismal forebodings. In this state of mind, it is not surprising that she now dreamed that her mother was lying at the point of death, and that she cried out with heart-rendering pathos:—

"Rena, my darlin,' why did you forsake your po' ole' mother? Come back to me, honey; I'll die ef I don't see you soon."

The stress of subconscious emotion engendered by the dream was powerful enough to wake Rena, and her mother's utterance seemed to come to her with the force of a fateful warning and a great reproach. Her mother was sick and needed her, and would die if she did not come. She felt that she must see her mother—it would be almost like murder to remain away from her under such circumstances.

After breakfast she went into the business part of the town and inquired what time a train would leave that would take her towards Fayetteville. Since she had come away from the town, a railroad had been opened by which the long river voyage might be avoided, and, making allowances for slow trains, the town of Fayetteville could be reached by an all-rail route in about twelve hours. Calling at the Post-Office for the family mail, she found there a letter from her mother, which she tore open in great excitement. It was written in handwriting she recognized, and was in effect as follows:—

My Dear Daughter:—I take my pen in hand to let you know that I am not very well. I have had a kind of misery in my side for two weeks, with palpitations of the heart, and I have been in bed for three days. I'm feeling mighty poorly, but Dr. Green says that I will get over it in a few days. Old Aunt Zilphy is staying with me, and looking after things tolerably well. I hope this will find you and Johnny enjoying good health. Give my regards to Johnny and I hope the Lord will bless him and you too. Cousin Billy Oxendine has had a rising on his neck and has had to have it lanced. Old man Tom Johnson was killed last week while trying to whip Black Jim Brown who lived down on the Wilmington road. Jim has run away. Mary B. has another young one, a boy this time. There has been a big freshet in the river and it looked for awhile that the new bridge would be washed away.

Frank comes over every day or two and asks about you. He says to tell you that he doesn't believe you are coming back any more, but he hopes that you remember him. He is very good to me and brings over shavings and kindlewood and made me a new well-bucket for nothing. It is a comfort to talk to him about you, though I haven't told him where you are living.

I hope this will find you and Johnny both well, and doing well. I should like to see you, but if it's the Lord's will that I shouldn't, I shall be thankful that you have done the best for yourselves and Johnny's child, and that I have given you up for your own good.

Your affectionate mother,
MOLLY NORTHCROSS

Rena shed tears over this simple letter, which to her excited imagination, merely confirmed the warning of her dreams. At the date of its writing her mother had been sick in bed with the symptoms of a serious illness. She had no nurse but a purblind old woman. Three days of progressive illness had evidently been quite sufficient to reduce her parent to the condition indicated by the third dream.

The thought that her mother might die without the presence of any one who loved her, pierced Rena's heart like a knife and lent wings to her feet. She determined to go at once to Fayetteville.

Returning home, she wrote a letter to her brother, enclosing their mother's letter, and stated that she had dreamed an alarming dream for three nights in succession; that she had left the house in charge of the servants and gone to Fayetteville; and that she would return as quickly as her mother was out of danger.

To Tryon she wrote that she had been called away to visit a sickbed, and would return very soon, perhaps by the time he got back to Charleston. These letters Rena posted on her way to the train, which she took at five in the afternoon. This would bring her to Fayetteville early in the morning of the following day.

Chapter Twenty Eight

WAR HAS BEEN called the court of last resort. A lawsuit may with equal aptness be compared to a battle—the parallel may be drawn very closely all along the line. First we have the *causus belli,* the cause of action; then the various protocols and proclamations and general orders, by way of pleas, demurrers, and motions; then the preliminary skirmishes at the trial table; and then the final struggle, in which might is quite as likely to prevail as right, victory most often resting with the strongest battalions, and truth and justice not seldom overborne by the weight of odds upon the other side.

The lawsuit which Walden and Tryon had gone to try did not, however, reach this ultimate stage, but, after a three day engagement, resulted in a treaty of peace. The case was compromised and settled, and Tryon and Walden set out on their homeward drive. They stopped at a farmhouse at noon, and while at the table saw the stage-coach from the town they had just left, pass, bound for their own destination. In the mail-bag under the driver's seat were Rena's two letters; they had been delivered at the town in the morning, and immediately remailed to Charleston, in accordance with orders left at the post-office the evening before. Tryon and Walden drove leisurely home through the pines, all unconscious of the squares of white paper moving along the road, a few miles before them, which a mother's yearning and a daughter's love had thrown, like the apple of discord, into the narrow circle of their happiness.

They reached Charleston at four o'clock. Walden got down from the buggy at his office. Tryon drove on to his hotel, to make a hasty toilet before visiting his sweetheart.

Walden glanced at his mail, tore open the envelope addressed in his sister's handwriting, and read the contents with something like dismay. She had gone away on the eve of her wedding, her lover knew not where, to be gone no one knew how long, on a mission which could not be frankly disclosed. A dim foreboding of disaster flashed across his mind. He thrust the letter into his pocket, with others yet unopened, and started towards his home. Reaching the gate, he paused a moment and then walked on past the house. Tryon would probably be there in a few minutes, and he did not care to meet him without first having had the opportunity for some moments of reflection. He must fix upon some line of action in this emergency.

Meanwhile Tryon had reached his hotel and opened his mail. The letter from Rena was read first, with profound disappointment. He had really made concessions in the settlement of that lawsuit—had yielded several hundred dollars of his just dues, in order that he might get back to Rena three days earlier. Now he must cool his heels in idleness for at least three days before she would return. It was annoying, to say the least. He wished to know where she had gone, that he might follow her and stay near her until she should be ready to come back. He might ask Walden—no, she might have had some good reason for not having mentioned her destination. She had probably gone to visit some of the poor relations of whom her brother had spoken so frankly, and she would doubtless prefer that he should not see her amid any surroundings but the best. Indeed, he did not know that he would himself care to endanger, by suggestive comparison, the fine aureole of superiority that surrounded her. She represented in her adorable person, and her pure heart the finest flower of the finest race that God had ever made—the supreme effort of creative power, of which there could be no finer. The flower would soon be his; why should he care to dig up the soil in which it grew?

Tryon went on opening his letters. There were several bills and circulars, and then a letter from his mother, of which he broke the seal:—

"My Dearest George:—This leaves us well. Blanche is still with me, and we are impatiently awaiting your return. In your absence she seems almost like a daughter to me. She joins me in the hope that your lawsuits are progressing favorably, and that you will be with us soon. . . .

"On your way home, if it does not keep you away from us too long, would it not be well for you to come by way of Fayetteville, and find out whether there is any prospect of our being able to collect our claim against old Mr. Duncan McSwayne's estate? You must have taken the papers with you, along with the rest, for I do not find them here. Things ought to be settled enough now for people to realize on some of their securities. Your grandfather always believed the note was good, and meant to try to collect it, but the war interfered. He said to me, before he died, that if the note was ever collected, he would use the money to buy a wedding present for your wife. Poor father! He is dead and gone to heaven; but I am sure that even there he would be happier if he knew the note was paid and the money used as he intended.

"If you go to Fayetteville, call on my cousin, Dr. Ed Green, and tell him who you are. Give him my love. I haven't seen him for twenty years. He used to be very fond of the ladies, a very gallant man. He can direct you to a good lawyer, no doubt. Hoping to see you soon,

Your loving mother, ELIZABETH TRYON

P. S. Blanche joins me in love to you."

This affectionate and motherly letter did not give Tryon unalloyed satisfaction. He was glad to hear that his mother was well, but he had hoped that Blanche Leary might have finished her visit by this time. The reasonable inference from the letter was that Blanche meant to await his return. Her presence would spoil the fine romantic flavor of the surprise he had planned for his mother. It would never do to expose his bride to an unannounced meeting with the woman whom he had tacitly rejected. There would be one advantage in such a meeting: the comparison of the two women would be so much in Rena's favor that his mother could not hesitate for a moment between them. The situation, however, would have elements of constraint, and he did not care to expose either Rena or Blanche to any disagreeable contingency. It would be better to take his wife on a wedding trip, and notify his mother, before he returned home, of his marriage. In the extremely improbable case that she should disapprove his choice after having seen his wife, the ice would at least have been broken before his arrival at home.

"By jove!" he exclaimed suddenly, striking his knee with his hand, "why shouldn't I run up to Fayetteville while

Rena's gone? I can leave here at five o'clock, and get there some time tomorrow morning. I can transact my business during the day and get back the day after tomorrow; for Rena might return ahead of time, just as we did, and I shall want to be here when she comes; I'd rather wait a year for a legal opinion on a doubtful note than to lose one day with my love. The train goes in forty minutes. My bag is already packed. I'll just drop a line to George and tell him where I've gone."

He put Rena's letter into his breast pocket, and turning to his trunk, took from it a handful of papers relating to the claim in reference to which he was going to Fayetteville. These he thrust into the same pocket with Rena's letter; he wished to read both letter and papers while on the train. It would be a pleasure merely to hold the letter before his eyes and look at the lines traced by her hand. The papers he wished to study, for the more practical purpose of examining into the merits of his claim against the estate of Duncan McSwayne.

When Walden reached home, he inquired if Mr. Tryon had called.

"No, suh," the nurse answered, to whom he had put the question; "He ain't been heah yet, suh."

Walden was surprised and much disturbed.

"The baby's been cryin' fo' Mis' Rena," the nurse suggested, "an I spec' he'd lak tu see you, suh. Shall I fetch him?"

"Yes, bring him to me."

He took the child in his arms and went out upon the piazza. Several porch pillows lay invitingly near. He pushed them toward the steps with his foot, sat down on one, and placed little Albert upon another. He was scarcely seated when a messenger from the hotel came up the walk from the gate and handed him a note. At the same moment he heard the long shriek of the afternoon train leaving the station on the opposite side of the town.

He tore the envelope open anxiously, read the note, smiled a weak and sickly smile, and clinched the paper in his hand unconsciously. There was nothing he could do. It had been done for him—by the strange hand of fate. The train had gone; there was no telegraph to Fayetteville and no letter could leave Charleston for twenty-four hours, going to Fayetteville. The best laid schemes of mice and men go wrong at times—the staunchest ships are sometimes wrecked or skirt the breakers perilously. Life is a sea, full of strange currents and uncharted reefs—whoever leaves the traveled path must run the danger of destruction. Walden was a lawyer, however, and accustomed to balance probabilities.

"He may easily be in Fayetteville a day or two without meeting her. She will spend most of her time at mother's bedside, and he will be occupied with his own affairs."

If Tryon should meet her—well, he was very much in love and he had spoken very nobly of birth and blood. Walden would have preferred, nevertheless, that Tryon's theories should not be put to this particular test. Rena's scruples had so far been successfully combated; the question would be open again, and the situation unnecessarily complicated, if Tryon should meet Rena in Fayetteville.

"Will he or will he not?" Walden asked himself. He took a coin from his pocket and spun it upon the floor. "Heads, he sees her; tails, he does not."

The coin spun swiftly and steadily, leaving upon the eye the impression of a revolving sphere. Little Albert, left for a moment to his own devices, had crept behind his father and was watching the whirling disk with great pleasure. He felt that he would like to possess this interesting object. The coin began to move more slowly, losing momentum, and was wabbling to its fall, when the child stretched forth his chubby fist and caught it ere it touched the floor.

Chapter Twenty Nine

Tryon arrived in the early morning and put up at the Fayetteville Hotel, a very comfortable inn. After a bath, breakfast, and a visit to the barber-shop, he inquired of the hotel clerk the way to the office of Dr. Green, his mother's cousin.

"On the corner, sir," the clerk replied, "by the market house just over the drugstore. The doctor drove past here only half an hour ago. You'll probably catch him in his office."

Tryon found the office without difficulty. He climbed the stair but found no one in except a colored boy, seated in the outer office, who rose promptly as Tryon entered.

"No, suh," the boy replied to Tryon's question, "he ain't in now. He's gone out to see a patient, suh, but he'll be back soon. Won't you set down in de private office an' wait fo' 'im, suh?"

Tryon had not slept well during his journey and felt somewhat fatigued. Through the open door of the next room he saw an inviting armchair, with a window at one side, and upon the other, a table strewn with papers and magazines.

"Yes," he replied in answer to the boy's invitation. "I'll wait."

He entered the private office, sank into the armchair, and looked out of the window upon the square below. The view was mildly interesting. The old brick market-house with the tower was quite picturesque. On a wagon-scale at one end of the public square, a weightmaster was weighing a load of hay. In the booths under the wide arches, several old Negro women were frying fish on little charcoal stoves—the odor would have been appetizing to one who had not breakfasted. On the shady-side stood half a dozen two-wheeled carts, loaded with lightwood and drawn by two diminutive steers, or superanuated army mules, branded on the flank with the cabalistic letters "C. S. A.," which represented a vanished dream, or "U. S. A.," which, as any Negro about the market-house would have borne witness, signified a very concrete fact. Now and then a lady or a gentleman passed with leisure step—no one ever hurried during those days in Fayetteville—or some poor white sandhiller slouched listlessly along toward a store or bar-room.

Tryon mechanically counted the slabs of ginger bread on the nearest market-stall, and calculated the cubical contents of several of the meagre loads of wood. Having exhausted this view, he turned to the table at his elbow and picked up a medical journal, in which he read, first, an account of a marvelous surgical operation. Turning the leaves idly, he came upon an article by a Southern writer, upon the perennial race problem that had vexed the country for a century. The writer maintained that owing to a special tendency of the Negro blood, however diluted, to revert to the African type, any future amalgamation of the white and black races, which foolish and wicked Northern Negrophiles predicted as the ultimate result of the new conditions confronting the South, would therefore be an ethnological impossibility; for the smallest trace of Negro blood would inevitably drag down the superior race to the level of the inferior, and reduce the fair Southland, already devastated by the hand of the invader, to the frightful level of Haiti, the awful example of Negro incapacity. To defend their beloved land, now doubly sanctified by the blood of her devoted sons who had fallen in the struggle to maintain her liberties and preserve her property, it behooved every true Southerner to stand firm against the abhorrent tide of radicalism, to maintain the supremacy and purity of his all pervading, all-conquering race, and to resist by every available means, the threatened domination of an inferior and degraded people, who were set to rule hereditary freeman ere they had themselves scarce ceased to be slaves.

When Tryon had finished the article, which seemed to him a well-considered argument, albeit a trifle bombastic, he threw the book upon the table. Finding the armchair wonderfully comfortable, and feeling the fatigue of his journey, he yielded to a drowsy impulse, leaned his head on the cushioned back of the chair, and fell asleep. According to the habit of youth, he dreamed and pursuant to his own individual habit, he dreamed of Rena. They were walking in the moonlight, along the quiet road in front of her brother's house. The air was redolent with the perfume of flowers. His arm was around her waist. He had asked her if she loved him, and was awaiting her answer in tremulous but confident expectation. She opened her lips to speak. The sound that came from them seemed to be:—

"Is Dr. Green in? No? Ask him, when he comes back, to please call at our house as soon as he can."

Tryon was in that state of somnolence in which one may dream and yet be aware that one is dreaming,—the state in which one, during a dream, dreams that one pinches one's self to be sure that one is not dreaming. He was therefore aware of a ringing quality about the words he had just heard that did not comport with the shadowy converse of a dream—an incongruity in the remark, too, which marred the harmony of the vision. The shock was sufficient to disturb Tryon's slumber, and he struggled slowly back to consciousness. When fully awake he thought he heard a light footfall descending the stairs. He got up and going to the door, met the boy who had heard him arise, and was on the way to the door to meet him.

"Was there someone here?" he asked the boy, who was smiling up into his face as if anxious to be of service to him.

"Yas, suh," the boy replied, nodding his head up and down. "A young cullud 'oman wuz in jes' now, axin' fo' de doctuh."

Tryon felt a momentary touch of annoyance that a Negro woman should have intruded herself into his dream at its most interesting point. Nevertheless, the voice had been so real, his imagination had reproduced with such exactness the dullest tones so dear to him, that he turned his head involuntarily, and crossing over to the window of the private office, looked out the window. He could just see the flutter of a woman's skirt disappearing around the corner.

A moment later the doctor came bustling in, a plump, rosy man, now in his fifties, wearing a frank open countenance and an air of genial good nature. Such a doctor, Tryon fancied, ought to enjoy a wide popularity. His mere presence would suggest life and hope and healthfullness.

"My dear boy," the doctor exclaimed cordially, after Tryon had introduced himself, "I'm delighted to meet you —or any one of the old blood. Your mother and I were sweethearts, long ago, when we both were pinafores, and went to see our grandfather at Christmas; and I met her more than once, and paid her more than one compliment, after she had grown to be a fine young woman. You're like her, too, but not quite so handsome—you've more of what I suppose to be the Tryon favor, though I never met your father. So one of old Duncan McSwayne's notes went so far as that? Well, well, I don't know where you won't find them. One of them turned up here the other day from New York.

"The man you want to see," he added later in the conversation, "is old Judge Straight. He's getting somewhat stiff in the joints, but he knows more law, and more about the McSwayne estate, than any other two lawyers in town. If anybody can collect your claim, Judge Straight can. I'll send my boy Dave over to his office. Dave," he turned and called loudly to the sleepy looking colored office boy.

"Yassuh?" Dave replied, waking quickly and hustling to his feet, stood before the doctor.

"Run over to Judge Straight's office and see if he's there."

"Yassuh," Dave replied and dashed quickly away. Doctor Green turned back to Tryon and continued.

"There was a freshet here a few weeks ago, and they had to open the flood-gates and let the water out of the mill pond, for if the dam had broken, as it did twenty years ago, it would have washed the pillars from under the judge's office and let it down in the creek, and—"

It was Dave, who had been to the judge's office.

"Uh, Dr. Green, Jedge Straight ain't in his office jes' now, suh. Naw, suh, he ain't in his office."

"Did you inquire of anybody when he'd be back?"

Dave's face fell. He swallowed guiltily, then, shaking his head:

"Naw, suh. You didn't tell me to ask dat, suh."

Dr. Green shook his head hopelessly, looked across at Tryon, who smiled at the humor of it, then turned back to Dave with a deep frown on his face.

"Well, go back now and inquire."

"Yassuh." Dave replied, as if relieved, and turning dashed back down the stairs again.

"The niggers," Dr. Green turned back to Tryon to explain. "Are getting mighty trifling since they've been freed. Before the war that boy would have been around there and back before you could have said Jack Robinson. Now, the lazy rascal takes his time—just like a white man."

Dave returned now, more promptly than from his first trip. "Jedge Straight's dare now, yassuh. 'E done come in."

"I'll take you right around and introduce you," the doctor said, rising to his feet with Tryon following suit. The doctor was a talkative man and never seemed to stop long enough to get his breath. "I don't know whether the judge ever met your mother or not, but he knows a gentleman when he sees one, and will be glad to meet you and look after your affair." They were leaving the office and approaching the stairway, when something seemed to occur to him and he caught Tryon by the arm, paused, and turned back.

"See to the patients, Dave, and say I'll be back shortly, and don't forget any messages left for me. Look sharp now!" he exclaimed, raising his hand in a gesture of warning and looking hard at Dave, who just grinned back at him and sat down in a comfortable seat, preparatory to taking another nap. "You know your failing!" Again Dave grinned, and before the men reached the bottom of the stairway he lay back and was fast asleep.

They found Judge Straight in his office. He was seated by the rear window and had fallen into a gentle doze. The air of Fayetteville was conducive to slumber. A visitor from some hustling city might have rubbed his eyes, on any but a market-day, and imagined the whole town asleep; that the people were somnambulists and did not know it. The judge, an old hand, roused himself so skillfully, at the sound of approaching footsteps, that his visitors could not guess but that he had been wide awake. He shook hands with the doctor, and acknowledged the introduction to Tryon with a rare, old-fashioned courtesy, which the young man thought a very charming survival of the manners of a past and happier age.

"No," the judge replied, in answer to a question by Dr. Green, "I never met his mother; I was a generation ahead of her. I was at school with her father, however, fifty years ago—fifty years ago! No doubt that seems to you a long time, young man?"

"It is a long time, sir," Tryon replied. "I must live twice as long as I have to cover it."

"A long time and a troubled time," the judge sighed. "I

could wish that I might see this unhappy land at peace with itself before I die. Things are in a sad tangle; I can't see the way out. But the worst enemy has been slain, in spite of us. We are well rid of slavery."

"But the Negro we still have with us," the doctor remarked, his face really serious for the first time. "For here comes my man, Dave. What is it now, David?" his question was sharp and his eyes were hard on the boy. He had a suspicion.

"Doctuh Green," Dave said. "Ah fugot to tell you, suh, dat dat young 'oman wuz at de office agin' befo' you come in, and said fo' you to go rat down an' see uh mammy ez soon as you could."

"Ah, yes, and you've just remembered it! I'm afraid you're entirely too forgetful for a Doctor's office. You forgot about old Mrs. Latimer, the other day, and when I got there she had almost choked to death. Now get back to the office," he said sharply, waving a threatening finger at Dave, who shied away with that silly grin as before on his face. "And remember that the next time you forget anything, I'll hire another boy; remember that!"

Bowing apologetically, Dave backed out of the office and in the door, turned and ran away. Doctor Green, with flashing eyes, had watched him out of sight, now turned back to his companions.

"That boy's head," he remarked, touching both his temples, "reminds me of nothing so much as a dried gourd, with a hand-full of cow peas rattling around in it, in lieu of gray matter. An old woman out in Redbank got a fishbone in her throat, the other day, and nearly choked to death before I got there. A white woman, sir, came very near losing her life because of a lazy, trifling Negro."

"I should think you would discharge him, sir," suggested Tryon.

"What would be the use?" the doctor rejoined. "All Negroes are alike, irresponsible, except that now and then there's a pretty woman along the borderline. Take this patient of mine, for instant—I'll call on her after dinner. Her case is not serious. Thirty years ago she would have made any man turn his head to look at her. You know who I mean, don't you, judge?"

"Yes, I think so," the judge said promptly. "I transact a little business for her now and then myself."

"I don't know whether you've seen the daughter or not —I'm sure you haven't for the past year or so, for she's been away. But she's in town now; and, by jove, the girl is really beautiful. And I'm a judge of beauty. Do you remember my wife thirty years ago, judge?"

"She was a very handsome woman, Ed," the other replied judicially. "If I had been twenty years younger I should have cut you out."

"You mean you would have tried," the doctor replied with a laugh, which brought a smile from the other two men. "But as I was saying," the doctor went on. "The girl is a beauty; I reckon we might guess where she got some of it, eh, Judge? Human nature is human nature, but it's a damned shame that a man should beget a child like that and leave it to live the life open for a Negro. If she had been born white, the young fellows would be tumbling over each other to get her. Her mother would have to look after her very closely as things are, if she stayed here; but she disappeared mysteriously a year or two ago and has been at the North, I'm told, passing for white. She'll probably marry a Yankee; he won't know any better, and it will serve him right—she's only too white for them. She has a very striking figure, something on the Greek order, stately and slow-moving. She has the manners of a lady, too—a beautiful woman, if she is a nigger!"

"I quite agree with you, Ed," the judge remarked dryly, "that the mother had better look closely after the daughter."

"Ah, no, Judge," the other replied, with a flattered smile, "my admiration for beauty is purely abstract. Twenty-five years ago when I was young—"

"When you were younger," the judge corrected, and smiled enigmatically.

"When you and I were young," the doctor continued ingeniously. "Twenty-five years ago I could not have answered for myself. But would advise the girl to stay at the North, if she can. She's certainly out of place around here."

Tryon found the subject a little tiresome, and the doctor's enthusiasm not at all contagious. He could not have possibly been interested in a colored girl, under any circumstances. He was sure of that. And he was engaged to be married to the most beautiful white woman on earth. To mention a Negro woman in the same room where he was thinking of Rena seemed little short of profanation. His friend, the doctor, was a jovial fellow, but it was surely doubtful taste to refer to his wife in such a conversation. He was very glad when the doctor dropped the subject and permitted him to go more into detail about the matter which formed his business in Fayetteville. He took out of his pocket the papers concerning the McSwayne claim and laid them on the judge's desk.

"You'll find everything there, sir,—the note, the contract and some correspondence that will give you the hang of the thing. Will you be able to look them over today? I should like," he added, a little nervously, "to go back tomorrow."

"What!" Dr. Green exclaimed, vivaciously, "insult our town by staying only one day? It won't be long enough to get acquainted with our young ladies. Fayetteville girls are famous for their beauty. But perhaps there's a loadstone in South Carolina to draw you back? Ah, you change color! To my mind there's nothing finer than the ingenuous blush of youth. But we'll spare you if you'll answer one question —is it serious?"

"I'm to be married in two weeks, sir," Tryon replied, blushing deeper. The statement sounded very pleasant, in spite of the slight embarrassment caused by the inquiry.

"Good boy!" the doctor rejoined, taking his arm familiarly—they were both standing now. "You ought to have married a Fayetteville girl, but you people down toward the eastern counties seldom come this way, and we are evidently too late to catch you."

"I'll look your papers over this morning," the judge said, "and when I come from dinner will stop at the courthouse and examine the record and see if there's anything we can get hold of. If you'll drop in around three or four o'clock, I may be able to give you an opinion."

"Now, George," the doctor exclaimed, "we'll go back to the office for a spell, and then I'll take you home with me to luncheon."

Tryon hesitated.

"Oh, you must come! Mrs. Green would never forgive me if I didn't bring you. Strangers are rare birds in our society, and when they come we make them welcome. Our enemies may overturn our institutions, and try to put the bottom rail on top, but they cannot destroy our Southern hospitality. There are so many carpet-baggers and other social vermin creeping into the South, with the Yankees trying to force the niggers on us, that it's a genuine pleasure to get acquainted with another real Southern gentleman, whom one can invite into one's house without fear of contamination, and before whom one can express his feelings freely and be sure of perfect sympathy."

Chapter Thirty

When Judge Straight's visitor had departed, he took up the papers which had been laid loosely on the table as they were taken out of Tryon's breast pocket, and commenced their perusal. There was a note for $500, many years overdue, but not yet outlawed by lapse of time; a contract covering the transaction out of which the note had grown; and several letters, and copies of letters modifying the terms of the contract. The judge had glanced over most of the papers, and was getting well into the merits of the case, when he unfolded a letter:—

My Dearest George:—I'm going away for about a week, to visit the bed-side of an old friend, who is very ill, and may not live. Do not be alarmed about me, for I shall very likely be back by the time you are.

Yours lovingly,
ROWENA WALDEN

The judge was unable to connect this with the transactions which formed the subject of his examination. Age had dimmed his perceptions somewhat, and it was not until he had finished the letter, and read it over again, and noted the signature at the bottom the second time, that he perceived that the writing was in a woman's hand, that ink was comparatively fresh, and that the letter was dated only a couple of days before. While he still held the sheet in his hand, it dawned upon him slowly that he held also one of the links in a chain of possible tragedy which he himself, he became uncomfortably aware, had had a hand in forging.

"It is the Walden woman's daughter, as sure as fate! Her name is Rena. Her brother goes by the name of Walden. She has come to visit her sick mother. My young client, Green's relation, is her lover—is engaged to marry her! Is in town, and is likely to meet her!"

The judge was so absorbed in the situation thus suggested that he laid the papers down and pondered for a moment the curious problem involved. He was quite aware that two races had not dwelt together, without their blood in greater or less degree; he was old enough, and had seen curious things enough to know that in this mingling the current had not always ran in one direction. Certain old decisions with which he was familiar; old scandals that had crept along obscure channels; old facts that had come to the knowledge of an old practitioner, who held in the hollow of his hand the honor of more than one family, made him know that there was dark blood among the white people—not a great deal, and that very much diluted, as, so long as it was sedulously concealed or vigorously denied, or lost in the midst of tradition, or ascribed to a foreign or an aboriginal strain, having no perceptible effect upon the racial type.

Such people were, for the most part, merely on the ragged edge of the white world, seldom rising above the level of overseers or slave-catchers, or sheriff officers, who usually could be relied upon to resent the drop of black blood that tainted them, and with the zeal of the proselyte to visit their hatred of it upon the unfortunate blacks that fell into their hands. One curse of slavery was, and one part of its baleful heritage is, that it poisoned the fountains of human sympathy. Under a system where men might sell their own children without social reprobation or loss of prestige, it was not surprising that some of them should hate their distant cousins. There were not in Fayetteville half a dozen persons capable of thinking Judge Straight's thoughts upon the question before him, and perhaps not another who would have adopted the course he now pursued toward this anomalous family in the house behind the cedars.

"Well, here we are again, as the clown in the circus remarks," the Judge murmured. "Almost fifteen years ago in a moment of sentimental weakness, and of quixotic loyalty to an old friend, who, by the way, had not cared enough for his own children to take them away from the South, as he might have done or to provide for them in his will which he perhaps intended to do, I violated the traditions of my class and stepped from the beaten path to help the misbegotten son of my old friend out of the slough of despond, in which he had learned, in some strange way, that he was floundering. And now, the ghost of my good deed returns to haunt me, and makes me doubt whether I have wrought more evil than good. I wonder," he mused, "if he will find her out?"

The judge was a man of imagination; he had read many books and had personally outlived some prejudices. He let his mind run on the various phases of the situation.

"If he found her out, would he by any possibility marry her?"

He thought silently for a few moments, weighing the pros and the cons of the situation, then shaking his head negatively, resumed talking lowly to himself.

"It is not likely. If he makes the discovery here, the facts would probably leak out in the town. It is something that a man might do in secret but only a hero or a fool would do openly."

The Judge sighed as he contemplated another possibility. He had lived for seventy years under the old regime. The young man was a gentleman—so had been the girl's father. Conditions were changed, but human nature was the same. Would the young man's love turn to disgust and repulsion, or would it merely sink from the level of worship to that of desire? Would the girl, denied marriage, accept anything else? Her mother had—but again, conditions were changed, in so far as the girl was concerned; there was a possible future for her under the new order of things; but white people had not changed their opinion of the Negroes, except for the worse. The general belief was that they were just as inferior as before, and had, moreover, been spoiled during reconstruction, by a disgusting assumption of equality, driven into their thick skulls by Yankee malignity bent upon humiliating a proud though vanquished foe.

If the Judge had had sons and daughters of his own, he might not have done what he now proceeded to do. But the old man's attitude toward society was chiefly that of an observer, and the narrow stream of sentiment left in his heart chose to flow toward the weaker party in this unequal conflict—a young woman fighting for love and opportunity against the ranked forces of society, against immemorial tradition, against pride of family and of race.

"It may be the unwisest thing I ever did," he said to himself, turning to his desk and picking up a quill pen, "and may result in more harm than good; but I was always from childhood in sympathy with the under dog. There is certainly as much reason in my helping the girl as the boy, for being a woman, she is less able to help herself."

He dipped his pen into the ink and wrote the following lines:—

Madam:—If you value your daughter's happiness, keep her at home for the next day or two.

This note he dried by sprinkling it with sand from a box near at hand, signed with his own name, and with a fine courtesy, addressed to, "Mrs. Molly Northcross." Having first carefully sealed it in an envelope, he stepped to the open door and spied a group of Negro boys, one of whom the Judge called by name.

"Here, Billy," he said, handing the boy the note, "take this to Mrs. Molly Northcross. Do you know where she lives—out on the old Wilmington Road, in the house behind the cedars?"

"Yas, suh, ah knows de place."

"Make haste now. When you come back and tell me what she says, I'll give you a dime." He handed the boy the note, and then as he was doing so, he had a more considered thought. He paused, looked at the boy with this thought in mind.

"On second thought, Billy, I'm afraid I may be gone to lunch when you come back, so here's your money," he added, handing the lad the coin.

Just here, however, the Judge made his mistake. Very

few mortals can spare the spring of hope, the motive force of expectation. The boy kept the note in his hand, winked at his companions, who had gathered as near as their awe of the judge would permit, and started down the street. As soon as the Judge had disappeared, Billy beckoned to his friends, who speedily overtook him. When the party turned the corner of Front street and were safely out of sight of Judge Straight's office, the capitalist entered a grocery and invested his unearned increment in gingerbread. When the ensuing saturnalia was over, Billy finished the game of marbles which the Judge had interrupted, and then set out to execute his commission. He had nearly reached his objective point when he met upon the street a young, apparently white lady, whom he did not know, and for whom, the path being narrow at that point, he stepped out into the gutter. He reached the house behind the cedars, went round to the back door, and handed the envelope to Mis' Molly, who was seated on the rear piazza, propped up by pillows in a comfortable rocking chair.

"Laws—a mussey:" she exclaimed weakly, "what is it?"

"It's a lettuh, ma'am," and to the boy, whose expanding nostrils had caught a pleasant odor from the kitchen, and who was therefore in no hurry to go away.

"Who's it fer?" she asked.

"Hit's for' you, ma'am," the lad replied.

"Who's it frum?" she inquired, turning the envelope over and over, and examining it with the impotent curiosity of one who cannot read.

"F'um ole' Jedge Straight, ma'am. He tole me tu fetch it to yuh." Then, after another sniff, he turned to Mis' Molly solicitously.

"Is you got a roasted 'tater you could gimme, ma'am?"

"Sholy, chile. I'll have aunt Zilphy fetch you a piece of 'tater pone, ef you'll hole on a minet."

She called to aunt Zilphy, who soon came hobbling out of the kitchen with a large square of the delicacy,—a flat cake made of mashed sweet potatoes, mixed with beaten eggs, sweetened and flavored to suit the taste, and baked in a dutch oven upon the open hearth.

The boy took the gratuity, thanked her, and turned to go. Mis' Molly was still scanning the superscription of the letter. "Ah wonduh," she murmured, "whut ole Jedge Straight c'n be writin' tu me 'bout? Oh, boy!"

"Yes'm?" the messenger answered, looking back.

"Can you read writin'?"

"No'm."

"All right. Never mind."

She laid the letter carefully on the chimney piece of the kitchen.

"I reckon it's somethin' mo' 'bout the taxes," she thought, "or maybe somebody wants to buy one of my lots. Rena'll be back 'terectly, and she'll read it and fin' out. I'm glad my children have been to school. They never could have got where they are now if they hadn't."

Chapter Thirty One

MENTION HAS BEEN made of certain addressed envelopes John Walden, on the occasion of his visit, had left with his illiterate mother by the use of which she might communicate with her children from time to time. On one occasion Mis' Molly, having had a letter written, took one of these envelopes from the chest where she kept her most valued possessions, and was about to enclose the letter when some one knocked at the door. She laid the envelope and letter on a table in her bedroom, and went to answer the knock on the door. The wind, blowing across the room through the open windows, picked up the envelope and bore it into the street. Mis' Molly on her return, missed it, looked for it, and being unable to find it, took another envelope. An hour or two later another gust of wind lifted the bit of paper from the ground and carried it into the open door of the cooper shop. Frank picked it up, and observing that it was clean and unused, read the superscription.

In his conversations with Mis' Molly, which were often about Rena—the subject uppermost in both their minds,—he had noted the mystery maintained by Mis' Molly about her daughter's whereabouts, and had often wondered at this peculiar silence. As we know, Frank was an intelligent fellow, and could put this and that together. The envelope was addressed to a place in South Carolina. He was aware, from her remarks, that Rena had gone to live in

South Carolina. Her son's name was John—that he had changed his last name was more than likely. Frank was not long in reaching the conclusion that Rena was to be found near the town named on the envelope, which he carefully preserved for future reference.

For a whole year Frank had yearned for a smile or a kind word from the only woman in the world that mattered.

Although of a dark complexion, Frank Fowler was little short of handsome, and there were plenty of girls in and around Fayetteville who would have welcomed his attentions. After Rena disappeared so mysteriously, and, knowing that they had been greatly devoted to each other, Frank's parents were hoping that he would give up the thoughts of Rena, whom they had learned enough regarding, to feel that she had gone back with her brother, and since they knew he was passing for white, could only conclude that he had taken her back to do the same thing. This angered them. There is always a division between dark colored people and light ones, and the dark ones are forever ready to accuse the other—that is the lighter ones, of being "stuck-up" and "think they are better than us." It also angers the dark ones, this thought.

Convinced that Frank was still thinking about Rena, and, perhaps living in the hope that something would happen and that she would return, Frank Fowler's father took it upon himself to speak seriously to his son about the situation.

"It's time now, Frank, for you to be looking around and considering some nice girl who will appreciate your effort to better yourself and perhaps make some girl a good husband. While the Northcross' haven't been bad neighbors, and we were all led for a long time to think that you and Rena would—find something in common with each other, it is obvious that her brother has overruled you. So why not write her off your memory and pay some attention to girls who are not expecting to "pass for white?"

When Rena came back unexpectedly at the behest of her dreams, Frank heard again the music of her voice, felt the joy of her presence and the benison of her smile. There was, however, a subtle difference in her bearing. Her words were not less kind, but they seemed to come from a remoter source. She was kind as the sun is warm or the rain refreshing; she was especially kind to Frank, because he had been good to her mother. If Frank felt the difference in her attitude, he ascribed it to the fact that she had been white, and had taken on something of the white attitude toward the Negro; and Frank, with an equal unconsciousness, clothed her with the attributes of the superior race. Only her drop of black blood, he conceived, gave him the right to feel toward her as he would never have felt without it; and if Rena guessed her faithful devotee's secret, the same reason saved his worship from presumption. A smile and a kind word were little enough to pay for a life's devotion.

On the third day of Rena's presence in Fayetteville, Frank was driving up Front street in the early afternoon, when he nearly fell off his cart in astonishment as he saw, seated in Dr. Green's buggy, which was standing in front of the Fayetteville Hotel, the young man whom he had seen, only the day before, at Rena's house, in a photograph standing beside Rena, and under which he had read, "From Rena to George with love," and had concluded rightly, that this was the man who had come into her life when she went to live with her brother; to do as he was doing, pass for white. He paused to take a closer look at the man, and then sat back convinced beyond a reasonable doubt. He tried to figure out the combination, but could reach only one conclusion: he was Rena's engaged sweetheart, here by some strange and mysterious train of events, now languishing for a while at least, in Fayetteville!

Frank was quite certain that Rena didn't know of his presence in the town. Frank had been over to see Mis' Molly in the morning, and had offered his services to the sick woman, who had rapidly become convalescent upon her daughter's return. Mis' Molly had spoken of some camphor that she needed. Frank had volunteered to get it. Rena had thanked him and spoken of going to the drugstore during the afternoon. It was her intention to leave Fayetteville the next day and return to Charleston.

Frank realized in a flash if Tryon saw Rena, it would surprise him; surprise her; the situation would very shortly explain itself—and then! He sighed and shook his head.

Suddenly, then, Frank was assailed by a new thought; a very strong temptation. Was it the devil working within him? If, as he surmised, the joint presence of the two lovers in Fayetteville was a mere coincidence, a meeting between them would almost surely result in his discovery of Rena's secret. Meanwhile, the voice of the tempter was whispering softly into his ear:

"If she's found out," the voice was saying, "she'll come back to her mother—and to you. . . ."

He hesitated only briefly, realizing of a sudden that he had never done anything to be ashamed of. His love for her was not of the selfish kind. He put temptation aside, and applied the whip quickly to the back of his mule, with a vigor that astonished the animal and moved him to unwonted activity. In an unusually short space of time, he drew up before Mis' Molly's back-gate, sprang from the cart, and ran up to Mis' Molly on the back porch.

"Is Rena here?" he demanded breathlessly.

"No, Frank, she went uptown about an hour ago to see the Doctor and to git me some camphor gum."

Frank uttered a groan, rushed from the house, sprang into the cart and goaded the terrified mule into a gallop which carried him back to the market house in half the time it had taken him to reach Mis' Molly's.

"I wonder what in the worl's the matter with Frank," Mis' Molly mused in vague alarm. "Ef he hadn't been in such a hurry, I'd a axed him tu read Jedge Straight's letter." She sighed, and adjusted her position uneasily, and then said to herself: "Well, Rena'll be home soon."

When Frank reached the doctor's office, the first thing he noted was that the doctor's buggy had moved from in front of the hotel to the front of the doctor's office, and Rena's lover was still seated in it as before. We have explained previously, that the Doctor's office was located over the drugstore which stood on a corner.

Frank ran upstairs and was met by Dave, whom he asked if Rena had been there.

"Yeah," Dave replied, and came forward and paused at top of steps that led downstairs. Pointing with a finger, he went on: "She wuz heah a lil' while ago, and said she wuz gwine downstairs to de drugsto'. I wouldn't be 'sprised ef you didn't fin' heh down dare now."

Let us return, before going further, to Dr. Green and his guest, after leaving Judge Straight's office. The Doctor recalled that he had a patient in the hotel whom he was in the habit of stopping in to see once a day, and, happening to think about it, he drove up in front of the hotel and asking Tryon to excuse him for a few minutes, jumped out of the buggy and went into the hotel.

After calling on his patient, he returned to the buggy, drove around the corner and ran up to his office, attended to a few things, returned and getting back into the buggy, he headed for his home.

The drive by which Dr. Green took Tryon to his own house led up Front street about a mile, the most aristocratic portion of the town, situated on the hill known as Haymount, or, more briefly, "The Hill."

The Hill had lost some of its former glory, however, for the blight of a four years war was everywhere. After reaching the top of the wooded eminence, the road skirted some distance, the brow of the hill. Below them lay the picturesque old town, a mass of vivid green, dotted here and there with gray-roofs that rose above the tree tops. Two long ribbons of street stretched away from the hill to the faint red lines that market the high bluffs beyond the river at the further side of town.

The market-house tier and the slender spires of half a dozen churches were sharply outlined against the green background. The face of the clock in the courthouse tower was visible, but the hour could have been read only by eyes of phenomenal sharpness. Around them stretched ruined walls, dismantled towers and crumbling earthworks

—footprints of the god of war, one of whose temples had crowned this height.

For many years before the rebellion, a Federal arsenal had been located at Fayetteville. Seized by state troops during the secession of North Carolina, it had been held by the Confederates until the approach of Sherman's victorious army, whereupon it was evacuated and partly destroyed. The work of destruction begun by the retreating garrison was completed by the conquerors, and now only ruined walls and broken cannon remained of what had once been the chief ornament and pride of Fayetteville.

The front of Dr. Green's spacious brick house, which occupied an ideally picturesque site, was overgrown by a network of clinging vines, contrasting most agreeably with the mellow red background. A low brick wall, also overrun with creepers, separated the premises from the street and shut in a well kept flower garden, in which Tryon, who knew something of plants, noticed many rare and beautiful specimens.

Mrs. Green greeted Tryon cordially. He did not have the doctor's memory with which to fill out the lady's cheeks or restore the lustre of her hair or the sparkle of her eyes, and thereby justify her husband's claim to be a judge of beauty; but her kind-hearted hospitality was obvious, and might have made even a plain woman seem handsome. She and her two fair daughters, to whom Tryon was duly presented, looked with much favor upon their handsome young kinsman; for among the people of Fayetteville, perhaps by virtue of the prevalence of Scottish blood, the ties of blood were cherished as things of value, and never forgotten except in the case of the unworthy—an exception, by the way, which one need hardly go far to seek.

The Fayetteville people were not exceptional in the weaknesses and meanesses which are common to all mankind, but for some of the finer social qualities they were conspicuously above the average. Kindness, hospitality, loyalty, a chivalrous deference to women,—all these things might be found in large measure by those who saw Fayetteville with the eyes of its best citizens, and accepted their standard of politics, religion, manners, and morals.

The doctor, after the introductions, excused himself for a moment. Mrs. Green soon left Tryon with the young ladies and went to look after luncheon. Her first errand, however, was to find the doctor.

"Is he well off, Ed?" she asked her husband in an anxious whisper.

"Lots of land and plenty of money, if he is ever able to collect it. He has inherited two estates."

"He's sure a good-looking fellow," she mused. "Is he married?"

"There you go again," her husband replied, shaking his forefinger at her in mock reproach. "To a woman with marriageable daughters, all roads lead to matrimony, the centre of a woman's universe. All men must be sized up by their matrimonial availability. No, he isn't married."

"That's nice," she rejoined reflectively. "I think we ought to ask him to stay with us while he is in town, don't you?"

"He's not married," the doctor rejoined slyly; "but the next thing, he's engaged."

He noticed his wife start, ever so slightly, and then she changed, promptly. The next words confirmed the fact that she had.

"Come to think of it," she said, "I'm afraid we wouldn't have the room to spare, and the girls would hardly have time to entertain him. But we'll have him up several times while he is here. I like his looks. I wish you had sent me word that you were bringing him. I'd have had a better luncheon."

"Make him a salad," the doctor suggested, "and get out a bottle of the best claret. Thank God! The Yankees didn't get into my wine cellar. The young man must be treated with genuine Southern hospitality—even if he were a mormon and married ten times over."

"Indeed, he would not, Ed—the idea! I'm ashamed of you. Now, get out, hurry back to the parlor and talk to him. The girls may want to primp a little before luncheon; we don't have a young man to call every day."

"Beauty unadorned," the doctor replied, "is adorned the most. My profession qualifies me to speak upon the subject. They are the two handsomest young women in Fayetteville, and the daughters of the most beautiful—"

"Don't you dare say the word," Mrs. Green interrupted, raising her hand, but with placid good nature. "I shall never grow old while living with a big boy like you. But I must go and make the salad."

At dinner the conversation ran on the family connections and their varying fortunes in the late war. Some had died upon the battlefield, and slept in unknown graves; some had been financially ruined by their faith in the "lost cause," having invested their all in the securities of the

Confederate government. Few had anything left but land, and land without slaves to work it was a drug on the market.

"I was offered a thousand acres the other day, at twenty-five cents an acre," the doctor remarked. "The owner is so land poor that he can't pay the taxes. They have taken our Negroes and our liberties. It may be better for our grandchildren that the Negroes are free, but it was confoundedly hard on us for the North to free them without giving us anything for them."

"I have heard, Dr. Green," Tryon suggested at this point, "that while Abraham Lincoln was campaigning for election, that he often suggested compensating the slaveholders for the Negroes and setting them free. That seemed like a fair and reasonable idea, since the North was swept so by the Abolitionist fever."

"Yes, you are right, and Abraham Lincoln did say a great deal about that very thing and often; and now, years later, when we've had a chance to cool off, the war and the defeat that followed, cooled us all off, but while he was saying it, nobody would listen, and he could get nowhere with the idea. The South insisted that the North let her alone about the slave question, but the North had the Abolition fever and refused to call off her Abolition dogs. I do believe at this time, however, that if the South hadn't rushed to secede and set up the Confederacy even before Lincoln had a chance to take his seat, that he would have, sooner or later, gotten the country to listen to reason, do what he often suggested, floated a big bond issue and paid us for our niggers, and there would have been no war and we would have all the money we blowed in trying to beat the Yankees—when we never had a chance, the niggers would have been freed and would now be working for us instead of trying to boss us as the carpet-baggers have them doing."

"Well," Tryon said with a sigh. "I guess it's too late to cry over spilled milk."

"We've got plenty crying to do and no money to buy handkerchiefs to wipe the tears," Dr. Green opined. "They exalt our slaves, but it is only temporarily. But they have not broken our spirit and cannot take away our superiority of blood and breeding. In due time we shall overthrow the stupid niggers and regain full control. The Negro is an inferior creature; God has marked him with the badge of servitude, and has adjusted his intellect to a servile condition. We will not long submit to his domination. I give you a toast, sir:"

Raising his glass, filled with fine claret:

"The Anglo-Saxon Race: may it remain forever, as now, the head and front of creation, never yielding its rights, and ready always to die, if need be, in defense of its liberties!"

"With all my heart, sir," Tryon replied, who felt in this company a thrill of that pleasure which accompanies conscious superiority. "With all my heart, sir, if the ladies will permit."

"We will join you," all three replied in chorus, lifting their glasses. The toast was drunk with great enthusiasm.

"And now, my dear George," the doctor exclaimed, "to change one good subject for another, tell us who is the favored young lady?"

"A Miss Rowena Walden, sir," Tryon replied promptly and proudly, vividly conscious of four pairs of eyes fixed upon him, but, apart from the momentary embarrassment, welcoming the subject as the one he would most like to speak upon.

"A good, strong old English name," the doctor observed, nodding his head up and down agreeably.

"The heroine of 'Ivanhoe!' " Miss Harriet, one of the daughters, exclaimed, ecstatically.

"Walden the Kingmaker!" Miss Mary said, enthusiastically. "Is she tall and fair, and dignified and stately?"

"She is tall, dark rather than fair, and full of tender grace and sweet humility."

"She should have been named Rebecca, instead of Rowena," Miss Mary rejoined, who was well up in her Scottish lore.

"Tell us something about her people," Mrs. Green asked, to which inquiry the daughters looked assent.

In this meeting of the elect of his own class and kindred, Tryon felt a certain strong illumination upon the value of birth and blood. Finding Rena among people of the best social standing, the subsequent intimation that she was a girl of no family had seemed a small matter to one so much in love. Nevertheless, in his present company he felt a decided satisfaction in being able to present for his future wife a clean bill of social health.

"Her brother is the most prominent lawyer of Charleston, South Carolina. They live in a fine old family mansion and are among the best people of the town."

"Quite right, my boy," the doctor assented. "None but the best are good enough for the best. You must bring her to Fayetteville some day. But bless my life," he broke off to exclaim, consulting his watch suddenly. "I must be going!"

He got quickly to his feet, turned to look at Tryon who stood up, too.

"Will you stay with the ladies awhile, or go back downtown with me?"

"I think I had better go with you, sir. I shall, if you recall, have to see Judge Straight."

"Very well, but you must come back to supper, and we'll have a few friends in to meet you. You must see some of the best people."

The Doctor's buggy was waiting at the gate. As they were passing the hotel on their drive downtown, the clerk came out to the curbstone and called to the Doctor.

"There's a man here, doctor, who's been taken suddenly ill. Can you come in a minute and look at him, sir?"

"I suppose I'll have to," the doctor said with a bit of a frown. After finding his kit, he turned to Tryon.

"Will you wait for me here, George, or will you drive on down to the office? I can walk the rest of the way."

"I think I'll wait here, doctor," Tryon replied. "I'll step up to my room a minute and be back by the time you're ready."

It was while they were standing before the hotel, previous to alighting from the buggy, that Frank Fowler, passing by in his cart, saw Tryon and set out as fast as he could to warn Mis' Molly and Rena of his presence in the town.

Tryon went up to his room, returned after awhile, and took his seat in the buggy, where he waited fifteen minutes before the doctor was ready. When they drew up in front of the office, the doctor's man, Dave, was standing in the doorway, looking up the street with an anxious expression, as though struggling hard to keep something upon his mind. The Doctor got out and approached him.

"Anything wanted, Dave?" he asked.

"Dat young 'oman's been heah agin', suh, and wants tu see you bad. She's in de drugsto' now, suh."

The doctor, without another word, went into the drugstore.

"Bless Gawd!" Dave said to himself with a deep sigh. "Ah remembered dat. Dis heah recomembrance a mine is gwine git me intu trouble ef I don't look out, and dats a fac' sho'."

Tryon sat looking at the boy with an amused smile on his face, wondering to himself if the Negro race was as stupid as they were accused of being; or if the whites, by classifying them as inferior for so long that they had simply convinced them against their will of being stupid. At this point the Doctor came back to the buggy and touching Tryon, whispered in an undertone.

"Just keep your seat, George, until I have finished with the young woman, and then we'll go around to Judge Straight's. Or, if you'll drive along a little further, you can see the girl through the window. She's sure worth looking at if you like a pretty face."

Tryon liked one pretty face: moreover, tinted beauty had never appealed to him. More to show a proper regard for what interested the doctor than from any curiosity of his own, he drove forward a few feet, until the side of the buggy was opposite the drugstore window, and then looked in through the window.

Between the colored glass bottles in the window he could

see a young woman, a tall and slender girl, like a lily on its stem. She stood talking with the doctor, who held his hat in his hand with as much deference as though she were the proudest dame in town. Her face was partly turned away from the window, but as Tryon's eyes fell upon her, he gave a great start. Surely, no two women could be so much alike. The height, the graceful droop of the shoulders, the swan-like poise of the head, the well-turned little ear—surely, no two women could have them all identical! But, pshaw! The notion was absurd, it was merely the reflex influence of his morning dream.

She moved slightly; it was Rena's movement. Surely he knew the gown, and the style of hair-dressing! She rested her hand lightly on the back of a chair. The ring that glittered on her finger could be none other than his own.

The doctor bowed. The girl nodded in response, and, turning, left the store. Tryon leaned forward from the buggy seat and kept his eyes fixed on the figure that moved across the floor of the drugstore. As she came out, she turned her face casually toward the buggy,—and there could no longer be any doubt as to her identity!

When Rena's eyes fell upon the young man in the bugby, she saw a face as pale as death, with startling eyes, in which love, which once had reigned, had now given place to astonishment and horror. She stood a moment as if turned to stone. One appealing glance she gave—a look that might have softened the adamant. When she saw it brought no answering sign of love, or sorrow or regret, the color faded from her cheek, the light from her eyes, and she fell fainting to the ground.

Chapter Thirty Two

THE FIRST EFFECT of Tryon's discovery was, figuratively speaking, to knock the bottom out of things for him. It was much as if a boat on which he had been floating smoothly down the stream of pleasure had sunk suddenly, and left him struggling in deep waters. The full realization of the truth, which followed speedily, had for the moment reversed his mental attitude towards her, and love and yearning had given place to anger and disgust. His agitation could hardly have escaped notice had not the doctor's attention, and that of the crowd that quickly gathered, been absorbed by the young woman who had fallen.

During the time occupied in carrying her into the drugstore, restoring her to consciousness, and sending her home in a carriage, Tryon had time to recover in some degree his self-possession. When Rena had been taken home, he slipped away for a long walk, after which he called at Judge Straight's office and received the judge's report upon the matter presented. Judge Straight had found the claim, in his opinion, a fairly good one; he had discovered property from which, in case the claim was allowed, the amount might be realized. The Judge, who had already been informed of the incident at the drugstore, observed Tryon's preoccupation and guessed shrewdly at its cause, but gave no sign. Tryon left the matter of the note unreservedly in the lawyer's hands, with instructions to communicate to him, any further developments.

Returning to the doctor's office, Tryon listened to that genial gentleman's comments on the accident, his own concern in which he, by a great effort, was able to conceal. The doctor insisted upon his returning to the Hill for supper. Tryon pleaded illness. The doctor was solicitous, felt his pulse, pronounced him feverish, and prescribed a sedative. Tryon sought refuge in his room at the hotel, from which he did not emerge again until morning.

His emotions were varied and stormy. At first he could see nothing but the fraud of which he had been made the victim. A Negro girl had been foisted upon him for a white woman, and he had almost committed the unpardonable sin against his race of marrying her. Such a step, he felt, would have been criminal at any time; it would have been the most odious treachery of this epoch, when his people had been subjugated and humiliated by the Northern invaders, who had preached Negro equality and abolished the wholesome laws decreeing the separation of the races. But no Southerner who loved his poor, down-trodden country, or his race, the proud Anglo-Saxon race which traced the clear stream of its blood to the cavaliers of England, could tolerate the idea that even in distant generations that unsullied current could be polluted by the blood of slaves. The very thought was an insult to the white people of the South. Of Tryon's liberalism, of which he had spoken so nobly and so sincerely, had been confined unconsciously, and as a matter of course, within the boundaries of his own race. The Southern mind, in discussing abstract questions, relative to humanity, makes always, consciously or unconsciously, the mental reservations that the conclusions reached do not apply to the Negro, unless they can be made to harmonize with the customs of the country.

But reasoning thus was not upon a mind of nature reasonable above the average. Tryon's race impulse and social prejudice had carried him too far, and the swing of the mental pendulum brought his thoughts rapidly back in the opposite direction. Tossing uneasily on the bed, where he had thrown himself without undressing, the air of the room oppressed him, and he threw open the window. The cool night air calmed his throbbing pulses. The moonlight streaming through the window, flooded the room with a soft light, in which he seemed to see Rena standing before him as she had appeared that afternoon, gazing at him with eyes that implored charity and forgiveness. He burst into tears, bitter tears, that strained his heartstrings. He was only a youth, she was his first love—and he had lost her forever! She was worse than dead to him; for if he had seen her lying in her shroud before him, he could at least have cherished her memory; now, even this consolation was denied him.

The town clock—which so long as it was wound up regularly, reeked nothing of love or hate, joy or sorrow—solemnly tolled the hour of midnight, and sounded the knell of his lost love. Lost she was, as though she had never been, as indeed she had no right to be. He resolutely determined to banish her from his mind: See her again, he could not; it would be painful to them both; it could be productive of no good to either. He had felt the power and charm of love, and no ordinary shock could have loosened its hold; but this catastrophe, which had so rudely swept away the ground work of his passion, had stirred into new life, all the slumbering pride of race and ancestry which characterized his caste. How much of this superiority was essential and how much accidental; how much of it was due to the ever-suggested comparison with a servile race; how much of it was ignorance and self-conceit; to what extent the boasted purity of his race would have been contaminated by the fair woman whose image filled his memory. Of these things he never thought. He was not influenced by sordid considerations; he would have denied that his course was controlled by any narrow prudence. If Rena had been white (for in his creed there was no compromise), he would have braved any danger for her sake. Had she been merely of illegitimate birth, he would have overlooked the bar sinister. Had her people been poor and of low state, he would have brushed aside mere worldly considerations, and would have bravely sacrificed convention for love; for his liberality was not a mere form of words. But the one objection which he could not overlook, was unhappily, the one that applied to the only woman who had as yet, moved his heart. He tried to be angry with her, but after the first hour he found it impossible. He was a man of too much imagination not to be able to put himself, in some measure at least, in her place; to perceive for her the step which had placed her in Tryon's world, was the working out of nature's great law of self-preservation for which he could not blame her. But for the sheerest accident—no, rather, but for a providential interference, he would have married her, and might have gone to the grave unconscious that she was other than what she seemed.

The City clock struck the hour of two. With a shiver

he closed the window, undressed by the moonlight, drew down the shade, and went to bed. He fell into an unquiet slumber, and dreamed again of Rena. He must learn to control his waking thoughts, that he knew; but his dreams could not be curbed. In that realm Rena's image was for many a day to remain supreme. He dreamed of her sweet smile, her soft touch, her gentle voice.

In all her fair young beauty she stood before him, and then by some hellish magic she was slowly transformed into a hideous black hag. With agonized eyes he watched her beautiful tresses become mere wisps of coarse wool, wrapped round with dingy cotton strings; he saw her clear eyes grow bloodshot, her ivory teeth turn to unwholesome fangs. With a shudder he awoke, to find the cold gray dawn of a rainy day stealing through the window.

He rose, dressed himself, went down to breakfast, then entered the writing room and penned a letter which, after reading it over, he tore into small pieces and threw into the waste-basket. A second shared the same fate. Giving up the task, he left the hotel and walked down to Dr. Green's office.

"Is the doctor in," he asked of Dave, the colored boy attendant.

"No, suh," the boy replied, "He's gone tu see a young cullud gal what fainted when de doctuh was wid you yistidy."

Tryon sat down at the doctor's desk and hastily scrawled a note, stating that business compelled his immediate departure. He thanked the doctor for courtesies extended, and left his regards for the ladies. Returning to the hotel, he paid his bill and took a hack for the wharf, from which a boat was due to leave at nine o'clock.

As the hack drove down Front street, Tryon noted idly the houses that lined the street. When he reached the more scattered district of the town, there was nothing to attract his attention until the carriage came abreast of a row of cedar trees, beyond what could be seen, the upper part of a large house with dormer windows. Before the gate stood a horse and buggy, which Tryon thought he recognized as Doctor Green's. The driver stopped and looked at him.

"Why have you stopped here?"

"Didn't yuh wish tu see de doctuh?" the driver asked.

"I told you to drive me to the boat," Tryon said to him a bit sharply. "Will you therefore turn around and drive me there?"

"Yassuh, yassuh! I guess I made a mistake." He turned round then. Meanwhile, Tryon's curiosity was aroused.

"Can you tell me who lives there?" and he jerked his thumb over his shoulder at the house they were just leaving.

"Yassuh, yas, suh! A cullud 'oman, suh," the man replied, "A Mis' Molly Northcross and her daughter, Rena, suh."

A planned, and all around masquerade—even to changing her name to fool him, or the white race, perhaps engineered years ago by her brother. Tryon smiled and shook his head. The vivid impression he received of this house and the spectre which rose before him of a pale, broken-hearted girl within its gray walls, weeping for a lost lover and a vanished dream of happiness, did not argue well for Tryon's future peace of mind. Rena's image was not to be easily expelled from his heart.

Chapter Thirty Three

BACK IN CHARLESTON, Walden awaited events with some calmness and some philosophy. He could hardly have had one without the other; and it required much philosophy to make him wait a week in patience for information upon a subject in which he was so vitally interested. The delay pointed to disaster. Bad news being expected, delay at least put off the evil day. At the end of the week he received two letters—one addressed in his own handwriting and postmarked, Fayetteville, N. C.; the other in the handwriting of George Tryon. He opened the Fayetteville letter first, which ran as follows:—

My Dean Son,—Frank is writing this letter for me. I am not well, but thank the Lord, I am better than I was.

Rena has had a heap of trouble on account of me and my sickness. If I could of dreamt that I was going to do so much harm, I would have died and gone to meet my God without writing one word to spoil my girl's chances in life; but I didn't know what was going to happen, and I hope the Lord will forgive me.

Frank knows all about it and so I am having him to write this letter for me as Rena is not well enough yet. Frank has been very good to me and to Rena. He was even down to Charleston and saw you and Rena there, and the fine house you live in, but he didn't let either of you see him. He never said a word about it to anybody, not even me, until after what has just happened. He didn't want to make any move that might hurt Rena. He is the best friend I have got in town, because he does so much for me, and won't accept anything in return. (He tells me not to put this in about him, but I want you to know it.)

And now about Rena. She came to see me and I got better right away, for it was longing for her as much as anything else that made me sick, and I was mighty miserable. When she had been here three days and was going back the next day, she went up town to see the doctor for me, and while she was up there she fainted and fell down in the street, and Dr. Green sent her home in a carriage and came down to see her. He couldn't tell what was the matter with her, but she has been sick ever since and out of her head, some of the time and keeps on calling on somebody by the name of George, which was the young white man she told me she was going to marry. It seems that he was in town the day Rena was took sick, for Frank saw him on the street and ran all the way down here to tell me, so that she could keep out of his way, while she was still uptown, waiting for the doctor and getting me some camphor gum for my camphor bottle. Old Judge Straight must have known something about it, for he sent me a note to keep Rena in the house, but the little boy he sent it by didn't bring it until Rena was already gone uptown, and, as I couldn't read, of course I didn't know what it said. Dr. Green heard Rena running on while she was out of her head, and I reckon he must have suspected something, for he looked kind of queer and went away without saying anything. Frank says she met this man on the street and when he found out she wasn't white, he said or did something that broke her heart and she fainted and fell down.

I am writing you this letter because I know you will be worrying about Rena not coming back. If it wasn't for Frank, I hardly know how I could write you. Frank is not going to say anything about Rena passing for white and meeting the man, and neither am I; and I don't suppose Judge Straight will say anything, because he is our good friend; and Dr. Green won't say anything about it, because Frank says that Dr. Green's cook Nancy, says that this young man George stopped with him and was some cousin or relation to the family, and they wouldn't want people to know that any of their kin was thinking about marrying a colored girl. The white folks have all been mad since J. B. Thompson married his black house-keeper when she got religion and wouldn't live with him any more unless he married her. The white people was so mad about what she did that they are preparing a bill, so I hear, to present to the legislature, prohibiting whites and colored from marrying from now on.

All the rest of the connections are well. I have just been in to see how Rena is. She is feeling some better, I think, and says give you her love and she will write you a letter in a few days, as soon as she is well enough. She burst out crying while she was talking, but I reckon that is better than being out of her head. I hope this may find you well, and that this man of Rena's won't say or do anything down there to hurt you. He has not written to Rena or sent her any word. I reckon he is very angry.

Your affectionate mother,
MOLLY NORTHCROSS

This letter, while confirming Walden's fears, relieved his suspense. He at least knew the worst, unless there be something still more disturbing in Tryon's letter, which he now proceeded to open, and which ran as follows:—

JOHN WALDEN, ESQ.

Dear sir,—When I inform you as you are doubtless informed ere the receipt of this, that I saw your sister in Fayetteville last week and learned the nature of those antecedents of yours and hers at which you hinted so obscurely in a recent conversation, you will not be surprised to learn that I take this opportunity of renouncing any pretentions to Miss Walden's hand, and request you to convey this message to her, since it was through you that I formed her acquaintance. I think perhaps that few white men would deem it necessary to make an explanation under the circumstances, and I do not know that I need say more than, that no one, considering where and how I met your sister, would have dreamed of even the possibility of what I have learned. I might with justice reproach you for trifling with the most sacred feelings of a man's heart; but I realize the hardship of your position, and hers, and can make allowances. I would never have sought to know this thing; would doubtless been happier had I gone through life without finding it out; but having the knowledge, I cannot ignore it, as you must understand perfectly well. I regret that she should be distressed or disappointed . . . She has not suffered alone.

I need scarcely assure you that I shall say nothing about this affair and that I shall keep your secret as though it were my own. Personally, I shall never be able to think of you as other than a white man, as you may gather from the tone of this letter; and while I cannot marry your sister, I wish her every happiness, and I remain

      Yours very truly,
      GEORGE W. TRYON

Walden could not know that this formal epistle was the last of a dozen that Tryon had written and destroyed during the week since the meeting in Fayetteville. Hot, blistering letters, cold, cutting letters, scornful, crushing letters. Though none of them was sent, except this last, they had furnished a safety-valve for his emotions, and had left him in a state of mind that permitted him to write the foregoing.

Chapter Thirty Four

Rena was convalescing from a two-weeks illness when her brother came to see her. He arrived in Fayetteville by an early morning train before the town was awake; and walked unnoticed from the station to his mother's house. His meeting with his sister was not without emotion: he embraced her tenderly, and Rena became for a few minutes a very Niobe of grief.

"Oh, it was cruel, cruel!" she sobbed. "I shall never get over it."

"I can understand it, my dear, I can understand it full well," Johnny replied soothingly. "I can understand it only too well and I am to blame for it. If I had never taken you away from here, you would have escaped this painful experience. But do not despair; all is not lost. Tryon will not marry you as I had hoped he might, while I feared the contrary; but he is a gentleman and will be silent. Come back and try again."

"No, Johnny, I couldn't go through it a second time. I managed very well before, when I thought our secret was unknown; but now I could never be sure. It would be borne on every wind, for aught I know, and every rustling leaf might whisper it. The law, you said, made us white; but not the law nor even love, can conquer prejudice. *He* spoke of my beauty, my grace, my sweetness: I looked into his eyes and believed him. And yet he left me without a word! What would I do in Charleston now? I came away engaged to be married, with even the day set; I should go back, forsaken and discredited; even the servants would pity me."

"Little Albert is pining for you," Walden suggested. "We could make some explanation that would spare your feelings."

"Ah, do not tempt me, Johnny! I love the child and I am grieved to leave him. I am grateful, too, for what you have done for me. I am not sorry that I tried it. It opened my eyes and I would rather die of knowledge than live in ignorance. But I could not go through it again, Johnny; I am not strong enough. I could do you no good; I have made you trouble enough already. Get a mother for little Albert—Mrs. Newberry would marry you, secret and all, and would be good to the child. Forget me, Johnny, please, and take care of yourself. Your friend has found you out through me—he may have told, or might possibly tell in time, a dozen people. You think he will be silent. I thought he loved me and he left me without a word, and with a look that told me how he hated and despised me. I would not have believed it—even of a white man."

"You do him an injustice," her brother said, producing Tryon's letter.

"He was not left unscathed. He sent you a message."

She turned her face away, but listened while he read the letter.

"He did not love me," she cried angrily when he had finished. "Or he would not have cast me off—he would not have looked at me so. The law would have let him marry me. I seemed as white as he is. He might have gone anywhere with me, and no one would have started at us curiously; no one need have known. The world is wide—there must be some place where a man can live happily with the woman he loves."

"Yes, Rena, there is; and the world is wide enough for you to get along without Tryon. That is what I am thinking of now, and what I think that you and I should discuss, make plans for, and concentrate on doing."

"For a day or two," she went on, not seeming to have heard or taken his last words seriously, "I had hoped he might come back. But his expression in that awful moment grew upon me, haunted me day and night, until I shuddered at the thought of my ever seeing him again. He looked at me as though I was not even a human being. I had grown fond of him, against my will, for I never felt it was exactly right to fall in love with a white man, but I no longer admire him. I would not marry him if I were white, or he were as I am. He did not love me or he would have acted differently. He might have loved me and have left me—but he could not have loved me and looked at me so."

She began to cry again, and in a few seconds was weeping hysterically. There was little he could say to comfort her. Presently, as if by force of will, she hushed and dried her tears. Walden was reluctant to leave her in Fayetteville. Her childish happiness had been that of ignorance; she could never be happy there again. She had flowered in the sunlight; she must not pine away in the shade.

"If you won't come back with me, Rena, I'll send you to some school at the North, where you can acquire a liberal education, and prepare yourself for some career of usefulness. You may marry a better man even than Tryon."

"No, if I ever marry, it will not be to a white man. I will never be able, as I think about it, to forget the look of hatred, vile contempt and downright cruelty, if he finds that I am colored. You have been successful in what you did, and the family will have to be satisfied at that, but I will never run the risk of having another white man look at me as Tryon did, never, until the longest day I live! Besides, Johnny, I'll never leave mother again; she is too innocent and too old to make another sacrifice as she tried to this time for our benefit. God is against it; I'll stay with my own people."

"God has nothing to do with it," Walden retorted, a bit impatiently. "God is too often a stalking horse for human selfishness. If there is anything to be done, so unjust, so despicable, so wicked that human reason revolts at it, there is always some smug hypocrite to exclaim, 'It is the will of God.'"

"God made us all," Rena continued dreamily, "and for some good purpose, though we may not always see it. He made some people white, and strong, and masterful, and—heartless! He made others black and homely, and poor and weak—"

"And a lot of others—'poor white' and shiftless," Walden smiled, and then burst into laughter.

"He made us, too," continued Rena, intent upon her own thought, "And He must have had a reason for it. Perhaps He meant us to bring the others together in his own good time. A man may make a new place for himself—a woman is born and bound to hers. God must have meant me to stay here, or He would not have sent me back. I shall accept things as they are. Why should I seek the society of people whose friendship—and love—one little word can turn to scorn? I was right, Johnny; I ought to have told him. Suppose he had married me and then had found out?"

To Rena's argument of fore-ordination Walden attached no weight whatever. He had seen God's heel planted for four long years upon the land which had nourished slavery. Had God ordained the crime that the punishment might follow? It would have been easier for omnipotence to prevent the crime. The experience of his sister had stirred up a certain bitterness against white people—a feeling which he had put aside years ago, with his dark blood, but which sprang anew into life when the fact of his own origin was brought home to him so forcibly through his sister's misfortune. His sworn friend and promised brother-in-law had thrown him over promptly, upon discovery of the hidden drop of dark blood. How many others of his friends would do the same, if they but knew of it? He had begun to feel a little of the spiritual estrangement from his associates that he had noticed in Rena during her life at Charleston. The fact that several persons knew his secret had spoiled the fine flavor of perfect security hitherto marking his position. George Tryon was a man of honor among white men, and had deigned to extend the protection of his honor to Walden as a man, though no longer as a friend; to Rena as a woman, but not as a wife. Tryon, however, was only human, and who could tell when their paths in life might cross again, or what future temptation might feel to use a damaging secret to their disadvantage?

Walden had cherished certain ambitions, but these he

must now put behind him. In the obscurity of private life, his past would be of little concern; in the glare of a political career, one's antecedents are public property, and too great a reserve in regard to one's past is regarded as a confession of something discreditable.

Frank, too, knew the secret—a good faithful fellow, even when there was no thought of fidelity; he ought to do something for Frank to show their appreciation of his conduct. But what assurance was there that Frank would always be discreet about the affairs of others? Judge Straight knew the whole story, and old men are sometimes garrulous. Dr. Green suspected the secret; he had a wife and daughters. If old Judge Straight could have known Walden's thoughts, he would have realized the fulfillment of his prophecy. Walden, who had done so well for himself, had weakened the structure of his own life by trying to share his good fortune with his sister.

"Listen, Rena," he said, with a sudden impulse, "we'll go to the North or the West—I'll go with you—far away from the South or Southern people, and start life over again. It will be easier for you, it will not be bad for me—I am young, and have means. There are no strong ties to bind me to the South. I would have a larger outlook everywhere."

"And what about our mother?" Rena asked, looking in the direction of the room where their mother was seated.

It would be necessary to leave her behind, they both perceived clearly enough, unless they were prepared to surrender the advantage of their whiteness and drop back to the lower rank. The mother bore the mark of the Ethiopian—not pronouncedly, but distinctly; neither would

Mis' Molly, in all probability, care to leave home and friends and the graves of her loved ones. She had no mental resources to supply the place of these; she was, moreover, too old to be transplanted; she would not fit into Walden's scheme for a new life.

"I left her once," Rena said, "and it brought pain and sorrow to all three of us. She is not strong and I will not leave her here to die alone, This shall be my home while she lives, and if I leave it again, it shall be for only a short time, to go where I can write to her freely, and hear from her often. Don't worry about me, Johnny. I shall do very well."

Walden sighed. He was sincerely sorry to leave his sister, and yet saw that, for the time being, her resolution was not to be shaken. He must bide his time. Perhaps in a few months she might tire of the old life. His door would always be open to her, and he would charge himself with her future.

"Well, then," he said, concluding the argument, "we'll say no more about it for the present. I'll write to you later. I was afraid that you might not care to go back just now, so I brought your trunk along with me."

He gave his mother the baggage check. She took it across to Frank, who during the day, brought the trunk from the depot. Mis' Molly offered to pay him for doing so, but as usual, he would accept nothing.

"My son, Johnny is here," Mis' Molly said, "and he wants to see you. Come into the settin' room. We don't want folks to know that he's in town; but you know all our secrets, and we can trust you like one of the family."

Frank followed Mis' Molly into the sitting room where Johnny rose to his feet as they approached, smiling.

"I'm glad to see you again, Frank," Walden said, extending his hand and clasping Frank's warmly. "You've grown up since I saw you last, but it seems you are still our good friend."

"Our *very* good friend," Rena interjected with a happy smile.

"Thank you, Frank, and I want you to understand how much I appreciate—"

"—How much *we all* appreciate it," Rena corrected, and seemed more happy still.

"I'm afraid you are all saying too much about nothing. We've been neighbors all our lives; there are no men around to help the ladies out, and it costs me nothing but a little time, which I have to spare, so why shouldn't I be a —good neighbor?" He looked from one to the other and bowed astutely. Rena felt proud. Here was the man she could always trust—always had trusted.

Walden, as if speaking for the family, again thanked him for his kindness and turned his attention to his mother and sister, then, Frank, still deprecating the idea, turned and left. Johnny Walden left by boat the same night; and a new life lay before Rena Northcross, back in her old home and to her old name.

Chapter Thirty Five

WHEN THE FIRST great shock of his discovery wore off, the fact of Rena's origin lost some of its initial repugnance to Tryon—indeed, the repulsion was not to the woman at all, as their past relations bore evidence, but merely to the thought of her as a wife. It could hardly have failed to occur to so reasonable a man as Tryon, that Rena's case could scarcely be unique. Surely in the past centuries of free manners and easy morals that had prevailed in remote parts of the South, there must have been many white persons whose origin would not have born too microscopic an investigation. Family trees seldom have not a crooked branch; or, to use a more opposite figure, many a flock has its black sheep. Being a man of lively imagination, Tryon soon found himself forming all sorts of hypothetical questions about a matter which he had already definitely concluded. If he had married Rena in ignorance of her secret, and had learned it afterwards, would he have put her aside? If, knowing her history, he had, nevertheless, married her and she had subsequently displayed some trait of character that would suggest the Negro, could he have forgotten, or forgiven the taint? Could he have still held her in love and honor? If not, could he have given her the outward pretense of affection or could he have been no more than coldly tolerant? He was glad that he had been spared this ordeal. With an effort he put the whole matter definitely and conclusively aside, as he had done a hundred times already.

Yet, no sooner than he had done this, again appeared her face, as he had seen it before the drug store when she turned and their eyes met; there was that pathetic and pitiful expression, touching deep down into his heart and seeming to say, "Oh, George, I'm so sorry. Now you have found out, but I didn't want you to. I would have done anything to have saved you this. Now you know and you are going to hate and despise me; yet, I am the same Rena you have been thinking about all the time. The fact that I am the same, as you have found out, I am still just as I was before you found out. Can you not therefore find it in your heart in this brief and fleeting moment to think of me as you have and speak to me and call me to you— only for a little while, George? Afterwards, there will be such a long time for you to hate me; but I feel that I could endure it more easily if I could feel in this one look that you have not begun to scorn and hate me so much."

Always, it was those eyes that haunted him, those soft and tender, pitiful and helpless eyes—but afterwards, as they recurred to him and he could not call her back, it pained him. And the more he fought to cast this memory off, the keener the pain. He could only think of her as the tenderest, the sweetest and the most lovely girl he ever knew. All that was wrong about her was that which she could not help; God himself could not help or change it —a Negress!

Yet, when he could be reasonable—even with himself, he found himself arguing: "She is more white than dark;

she is more of myself than of that hateful drop of dark blood that makes marrying her impossible!"

Oh, what a cruel world. The world that the white man, his race, had made. Some white man, and he must have been rich, a gentleman and proud, was Rena's father. She could not have been the offspring of either a slave-catcher, an over-seer, or a poor white man at all. And yet—"what's the use" he would conclude and after trying to blank his mind and imagination, only to find himself living right through it all, over and over again.

Returning to his home after an absence of several months in South Carolina it was quite apparent to his mother's watchful eye that he was in serious trouble. He was absent-minded, monosyllabic, sighed deeply and often, and could not always conceal the traces of secret tears. For Tryon was young and possessed of a sensitive soul—a source of happiness or misery, as the Fates decree, to those thus endowed, the heights of rapture are accessible, the abysses of despair yawn threateningly; only the dull monotony of contentment is denied.

Mrs. Tryon vainly sought by every gentle art a woman knows, to win her son's confidence. "What is the matter, George, dear?" she would ask, stroking his hot brow with her small, cool hand as he sat, nursing his grief. "Tell your mother, George. Who else could comfort you so well as she?"

"Oh, it's nothing, mother—nothing at all."—he would reply with a forced attempt at lightness. "I guess I am somewhat on the anxious seat about—our business and estate. People owe us; the country is still unsettled; nobody seems to know definitely just what is going to happen, politically and otherwise. I guess I think about it—too much. I shall try to think less about it in the future."

His mother knew he was lying; that it was something entirely different from that, and when he dared to meet her sympathetic eyes, he knew that the excuse or the lie had not gotten over. "It's only your fond imagination, dear; you, the best of all mothers." Then he would take her in his arms and press her to him tightly.

This would quiet matters for the time being, but just as quickly as he was alone again, back into his mind came Rena.

It was Mrs. Tryon's turn, when she saw it, to shed a clandestine tear. Before her son had gone away on this trip to South Carolina, he had kept no secrets from her; his heart had been an open book, of which she knew every page; now, some painful story was inscribed therein. What could be more painful to a young man's heart than an impossible love? If she could have known the story, his story, she felt sure that she could at least have comforted him. If she could have abdicated her empire to Blanche Leary, or have shared it with her, she would have yielded gracefully; but very palpably some other influence than Blanche's had driven joy from her son's countenance and lightness from his heart.

Miss Blanche Leary, whom Tryon found in the house on his return, was a demure, and pretty little blonde, with an amiable disposition, a talent for society, and a pronounced fondness for George Tryon. A poor girl of an excellent family, impoverished by the war, she was distantly related to Mrs. Tryon, had for a long time enjoyed that lady's favor, and was her choice for George's wife when he should be old enough to marry. A woman less interested than Miss Leary would have perceived that there was something wrong with Tryon. Miss Leary had no doubt that there was a woman at the bottom of it—for over what else should a youth worry but love? Or, if one's love affairs ran smoothly, why should one worry about anything at all? Miss Leary, in the nineteen years of her mundane existence, had not been without mild experiences of the heart, and had hovered for some time on the verge of disappointment with respect to Tryon himself. A sensitive pride would have driven more than one woman away at the sight of the man of her preference sighing like a furnace for some absent fair one. But Mrs. Tryon was so cordial, and insisted so strenuously on her remaining, that Blanche's love, which was strong, conquered her pride, which was no more than a reasonable young woman should do who places success above mere sentiment. She remained in the house and bided her opportunity.

If George practically ignored her for a time, she did not throw herself at all in his way. She went on a visit to some girls in the neighborhood and remained away a week, hoping that she might be missed. Tryon expressed no regret at her departure and no particular satisfaction upon her return. If the house was duller in her absence, he was but dimly conscious of the difference. He was still fighting a battle in which a susceptible heart and a reasonable mind had locked horns in a well-nigh hopeless conflict. Reason, common sense, the instinctive ready made judgments of his training and environment—the deep seated prejudices of race and caste—commanded him to dismiss Rena from his thoughts. His stubborn heart simply would not let her go.

Chapter Thirty Six

ALTHOUGH THE WHOLE fabric of Rena's life toppled and fell with her lover's defection, her sympathies, broadened by culture and still more by her recent emotional experience, did not shrink as would have been the case with a more selfish soul, to the mere limits of her personal sorrow, great as this seemed at the moment. She had learned to love, and where the love of one man failed her, she turned to humanity as a stream obstructed in its course overflows the adjacent country. Her early training had not directed her thoughts to the darker people with whose fate her own was bund up so closely, but rather away from them.

As detailed earlier in this story, she and Frank Fowler, the darker one, had seemed to understand that in due time, one would wed the other. It was also detailed earlier in the story, that her mother secretly objected to Frank, her one and only reason being that he was dark, and light people during that period and many generations thereafter, and many still shy from it up to this day, do not favor dark people in their families. Mis' Molly did not, and while she really loved Frank as a friend and neighbor; admired him for his ability and all that went with it, she had never wanted Frank for her son-in-law.

Rena's experience over on the "other side" as Mis' Molly was wont to refer to it afterwards, had a delaying effect on Rena's previous ambition, to become Frank's wife at the first opportunity, and for this fact which Mis' Molly could see, she was greatly relieved and hoped she wouldn't take the notion to do so at any early date.

The fact is, Rena had been reared and taught to even dislike dark Negroes because they were not so white as she was, and, since most Negroes who were free before the war were more or less light in color, they had been able to develop a little circle of their own, which in no way encouraged darker Negroes to seek entry into same. Moreover, the fact that most of the dark ones had been slaves while Rena and her folks were free, added to that superior feeling.

Her life in her brother's home in Charleston, by removing her from immediate contact with them, had given her a somewhat different point of view—one which emphasized their shortcomings, and thereby made vastly clearer to her the gulf that separated them from the new world in which she lived; so that when misfortune threw her back among them, the reaction brought her nearer than before. When once she had seemed able to escape from them, they were now, it appeared, of her inalienable race. Thus doubly equipped, she was able to view them at once with the mental eye of an outsider and the sympathy of a sister: she could see their faults and judge them charitably; she knew and appreciated their good qualities. With her quickened intelligence, she could perceive how great was their need and how small was their opportunity; and with this illumination came the desire to contribute to their help. She had not the breadth of culture to see all its ramifications the great problem which still puzzles statesmen and philosophers; but she was conscious of the wish, and of the power, in a small way, to do something for the advancement of those who had just set their feet upon the ladder of progress.

The new-born desire to be of service to her re-discovered people was not long without an opportunity for expression. Yet the Fates willed that her future should be but another link in a connected chain: she was to be as powerless to put aside her recent past as she had been to escape from the influence of her earlier life. There are sordid souls that eat and drink and breed and die and imagine they have lived. But Rena's life since her great awakening had been that of the emotions, and her temperament made of a continuous life. Her successive states of consciousness were not detachable, but united to form a single if not harmonious whole. To her sensitive spirit, today was born of yesterday, tomorrow would be but the off-spring of today.

One day, along towards noon, her mother received a visit from Mary B. Pettifoot, a second cousin who lived on Back Street, only a short distance from the house behind the cedars. Rena had gone out so that the visitor found Mis' Molly alone.

"I heard you say, Cousin Molly," Mary B. said (no one ever knew what the B in Mary's name stood for—it was a mere ornamental flourish) "that Rena was talkin' 'bout teachin' school. I've got a good chance for her, if she ceah's to take it. My Cousin, Jeff Wain, 'rived in town dis mawnin', f'm way down in Sampson County, tu git a teachuh fo' de niggah school in his distric'. I suppose he mighta got one from 'round Newbern, ah Goldsboro, ah some ob dem places East, but he 'lowed he'd lak tu visit some ob his kin an' ole' frien's, an' so kill two birds wid one stone."

"I seed a strange mulattuh man, wid a bay hoss and a new buggy, drivin' by heah dis mawning' early, from down to'ds de river," Mis' Molly rejoined. "Ah wonduh's if dat wuz 'im?"

"Did he have on a linen duster?" Mary B. asked.

"Yeah, an' 'peared to be a very well sot up man," Mis' Molly replied, becoming enthusiastic, with growing interest. "He looked to be 'bout thirty-five yeahs old I reckon."

"Dat wuz him," Mary B. assented. "He's got a fine hoss an' buggy, an' a gol' watch 'n' chain, owns a big plantation, an lots a hosses an' mules, an' cows an' hogs. He raise fifty bales a cotton las' yeah, an' he's been to de legislatuh."

"My gracious!" Mis' Molly exclaimed, struck with awe at this catalogue of the stranger's possessions. He was evidently worth more than a great many "rich" white people —all white people in North Carolina in those days were either "rich" or "poor," the distinction being one of caste rather than of wealth. "Is he married?" Mis' Molly now inquired with interest.

"No—single. You might 'low it was quare that he shouldn' be married at his age; but he was crossed in love oncet," Mary B. heaved a self-conscious sigh, "an' has stayed single eveh sence. That wuz ten yeahs ago, but as some husban's is long-lived, an' thauih ain' no mo chance fo' 'im now than there wuz then, I reckon some nice gal mought stan' a good show a ketchin' 'im ef she played heh kyards right."

To Mis' Molly this was news of considerable importance. She had not thought a great deal of Rena's plans to teach;

she considered it lowering for Rena, after having been white to go among the Negroes any more than was unavoidable. This opportunity meant more than mere employment for her daughter. She had felt Rena's disappointment keenly, from the practical point of view, and, blaming herself for it, held herself all the more bound to retrieve the misfortune in any possible way. If she had not been sick, Rena would not have dreamed the fateful dream that had brought her to Fayetteville; for the connection between the vision and the reality was even closer in Mis' Molly's eyes than in Rena's. If the mother had not sent the letter announcing her illness and confirming the dream, Rena would not have ruined her promising future by coming to Fayetteville. But the harm had been done, and she was responsible, ignorantly of course, but none the less truly, as far as possible. Her highest ambition since Rena had grown up, had been to see her married and settled comfortably in life—at least to some kind of man light in color. She had no hope that Tryon would come back. Rena had declared that she would make no further effort to get away from her people; and, furthermore, that she would never marry. To this latter statement Mis' Molly attached but little importance. That a woman should go single from the cradle to the grave did not accord with her experience in life of the customs of North Carolina. She respected a grief she could not entirely fathom, yet did not for a moment believe that Rena would remain unmarried.

"You'd better fetch him 'roun' to see me, Ma'y B." she said, "an let me see what he looks lak. Ah'm puticulah 'bout my gal. She says she ain't goin' tu marry nobody, but ob cose we know dat's all foolishness."

"Ah'll fetch him 'roun' dis ebenin' 'bout three o'clock," the visitor said, rising. "Ah mus' hurry back now and keep him comp'ny. Tell Rena to put on her bes' bib and tucker; fo' Mistah Wain is puticulah too, an' I've already been braggin' 'bout heh looks."

When Mary B., at the appointed hour, knocked on Mis' Molly's front door—the visit being one of ceremony, she had taken her cousin round to the Front Street entrance and through the flower garden where Mis' Molly was prepared to receive them. After a decent interval, long enough to suggest that she had not been watching their approach and was not over-eager about the visit, she answered the knock and admitted them into the parlor. Mr. Wain was formally introduced, and seated himself on the ancient haircloth sofa, under the famed fashion-plate, while Mary B. sat by the open door and fanned herself with a palm-leaf fan.

Mis' Molly's impression of Wain was favorable. His complexion was of a light brown—not quite as fair as Mis' Molly would have preferred; but any deficiency in this regard, or in the matter of the stranger's features, which, while not unpleasing, leaned toward the broad mulatto type, was more than compensated in her eyes by very straight black hair, and, as soon appeared, a great facility of complimentary speech. On his introduction, Mr. Wain bowed low, assumed an air of great admiration, and expressed his extreme delight in making the acquaintance of so distinguished-looking a lady.

"You're flatterin' me, Mr. Wain," Mis' Molly returned with a grateful smile. "But you want to meet my daughter befo' you begin thow'in' bokays. Excuse my leavin' you. I'll go fetch heh."

She returned in a moment, followed by Rena. "Mr. Wain, 'low me to introduce you to my daughter, Rena. Rena, this is Mary B's cousin on her pappy's side, who's come up fum Sampson County to git a school-teacher."

Rena bowed gracefully. Wain stared a moment in genuine astonishment, and then bent himself nearly double, keeping his eyes fixed meanwhile, upon Rena's face. He had expected to see a pretty yellow girl, but had been prepared for no such radiant vision of beauty as this which now confronted him.

"Does—does yuh mean tu say, Miz Northcross, dat—dat dis young lady is yo' own daughter?", he stammered, rallying his forces for action.

"Why not, Mr. Wain?" Mis' Molly asked, bridling with mock resentment. "Does yuh mean tu 'low that she was changed in her cradle, er is she too goodlookin' to be my daughter?"

Promptly into his fat head, Jeff Wain saw a chance to drive home a telling blow of flattery, with a view to winning Mis' Molly over to his side right quickly.

"My deah Miz Northcross! It would be wastin' wo'ds to say dat dey ain' no lady too good-lookin' tu be yo' daughtah; but youah lookin' so young yo' se'f dat I'd ruther tookin' heh fo' yo' sistah."

That did it! Mis' Molly was so flattered that she actually blushed all over, closing her eyes and moving from right to left, left to right before she was able to go on.

"Yas," Mis' Molly rejoined, trying very much to be

proper, "they really ain' many yeahs between us. I wuz ruther young mah se'f when she war bo'n."

"An, mo'ober," Wain went on, "Hit takes me a minet ah so tu git mah mind use tu thinkin' ob Miss Rena as a cullud young lady. Ah mought ah seed heh a hund'ed times, an' I'd a nevuh dreamt but w'at she wuz a white young lady, fum one ob de bes' families."

That just about broke it up completely, as far as Mis' Molly was concerned. Mr. Wain was in her favor for good, and any influence that she possessed over Rena, was geared to go to his assistance.

"Yas, Mr. Wain," Mis' Molly replied complacently, "all three ob mah chillun wuz white, an' one ob 'em has been on the other side fo' many years. Rena has been to school an' has traveled—and has had chances—better chances than anybody roun' heah knows."

"She's jes' the lady ah'm lookin' fo', tu teach ouh school," Wain rejoined with emphasis. "Wid heh schoolin' and mah recommen', she c'n git a fus' grade ce'tifikt and draw fo'ty dollahs a month; and a lady ob heh culoh can keep a lot ob little niggahs straightuh dan' uh darker lady could. We jes' got to hab heh tu teach ouh school—ef we c'n git heh."

Rena's interest in the prospect of employment at her chosen work was so great that she paid little attention to Wain's compliments. Mis' Molly led Mary B. away to the kitchen on some pretext, and left Rena to entertain the gentleman. She questioned him eagerly about the school and he gave the most glowing accounts of the elegant school-house, the bright pupils and the congenial society of the neighborhood. He spoke almost entirely in superlatives, and, after making due allowances for what Rena perceived to be a temperamental tendency to exaggeration, she concluded that she would find in the school, a worthy field of usefulness and in this polite and good-natured, though somewhat wordy man, a coadjutor on whom she could rely in her first efforts; for she was not over-confident of her powers, which seemed to grow less as the way opened for their exercise.

"Do you think I am capable of holding the position," she asked the visitor, after stating some of her qualifications.

"Oh, dere's no doubt 'bout it, Miss Rena," Wain replied, having listened with an air of great wisdom, though secretly aware that he was too ignorant of letters to form a judgment; "you c'n teach the school all right, and could ef you didn't know ha'f as much. You won't have no trouble managin' the chillun nuther. Ef any ob dem gets onruly, jes' call me an' I'll lam de hide ofn'um. Ah'll show 'em how tu walk Spanish. Ah'm chuhman ob de school committee, and, as fo' said, I'll lam de hide off'n any scholar dat don' behave. You c'n trus' me fo' dat, sho' as ah'm a settin' heah."

"Then," Rena said, with a little pleasant and seemingly satisfied sigh, "I'll undertake it, and do my best. I'm sure you'll not be too exacting."

"Yo' bes', Miss Rena'll be de bes' dey is. Don't you worry na fret. Dem niggahs won't hab no other teachuh aftuh dey've once laid eyes on yuh: Ah'll guarantee dat. Dere won't be no trouble, not a bit."

Back in the rear in the meantime:

"Well, Cousin Molly," Mary B. said to Mis' Molly in the kitchen, "How does the plan strike you?"

"Ef Rena's satisfied, I am," Mis' Molly replied, "But you'd better say nothin' 'bout ketchin a beau, or any such foolishness, er else she'd be just likely not to go to Sampson County."

"Befo' Cousin Jeff goes back," Mary B. confided, "I'd lak tu gib him a pahty, but mah house is too small. I wuz wonder'n ef I could—borry yo' house?"

"Showly Mary B. Ah'm interested in Mr. Wain on Rena's account, an hits as little as I can do to let you use my house an hep you git things ready."

The date of the party was set for Thursday night, as Wain was to leave Fayetteville on Friday morning, taking with him the new teacher. The party would serve the double purpose of a compliment to the guest and a farewell to Rena, and it might prove the precursor, the mother secretly hoped, of other festivities to follow at some later date.

Rena looked forward to the trip with strange relief, compared to the time she went away with her brother, to pass for white and get her big opportunity in life, according to her brother. Sampson County was down towards the Southeastern corner of the State, where the percentage of Negroes was much higher than around Fayetteville, due to larger plantations being located in that section of the State, and this made Rena more anxious to begin her work there, where she could learn more about the manners and customs of her people.

Chapter Thirty Seven

ONE WEDNESDAY MORNING, about six weeks after his return home, Tryon received a letter from Judge Straight with reference to the note left with him at Fayetteville for collection. This communication properly required an answer, which might have been made in writing within the compass of ten lines. No sooner, however, had Tryon read the letter than he began to perceive reasons why it should be answered in person. He had left Fayetteville under extremely painful circumstances, vowing that he would never return; yet now the barest pretext, by which no one could have been deceived except willingly, was sufficient to turn his footsteps thither again. He explained to his mother—with a vagueness which she found somewhat puzzling, but ascribed to her own feminine obtuseness in matters of business—the reasons that imperatively demanded his presence in Fayetteville. With an early start he could drive there in one day—he had an excellent roadster, a light buggy, and a recent rain had left the road in good condition. A day would suffice for the transaction of his business, and the third day, would bring him home again. He set out on his journey on Thursday morning, with this program very clearly outlined.

Tryon would not have first admitted even to himself that Rena's presence in Fayetteville had any bearing whatever on his projected visit. The matter about which Judge

Straight had written, might, it was clear, be viewed in several aspects. The judge had written him concerning one of immediate importance. It would be much easier to discuss the subject in all its bearings, and clean up the whole matter, in one comprehensive interview.

The importance of this business, then, seemed very urgent for the first few hours of Tryon's journey. Ordinarily a careful driver and merciful to his beast, his eagerness to reach Fayetteville increased gradually until it became necessary to exercise some self-restraint in order not to urge his faithful mare beyond her powers; and soon he could no longer pretend obliviousness of the fact that some attraction stronger than the whole amount of Duncan McSwayne's note was urging him irresistibly toward his destination. The old town beyond the distant river, his heart told him clamorously, held the object in all the world to him most dear. Memory brought up in vivid detail every moment of his brief and joyous court-ship. Each tender word, each enchanting smile, every fond caress. He lived his past happiness over again down to the moment of that fatal discovery. What horrible fate was it that had involved him—nay, that had caught this sweet, delicate girl in such a blind alley? A wild hope flashed across his mind; perhaps the ghastly story might not be true; perhaps, after all, the girl was no more a Negro than she seemed. He had heard sad stories of white children, born out of wedlock, abandoned by sinful parents to the care or adoption of colored women, who had reared them as their own, the children's future basely sacrificed to hide the parent's shame. He would confront this reputed mother of his darling and wring the truth from her. He was in a state of mind where any sort of fairy tale would have seemed reasonable. He would almost have bribed some one to tell him that the woman he had loved, the woman he still loved (he felt a thrill of lawless pleasure in the confession), was not the descendant of slaves—that he might marry her, and not have to have before his eyes forever anon the gruesome fear that some one of their children might show even the faintest mark of the despised race.

At noon he halted at a convenient hamlet, fed and watered his mare, and resumed his journey after an hour's rest. By this time he had about well nigh forgotten the legal business which formed the ostensible occasion for his journey, and was conscious only of a wild desire to see the woman whose image was beckoning him on to Fayetteville as fast as his horse could take him.

At sundown he stopped again, about ten miles from the town and cared for his tired beast. He knew her capacity, however, and calculated that she could stand the additional ten miles without injury. The mare set out with reluctance but soon settled resignedly into a steady jog.

Memory had hitherto assailed Tryon with the vision of past joys. As he neared the town, imagination attacked him with still more moving images. He had left her, this sweet flower of womankind—white or not, God had never made one fairer! He had seen her fall to the hard pavement, with he knew not what resulting injury. He had left her tender frame—the touch of her finger tips had made him thrill with happiness—to be lifted by strange hands, while he with heartless pride had driven deliberately away, without a word of sorrow or regret. He had ignored her as completely as if she had never existed. That he had been deceived was true. But had he not sided in his own deception? Had not Walden told him distinctly that they were of no family, and was it not his fault that he had not followed up the clue thus given him? Had not Rena compared herself to the child's nurse, and had he not assured her that if she were the nurse, he would marry her the next day? The deception had been due more to his own blindness than to any lack of honesty on the part of Rena and her brother. In the light of his present feelings they seemed to have been absurdly outspoken. He was glad that he had kept his discovery to himself. He had considered himself very magnanimous not to have exposed the fraud that was being perpetrated upon society; it was with a very comfortable feeling that he now realized that the matter was as profound a secret as before.

"She ought to have been born white," he muttered to himself, adding weakly, "I would to God that I had never found her out!"

Drawing near the bridge that crossed the river to the town, he pictured to himself a pale girl, with sorrowful, tear-stained eyes, pining away at the old house behind the cedars for love of him, dying, perhaps, of a broken heart. He would hasten to her; he would dry her tears with kisses; he would express sorrow for his cruelty.

The tired mare had crossed the bridge and was toiling slowly up Front Street; she was near the limit of her endurance, and Tryon did not urge her.

They might talk the matter over and if they must part, part at least they would in peace and friendship. If he could not marry her, he would never marry any one else; it would be cruel for him to seek happiness while she was denied it, for, having once given her heart to him, she could never, he was sure—so instinctively fine was her nature—she could never love any one less worthy than himself, and would therefore, probably never marry. He knew from a Charleston acquaintance, who had written him a letter, that Rena had not reappeared in that town.

He should discover—the chance was one in a thousand—that she was white; or if he should find it too hard to leave her, ah, well! he was a white man, one of a race born to command. He would *make* her white; no one beyond the old town would ever know the difference. If, perchance, their secret should be disclosed, the world was wide; a man of courage and ambition inspired by love might make a career anywhere. Circumstances made weak men; strong men mould circumstances to do their bidding. He would not let his darling die of grief, whatever the price must be paid for her salvation. She was only a few rods away from him now. In a moment he would see her; he would take her tenderly in his arms, and heart to heart they would mutually forgive and forget, and, strengthened by their love, would face the future boldly and bid the world do its worse.

Chapter Thirty Eight

THE EVENING OF the party arrived. The home had been thoroughly cleaned in preparation for the event, and decorated with the choicest of the garden. By eight o'clock the guests had gathered. They were all mulattoes. All people of mixed blood were called "mulattoes" in North Carolina. There were dark mulattoes and light mulattoes. Mis' Molly's guests were mostly of the light class, most of them more than half white, and few of them less. In Mis' Molly's small circle, straight hair was the only palliative of a dark complexion. Many of the guests would not have been casually distinguishable from white people of the poorer class. Others bore unmistakable traces of Indian ancestry, for Cherokee and Tuscarora blood was quite widely diffused among the Free Negroes of North Carolina, though wellnigh lost sight of by the curious customs of the white people to ignore anything but the Negro blood in those who were touched by its potent current. Very few of those present had been slaves. The free colored people of Fayetteville were numerous enough before the war to have their own "society," and human enough to despise those who did not possess advantages equal to their own.

Most of the Free Negroes did not become free by purchasing themselves as Henry Fowler did, and later his wife. They were free because some planter begat a child, or several children, by a slave woman, and their consciences irked them to see their own flesh and blood, herded with the slaves, so, at one time or another, they found some excuse to set them free. Once free, these descendants felt it the proper thing to ape their masters who almost never admitted publicly their acts; but it hadn't mattered. A Free Negro delighted in boasting his ancestry, if it did begin through clandestine intercourse—but getting back to Mis' Molly's party—

At this time, those who had been free before the war, still looked down on those who had been held in bondage. The only black man present at this party occupied a chair which stood on a broad chest in one corner, and extracted melody from a fiddle to which a whole generation of the best people of Fayetteville (white people) had danced to and made merry. Uncle Needham seldom played for colored gatherings, but made an exception in Mis' Molly's case; she was not white, but he knew her past; if she was not the rose, she had at least been near the rose. When the company had gathered, Mary B., as mistress of ceremonies, whispered to Uncle Needham, who tapped his violin sharply with the bow.

"Ladies and gent'emens, take yo' pa'tnuh's fo' a Vuhginny reel!"

Mr. Wain, as the guest of honor, opened the ball with his hostess. He wore a broadcloth coat and trousers, a heavy glittering chain across the spacious front of his white waistcoat, and a large red rose in his button hole. If his boots were slightly run down at the heel, so trivial a detail passed unnoticed in the general splendor of his attire. Upon a close or hostile inspection, there would have been some features of his ostensibly good-natured face—the shifty eye, the full and slightly drooping lower lip—which might have given a student of physiognomy food for reflection. But whatever the latent defects of Wain's character, he proved himself this evening a model of geniality, presuming not at all on his reputed wealth, but winning golden opinions from those who came to criticize, of whom, of course, there were a few, the company being composed of human beings.

When the dance began, Wain extended his large, soft hand to Mary B., yellow, buxom, thirty, with white and even teeth, glistening behind her full red lips. A younger sister of Mary B's was paired with Billy Oxendine, a funny little tailor, a great gossiper, and therefore a favorite among the women. Mis' Molly graciously consented, after many protestations of lack of skill and want of practice to stand up opposite Henry Pettifoot, Mary B's husband, a tall man with a slight stoop, a bald crown and full dreamy eyes—a man of much imagination and a large fund of anecdotes. Two other couples completed the set; others were restrained by bashfulness or religious scruples, which did not yield until later in the evening.

The perfumed air from the garden without and the cut roses within, mingled incongruously with the alien odors of musk and hair oil, of which several young barbers in the company were especially redolent. There was a play of sparkling eyes and dancing feet. Mary B. danced with the danguorous grace of an Eastern odalisque, Mis' Molly with the mincing, hesitating step of one long out of practice. Wain performed salutatory prodigies. This was a golden opportunity for the display in which his soul found delight. He introduced variations hitherto unknown to the dance. His skill and suppleness brought a glow of admiration into the eyes of the women, and spread a cloud of jealousy over the faces of several of the younger men, who saw themselves eclipsed.

Rena had announced in advance her intention to take no active part in the festivities. "I don't feel like dancing, Mama—I shall never dance again."

"Well, now, Rena," her mother argued, "ob cose you're too dignified, sence you been sociatin' wid white folks, to be hoppin' 'roun' an' kickin' up lak Ma'y B. an' these other yaller gals; but of co'se, too, you can't slight the comp'ny entirely, even ef it ain' exactly ouh party—you'll have to pay 'em some little attention, 'specially Mr. Wain, sence you're goin' down yonder with him."

Rena did what, conscientiously, she though politeness required. She went the round of the guests in the early part of the evening and exchanged greetings with them. To several requests for dances she replied that she was not dancing. She did not hold herself aloof because of pride; any instinctive shrinking she might have felt by reason of her recent association with persons of greater refinement was offset by her still more newly awakened zeal for humanity; they were her people; she must not despise them. But the occasion suggested painful memories of other and different scenes in which she had lately participated. Once or twice these memories were so vivid as almost to overpower her. She slipped away from the company and kept in the background as much as possible without seeming to slight any one.

The guests as well were dimly conscious of a slight barrier between Mis' Molly's daughter and themselves. The time she had spent apart from these friends of her youth had rendered it impossible for her ever to meet them again on the plane of common interests and common thoughts. It was much as though one, having acquired the vernacular of his native country, had lived in a foreign land long enough to lose the language of his childhood without acquiring that, fully, of his adopted country. Miss Rowena Walden could never again become the Rena Northcross who had left the house behind the cedars no more than a year and a half before. Upon this very difference were based her noble aspirations for usefulness—one must stoop in order that one may lift others. Any other young woman present would have been importuned beyond her powers of resistance. Rena's reserve was respected.

When supper was announced, somewhat early in the evening, the dancers found seats in the hall or on the piazza. Aunt Zilphy, assisted by Mis' Molly and Mary B., passed around the refreshments, which consisted of fried chicken, buttered biscuit, pound-cake and egg-nog. When the first edge of appetite was taken off, the conversation waxed animatedly. Homer Pettifoot related, with minute detail, an old, thread-bare hunting lie, dating, in slightly different forms, from the age of Nimrod, about finding twenty-five partridges sitting in a row on a rail, and killing them all with a single buckshot, which passed through twenty-four and lodged in the body of the twenty-fifth, from which it was extracted and returned to the shot pouch for future service.

This story was followed by a murmur of incredulity—of course, the thing was possible, but Homer's faculty for exaggeration was so well known that any statement of his was viewed with suspicion. Homer seemed hurt at this lack of faith, and was disposed to argue the point; but the sonorous voice of Mr. Wain on the other side of the room cut short his protestations, in much the same way that the rising sun extinguishes the light of lesser luminaries.

"I wuz a member of de fus' legislachu after de wah," Wain was saying. "When I wuz up fum' Sampson in de fall, I had to pass th'ough Smithfiel'. I got in town in the aftuhnoon, and put up at de bes' hotel. De lan'l'od didn't hab no 'spicion' but what I wuz a white man, and he gimme a room, an' I had suppuh an' breakfus', and went on tu Rolly nex' mawnin'. When de session wuz ovuh, I come along back, and when I got tu Smithfiel' I drive up to de same hotel. I noticed, as soon as ah got dare, dat de place had run down conside'able—dare wuz weeds growin' in de ya'd, de winduhs wuz doity, an' eve'thing 'roun' dare looked kinda lonesome and shiftless. De lan'lo'd met me at de do'; he looked mighty down in de mouth, an sezee:—

"Looka heah, w'at made you come and stop at mah place widout tellin' me you wuz a black man? Befo' you come th'ough dis town I had a fus' class bizness. But when fo'kes found out dat a nigger had put up heah, business drapped rat off, and I've had tu shet up mah hotel. You oughta be 'shamed of yo'se'f fo' ruinin' a po' man w'at hadn't never done no ha'm tu you. You've done a mean, low-lived thing, an' a jes' God'll punish you fo' hit.

"De po' man ascually bust intu teahs," Mr. Wain continued maganmously. "An' ah felt so sorry fo' him—he wuz a po' white man tryin' tu get up in de worl'—dat I hauled out mah pu'se an' gin' him ten dollars, an' he peahed monstrous glad to git hit."

"How good hearted! How kin'!" the ladies murmured. "Hit musta done credit to yo' feelin's."

"Don't b'lieve a word ob dem lies," one young man muttered to another, sarcastically. "He couldn't pass for white, onless it wuz a mighty da'k night."

"Ef he stopped in a white hotel anywhere in No'th Ca'lina, he slipped in and hid in a closet while the clerk wuz out," the other said which brought a laugh from both.

Upon this glorious evening of his life, Mr. Wain had one distinctly hostile critic, of whose presence he was blissfully unconscious. Frank Fowler had not been invited to the party—his family did not belong with Mary B's set. Rena had suggested to her mother that he be invited, but Mis' Molly had demurred on the ground that it was not her party, but Mary B's, and that she had no right to issue invitations. It is quite likely that she would have sought an invitation from Mary B., but, as we have previously explained, Frank was dark, that fact would not harmonize with the rest of the company, who would not have Mis' Molly's reasons for treating him well. The fact is, Frank had never been invited to attend a party conceived for light Negroes only, so was not disappointed, for he did not or had not expected to be invited. He knew that Rena would have invited him, but she had explained that they had simply let Mary B. hold the party at their house because hers was too small; and to make Frank feel better about it, Rena informed him that other than greeting the guests, she would take no part in the festivities. Upon leaving Frank then, Rena had smiled much like she used to, and when their hands happened to touch as he was turning to go, she caught his and squeezed it fondly, which was the first time she had in any way, relaxed into the old way.

Mis' Molly, in the meanwhile, conscious of Frank's great kindness, had given him fried chicken, cake and wine when he chanced to pass shortly before the party started, and asked him to come back, sit with her, and enjoy hearing Uncle Needham play that night. Frank was not without an honest pride. He was sensitive enough, too, not to care to go where he was not wanted. He would have curtly refused any such maimed invitation to any other place. But had not Rena explained, and squeezed his hand and looked into his eyes kindly, which was the only way she used to know how to look at him? He had long since decided to be patient with her. Conditions changed; if he began getting angry with all the yellow Negroes in Fayetteville, who thought simply because their skin was bright, that they were better than he, he would be a very unhappy man. So he had become philosophical a long time ago, and saved himself many a heartache.

But he was alone, as far as his family was concerned, in this matter of philosophy, his father, especially. He knew by heart and could recite without much effort, exactly what his father would say if he knew that his son planned to "drop in on the party." "You're a big fool, boy! To be ever seen around those yellow Negroes; hangin' round their back door. Just as if they were white people. I'd see them dead and in hell first!"

Frank resisted the invitation for quite awhile, in spite of Rena's personal encouragement for him to come, but at length he went around to the small porch which was rarely used. As he came up, Rena stepped forth to meet him and his heart was happy. There was a settee just large enough for two and as she sat down she patted the seat beside her for him to sit there, and he did.

Before Rena came up and while Frank stood outside looking at the dancers and the party in general, his eyes fell upon Jeff Wain. He did not know him, and had never seen him before, but having heard that he had come to Fayetteville to get a teacher, he studied Wain unseen. The longer he looked at Wain, the less he liked him; the less he trusted him. To his fancy, Wain's style and apparent skill were affectation, his good-nature mere hypocrisy, and his frequent glances at Rena, that of a sly hawk upon it prey or quarry.

He had heard that Wain was unmarried, and he could not see how, this being so, he could help wishing Rena for a wife. Frank had resigned himself to the possibility when she went to Charleston with her brother, of her probably marrying a white man—who would have raised her to a plane worthy of her merits. In Wain's shifty eye, however, he read the liar—his wealth and standing were probably as false as his seeming good humor. He doubted Rena's falling for such a man, but he was chagrined to see Mis' Molly, prodded on by Mary B., to be completely sold, apparently on this pompous looking creature.

"Nice party. I should think you would be dancing," he suggested to Rena as they sat there side by side.

"No, Frank, I don't feel like it. I don't plan to dance any tonight."

This answer was pleasing to Frank. If he could not hope to dance with her, and he didn't plan to upset the party by doing so, at least this snake in the grass from down the country, should not have that privilege.

"Won't you have some supper, Frank," Rena suggested, starting to rise. "I'll go get it for you myself."

He pulled her back into the seat.

"No, Rena, I don't care for anything. I didn't come over to eat; but I do like Uncle Needham's playing."

"Do you like it?"

"He's an artist; one of the best fiddlers, if he could be judged, in all North Carolina. His playing seems to—get under your skin."

"Makes you feel things, Frank." As she said this, she slid her hand into his and her fingers closed around his. Both sighed, inaudibly. Rena was beginning to come back into her own; into the way she used to be.

At this point he saw Mis' Molly going through the parlor, as if looking for some one. He knew that it must be Rena, and he knew she would not like to see them sitting there together, feeling as he did at least, so rising easily to his feet, with Rena protesting lowly, he stepped outside and into the shadows, paused and turned back just long enough to catch Rena's soft eyes, looking at him tenderly, then turning, he slipped away into the night.

Mis' Molly spied Rena as she turned back toward the parlor, and quickening her step, caught up with her daughter and laying a hand on her, "Rena," she said. "Mr. Wain wants to know if you won't dance one dance with him, just one, please."

Mary B. came up before Rena could answer, and joined the plea.

"Yas, Rena," Mary B. said, taking her hand and caressing it. "Jest one, darlint. I don't think you're treatin' my company jes' right, ef you don't."

"You're goin' all the way to Sampson County with him alone," her mother interjected, "An' it'd be just as well to be on friendly terms with him."

Wain himself had followed the women. "Sholy, Miss Rena, youah gwine to honah me wid one dance? I'd go away fum dis pahty sad at hea't ef I had'nt stood up oncet wid de young lady ob de house."

As Rena, weakly persuaded, placed her hand on Wain's arm and entered the house, a buggy came up Front Street, concealed by the intervening cedars until it reached a point from which the occupant could view, through the open front window, the interior of the parlor.

Chapter Thirty Nine

MOVED BY TENDERNESS and thoughts of self-sacrifice, which had occupied his mind to the momentary exclusion of all else, Tryon had scarcely noticed, as he approached the house behind the cedars, a string of lively music, to which was added, as he drew still nearer, the accompaniment of other festive sounds. He suddenly awoke, however, to the fact that these signs of merriment came from the house at which he had intended to stop; he had not meant that Rena should pass another night of sleepless sorrow, or that he himself should endure another needless hour of suspense.

He drew rein at the corner. Shocked surprise, a nascent anger, a vague alarm, an insistent curiosity, urged him nearer. Turning the mare into the side street and keeping close to the fence, he drove ahead in the shadow of the cedars until he reached a gap through which he could see into the open door of the brightly lighted hall.

There was evidently a ball in progress. The fiddle was squeaking merrily to a tune that he remembered well—it was associated with one of the most delightful evenings of his life, that of the Tournament ball, where he had met Rena. A mellow Negro voice was calling with a rhythmic accompaniment, the figures of a quadrille. Tryon, with parted lips and slowly hardening heart, leaned forward from the buggy-seat, gripping the rein so tightly that his nails cut into the opposing palm. Above the clatter of noisy conversation rose the fiddler's voice:—

"Swing yo' pa'dnuhs; don't be shy,
Look yo' lady in de eye!
Th'ow yo' ahms aroun' heh wais';
Take yo' time—dey ain' no has'e!"

To the middle of the floor, in full view through an open window, the woman advanced who all day long had been the burden of his thoughts—not pale with grief and hollow-eyed with weeping, but flushed with pleasure, while around her waist the arm of a burly, grinning mulatto, whose fat, foul face, was offensively familiar to Tryon.

With a muttered curse of concentrated bitterness, Tryon struck the mare a sharp blow with the whip. The sensitive creature, spirited in her great weariness, resented the lash and started off with the bit in her teeth. Perceiving that it would be difficult to turn in the narrow roadway without running into the ditch at the left, Tryon gave the mare rein and dashed down the street, scarcely missing, as the buggy crossed the bridge, a man standing abstractedly by the old canal, who sprang aside barely in time to avoid being run over.

Meanwhile Rena was passing through a trying ordeal. After the first few bars, the fiddler plunged into a well-known air, in which Rena, keenly susceptible to musical impressions, recognized the tune to which, as Queen of Love and Beauty, she had opened the dance at her entrance into the world of life and love, for it was there that she met George Tryon. The combination of music and movement brought up the scene with great distinction. Tryon, peering angrily through the cedars had not been more conscious than she of the external contrast between her partners on this and the former occasion. She perceived, too, as Tryon from the outside had not, the difference between Wain's wordy flattery (only saved by his cousin's warning from pointed and fulsome adulation), and the tenderly graceful compliments, couched in the romantic terms of chivalry, with which the night of the handkerchief had charmed her ear. It was only by an immense effort that she was able to keep her emotions under control until the end of the dance, when she fled to her chamber and burst into tears. It was not the cruel Tryon who had blasted her love with his deadly look that she mourned, but the gallant young knight who had worn her favor on his lance and crowned her queen of Love and Beauty.

Tryon's stay in Fayetteville was very brief. He drove to the hotel and put up for the night. During many sleepless hours his mind was in a turmoil with a very different set of thoughts from those which had occupied it on the way to town. Not the least of them was a profound self-contempt for his own lack of foresight. How had he been so blind as not to have read the character of this wretched girl who had bewitched him? Tonight his eyes had been opened—he had seen her with the mask thrown off, a true daughter of a race in which the sensuous enjoyment of the moment took precedence over taste, or sentiment, or any of the higher emotions. Her few months of boarding-school, her brief association with white people, had evidently been a mere veneer over the under-lying Negro, and their effects had slipped away as soon as the intercourse had ceased. With the monkey-like imitativeness of the Negro, she had copied the manners of white people while she lived among them, and had dropped them with equal facility when they ceased to serve a purpose. Who but a Negro, he conceived, could have recovered so soon from what had seemed a terrible bereavement?—She herself must have felt it at the time, for otherwise she would not have swooned. A woman of sensibility as this one seemed to have been, should naturally feel more keenly, and for a longer time than a man, an injury to the affections; but he, a son of the ruling race, had been miserable for six weeks about a girl who had so far forgotten as already to plunge headlong into the childish amusements of her own ignorant and degraded people. What more, indeed, he asked himself savagely—what more could be expected of the base-born of the plaything of a gentleman's idle hour, who to this ignoble origin added the blood of a servile race? And he, George Tryon had honored her with his love; he had very nearly linked his fate and joined his blood to hers by the solemn sanctions of church and State. Tryon was not a devout man, but he thanked God with religious fervor that he had been saved a second time from a mistake which would have wrecked his whole future. If he had yielded to the momentary weakness of the past night—the outcome of a sickly sentimentality to which he recognized now, in the light of reflection, that he was entirely too prone—he would have regretted it soon enough. The black streak would have been sure to come out in some form, sooner or later, if not in the wife, then in her children. He saw clearly enough in this hour of revulsion, that with his temperament and training, such a union could never have been happy. If all the world had been ignorant of the dark secret, it would always have been in his own thoughts, or at least never far away. Each fault of hers that the close daily association of husband and wife might reveal—the most flawless of sweethearts do not pass scatheless through the long test of matrimony—every wayward impulse of his children, every defect of mind, morals, temper, or health, would have been ascribed to the dark ancestral strain. Happiness under such conditions would have been impossible.

When Tryon lay awake in the early morning, after a few brief hours of sleep, the business which had brought him to Fayetteville seemed, in the cold light of reason, so ridiculously inadequate that he felt almost ashamed to have set up such a pretext for his journey. The prospect, too, of meeting Dr. Green and his family, of having to explain his former sudden departure, and of running a gauntlet of inquiry concerning his marriage to the aristocratic Miss Walden, of South Carolina; the fear that some one at Fayetteville might have suspected a connection between Rena's swoon and his own flight, these considerations so moved this impressionable young man that he called a bell-boy, demanded an early breakfast, ordered his horse, paid his reckoning, and started upon his homeward journey forthwith. A certain distrust of his own sensibility, which he felt to be curiously inconsistent with his most positive convictions, led him to seek the river bridge by a roundabout route, which did not take him past the house, where, a few hours before, he had seen the last fragment of his idol shattered beyond the hope of repair.

The party broke up at an early hour, since most of the guests were working people, and the travelers were to make an early start next day. About nine in the morning, Wain drove around to Mis' Molly's. Rena's trunk was strapped behind the buggy, and she set out, in the company of Wain, for her new field of labor.

"Oh, Mother," she whispered, as they stood wrapped in a close embrace, "I'm afraid to leave you. I left you once and it turned out so miserably."

"It'll turn out better this time, Honey," her mother replied soothingly. "Goodby, child. Take care of yo'se'f an yo' money, and write to yore mammy."

One kiss all around and Rena was lifted into the buggy. Wain seized the reins and under his skillful touch, the pretty mare began to prance and curvet with restrained impatience. Wain could not resist the opportunity to show off before the party, which included Mary B's entire family, and several other neighbors, who had gathered to see the travelers off.

"Good-by to Fayetteville! Good-by, folkses all!" he cried, with a wave of his disengaged hand.

"Good-by, Mother! Good-by, all!" Rena cried as with tears in her heart, and a brave smile on her face she left her home behind her for the second time.

When they had crossed the river bridge, the travelers came to a long stretch of rising ground, from the summit of which they could look back over the white sandy road for nearly a mile. Neither Rena nor her companion saw Frank Fowler behind the Chinquapin bush at the foot of the hill, nor the gaze of mute love and longing with which he watched the buggy mount the long incline. He had not been able to trust himself to bid her farewell. He had seen her go away once before with every prospect of happiness, and come back, a dove with a wounded wing, to the old nest behind the cedars. She was going away again, with a man whom he disliked and distrusted. If she had met misfortune before, what were her prospects for happiness now?

The buggy paused at the top of the hill, and Frank, shading his eyes with his hand, thought he could see her turn and look behind. "Look back, dear child, towards your home and those who love you," he whispered to himself with a deep sigh. For who knows more than this faithful worshiper what threads of the past Fate is weaving into your future, or whether happiness or misery lies before you?

Chapter Forty

THE ROAD TO Sampson County lay for the most part over the pine-clad sandhills; an alternation of general rises and gradual descents, with now and then a swamp of greater or less extent. Long stretches of the highway led through the virgin forest, for miles unbroken by a clearing or sign of human habitation.

They traveled slowly with frequent pauses in shady places, for the weather was hot. The journey made leisurely, required more than a day and might with slight effort be prolonged into two. They stopped for the night at a small village, where Wain found lodging for Rena with an acquaintance of his, and for himself with another, while a third took charge of the horse, the accommodations for travelers being limited. Rena's appearance and manners were the subject of much comment. It was necessary to explain to several curious white people that Rena was a woman of color. A white woman might have driven with Wain without attracting remark—most white ladies had Negro coachmen. That a woman of Rena's complexion should eat at a Negro table, or sleep beneath a Negro roof, was a seeming breach of caste which only black blood could excuse. The explanation was never questioned. No white person of sound mind would ever claim to be a Negro.

They resumed their journey somewhat late in the morning. Rena would willingly have hastened, for she was anxious to plunge into her new work; but Wain seemed disposed to prolong the pleasant drive, and beguiled the way, for a time, with stories of wonderful things he had done and strange experiences of a somewhat checkered career. He was shrewd enough to avoid any subject which would offend a modest young woman, but too obtuse to perceive that much of what he said would not commend him to a person of refinement. He made little reference to his possessions, concerning which so much had been said at Fayetteville; and his reticence was a point in his favor. If he had not been so much on his guard, and Rena so much absorbed by thoughts of her future work, such a drive would have furnished a person of her discernment a very fair measure of the man's character. To these distractions must be added the entire absence of any idea that Wain might have amorous designs on her; and any shortcomings of manners, or speech were covered by the broad mantle of charity which Rena in her new found zeal for the welfare of her people was willing to throw over all their faults. They were the victims of oppression; they were not responsible for its results.

Toward the end of the second day, while nearing their destination, the travelers passed a large white house standing back from the road at the foot of a lane. Around it grew wide spreading trees and well-kept shrubbery. The fences were in good repair. Behind the house and across the road stretched extensive fields of cotton and waving corn. They had passed no other place that showed such signs of thrift and prosperity.

"Oh, what a lovely place," Rena exclaimed, enthusiastically, pointing at it. "That is yours, isn't it?"

"No, we ain't got to my home yit," he answered. "Dat house belongs to der richest people 'round heah. Dat house is ober in de nex' county. We're right close to de line now."

Shortly after they turned off from the main highway they had been pursuing and struck into a narrower road to the left.

"De main road," Wain explained, "goes on to Clinton, 'bout five miles ah mo' away. Dis one we're turnin' into now will take us to my place, which is 'bout three miles further on. We'll git dare now in an houh ah so."

Wain lived in an old plantation house, somewhat dilapidated, and surrounded by an air of neglect, and shiftlessness, but still preserving a remnant of dignity in its outlines and comfort in its interior arrangements. It had belonged to a wealthy and successful planter, who had gone off to war and been killed.

Rena was assigned a large room on the second floor. She was somewhat surprised at the makeup of the household. Wain's mother, an old woman, much darker than her son, kept house for him. A sister with two children lived in the house. The element of surprise lay in the presence of two small children left by Wain's wife, of whom Rena now heard for the first time. He had lost his wife, he informed Rena sadly, a couple of years before.

"Yas, Miss Rena," he sighed, "de Lawd give her, and de Lawd tuck her away. Blessed be de name ob de Lawd." He accompanied this sententious quotation with a wicked look from under his half-closed eyelids that Rena did not see.

The following morning Wain drove her in his buggy over to the county town, where she took the teacher's examination. She was given a seat in a room with a number of other candidates for certificates, but the fact, leaking out from some remark of Wain's that she was a colored girl, objections were quietly made by several of the would-be-teachers to her presence in the room, and she was requested to retire until the white teachers should have been examined. An hour or two later she was given a separate examination, which she passed without difficulty. The examiner, a gentleman of local standing, was dimly conscious that she might not have found her exclusion pleasant, and was especially polite. It would have been strange, indeed, if he had not been impressed by her sweet face and air of modest dignity, which were all the more striking because of her social disability. He fell into conversation with her, became interested in her hopes and aims, and very cordially offered to be of service, if at any time he might, in connection with her school.

"You have the satisfaction," he said, "of receiving the only first-grade certificate issued today. You might teach a higher-grade of pupils than you will find at Sandy Run, but let us hope that you may in time raise them to your own level."

"Which I doubt very much," he muttered to himself as she went away with Wain. "What a pity," he said, watching her out of sight and shaking his head sadly, "that such a beautiful and such an intelligent woman, should be a nigger! If she were anything to me, though, I should hate to trust her anywhere near that saddle-colored scoundrel. He's a thoroughly bad lot, and will bear close watching."

Rena, however, was serenely ignorant of any danger from the accommodating Wain. Absorbed in her own thoughts and plans, she had not sought to look beneath the surface of his somewhat overdone politeness. In a few days she began her work as a teacher, and sought to forget, in the service of others, the dull sorrow that gnawed at her heart.

While she busied herself with enthusiasm to her new found work, she was entirely unconscious of the fact that Jeff Wain was planning also, and secretly, the most practical and quickest way to a courtship with her, with a possible view to ultimate matrimony. She was also unconscious of the fact that almost in sight of the small schoolhouse wherein she was teaching, had the trees been cleared away, reposed the great mansion where she would have now been living, and as mistress, had her masquerade not been revealed, and the fact that she was not a white girl, found out by George W. Tryon.

Chapter Forty One

BLANCHE LEARY, CLOSELY observant of Tryon's moods, marked a decided change in his manner after his return from his trip to Fayetteville. His former moroseness had given way to a certain defiant lightness, broken now and then by an involuntary sigh, but maintained so well, on the whole, that his mother detected no lapses whatever.

The change was characterized by another feature agreeable to both the women: Tryon showed decidely more interest than ever before in Miss Leary's society. Within a week he asked her several times to play a selection on the piano, displaying, as she noticed, a decided preference for gay and cheerful music, and several times suggested a change when she chose pieces of a sentimental tone. More than once, during the second week after his return, he went out riding with her; she was a graceful horsewoman, perfectly at home in the saddle, and appearing to advantage in a riding habit. She was aware that Tryon watched her now and then, with an eye rather critical than indulgent.

"He is comparing me with some other girl," she surmised. "I seem to stand the test very well. I wonder who the other is, and what was the trouble?"

Miss Leary exerted all her powers to interest and amuse the man she had set out to win, and who seemed nearer than ever before. Tryon, to his pleased surprise, discovered in her mind depths that he had never suspected. She displayed a singular affinity for the tastes that were his. He could not, of course, know how carefully she had studied them. The old wound, recently reopened, seemed to be healing rapidly, under conditions more conducive than before to perfect recovery. No longer, indeed, was he pursued by the picture of Rena discovered and unmasked—this he had definitely banished from the realm of sentiment to that of reason. The haunting image of Rena loving and beloved, among the harmonious surroundings of her brother's home, was not so readily displaced. Nevertheless, he reached, in several weeks, a point from which he could consider her as one thinks of a dear one removed by the hand of death, or smitten by some incurable ailment of mind or body. Erelong, he fondly believed, the recovery would be so far complete that he could consign to the tomb of pleasant memories even the most thrilling episodes of his ill-starred courtship.

"George," Mrs. Tryon said one morning while her son was in his cheerful mood, "I'm sending Blanche over to Major McLeod's to do an errand for me. Would you mind driving her over? The road may be rough after the storm last night, and Blanche has an idea that no one drives so well as you."

"Why, yes, Mother, I'll be glad to drive Blanche over. I want to see the major myself."

They were soon bowling along between the pines, behind the handsome mare that had carried Tryon so well at the Charleston Tournament. Presently he drew up sharply.

"A tree has fallen squarely across the road," he exclaimed. "We shall have to turn back a little way and go around."

They drove back a quarter of a mile and turned into a byroad leading to the right through the woods. The solemn silence of the pine forest is soothing or oppressive, according to one's mood. Beneath the cool arcade of the tall, overarching trees a deep peace stole over Tryon's heart. He had put aside indefinitely and forever an unhappy and impossible love. The pretty and affectionate girl beside him would make an ideal wife. Of her family and blood he was sure. She was his mother's choice, and his mother had set her heart upon their marriage. Why not speak to her now? And thus give himself the best possible protection against stray flames of love?

"Blanche," he said, looking at her kindly.

"Yes, George?" Her voice was very gentle, and slightly tremulous. Could she have divined his thoughts? Love is a great clairvoyant.

"Blanche, dear, I—"

A clatter of voices broke upon the stillness of the forest and interrupted Tryon's speech. A sudden turn to the left brought the buggy to a little clearing in the midst of which stood a small, log school house. Out of the school house a swarm of colored children were emerging, the suppressed energy of the school hour finding vent in vocal exercises of various sorts. A group had already formed a ring, and were singing with great volume and vigor:—

> "Miss Jane she loves sugar and tea,
> Miss Jane, she loves candy.
> Miss Jane she can whirl all around
> And kiss her love quite handy.

"De oak grows tall,
De pine grows slim,
So rise you up, my true love
An' let me come in."

"What a funny little darky," Miss Leary exclaimed, pointing to a diminutive lad, who was walking on his hands, with his feet balanced in the air. At sight of the buggy and its occupants this able acrobat, still retaining his inverted position, moved towards the newcomers, and, reversing himself with a sudden spring, brought himself up standing beside the buggy.

"Hoddy, Mar's George!" he exclaimed, grinning all over and removing his cap, showing a row of pretty white teeth as he did so.

"Hello, Plato," the young man replied. "What are you doing here?"

"Gwine tu school, Mar's Geo'ge," Plato replied, moving back and forth as if embarrassed in the lady's company. "Larnin' how tu read and write, suh, lak de white fo'kes."

At this point a larger boy and a mulatto drew up beside Plato, scowled up at Tryon, who did not notice him, and, then in an undertone: "W'at you callin' dat man marster fuh? You don't belong tu him no mo; you're free an' ain't got sense e'nough tu know hit."

Tryon threw a small coin to Plato, and holding another in his hand suggestively, smiled toward the tall yellow boy, who looked regretfully at the coin, but stood his ground; he would call no man master, not even for a piece of money.

During this little colloquy, Miss Leary had kept her face turned toward the schoolhouse. At this moment Rena, bareheaded, stepped outside and looked at the children playing. Miss Leary started, opened her lips and, pointing to Rena, cried:

"Oh, what a pretty girl!" she exclaimed. "There," she added, as Tryon turned his head toward her, "you are too late. She has retired into her castle."

With a little sigh of disappointment, she turned to look at Plato, a suggestion in her eyes.

"Oh, Plato?" she asked.

"Yas, Misses?" Plato replied, prancing around the buggy in great glee, on the strength of his acquaintance with the white folks.

"Is your teacher white?"

"No, ma'am, she ain't white; she's black. She looks lak she's white, but she ain't."

Tryon had not seen the teacher's face, but the incident had jarred the old wound; Miss Leary's description of the teacher, together with Plato's characterization, had stirred lightly sleeping memories. He was more or less abstracted during the remainder of the drive, and did not recur to the conversation that had been interrupted by coming upon the schoolhouse.

The teacher, glancing for a moment through the open door of the schoolhouse, had seen a handsome young lady staring at her. Miss Leary had a curiously intent look when she was interested in anything, with no intention whatever of being rude. Beyond the lady, Rena saw the back and shoulder of a man, whose face was turned the other way. There was a vague suggestion of something familiar about the equipage, but Rena shrank from this close scrutiny and withdrew out of sight before she had an opportunity to identify the vague resemblance to something she had known.

Miss Leary had missed by a hairs-breadth the psychological moment, and felt some resentment toward the little Negroes who had interrupted her lover's train of thought. Negroes have caused a great deal of trouble among white people. How deeply the shadow of the Ethiopian had fallen upon her own happiness, Miss Leary of course could not guess.

Chapter Forty Two

A FEW DAYS LATER Rena looked out of the window near her desk and saw a long basket phaeton, drawn by a sorrell pony, driven sharply into the clearing and draw up beside an oak sapling. The occupant of the phaeton, a tall, handsome, well preserved lady in middle life, with slightly gray hair, alighted briskly from the phaeton, tied the pony to the sapling with a hitching strap, and advanced to the schoolhouse door.

Rena wondered who the lady might be. She had a benevolent aspect, however, and came forward to the desk with a smile, not at all embarrassed by the wide-eyed inspection of the entire school.

"How do you do," she said, extending her hand to the teacher. "I live in the neighborhood and am interested in the colored people—a good many of them once belonged to me. I heard of your school, and thought I should like to make your acquaintance."

"It is very kind of you, indeed," murmured Rena respectfully.

"Yes," the lady continued, "I am not one of those who sit back and blame their former slaves because they were freed. They are free now—it is all decided and settled—and they should be taught at least enough to enable them to make good use of their freedom. But really, my dear—you mustn't feel offended if I make a mistake. I am going to ask you something very personal." She turned and looked suggestively at the gaping pupils.

"The school may take the morning recess now," the teacher announced. The children filed out in an orderly manner, most of them stationing themselves about the grounds in such places as would keep the teacher and the white lady in view. Very few white persons approved of the colored schools; no other white person had ever visited this one.

"Are you really colored?" the lady turned to her to ask, after the last child had left the room.

A year and a half earlier, Rena would have met the question by some display of self-consciousness. Now, she replied simply and directly.

"Yes, ma'am, I am colored."

"Well, it's a shame. No one would ever think it. If you chose to conceal it, no one would be the wiser. What is your name, child, and where were you brought up? You must have a romantic history."

Rena gave her name and a few facts in regards to her past. The lady was so much interested, and put forth so many and such searching questions, that Rena found it more difficult to suppress the fact that she had been white, than she had formerly had in hiding her African origin. There was about the girl an air of real refinement that pleased the lady; the refinement not merely of a fine nature, but of contact with cultured people; a certain reserve of speech and manner quite inconsistent with Mrs. Tryon's experiences with colored women. The lady was interested and slightly mystified. A generous, impulsive spirit —her son's own mother—she made minute inquiries about the school and the pupils, several of whom she knew by name. Rena stated that the two months term was nearing its end, and that she was training the children in various declamations and dialogues for the exhibition at the close.

"I shall attend it," the lady declared positively. "I'm sure you are doing a good work, and it's very noble of you to undertake it when you might have had a very different future. If I can serve you at any time, don't hesitate to call on me. I live in the big white house just before you turn out of the Clinton Road to come this way. I'm only a widow, but my son, George, lives with me and has some influence in the neighborhood. He drove by here yesterday with the lady he's going to marry. It was she who told me about you."

Was it the name, or some subtle resemblance in speech or feature, that recalled Tryon's image to Rena's mind? It was not so far away—the image of the loving Tryon—that any powerful witchcraft was required to call it up. His mother was a widow; Rena had thought, in happier days, that she might be such a kind lady as this. But the cruel Tryon who had left her—she pictured that his mother would be some hard, cold, proud woman, who would regard a Negro as but little better than a dog, and who would not soil her lips by addressing a colored person upon any other terms than as a servant. She knew, too, that Tryon did not live in Sampson County, thought the exact location of his house was not clear to her.

"And where are you staying, my dear?" the good lady asked.

"I'm boarding at Mrs. Wain's," Rena answered.

"Mrs. Wain's?"

"Yes, they live in the old Campbell place."

"Oh, yes—Aunt Nancy. She's a good enough woman, but we don't think much of her son, Jeff. He married my Amanda after the war—she used to belong to me—and ought to have known better. He abused her most shamefully and had to be threatened with the law. She left him a year or so ago and went away; I haven't seen her lately. Well, good-by, my child; I'm coming to your exhibition. If you ever pass my house, come in and see me."

The good lady had talked for half an hour, and had brought a ray of sunshine into the teacher's monotonous life, heretofore lighted by only the uncertain lamp of high resolve. She had satisfied a pardonable curiosity, and had gone away without mentioning her name.

Rena saw Plato untying the pony as the lady climbed into the phaeton. When she had driven away and was out of sight, Rena called Plato to her.

"Who was the lady, Plato?" she asked the boy, who had crossed quickly to her when she beckoned to him.

"Dat was mah ole mist'iss, ma'am," Plato returned, proudly. "Ole Mis' Liza."

"Mis' Liza who?"

"Mis' Liza Tryon. I use tu belong to heh. Dat wuz her son, my young Marse Geo'ge, w'at drive pas' hyuh yistidy wid 'is sweetheart."

At dinner at the Tryon's great house a few hours later, Mrs. Tryon after she was seated, turned to smile into the faces of her son and Blanche Leary, who was curious to hear about her visit.

"Well," Mrs. Tryon began, pleasantly, "I called on the girl you were so excited about yesterday, dear Blanche."

Leaning forward anxiously.

"Oh, you did, Mother? I'm so glad. And, how did you find her?"

"Just like you said—the most beautiful creature, I think, that I ever looked at, and just about the nicest; the most congenial."

"Oh, really!" Blanche exclaimed, enthusiastically. "I wish I could have been with you. Did she tell you her name?"

"She did, for I not only asked her that, but no end of other questions, I was that interested. Well, her name is Rowena Northcross." She paused briefly but neither was looking at George, or they could not have missed seeing that he started up, almost violently. He listened then, controlling his breathing and excitement with an effort.

"And she's really a colored girl?" from Blanche.

"The most amazing thing! She admitted it freely, too."

"That was very sweet of her, I think," Blanche said.

"That is what I thought, also," continued Mrs. Tryon. "She didn't seem to be uppish in the least, just a nice, lovely and sweet girl that no one could help but like. To be frank with you, I fell in love with her myself, and, if she hadn't admitted being colored, I would have invited her here to be my guest some week end. As it is, I asked her if she ever happened to pass by, to stop in and see me—and if she does, I plan to be nice to her, and I want you and George to be the same way—a perfect lady, even if she has to be a colored person."

"I'll be glad to be nice to her, Mrs. Tryon," Blanche said,

quickly. "I do hope she comes by, too, for I am curious to talk to her myself."

"I promised to come to her exhibition, the last day of school, and I want you, and George too, to go with me."

"Oh, I'll be so glad to, Mother." She turned to George, who was thinking about Rena. In spite of the fact that he had put her out of his heart, and had been trying to get her out of his mind, he was happy to hear what his own mother was saying—that Rena was a lady, all he had felt she was. In those moments he was thinking of her brother, too. He was beginning to see things clearly. He was beginning to understand that it had not been Rena's plan, or perhaps desire even, to go to Charleston and pass for white; to fool people and intrude herself on white people. It had all been her brother's scheme; he could see through it all now, and instead of trying to hate Rena, as he had not been very successful at doing, he should have been hating John for the masquerade. He heard Blanche saying something, and with a start, turned to her with a:

"Did you address me? What were you saying?"

Blanche repeated what she had asked, and he promised to think about it. The servants were serving their meal now, and all fell to eating and said no more about Rena, just then.

Chapter Forty Three

RENA HAD FOUND her task not a difficult one so far as discipline was concerned. Her pupils were of a docile race, and school to them had all the charm of novelty. The teacher commanded some awe because she was a stranger, and some, perhaps, because she was white; for the theory of blackness as propounded by Plato could not quite counterbalance in the young African mind the evidence of his own senses. She combined gentleness with firmness; and if these had not been sufficient, she had reserves of character which would have given her mastery over much less plastic material than these ignorant but eager young people. The work of instruction was simple enough, for most of the pupils began with the alphabet, which they acquired from Webster's blue-back spelling book, the palladium of Southern education at that epoch. The much abused carpet-baggers had put the spelling book within reach of every child of school age in North Carolina, a fact which is often overlooked when the carpet-baggers are held up to odium. Even the devil should have his due, and is not so black as he is painted. At the time that she learned that Tryon lived in the neighborhood, Rena had already been subjected to a trying ordeal. Wain had begun to persecute her with marked attentions. She had at first gone to board at his house, or, by courtesy, with his mother. For a week or two she had considered his attentions in no other light than those of a member of the school committee sharing her own zeal and being interested in seeing the school successfully carried on. In this character Wain had driven her to the town for her examination; he had busied himself about putting the schoolhouse in order, and in various matters, affecting the conduct of the school. He had jocularly offered to come and whip the children for her, and had found it convenient to drop in occasionally, ostensibly to see what progress she was making.

"Dese chillun," he would observe sonorously, in the presence of the school, "ought to be monst'ous glad tu have de chance ob settin' unduh yo' instruction, Miss Rena. I'm sho' eve'body in de neighbo'd 'preciates de privilege in habin' you in ouh midst."

Though slightly embarrassing to the teacher, these public demonstrations were endurable so long as they could be regarded as mere official appreciation of her work. Sincerely in earnest about her undertaking, she had plunged into it with all the intensity of a serious nature which love had stirred to activity. A pessimist might have sighed sadly or smiled cynically at the notion that a poor, weak girl, with a dangerous beauty and a sensitive soul, and troubles enough of her own, should hope to accomplish anything toward lifting the black mass, still floundering in the mud where slavery had left them, and where emancipation had found them—the mud in which, for aught that could be seen to the contrary, her little feet, too, were hopelessly entangled. It might have seemed like expecting a man to lift himself by his bootstraps.

But Rena was no philosopher, either sad or cheerful. She could not even have replied to this argument, that races must lift themselves, and the most that can be done by others is to give them opportunity and fairplay. This, the South at that period and for a generation or more afterward, was most unwilling to do. The white man himself had not dipped that deep into philosophical education. While there were a few like Mrs. Tryon, broadminded enough to be able to foresee that ultimately an educated and trained Negro would be in time an asset to the South helping to raise the general standard to a higher plane of thought and action, there were too many who thought the other way and succeeded in holding the whole South back, themselves included.

Rena's was a simpler reasoning; the logic by which the world is kept going onward and upward when philosophers at odds and reformers are not forthcoming. She knew that, for every child she taught to read and write, she opened, if ever so little, the door of opportunity, and she was happy in the consciousness of performing a duty which seemed all the more imperative because newly discovered. Her zeal indeed, for the time being, was like that of an early Christian, who was more willing than not, to die for his faith. Rena had fully and firmly made up her mind to sacrifice her life upon this altar. Her absorption in the work had not been without its reward, for thereby she had been able to keep the spectre of her lost love. Her dreams she could not control, but she banished Tryon as far as possible from her waking thoughts.

When Wain's attentions became obviously personal, Rena's new vestal instincts took alarm, and she began to apprehend his character more clearly. She had long ago learned that his pretensions to wealth were a sham. He was a nominal owner of a large plantation, it is true; but the land was worn out, and mortgaged to the limit of its security value. His reputed droves of cattle and hogs had dwindled to a mere handful of lean and listless brutes.

Her clear eye, when once set to take Wain's measure, soon fathomed his shallow, selfish soul and detected, or at least divined, behind his mask of good-nature a lurking brutality which filled her with vague distrust, needing only occasion to develop it into active apprehension—occasion which was not long wanting. She avoided being alone with him at home by keeping carefully with the women of the house. If she were left alone,—and they soon showed tendencies to leave her, on any pretext, whenever Wain came near—she would seek her own room and lock the door. She preferred not to offend Wain. She was far away from home and in a measure in his power, but she dreaded his compliments and sickened at his smile. She was also compelled to listen to his relations sing his praises.

"My son, Jeff," old Mrs. Wain would say, "is de bes' man you eber seed. His fus' wife had de easies' time an' de happies' time ob ary woman in dis settlement. He grieve' fo' heh a long time, but I reckon' 'es gittin' ovuh hit, an' de nex' 'oman w'at marries 'm 'll git a box ob pyo' gol', ef I does say hit as his own mammy."

Rena had thought Wain rather harsh with his household, except in her immediate presence. His mother and sister seemed more or less afraid of him, and the children often anxious to avoid him.

One day, he timed his visit to the schoolhouse, so as to walk home with Rena through the woods. When she became aware of his purpose, she called to one of the children who was loitering behind the others.

"Wait a minute, Jenny," she called to the child. "I'm going your way and you can walk along with me."

Wain with difficulty hid a scowl behind a smiling front. When they had gone a little distance, along the road through the woods, he clapped his hand upon his pocket.

"I decla' tu goodness," he exclaimed, registering much disappointment and chagrin, "ef I ain' los' my pocket knife! I tho't I felt something slip thu' dat hole in mah pocket jes' by the big pine stump in the schoolhouse ya'd. Jenny, chile, run back and hunt fo' mah knife, an' I'll given you a nickel—ef you fin' hit. Me an' Miss Rena'll walk on slow 'tel you ketches up."

Rena did not dare to object, though she was afraid to be alone with this man. If she could have had a moment to think, she would have volunteered to go back with Jenny and look for the knife, which, although a palpable subterfuge on her part, would have been one to which Wain could not object; but the child, dazzled by prospect of reward, had darted back so quickly that this way of escape was cut off. She was evidently in for a declaration of love, which she had taken infinite pains to avoid. Just the form it would assume, she could not foresee. She was not long left in suspense. No sooner was the child well out of sight than Wain threw his arms suddenly about her and smilingly attempted to kiss her.

Speechless with fear and indignation, she tore herself from his grasp with totally unexpected force, and fled incontinently along the forest path. Wain—who, to do him justice, had merely meant to declare his passion in what he had hoped might prove a not unacceptable fashion—followed in some alarm, expostulating and apologizing as he went. But he was heavy and Rena was light, and fear lent wings to her feet. He followed her until he saw her enter the house of Elder Johnson's, the father of several of her pupils, after which he sneaked uneasily homeward, somewhat apprehensive of the consequences of his abrupt wooing, which was evidently open to an unfavorable construction. When, an hour later, Rena sent one of the Johnson children for some of her things, with a message explaining that the teacher had been invited to spend a few days at Elder Johnson's, Wain felt a pronounced measure of relief. For an hour he had even thought it might be better to relinquish his pursuit. With a fatuousness, born of vanity, however, no sooner had she sent her excuse than he began to look upon her visit to Johnson's as a mere exhibition of coyness, which, together with her conduct in the woods, was merely intended to lure him on.

Right upon the heels of perturbation caused by Wain's conduct, Rena discovered that Tryon lived in the neighborhood; that not only might she meet him any day upon the highway, but that he had actually driven by the schoolhouse. That he knew or would know of her proximity there could be no possible doubt, since she had freely told his mother her name and her home. A hot wave of shame swept over her at the thought that George Tryon might imagine that she were following him, throwing herself in his way, and at the thought of the construction which he might place upon her actions. Caught thus between two emotional fires, at the very time when her school duties, owing to the approaching exhibition, demanded all her energies, Rena was subjected to a physical and mental strain that only youth and health could have resisted, and then only for a short time.

The fault of almost every sensitive and ambitious person, is the burden of imagination, often almost uncurable. When Rena learned that the fine house and plantation that she had admired so much on her way to Sampson County to teach, was the home and property of the Tryon family; and that is was the place George Tryon planned, while he was engaged to marry her, to bring her to live as his wife, her imagination went to work. It continued to burden her, regardless of all her efforts to throw it off in the days that followed. What annoyed her most, was the fear that he would feel that she had taken the school to be near him, in the hope, no doubt, of involving him, perhaps, in a new scheme of her own—and which happened to be the very way he was taking it.

Chapter Forty Four

TRYON'S SECOND FEELING, after his mother at the dinner table gave an account of her visit to the schoolhouse in the woods, was one of extreme annoyance. Why, of all created beings should this particular woman be chosen to teach the colored school at Sandy Run? Had she learned that he lived in the neighborhood, and had she sought the place hoping that he might consent to renew, on different terms, relations which could never be resumed upon their former footing?

Six weeks before, he would not have believed her capable of following him; but his last visit to Fayetteville had revealed her character in such a light that it was difficult to predict what she might do. It was, however, no affair of his. He was done with her; he had dismissed her from his own life, where she had never properly belonged; and he had filled her place, or would soon fill it, with another and worthier woman. Even his mother, a woman of keen discernment and delicate intuitions, had been deceived by this girl's specious exterior. She had brought away from her interview of the morning the impression that Rena was a fine, pure spirit, born out of place, through some freak of Fate, devoting herself with heroic self-sacrifice to a noble cause. Well, he had imagined her just as pure, and fine, and she had deliberately, with a Negro's low cunning, deceived him into believing that she was a white girl. The pretended confession of the brother, in which he had spoken of the humble origin of the family, had been, consciously and unconsciously, the most disingenious feature of the whole miserable performance. They had tried by a show of frankness to satisfy their own consciences. They doubtless have enough of white blood to give them a rudimentary trace of such a moral organ; and by the same act to disarm him against future recriminations, in the event of possible discovery. How was he to imagine that persons of their appearances and pretentions were tainted with Negro blood? The more he dwelt upon the subject, the more angry he became with those who had surprised his virgin heart and deflowered it by such low trickery. The man who brought the first Negro into the British colonies had committed a crime against humanity and a worse crime against his own race. The father of this girl had been guilty of a sin against society for which others—for which he, George Tryon—must pay the penalty. As slaves, Negroes were tolerable. As freeman they were excrescences, an alien element incapable of absorption into the body politic of white men. He would like to send them all back to the Africa from which their fore-fathers had come—unwillingly enough, he would admit, and he would like, especially to banish this girl from his own neighborhood; not indeed that her presence would make any difference to him; except as a humiliating reminder of his own folly and weakness with which he could very well dispense.

Of this state of mind Tryon gave no visible manifestation beyond a certain taciturnity, so much at variance with his recent liveliness that the ladies could not fail to notice it. No effort on the part of either was able to effect his mood and they both resigned themselves to await his lordship's pleasure to be companionable.

For a day or two Tryon sedulously kept away from the neighborhood of the schoolhouse at Sandy Run. He really had business which would have taken him in that direction, but made a detour of five miles rather than go near his abandoned and discredited sweetheart.

But George Tryon was wisely distrustful of his own impulses. Driving one day along the road to Clinton, he overhauled a diminutive black figure trudging along the road, occasionally turning a hand spring by way of diversion.

"Hello, Plato," Tryon called, "do you want a lift?"

"Sure, Mars' Geo'ge. Kin ah ride wid you?"

"Jump up, Plato."

Plato mounted into the buggy with the agility to be expected from a lad of his acrobatic accomplishments. The two almost immediately fell into conversation upon perhaps the only subject of common interest between both. Before the town was reached, Tryon knew, so far as Plato could make it plain, the estimation in which the teacher was held by pupils and parents. He had learned the hours of opening and dismissal of the school, where the teacher lived, her habits of coming to and going from the schoolhouse, and the road she always followed.

"Does she go to church or anywhere else with Jeff Wain, Plato?," Tryon asked.

"No, suh, she don' go nowhar wid nobody, excep'n ole Elduh Johnson ah Mis' Johnson, an' de chillun. She use to stop at Mis' Wain's, but she's stayin' wid Elduh Johnson now. She allus makes som'a de chillun go home wid heh fum school," Plato said, proud to find in George an appreciative listener, "sometimes one an' sometimes annuder. I'se been home wid her twice, an' it'll be mah tu'n agin' befo' long."

"Plato," Tryon said, after some thought and reflection, and turning to Plato impressively, as they drove into the town, "do you think you could keep a secret?"

"Yas, suh, Mistah Geo'ge, ef you says I shill."

Withdrawing a coin from his pocket, he held it before Plato's eyes, which opened wider at the sight of it.

"Do you see this 50c piece?" Tryon displayed a silver coin. It was new and very shiny.

"Yas, Mistah Geo'ge," Plato replied, anxiously, fixing his eyes on the coin. Fifty cents was a large sum of money in those times and in that place. His acquaintance with Tryon gave him the privilege of looking at money. When he grew up, as he now conceived, and times were good, he would be able to earn fifty cents, several days in each week.

"I'm going to give this to you, Plato."

Plato's eyes opened almost as wide as the back of a saucer. "Me, Mistah Geo'ge?" he asked in amazement.

"Yes, Plato. I'm going to write a letter while I'm in town, and want you to take it. Meet me here in half an hour, and I'll give you the letter. Meanwhile, you must promise to keep your mouth shut—shut tight, understand?"

"Aw, yas, Mistah Geo'ge," Plato assured him earnestly, with a grin that distended his nose unduly. That he did not keep it shut may be inferred from the fact that within the next half hour he had eaten and drunk fifty cents worth of candy, ginger-pop, and other available delicacies that appealed to the useful palate. Having nothing more to spend, and the high prices prevailing for some time after the war having left him capable of locomotion, Plato was promptly on hand at the appointed time and place.

Tryon placed a letter in Plato's hand, still sticky with molasses candy. Tryon had enclosed it in a second cover by way of protection. "Give that letter," he said, "to your teacher; don't say a word about it to a living soul; bring me an answer, and give it into my own hand, and you shall have another half dollar."

Tryon was quite aware that by a superstitious correspondence he ran some risk of compromising Rena. But he felt, as soon as he had indulged his first opportunity to talk to her an irresistible impulse to see her and speak to her again. He could scarcely call at her boarding-place—what possible proper excuse could a young white man have for visiting a colored woman? At the schoolhouse she would be surrounded by her pupils, and a private interview would be as difficult, with more eyes to remark, and more tongues to comment upon it. He might address her by mail, but did not know how often she went to the nearest post-office. A letter mailed in town must pass through the hands of a postmaster, notoriously inquisitive and evil-minded, who was familiar with Tryon's handwriting and had ample time to attend to other people's business. To meet the teacher alone on the road seemed scarcely feasible, according to Plato's statement. A messenger, then, was not only the least of several evils, but really the only practicable way to communicate with Rena. He thought he could trust Plato, though miserably aware that he could not trust himself where this girl was concerned.

The letter handed by Tryon to Plato, and by the latter

delivered with due secrecy and precaution, ran as follows:—

Dear Miss Walden:—You may think it strange that I should address you after what has passed between us; but learning from my mother of your presence in the neighborhood, I am constrained to believe that you do not find my proximity embarrassing, and I cannot resist the wish to meet you at least once more, and talk over the circumstances o four former friendship. From a practical point of view this may seem superfluous, as the matter has been definitely settled. I have no desire to find fault with you; on the contrary, I wish to set myself right with regard to my own actions, and to assure you of my good wishes. In other words, since we must part, I would rather we parted friends than enemies. If nature and society—or Fate, to put it another way—have decreed that we cannot live together, it is nevertheless possible that we may carry into the future a pleasant, though somewhat sad memory of a past friendship. Will you not grant me one interview? I appreciate the difficulty of arranging it: I have found it almost as hard to communicate by letter. I will suit myself to your convenience; and meet you at any time and place you may designate. Please answer by bearer, whom I think is trustworthy, and believe me whatever your answer may be,
       Respectfully yours,
        G. W. T.

Plato gave Rena Tryon's letter at the school. After reading the same carefully, she took it home and read it again, then decided to mail her reply.

The next day but one, Tryon received through the mail, the following reply to his letter:—

GEORGE TRYON, Esq.

Dear sir:—I have requested your messenger to say that I will answer your letter by mail, which I shall now proceed to do. I assure you that I was entirely ignorant of your residence in this neighborhood, or it would have been the last place on earth in which I should have set foot.

As to our past relations, they were ended by your own act. I frankly confess that I deceived you; I have paid the penalty and have no complaint to make. I appreciate the delicacy which has made you respect my brother's secret, and thank you for it. I remember the whole affair with shame and humiliation, and would willingly forget it.

As to a future interview, I do not see what good it will do either of us. You are white and you have given me to understand that I am black. I accept the classification, however unfair, and the consequences, however unjust, one of which is that we cannot meet in the same parlor, in the same church, at the same table, or anywhere, in social intercourse; upon a steamboat we would not sit at the same table; we could not walk together on the street, or meet anywhere publicly and converse, without unkind remark. As a white man this might not mean a great deal to you; as a woman, shut out already by my color from much that is desirable, my good name remains my most valuable possession. I beg of you to let me alone. The best possible proof you can give me of your good wishes is to relinquish any desire or attempt to see me. I shall have finished my work here in a few days. I have other troubles, of which you know nothing, and my meeting with you would only add to a burden which is already as much as I can bear. To speak of parting is superfluous—we have already parted. It was idle to dream of a future friendship between two people so widely different in station. Such a relation, if possible in itself, would never be tolerated by the lady whom you are to marry, with whom you drove by the schoolhouse the other day. A gentleman so loyal to his race and tradition as you have shown yourself, could not be less faithful to the lady to whom he has lost his heart and his memory in three short months.

No, Mr. Tryon, our romance is ended, and better so. We could never, under the circumstances later discovered, have been happy. I have found a work in which I may be of service to others who have fewer opportunities than mine have been. Leave me in peace, I beseech you, and I shall soon pass out of your neighborhood as I have passed out of your life, and as I hope to pass out of your memory.

Yours very truly,
ROWENA NORTHCROSS

Chapter Forty Five

To Rena's high-strung and sensitive nature, already under very great tension from her past experience, the ordeal of the next few days was a severe one. On the one hand, Jeff Wain's infatuation had rapidly increased, in view of her speedy departure. From Mrs. Tryon's remark about Wain's wife, Amanda, and from things Rena had since learned, she had every reason to believe that this wife was living, and that Wain must be aware of the fact. In the light of this knowledge, Wain's former conduct took on a blacker significance than upon reflection she had charitably clothed it, after the first flush of indignation. That he had not given up his design to make love to her was quite apparent, and, with Amanda alive, his attentions, always offensive since she had gathered their import, became in her eyes the expression of a villainous purpose of which she could not speak to others, and from which she felt safe only so long as she took proper precaution against it. In a week her school would be over, and then she would get Elder Johnson, or some one else than Wain, to take her back to Fayetteville. True, she might abandon her school and go at once; but her work would be incomplete, she would have violated her contract, she would lose her salary for a month, explanations would be necessary, and would not be forthcoming. She might feign sickness —indeed, it would scarcely be feigning, for she felt far from well; she had never, since her illness, quite recovered her former vigor—but the inconvenience to others would be the same, and her self-sacrifice, would have had, at its very first trial, a lame and impotent conclusion. She had as yet no fear of personal violence from Wain; but under the circumstances, his attentions were an insult. He was evidently bent upon conquest, and vain enough to think he might achieve it by virtue of his personal attraction. If he could have understood how she loathed the sight of his narrow eyes, with their puffy lids, his thick, tobacco-stained lips, his doubtful teeth and his unwieldy person, Wain, the monument of conceit that he was, might have shrunk even in his own estimation, to something like his real proportions. Rena believed that, to defend herself from persecution at his hands, it was only necessary that she never let him find her alone. This, however, required constant watchfulness. Relying upon his own powers, and upon a woman's weakness and aversion to scandal, from which not even the purest may always escape unscathed, and convinced by her former silence that he had nothing serious to fear, Wain made it a point to be present at every public place where she might be. He assumed, in conversation with her which she could not avoid, and stated to others, that she had left his house because of a previous promise to divide the time of her stay between Elder Johnson's house and his own. He volunteered to teach a class in the Sunday school, which Rena conducted at the Colored Methodist Church, and when she remained to service, occupied a seat conspicuously near her own. In addition to these public demonstrations, which it was impossible to escape, or, it seemed, with so thick-skinned an individual as Wain, even to discourage, she was secretly and uncomfortably conscious that she could scarcely stir abroad without the risk of encountering one of two men, each of whom was on the lookout for an opportunity to find her alone.

The knowledge of Tryon's presence in the community had been just about as much as Rena could bear. To it must be added the consciousness that he, too, was pursuing her, to what end she could not tell. After his letter to her brother, and the feeling therein displayed, she found it necessary to crush, once or twice a wild hope that, her secret being still unknown, save to a friendly few, he might return and claim her. Now, such an outcome would be impossible. He had become engaged to another woman—this in itself would be enough to keep him from her, if it were not an index of a vastly more serious barrier, a proof that he had never loved her. If he had loved her truly, he would never have forgotten her in three short months—three long months they had heretofore seemed to her, for in them she had lived a lifetime of experience. Another impossible barrier lay in the fact that, his mother had met her, and that she was known in the neighborhood. Thus cut off from any hope that she might be anything to him, she had no wish to meet her former lover; no possible good could come of such a meeting; and yet her fluttering heart told her that if he should come, as his letter foreshadowed that he might,—if he should come, the loving George of old, with soft words and tender smiles and specious talk of friendship—ah! her heart would break! She must not meet him—at any cost she must avoid him.

But this heaping up of cares strained her endurance to the breaking point. Toward the middle of the last week, she knew that she had almost reached the limit, and was haunted by a fear that she might break down before the week was over. Now her really fine nature rose to the emergency, though she mustered her forces with a great effort. If she could keep Wain at his distance and avoid Tryon for three days longer, her school labors would be ended and she might retire in peace and honor.

"Miss Rena," Plato said to her on Tuesday, "ain' it 'bout time I wuz gwine home wid you?"

"You may see me home tomorrow, Plato, dear," she said and smiled upon the boy sweetly. He did a handspring as if to reward her for the smile.

After school Plato met an anxious-eyed young man in the woods a short distance from the schoolhouse.

"Well, Plato, what news?"

"I'se gwine tu see her home tu'morrow, Mistah Geo'ge."

"Tomorrow!" Tryon exclaimed, a deep frown covering his face. "How very unfortunate! I wanted you to go to town tomorrow to take an important message for me. I'm sorry, Plato—you might have earned another dollar."

To lie is a disgraceful thing, and yet there are times when, to a lover's mind, love dwarfs all ordinary laws. Plato scratched his head disconsolately, but suddenly a bright thought struck him.

"Can't I go to town fo' you atter I've seed her home, Mistah Geo'ge?" He waited anxiously to hear Tryon's reaction to this suggestion.

"N-o, I'm afraid it would be too late," Tryon returned doubtfully, shaking his head as he did so.

"Den I'll have tu ax heh to lemme go nex' day," Plato said with resignation. The honor might be postponed, or, if necessary, foregone; the opportunity to earn a dollar was the chance of a lifetime and must not be allowed to slip.

"No, Plato," Tryon rejoined, shaking his head again, this time both regretfully and sadly. "I shouldn't want to deprive you of so great a pleasure." Tryon was entirely sincere in this characterization of Plato's chance; he would have given many a dollar to be sure of Plato's place and Plato's welcome. Rena's letter had reinflamed his smouldering passion; only opposition was needed to fan it to a white heat. Wherein lay the great superiority of his position, if he was denied the right to speak to the one person whom he most cared to address? He felt some realization of the tyranny of his caste, when he found it not merely pressing upon an inferior people who had no right to expect anything better, but also barring his way to something that he desired. He meant her no harm—but he must see her. He was conscious of a certain relief at the thought that he had not asked Blanche Leary to be his wife. His hand was unpledged. He could not marry the other girl, of course, but they must meet again. The rest he would leave to Fate, which seemed reluctant to disentangle threads which it had woven so closely.

"I think, Plato, that I see an easier way out of the difficulty. Your teacher, I imagine, merely wants some one to see her safely home. Don't you think, if you should go part of the way, that I might take your place for the rest, while you did my errand?"

"Why, sholy, Mistah Geo'ge, you could take ca'eh ob heh bettern' I could—bettern' anybody could—'co'se you could."

George Tryon was white and rich, and could do anything. Plato was proud of the fact that he once belonged to the Tryon family. He could not conceive of any one so powerful as George Tryon, unless it might be God, of whom Plato had heard more or less, and even here the comparison might not be quite fair to Mr. George, for he was the younger of the two. It would undoubtedly be a great honor for the teacher to be escorted home by Mister George. The teacher was a great woman, no doubt, and looked white; but George Tryon was the real article. Mr. George had never been known to go with a colored woman before, and the teacher would doubtless thank Plato for arranging that so great an honor should fall upon her. George Tryon had given him fifty cents twice, and would now give him a whole dollar. Noble Mr. George! Fortunate teacher! Happy Plato!

"Very well, Plato. I think we can arrange it so that you can kill the two rabbits with one shot. Suppose that we go over the road that she will take to go home."

They soon arrived at the schoolhouse. School had been out an hour, and the clearing was deserted. Plato led the way by the road through the woods to a point where, amid somewhat thick underbrush, another path intersected the road they were following.

"Now, Plato," Tryon said, pausing, "this would be a good spot for you to leave the teacher, and for me to take your place. This path leads to the main road, and will take you to town very quickly. I shouldn't say anything about it to the teacher at all; but when you and she get here, drop behind and run along this path until you meet me— I'll be waiting a few yards down the road—and then run to town as fast as your legs will carry you. As soon as you are gone, I'll come out and tell the teacher that I've sent you on an errand, and will myself take your place. You shall have a dollar and I'll ask her to let you go home with her the next day. But you mustn't say a word about it, Plato, or you won't get the dollar, and I'll not ask the teacher to let you go home with her again."

"All right, Mistah Geo'ge, I ain' gwine tu say no' mo' de'n ef de cat had mah tongue."

Chapter Forty Six

Rena was unusually fatigued at the close of her school on Wednesday afternoon. She had been troubled all day with a headache, which, beginning with a dull pain, had gradually increased in intensity until every nerve was throbbing like a trip-hammer. The pupils seemed unusually stupid, a discouraging sense of the insignificance of any part she could perform towards the education of three million people with a school term of two months a year hung over her spirits like a pall. As the object of Wain's attentions, she had begun to feel somewhat like a wild creature who hears the pursuers on its tracks, and has the fear of capture, added to the fatigue of flight. But when this excitement had gone too far and had neared the limit of exhaustion, came Tryon's letter, with the resulting surprise and consternation. Rena had keyed herself up to an heroic pitch to answer it; but when the inevitable reaction came, she was overwhelmed with a sickening sense of her own weakness. The things which in another sphere had constituted her strength and shield, were now her undoing; and exposed her to dangers from which they lent her no protection. Not only was her position in theory, but the pursuers were already at her heels. As the day wore on these dark thoughts took on an added gloom, until, when the hour to dismiss school arrived, she felt as though she had not a friend in the world. This feeling was accentuated by a letter which she had that morning received from her mother, in which Mis' Molly spoke very highly of Wain, and plainly expressed the hope that her daughter might like him so well that she would prefer to remain in Sampson County.

Having been near this pompous and deceiving creature for two months; and having learned from personal contact, what a scoundrel he was, having also heard him referred to as about the worst scoundrel the community possessed, she sighed unhappily, and tried to forgive her mother for what she was in no position to know—or even find out.

Plato, bright-eyed and alert, was waiting in the school yard until the teacher should be ready to start. Having warned several smaller children who had hung around after school as though to share his prerogative of accompanying the teacher, Plato had swung himself into the low branches of an oak at the edge of the clearing, from which he was hanging by his legs, head downward. He dropped from the reposeful attitude when the teacher appeared at the door, and took his place at her side.

A strange premonition of impending trouble caused the teacher to hesitate. She wished for some strange and unaccountable reason, that she could not understand, that she had kept more of the pupils behind. Something whispered that danger lurked in the road she customarily followed. Plato, as she looked down upon him, seemed insignificantly small and weak, and she felt miserably unable to cope with any difficult or untoward situation.

"Plato," she suggested, "I think we'll go around the other way tonight, if you don't mind."

Visions of George Tryon disappointed, of a dollar unearned and unspent flitted through the narrow brain which some one, with the irony of ignorance or of knowledge, had mocked with the name of a great philosopher. Plato was not an untruthful lad, but he seldom had the opportunity to earn a dollar. His imagination spurred on by the instinct of self-interest, rose quickly to the present emergency.

"I'se afraid you mought git snake-bit gwine roun' dat way, Miss Rena. Mah bre'r Jim, kilt a water-moccasin down here yistidy 'bout ten feet long."

Rena had a horror of snakes, with which the swamp by which the other road ran was infested. Snakes were a vivid reality; her presentiment was probably a mere depression of spirits due to her condition of nervous exhaustion. A cloud had come up and threatened rain, and the wind was rising ominously. The old way was the shorter; she wanted, above all things, to get to Elder Johnson's and go to bed. Perhaps sleep would rest her tired brain—she could not imagine herself feeling worse, unless she should break down all together.

She plunged into the path and hastened forward so as to reach home before the approaching storm. So completely was she absorbed in her own thoughts, that she scarcely noticed that Plato himself seemed preoccupied. Instead of capering along like a playful kitten or puppy, he walked by her side unusually silent. When they had gone a short distance and were approaching a path which intersected their road at something near a right angle, the teacher missed Plato. He had dropped behind a moment before;

now he had disappeared entirely. Her vague alarm of a few moments before returned with redoubled force.

"Plato!" she called frantically, pausing to look all around her for him. "Plato!" she all but yelled this time.

There was no response, save the soughing of the wind through the swaying treetops. She stepped hastily forward, wondering if this were some childish prank. If so, it was badly timed, and she would let Plato feel the weight of her displeasure.

Her forward step had brought her to the junction of the two paths, where she paused doubtfully. The route she had been following was the most direct way home, but led for quite a distance through the forest, which she did not care to traverse alone. The intersecting path would soon take her to the main road where she might find either shelter, or company, or both. Glancing around again in search of her missing escort, she became aware that a man was approaching her from each of the two paths. In one she recognized the eager and excited face of George Tryon, flushed with anticipation for their meeting, and yet grave with his uncertainty of his reception. Advancing confidently along the other path, she saw the face of Jeff Wain, drawn, as she imagined in her anguish, with evil passions which would stop at nothing.

What should she do? There was no sign of Plato—for aught she could see or hear of him, the earth might have opened and swallowed him up. Some deadly serpent might have stung him. Some wandering rabbit might have tempted him aside. Another thought struck her. Plato had been very quiet—there had been something on his conscience—perhaps he had betrayed her! But to which of the two men? And to what end?

The problem was too much for her overwrought brain. She turned and fled. A wiser instinct would have led her forward. In the two dangers she might have found safety. The road after all was a public way. Any number of persons might meet there accidently. But she saw only the darker side of the situation. To turn to Tryon for protection before Wain, by some overt act, manifested the evil purpose which she as yet only suspected would be, she imagined would acknowledge a previous secret acquaintance with Tryon, thus placing her reputation at Wain's mercy, and to charge herself with a burden of obligation toward a man whom she wished to avoid and had refused to meet. If, on the other hand, she should go forward to meet Wain, he would undoubtedly offer to accompany her homeward. Tyron would inevitably observe the meeting, and suppose it prearranged. Not for the world would she have him think so. Why she should care for his opinion, she didn't stop to argue. She turned and fled, and to avoid possible pursuit, struck into the underbrush at an angle which she calculated would bring her in a few rods to another path which would lead quickly into the main road. She had run only a few yards when she found herself in the midst of a clump of prickly shrubs and briars. Meantime, the storm had burst; the rain fell in torrents. Extricating herself from the thorns, she pressed forward, but instead of coming out upon the road, found herself penetrating deeper and deeper into the forest.

The storm increased in violence. The sky grew darker and darker. It was near evening, the clouds were dense, the thick woods increased the gloom. Suddenly a blinding flash of lightning pierced the darkness, followed by a sharp clap of thunder. There was a crash of falling timber. Terror-stricken, Rena flew forward through the forest, the underbrush growing closer and closer as she advanced. Suddenly the earth gave way beneath her feet and she sank into a concealed morass. By clasping the trunk of a neighboring sapling she extricated herself with an effort, and realized with a horrible certainty that she was lost in the swamp!

Turning, she tried to retrace her steps. A flash of lightning penetrated the gloom around her, and barring her path, she saw a huge black snake—harmless enough, in fact, but to her excited imagination, frightful in appearance. With a wild shriek she turned again, staggered forward a few yards, stumbled over a projecting root, and fell heavily to the earth.

When Rena disappeared in the underbrush, Tryon and Wain had instinctively set out in pursuit of her, but owing to the gathering darkness, the noise of the storm and the thickness of the underbrush, they missed not only Rena but each other, and neither was aware of the other's presence in the forest. Wain kept up the chase until the rain drove him to shelter. Tryon, after a few minutes, realized that she had fled to escape him, and that to pursue her would be to defeat rather than promote his purpose. He desisted, therefore, and returning to the main road, stationed himself where he could watch Elder Johnson's house, and having waited for awhile without any sign of Rena, concluded that she had taken refuge in some friendly cabin. Turning home disconsolately as night came on, he intercepted Plato on his way back from town and pledged him to inviolable secrecy so effectually that Plato, when subsequently questioned, merely answered that he had stopped a moment to gather some chinquapins, and when he had looked around the teacher was gone.

Rena having not appeared at supper time and for an hour later, the Elder, somewhat anxious, made inquiries about the neighborhood, and finding his guest at no place where she might be expected to stop, became very much alarmed. Wain's home was the last to which he went. He had surmised that there was some mystery connected with her leaving Wain's, but had never been given any definition about the matter. In response to his inquiries, Wain expressed surprise, but betrayed a certain self-consciouness which did not escape the elder's eye. Returning home, he organized a search party from his own family and several near neighbors, and set out with dogs and torches to scour the woods for the missing teacher. A couple of hours later, they found her lying unconscious, only a few rods from a well defined path which would have soon led her to the open highway. Strong arms lifted her gently and bore her home. Mrs. Johnson undressed her and put her to bed, administering a home remedy, of which whiskey was the principal ingredient, to counteract the effects of the exposure. There was a doctor within five miles, but no one thought of sending for him, nor was it at all likely that it would have been possible to get him for such a case at such an hour.

Rena's illness, however, was more deeply seated than her friends could imagine. A tired body, in sympathy with an overwrought brain, had left her peculiarly susceptible to the nerves because of her forest experience. The exposure for several hours in her wet clothing to the damps of miasma of the swamp had brought on an attack of brain fever. The next morning, she was delirious. One of the children took word to the schoolhouse that the teacher was sick and there would be no school that day. A number of curious and sympathetic people came from time to time and suggested various remedies, several of which, old Mrs. Johnson, with Catholic impartiality, administered to the helpless teacher, who from delirium gradually sank into a heavy stupor scarcely distinguishable from sleep. It was predicted that she would probably be well in the morning; if not, it would then be time to consider seriously the question of sending for the doctor.

Chapter Forty Seven

AFTER TRYON'S FAILURE to obtain an interview with Rena through Plato's connivance, he decided upon a different course of procedure. In a few days her school term would be finished. He was not less desirous to see her, was indeed as much more eager as opposition would be likely to make a very young man who was accustomed to having his own way, and whose heart, as he had discovered, was more deeply and permanently involved than he had imagined. His present plan was to wait until the end of the school term; then, when Rena went to Clinton on the Saturday or the Monday to draw her salary for the month, he would see her in the town, or, if necessary, would follow her to Fayetteville. No power on earth should keep him from her long, but he had no desire to interfere in any way with the duty which she owed to others. When the school session was over and her work completed, then he would have his innings. Writing letters was too unsatisfactory a method of communication—he must see her face to face.

The first of his three days of waiting had passed, when, about ten o'clock in the morning of the second day, which seemed very long in prospect, while driving along the road toward Clinton, he met Plato, with a rabbit trap in his hand.

"Well, Plato," he asked, "why are you absent from the classic shades of the academy today?"

"Hoddy, Mistah Geo'ge. W'at was dat you say?"

"Why are you not at school today?"

"Ain' got no teacher, Mistah Geo'ge. Teacher's gone!"

"Gone!" Tryon exclaimed, with a sudden leap of the heart. "Gone where? What do you mean, anyhow?"

"Teacher got los' in de swamp night befo' las', 'cause Plato wa'nt dere to show her de way out'n de woods. El- duh Johnson foun' heh wid dawgs and tawches an' fotch heh home, an' put heh tu bed. No school yistidy. She wuz out'n heh haid las' night, and dis' mawnin' she wuz gone."

"Gone—but where?"

"Dey don' nobody know wha', suh."

Leaving Plato abruptly, Tryon hastened down the road toward Elder Johnson's cabin. This was no time to stand on punctillo. The girl had been lost in the woods in the storm, amid the thunder and lightning and the pouring rain. She was sick with fright and exposure, and he was the cause of it all, and now he felt the responsibility keenly. She hadn't known he lived in the vicinity; had come down to teach the little Negro school honestly and willingly, to help her distressed and ignorant people. She was acting in the best Christian interests and no person had a right to interfere with such work—and he had! By bribery, corruption and falsehood, he had brought misery and suffering.

White men of honor and character did not submit to such low things. Their honor was too high; and they would, under no circumstances whatever, be guilty of such an unprincipled thing. As it was, Rena, now at last before his eyes, the innocent, for she would have never come to Charleston and deceived him had it not been for her brother. He had learned since that she went back to see her sick mother on an errand of mercy; and it was even on an errand of mercy that took her inadvertently to the drugstore, where he made the discovery—and acted so beastly as a result of it. As he rushed to Elder Johnson's to inquire about her; and to offer his services in the search for her, George Tryon felt guilty and almost hated himself for the thing that he knew now he was responsible for. He must learn at once what became of her.

Reaching Elder Johnson's house, he drew up by the front fence and gave the customary "halloa," which summoned a woman to the door.

"Good-morning," he said, nodding unconsciously, with the careless politeness of a gentleman to his inferiors. "I'm Mr. Tryon. I have come to inquire about the sick teacher."

"Why, suh," the woman replied respectfully, "she got los' in de woods night befo' las', an' she wuz outen heh min' mos ob de time yistidy. Las' night, she musta got outa bed an' run away w'en eveh body wuz sound asleep, fo' dis mawning' she wuz gone, an' none a us knows wha' she is."

"Has any search been made for her?"

"Yas, suh, my husban' an' de chillun has been huntin' roun' all de mawnin', an' he's gone now to borry a hoss tu go fudder. But Lawd knows dey ain' no tellin' wha' she'd go, lessen' she got heh min' back atter she lef.'"

Tryon's mare was in good condition. He had money in his pockets and nothing to interfere with his movements. He set out immediately on the road to Fayetteville, keeping a lookout by the roadside, and stopping each person he met to inquire if a young woman, apparently ill, had been seen traveling along the road on foot. No one had met such a traveler. When he had gone two or three miles, he drove through a shallow branch that crossed the road. The splashing of his horse's hoofs in the water prevented him from hearing a low groan that came from the woods by the roadside.

He drove on, making inquiries of each farmhouse and of every person whom he encountered. Shortly after crossing the branch, he met a young Negro with a cartload of tubs and buckets and piggins, and asked him if he had seen on the road a young white woman with dark eyes and hair, apparently sick or demented. The young man answered in the negative, and Tryon pushed forward anxiously.

At noon he stopped at a farmhouse and swallowed a hasty meal. His inquiries here elicited no information, and he was just leaving when a young man came in late to dinner and stated, in response to the usual question, that he had met, some two hours before, a young woman who answered Tryon's description, on the Lillington Road, which crossed the main road to Fayetteville a short distance beyond the farm house. He had spoken to the woman. At first she had paid no heed to his question. When addressed a second time, she had answered in a rambling and disconnected way, which indicated to his mind that there was something wrong with her.

Tryon thanked his informant and hastened to the Lillington Road. Stopping as before to inquire, he followed the woman for several hours, each mile of the distance taking him farther away from Fayetteville. From time to time he heard of the woman. Toward nightfall he found her. She was white enough with the sallowness of the sandhill poor white. She was still young, perhaps, but poverty and a hard life made her look older than she ought. She was not fair and she was not Rena. When Tryon came up to her, she was sitting on the doorsill of a miserable cabin, and held in her hand a bottle, the contents of which had never had paid on it any revenue tax. She had walked twenty miles that day, and had beguiled the tedium of the journey by occasional potations, which probably accounted for the incoherency of speech which several of those who met her had observed. When Tryon drew near she tendered him the bottle with tipsy cordiality. He turned in disgust and retraced his steps to the Fayetteville Road, which he did not reach until nightfall. As it was too dark to prosecute the search with any chance of success, he secured lodging for the night, intending to resume his quest early in the morning.

Frank Fowler's heart was filled with longing for a sight of Rena. It had cost him many a heartache to let her go and give her up; they had been play mates first, then school mates, then love mates, with plans to marry by and by, although there had never been a declaration of love, nor any date discussed as to when they would some day marry. It was just understood, and there it had rested until the night Johnny Northcross, who had disappeared so mysteriously, nearly fourteen years before, and had come back twelve years later—as mysteriously as he had disappeared.

We know the story only too well of what happened then. Her stay in Charleston, her engagement to a white gentleman, through her brother, and of her return to Fayetteville to see her sick mother; the discovery of her secret by the white man, had changed Rena very much. While he was confident that she still cared for him, there was a change and he had not attempted to intrude himself upon her, giving her time to come back as nearly as possible, to what she once was.

He had always known that Mis' Molly hadn't wanted him for a son-in-law because he was dark; and he had observed her favoritism toward Jeff Wain, because that one was brighter, had beautiful straight, or almost straight black hair,—and was a bigger liar, because he had fooled Mis' Molly into believing that he was rich and powerful in the county wherein he lived.

When Rena had departed for Sampson County to teach, Frank had reconciled himself to her absence by the hope of her speedy return. He often stopped to talk to Mis' Molly about her. Several letters had passed between mother and daughter, and in response to Frank's inquiries Mis' Molly uniformly stated that Rena was well and doing well, and sent her love to all inquiring friends. But Frank observed that Mis' Molly, when pressed for the date of Rena's return, grew more and more indefinite; and finally the mother, in a burst of confidential friendship, told Frank of all her hopes with reference to the stranger from down the country.

"Yas, Frank," she concluded, "it'll be her own fault ef she don' become a lady of proputty, fo' Mistah Wain is rich, an' owns a big plantation, an' hiahs a lotta hands, an' is a big man in the county. He's crazy to git heh, an' it all lays in her own han's."

Frank did not find this news reassuring. He felt that Wain was a liar and a scoundrel. He had no more than his intuitions upon which to found this belief, but it was none the less firm. If this estimate of the man's character was correct, then his wealth might be a fiction, pure and simple. If so, the truth should be known to Mis' Molly, so that instead of encouraging a marriage with Wain, she would see him in his true light, and interpose to rescue her daughter from his importunities. A day or two after this conversation, Frank met in the town a Negro from Sampson County, made his acquaintance, and inquired if he knew a man by the name of Jeff Wain.

"Aw, Jeff Wain!" the countryman replied, slightingly. "Yas, ah knows him, an' don' know no good ob 'im. One ob dese heah biggity, braggin' niggahs—talks lak he owns de whole country, an' ain' wof no mo'd'n I is—jes' a big bladder wid a handful ob shot rattlin' 'roun' in it. Had a wife when I wuz dare, an' beat heh an' 'bused heh so she had tu run away."

This was alarming information. Wain had passed in the town as a single man, and Frank had had no hint that he had ever been married. There was something wrong somewhere. Frank determined that he would find out the truth, and, if possible, do something to protect Rena against the obviously evil designs of the man who had taken her away. In spite of the fact that Mis' Molly had not told him, and did not seem to want to tell him, when Rena's school would be out, he had in a round-about way learned that the term was for only two months, and reckoned correctly, that the school should let out the coming Friday.

He decided to go there and hang around one or two days

prior to that time, during which he could busy himself finding out still more about Jeff Wain.

Accordingly, he set about preparing to drive to Sampson County in his wagon, with his best mule. Not knowing just whether he could secure a place to stay all night, he decided to take along enough bed clothes to make a pallet and he could sleep in the wagon. He also took his gun with sufficient ammunition to shoot a rabbit, some partridges and possibly a squirrel or two and set out quietly for Sampson County, with the purpose of bringing Rena back home, if it be agreeable with her.

He went about thirty miles the first day, and camped by the roadside for the night, resuming the journey at dawn. After driving for an hour through the tall pines that overhung the road like the stately arch of a cathedral aisle, weaving a carpet for the earth with their brown spines, and cones, and soothing the ear with their ceaseless murmur, Frank stopped to water his mule at a point where the white, sandy road, widening as it went, sloped downward to a clear running branch. On the right a bay-tree bending over the stream mingled the heavy odor of its flowers with the delicate perfume of a yellow jasmine vine that had over-run a clump of saplings on the left. From a neighboring tree a silver-throated mocking-bird poured out a flood of riotous melody. A group of minnows, startled by the sloshing of the mule's feet in the water, darted away into the shadow of the thicket, their quick passage leaving the amber water filled with laughing light.

The mule drank long and lazily, while over Frank stole thoughts in harmony with the peaceful scene—thoughts of Rena, young and beautiful, her friendly smile, her pensive dark eyes. He would soon see her now, as he visualized it, and if she had any cause for fear and unhappiness, he would place himself at her service—for a day, a week, a month, a year—a lifetime, if need be.

His reverie was broken by a noise ahead of him, and he strained his neck to see what it was. Then he started. A wretched looking old Negro woman stepped out of the thick underbrush into the road, and paused to look around, her large white eyes seeming filled with fear and excitement. The eyes finally rested on him and he started again.

"Della!" he cried suddenly, for it was no other than Della, the Conjure Woman, who used to dwell on the edge of the swamps near where he was born. He recalled as he looked from the creek up at her, that it had been years since he had seen her. He thought she had died, but there was the same wretched looking witch-woman, standing in the road, looking down at him. His mule had finished drinking by now, and he urged her forward and upon the bank of the branch and beside Della.

"Who is you?" she said, peering up at him closely. "Seems I've seen you befo' somewha."

"I'm Henry Fowler's son, Frank, Della. What are you doing here? I haven't seen you for a long time. I thought you—were dead."

The old woman grinned, opened her eyes wider, which made her seem more wretched still, showed her haggled teeth, then as quickly became serious.

"I left Fayetteville and came down heah a long time ago. I had a sister who was older—she has died since, and she lived where I now live. I came to take care of her and she died, so I've lived there alone since. But I'm wasting time. Something terrible's happened. A putty young gal is at mah house, sick, terribly sick. I found her on the edge of the swamp this mawnin' while I was looking fo' snake root and grapes. She's awfully sick—terribly sick and needs a doctuh, boy, the child needs a doctuh. She's out of heh head, and needs a real doctuh. I cain' do heh no good."

"Rena!" Frank cried, "could this be—Rena?"

"That's heh name—she was teaching school down the road fudder. Ah hurd dem call heh name, and it wuz Rena, dat's hit, Rena. Well, boy, she's terrible sick, fever, maybe pneumonia, who knows."

"Get into my cart and take me to her, Della. I don't know what this is all about, but I was on my way to Sandy Run to take her back to Fayetteville and to her mother. Come with me and I'll drive to your cabin. Which way?" Della pointed to the right. After a few steps they came to a narrow lane, barely wide enough for the cart, that wound and twisted through the woods. They must have gone almost a mile when they came to a little clearing, and a cabin in the woods. From a mud and stick chimney, smoke curled upward, indicating habitation.

Frank piled out of the cart and followed Della inside the cabin, where, in a corner, lay Rena, stretched on a homemade bed, but on a feather mattress, tossing and tumbling restlessly, and out of her head as he could see.

Frank leaned over her, placed his hand on her forehead to find it hot and burning with fever.

"Rena, Rena, my poor child, it is you. How did this happen?"

Della came closer. She pressed a cold wet towel on her forehead, looked up at Frank and went on to explain.

"She took sick the other day, got lost in the storm, wandered into the woods and fainted. They found her late that night and took her to Elder Johnson's where she was boarding. She was sick all day yesterday, and las' night she disappeared as tho' the earth opened and swallowed her. They were here today looking for her, and it was after they left that I went out to find snake-root and scuppernon grapes, that I found her and brought her heah."

"This is shocking. Is there a doctor near?"

"There is a doctuh in Clinton, but ef I was you, I'd put her in that cart of yours and take her home—start right away. Once home, where she can have treatment and with old Doctuh Green, Molly's physician, she has a chance; but hurry, Frank. That child is sick, I tell you, mighty sick."

Frank was glad that he had brought comforts, and could construct a very comfortable bed in his cart, where they placed the sick girl, whereupon he turned around, and set out for Fayetteville, retracing his steps and determined to travel late into the night—until he reached Fayetteville and the house behind the cedars.

Chapter Forty Eight

REALIZING THAT RENA, out of her head, would toss and tumble, and that Frank would have great difficulty keeping any covering over her, Della pinned the covers around Rena's body, allowing enough room for her to turn over, to even toss and still remain covered, after which Della sent Frank on his way back to Fayetteville with his precious treasure. They bathed her face and neck with cold water from a spring, and while Rena continued to talk wildly at intervals, Frank was relieved to observe that, after a time, she sank into a restful sleep and continued that way for many miles on their way back to Fayetteville.

As they journeyed on the long trek back to the house behind the cedars, Frank could hear Rena talking wildly, but from which he could gather what had happened—at least an idea, before she became sick.

"Yes, I know you, Jeff Wain, and I want nothing to do with you, so go away from here!"

Silence, then, but after a time:

"You wicked creature. I saw you coming down the road to meet me with a cunning smile on your face. Forcing yourself on me when I had tried to convince you in every way I knew how, that I was not interested in you—or your lies. The people all around you told me about you—

just what you were, a scoundrel, so get away, don't touch me."

Frank listened with keen interest. He had brought an umbrella to divert the sun, and to use for shelter in the event of rain. He opened this and sat it up so that it shaded her face and much of her body from the burning sun, and continued down the Fayetteville highway, and listened to Rena as she continued, at intervals, to talk.

"George, George, dear George. Regardless of the way you treated me, at least you've always been a gentleman, with no sordid or ill-conceived purposes in your mind. I saw you also coming to meet me, in the path on the right, Jeff Wain, unseen by you, was coming to meet me down the path at the left. Neither of you, I was aware, knew of the other's presence or purpose. I couldn't stand to meet you, George. You did not love me; you only wanted to satisfy a maddening desire to talk, to ask me questions. You did not love me, you only once thought you did. The fact is you hate me, you despise me, all because I am black; you don't love me; you hate and despise me."

After that, she would toss and tumble, sometimes so violently until Frank had to hold her in the cart with both hands. His faithful mule seemed to understand and jogged on toward Fayetteville faithfully, trotting when the road was level or sloped downward and walking when it ran otherwise.

Toward noon he was met by a young white man, who peered inquisitively under the raised umbrella, and started suddenly.

"Hello!" he exclaimed, suspiciously, "who've you got here?"

"A sick woman," Frank answered.

The inquisitor, still suspicious, looked again, this time closer.

"Why, she's white, or I'm a sinner!," he cried, stepping back and looking at Frank more closely. Knowing that he might encounter such, Frank was calm. "Look a-here, nigger, what are you doin' with this white woman?"

"She's not white, Mr.—she's simply a very bright mulatto."

"Yeah, *mighty* bright," the stranger continued, still suspicious, but still by his tone, not positive. "Where are you goin' with her?"

"I'm taking her to her mother in Fayetteville."

Still not entirely satisfied, the stranger finally, with a grunt of possible doubt, passed on and Frank continued on his way.

Towards evening, Frank heard hounds baying in the distance. A red fox weary with running, brush drooping, crossed the road ahead of the cart. Presently, the hounds straggled across the road, followed by three or four hunters on horesback, who stopped at sight of the canopied cart. They stared at the sick girl and demanded to know who she was.

"I don't b'lieve she's black at all," one of them declared after Frank's explanation. "I don't like this nigger's eye; I think he's up to some devilment. What ails the girl, anyhow?"

"She's down with a serious attack of fever," Frank explained. "I suggest that you feel her forehead."

The disagreeable one did, and jerked his hand back with a frown on his face. They stepped away a few paces and consulted each other.

"I reckon' it's all right. She's burning up with fever all right, so guess we'd better let the nigger alone." At this moment the hounds could be heard, baying clamorously in the distance. The hunters jumped back on their horses and followed the hounds, and again Frank was left to proceed on his peaceful way.

Frank drove all day and all night, stopping for brief periods every few hours to feed and water his faithful mule and take some refreshments for himself. At dawn, from the top of the long white hill, he sighted the river bridge below. At sunrise he rapped at Mis' Molly's door.

After rising at dawn, Tryon's first step, after a hasty breakfast, was to turn back towards Clinton. He had wasted half a day in following the false clue on the Lillington Road. It seemed, after reflection, unlikely that a woman seriously ill should have been able to go any considerable distance before her strength gave out. In her delirium, she might have wandered in a wrong direction, imagining any road to lead to Fayetteville. It would be a good plan to drive back home, continuing his inquiries meantime, and ascertain whether or not she had been found by those who were seeking her, including many whom Tryon's inquiries had placed upon the alert. If she should prove still missing, he would resume the journey to Fayetteville and continue the search in that direction. She had probably not wandered far from the high road; even in delirium she would be likely to avoid the deep woods, with which her illness was associated.

He had retraced more than half the distance to Clinton

when he encountered, at the side of the road, Elder Johnson, Della and several other Negroes, whom he went up to to make inquiry, and who told him that she had been found and had been taken directly back to Fayetteville from Della's cabin in the woods.

If anything could have taken more complete possession of George Tryon at twenty-four than love successful and triumphant, it was love thwarted and denied. Never in the few deep, delirious weeks of his courtship had he felt so strongly drawn to the beautiful sister of the popular lawyer, as he was now driven by an aching heart toward the same woman stripped of every adventitious advantage and placed, by custom, beyond the pale of marriage with women of his own race. Custom was tyranny. Love was the only law. Would God have made hearts to yearn for one another if He had meant them to stay forever apart? If this girl should die it would be he who killed her, by his cruelty, no less surely than if with his own hand he had struck her down. He had been so dazzled by his own superiority, so blinded by his own glory, that he had ruthlessly spurned and spoiled the image of God in this fair creature, whom he might have had for his own treasure. Whom, please God, he would yet have, at any cost, to love and cherish while they both should live. There were difficulties—they had seemed insuperable, but love would surmount them. Sacrifices must be made, but if the world without love would be nothing, then why not give up the world for love? He would hasten to Fayetteville. He would find her; he would tell her that he loved her, that she was all the world to him, that he had come to marry her, and take her away where they might be happy together. He pictured to himself the joy that would light up her face; he felt her soft arms around his neck, her tremulous kisses upon his lips. If she were still ill when he arrived, his love would woo her back to health. If disappointment and sorrow had contributed to her illness, joy and gladness should lead to her recovery.

He urged the mare forward; if she would but keep up her pace, he would reach Fayetteville by nightfall.

Dr. Green came out of the front door of the house behind the cedars, his kit in his hand, his face serious. Waiting on the outside, their faces anxious, stood Mis' Molly, Frank, Mary B. and Homer Pettifoot and Billy Oxendine, who, having heard of Rena's illness and return home, wanted to know more.

"Now, folks," Dr. Green said, removing his hat and wiping the perspiration from his forehead. "Rena is an awfully sick girl. All the exposure and the long ride while ill from Sampson County back here, has developed into the most serious attack of typhoid pneumonia, from which she will be fortunate if she ever recovers. In the meantime, she must not be allowed to see or talk to anybody until she passes the crisis, in about ten days. She's a very, very sick girl. I'll send my visiting nurse to look after her as much as she can, otherwise you will have to do so, Molly. I'll come to see her twice a day myself. But understand—and if you fail to do what I say, Rena may never recover."

Naturally they all agreed to follow his instructions and he left. As he came to the crossroads after leaving the house behind the cedars, he ran into George Tryon, coming in from Sampson County. George had intended to avoid the doctor, but this inadvertent meeting left this out of the question.

After exchanging greetings, the doctor said, bluntly:

"I know your story, George, also my family, and we know that you'd rather not be embarrassed by our knowing. But the girl you are in love with lies at this moment at the point of death, and your trip here to see her is all in vain. I have just left orders that she is not to see anybody —least of all you—I didn't say anything about you, but it is obvious that under the circumstances, you are the last person that she should see. So come on with me and we will talk more about it at my office."

Accordingly, therefore, George Tryon, after a long talk with Dr. Green, spent the night in Fayetteville and returned to Sampson County the next morning, declaring to himself secretly, however, to return in two weeks to see Rena, when he would go directly to her home.

It was ten days to a day, following Frank's return to Fayetteville when he brought Rena home, that he called on her and they had a long talk. She was sitting up in her bedroom with blankets around her, and had sent for Frank and was anxious, both to see and talk with him.

"Frank," she said, beckoning for him to move his chair close to hers. After he did so, she took his hand and stroked it affectionately with her free hand.

"Before this all started, Frank, you and I were very happy here—happier than I have ever been since, and I know now that my whole career as planned by my brother and my mother, was all vain and impossible. I know

now that the idea of crossing over and passing for white, was impossible. North Carolina is not large enough but that sometime, somewhere and somehow, paths must cross and the masquerade would sooner or later be discovered—as it very quickly was—and the bottom would fall out of it all—as it did.

"My poor mother, then, who really loves you, but is so influenced by the customs around her, and which she grew up under, planned to marry me off to Jeff Wain, down in Sampson County, not knowing as I suspected all along, and very quickly found out, that the man was a scoundrel, and just abut every other impossible thing that a man could be. I never would have married him. All the while, Frank, you—the faithful one, the ambitious one, and the only unselfish one of them all—has been neglected. I am happy that I am recovering. When I am fully well again, I want to do something, even though it be ever so little, for my people—your people, our people. Meanwhile, what are your plans, Frank? Before all this started, I am sure you were about to launch on a career for wider accomplishments. Now tell me, dear, and take your time, just what have you decided, and what do you want to do. If you are still interested in me as you once were, then what do you want me to do?"

"I will answer your last suggestion first, Rena. I will come right to the point. I—want you to—marry me dear. If you love me."

"Oh, Frank! I still love you. I have always loved you. While to please my brother, and to do as I knew he wanted me to, I—thought I was about to learn to love somebody else, but I soon discovered that it was only you, Frank, you dear. Please kiss me, Frank."

After they had exchanged, not one, but many kisses, Frank told Rena of his plans.

"We will get married, Rena, whenever you are strong again, and say the word, after which I want to take you away, dear."

"Away, Frank," she said, in some surprise. "Where, Frank?"

"To a city at the North, dear, a booming and growing town called Chicago."

"To Chicago, Frank? That is far away, and cold," she shuddered sweetly.

"It is a growing town, a good place for my work, building and contracting."

"I'm sure it must be all that Frank, I read so much about it."

"Are you willing to go there with me, Rena?"

She smiled tenderly and squeezed his hand.

"I would go anywhere with you, Frank."

"In Chicago, we will be free, Rena, do you understand what I mean?"

Rena nodded her head in the affirmative, and Frank understood. They meant color discrimination and the caste system among Negroes which didn't exist there. Both knew that it was enough to be hated by the white race. To hate each other because one happened to be dark and the other light, made future life for them in Fayetteville, not what they wanted to experience.

"I have been in touch with a friend in Chicago, who wishes me to come there as soon as possible and go into business with him, contracting and building, and—"

"—You'll need a—bookkeeper, Frank?"

"Just like it used to be, Rena," he said, and placing an arm about her shoulders gently, he kissed her long and tenderly.

George Tryon was delayed by urgent business matters in returning to Fayetteville, but return he did, reaching there one night, about two weeks after the declarations above. As he drove into the lane that led up to the house behind the cedars and paused when he saw that it was all lighted up, he was surprised, and as Billy Oxendine strode past him on the way there, he stopped him, pointed to the house and inquired:

"What goes on there?"

Billy looked at the house, and then up into the white man's face, and replied:

"A wedding, suh."

"A wedding?" Tryon repeated, "Whose wedding?"

"Miss Rena Northcross, suh. She's marrying Frank Fowler, her childhood sweetheart."

"Childhood sweetheart," George Tryon repeated as Billy Oxendine continued on toward the house.

"Humph!" Tryon exclaimed, to himself, stupidly.

He turned the mare round then, drove out of the lane and turned into the highway that led to town, where he would spend the night, and return to Sampson County the next morning for good. And as he turned into the highway and crossed the bridge, George Tryon continued to think how stupid he was. "Childhood sweetheart," he kept repeating, and wondering who that could be, but if she was marrying a childhood sweetheart, she must have been in love before she ever met him.